PRAISE FOR TE
GREEN LION
CHILD OF SATURN
THE MOON IN HIDING
THE WORK OF THE SUN

"Four Stars. One of fantasy fiction's most interesting trilogies. . . . Breathtaking . . . fascinating!"

—*Rave Reviews*

"A nicely balanced mix of intrigue and sorcery. . . . . Give this one a try!"

—*Locus*

"CHILD OF SATURN marks the appearance of a new and exciting talent."

—Tad Williams
author of THE DRAGONBONE CHAIR

"A very promising debut."

—*Booklist*

"A grand story told with a sly wit."

—Raymond E. Feist

AND DON'T MISS TERESA EDGERTON'S
THRILLING FANTASY ADVENTURE . . .
GOBLIN MOON

Ace Books by Teresa Edgerton

THE GREEN LION TRILOGY

CHILD OF SATURN
THE MOON IN HIDING
THE WORK OF THE SUN

GOBLIN MOON
THE GNOME'S ENGINE

TERESA EDGERTON
THE
GNOME'S ENGINE

ACE BOOKS, NEW YORK

This book is an Ace original edition,
and has never been previously published.

THE GNOME'S ENGINE

An Ace Book / published by arrangement with
the author

PRINTING HISTORY
Ace edition / August 1991

All rights reserved.
Copyright © 1991 by Teresa Edgerton.
Cover art by Den Beauvais.
Interior art © 1991 by Anne Meyer Maglinte.
This book may not be reproduced in whole or in part,
by mimeograph or any other means, without permission.
For information address: The Berkley Publishing Group,
200 Madison Avenue, New York, NY 10016.

ISBN: 0-441-52057-X

Ace Books are published by The Berkley Publishing Group,
200 Madison Avenue, New York, New York 10016.
The name "ACE" and the "A" logo
are trademarks belonging to Charter Communications, Inc.

PRINTED IN THE UNITED STATES OF AMERICA

10 9 8 7 6 5 4 3 2 1

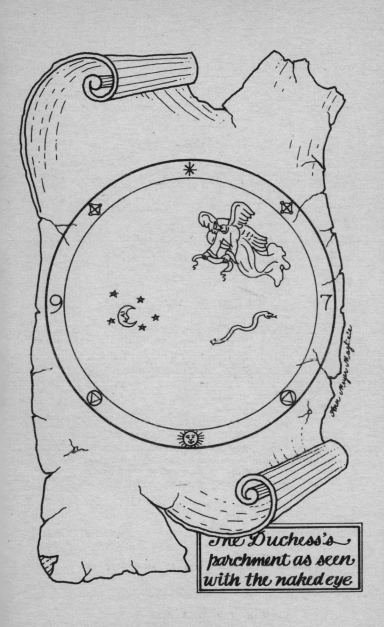

9   7

The Duchess's
parchment as seen
with the naked eye

Figures seen when viewed through magic spectacles

Of the Stone Seramarias

There is a Stone called Seramarias which does not occur in Nature. Its properties are Marvelous, for it neutralizes Poisons, attracts other Gem-stones as a Lodestone attracts Iron, and Gifts the One who wears it with the power of Prophecy.

Many other Applications, equally Remarkable, have been ascribed.

When Soaked in one dram Water and two drams Wine for a period of Seven days—that it may thus Communicate its own Sovereign Virtue—the Stone yields up the Elixir, which if an Honest Man should drink but a Sip each day, his Life shall be Prolonged past its Natural Span. Further Pseudopholus Benedictus hath written: "In the hands of the Philosopher, Seramarias cures all Ills, cools all Wicked Passions, and Elevates the Mind."

Yet it is also True that for a Greedy Love of the Fire and Lustre of the Stone, men seek Seramarias and thereby lose their Peace. ~~~~

From Catalana's *Book of Silences: being the Memoirs and Reflections of the Sage, Don Gaspar Eirenius Catalana*, translated from the Spagnish by Dr. Thos. Scotus Kelly, Fr. Mezz., M.S.O.

1.

In the nature of a Prologue.

Even by moonlight, it was evident the crumbling Zar-Wildungen mansion had seen better days. A rambling structure of white stone, caught in a woven net of ivy and flowering vines, the house yet maintained a certain slumberous dignity, as though it existed in a kind of architectural trance, a ponderous sleeping beauty dreaming away the centuries in a prison of leaves and flowers.

So the ancient building appeared from without—heavy, drowsy, and dull. Inside, it was all very different: grim-faced servants scurried from room to dusty room in the frantic performance of their duties, relaying orders in tense, hurried whispers; a constant traffic of footmen and page-boys moved between the butler's pantry and the kitchen, picking up dishes which had grown cold awaiting the Duchess's pleasure and whisking them downstairs to be reheated. The little Duchess, in one of her rare violent rages, had cast the entire household into turmoil.

Seemingly oblivious to the flurry of activity down below, she paced the floor of her elegant gilded bedchamber, the full skirts of her satin gown rustling with every agitated movement. Her cheeks glowed and her chest rose and fell in short panting breaths. Cast carelessly aside on the floor near the marble fireplace lay a crumpled piece of paper: the letter which, many hours earlier, had served to ignite her volatile temper.

"My spies . . ." she raged aloud—though there was no one in the room to hear her but Sebastian the miniature indigo ape, who had taken refuge on the mantelpiece. " . . . My spies are fools and incompetents. Two young ladies—nay, two ignorant, inexperienced girls—have defeated them all!"

She clenched her hands into fierce little fists. A year had passed since those wicked, provoking girls had disappeared, a year in which they had successfully eluded the Duchess and all her twoscore spies, a year of false leads and repeated disappointments, like the one she had received today . . .

She threw herself down on a dainty loveseat by the window, put a hand to her aching head. As her fury began to abate, a vast, suffocating weariness stole over her, and her eyes filled with sudden tears.

Only those like her, of fairy blood, the Duchess thought, could understand her bitter frustration—her every scheme balked, her rightful vengeance denied her. Only another miserable hybrid like herself could understand what it was to be pulled and harassed by so many conflicting desires. A shudder passed over her delicate frame. From her father, a full-blooded Fee, she had inherited this consuming hunger for vengeance, a constitutional inability to forgive any insult, no matter how minor or unintentional; but a human taint, by way of her mother, robbed her of the fierce, sustaining passion which ought to uphold her now, and disheartened her, instead, with a morbid conviction that when victory over her enemies finally came, it would be a hollow triumph at best.

"What a wretched creature I am; not one thing or the other," she exclaimed rucfully. "And it is wearisome . . . wearisome beyond all measure."

As if responding to this quieter mood, the blue ape climbed down from the mantel, loped awkwardly across the floor, scrambled up to the back of the loveseat, and gazed down at her with his clouded old eyes. The Duchess regarded him through her tears. "Poor little Sebastian, poor lonely fellow. If *I* am a freak, then what are you?"

"*An indigo ape, very rare indeed . . . an undoubted novelty.*" That was how she explained him to her friends. Only the Duchess (and possibly Sebastian himself) knew how very rare he was—that there had never been, and probably never would be, another of his kind. "*Do* you know, Sebastian? Have you any inkling that you are utterly unique . . . or do you live your life in merciful ignorance?" Even she, after so many years, could not be sure how much Sebastian knew, how far his comprehension might extend.

And even if he understood his own condition, she thought wistfully, she could hardly suppose that he understood hers.

The Duchess took out a lacy handkerchief and wiped her eyes. Outwardly, she knew, she bore little trace of her mixed heritage. Something less than five feet tall and porcelain fair, she was otherwise so entirely human in appearance that few suspected more than the tiniest hint of fairy blood. But it was a maxim, among those of mixed race, that hybrids who bore the most freakish outward signs of their mongrel heritage inevitably possessed a greater degree of inner harmony, a more placid and sober disposition—while those like the Duchess, who appeared most markedly either Man or fay, dwarf or gnome, carried all their turmoil within them.

The Duchess spread out her handkerchief on her lap to dry. She reached up to stroke Sebastian's long blue hair. The little creature whimpered softly in his throat. The Duchess shook her head mournfully. Though worlds apart, it was plain the two of them shared a common grief. "No," she said, with a sigh. "Ignorant you may well be, but I cannot suppose that you are happy."

And thinking of Sebastian and all his sorrows, memories of her own vexatious circumstances came flooding back: her beautiful, intricate scheme of revenge (sixteen years in preparation) all brought to nothing—no, worse! the one insult, unrequited, giving birth to a whole host of bitter grievances, all of which *had* to be revenged . . . the defection of her sensitive young lover, Francis Skelbrooke . . . the theft of her magic parchment—of immense antiquity and incalculable worth . . . most painful of all, perhaps, the child she had wished for, to rear as her own, so treacherously denied her. Oh yes, her wrongs were many and all of them serious.

One white fist clenched and unclenched. "What a price I shall exact when finally I catch up with those young women. How I shall make them *pay!*"

2.

Wherein the Reader may, perchance, Recognize a number of old Friends.

The little colonial town of Lootie's Bay was a town first built, and still mostly inhabited, by dwarves and gnomes. The houses stood in precise rows, all made of stone or brick, with little dwarf gardens behind—tidy plots of grass bordered with useful herbs and shrubs, each one boasting a fine fountain or a statue at the center—and the cobbled streets were broad and straight, with crossing and corners all mathematically correct, for the gnomes cherished a fondness for numbers and geometry, just as the dwarves were devoted to earth, water, and stone.

A deep water harbor with elegant stonework piers and a small fishing fleet supported the handful of full-sized Men who lived there. For the most part, however, Lootie's Bay was a town of merchants and skilled artisans: weavers, pewtersmiths, potters, jewelers; glaziers, joiners, masons, and shipbuilders.

About two blocks from the seawall, on Hartishorn Lane, stood a neat little shop:

MAPS AND PHILOSOPHIC INSTRUMENTS
Sammuel Digby Jonas, Proprietor

A gnome of immense respectability, Mr. Jonas made his living principally as a lensmaker—as a prodigious pair of gold-rimmed spectacles mounted over his door attested—and by selling charts and navigational instruments to mariners. But he had a penchant for invention which led him to construct elaborate and fantastical devices for which even he could find no practical use, and he kept a workroom at the back of the shop, where he and his new assistant, a brawny six-foot youth who went by the name of Jedidiah Thorn, regularly conducted experiments with prisms and magnets, speculums and glass pumps, microscopes and burning glasses.

To the town at large, this Jedidiah Thorn presented something of a mystery (though anything less sinister than Mr. Thorn, with his honest face and his candid brown eyes, could scarcely be imagined). He had arrived in Lootie's Bay, along with his sister Sera and their cousin Miss Winter, during the season of Ripening. Where he lived before that, or what his occupation, he never revealed, though it was known that he brought letters of reference with him, which he presented to the Mayor, Mr. Bullrush the glassblower . . . references which evidently proved entirely satisfactory, for Mr. Bullrush had recommended him to Mr. Jonas, and the two young ladies now lived in the Bullrush household. The folk of Lootie's Bay experienced some little difficulty in placing Jed Thorn as to rank and birth: he dressed and spoke like a gentleman, but his manners were easy and unaffected, lacking all pretension. His sister, however, was unmistakably a lady.

As the days dwindled and the year faded, the young Man and the gnome spent more and more of their time in the back room working by lanthorn-light, apparently engrossed in some new philosophic inquiry. Just precisely the nature of that inquiry, nobody seemed to know, but his friends waited for Mr. Jonas to produce a paper—a paper he would read aloud at some ceremonial function of the Glassmaker's Guild, and then consign to live burial in the dusty guildhall archives. Such had always been the course of Mr. Jonas's inquiries in the past, so naturally, his neighbors expected nothing more to come of this one.

Then one day, late in the season of Fading, a note came 'round to the Bullrush residence, inviting Miss Thorn and Miss Winter to take tea at the shop on Hartishorn Lane, a letter which piqued the curiosity of the recipients, with its calculated air of mystery. *Extraordinary revelations*, promised the letter (penned in Mr. Jonas's hand), and it ended with a solemn declaration: *I know that we may rely on your absolute discretion*.

The house of Mr. Bullrush the Mayor was an imposing structure of mellow pink brick, three stories high with a roof of smoke-blue slates, and a marble porch with a roof supported by dwarf caryatids. The schoolroom was in the attic, nestled directly under the slates, and there the Bullrush children and their portly Vole cousins conned their daily lessons under the keen eye of the formidable Sera Thorn.

On the afternoon in question, lessons being over, Sera left her young charges to a nursery tea with the babies and their nursemaids, and went down to her bedchamber. There she changed into a gown of striped muslin and tied a wide-brimmed straw hat over her glossy brown curls. She scowled at her reflection in the oval looking glass over her dressing table. There was a shade under her dark eyes that spoke of sleepless nights. She was oddly out of sorts these days without knowing why, her nerves so charged that she often started or dropped things for no discernible reason at all—nor had Mr. Jonas's tantalizing letter done anything to lift her spirits or to improve her temper.

"Extraordinary revelations, indeed!" Sera said under her breath, as she descended to the first floor. "Like as not, it is merely another preposterous mechanism that Jed and Mr. Jonas mean to unveil . . . I do hope that it proves to be nothing more."

Going down another flight, she met Elsie ascending. "My dear, you aren't even ready!" she said, pausing with one hand on the rail. "I thought you meant to accompany me."

"No, Sera." Elsie Winter regarded her cousin regretfully. "Madam Bullrush is expecting visitors . . ." (Elsie was Madam's paid companion) " . . . all the most formidable dames in the town, and Mr. Tynsdale, that horrid preacher, so of course she asked me to stay and help entertain them. What else could I say but yes?"

Sera shook her head and continued on her way. She did not envy her cousin her position in the house. Though the role of governess occasionally chafed Sera, it was better by far than serving as companion to a fretful old lady.

Descending a long flight of shallow marble steps to the street, she headed in the direction of Mr. Jonas's shop. The streets were always crowded at this hour with brisk merchants, craftsmen, and clerks hurrying home to tea; with bustling dwarf nursemaids and little gnome mothers in high-crowned bonnets, ushering their tiny charges back to the nursery after an afternoon stroll in the park. Sera was fond of Lootie's Bay, and sympathized with the impatient New World industry of the inhabitants. But she had to admit that she grew just a bit tired of fragile dwarf knick-knacks and miniature furnishings, of ducking her head whenever she passed through a doorway or walked under a shop sign suspended over the street, and most *particularly* tired of feeling bigger and gawkier than she had ever felt in her life.

As Sera crossed the square, she experienced an unnerving sensation—a sort of prickling at the back of her neck—that someone followed her. But even when a familiar long black shadow loomed up on the cobblestones beside hers, Sera did not glance back. She remembered, with a shudder, all the times that she had done so . . . only to discover there was no one on the street to whom such a *long* thin shadow could possibly belong.

Scolding herself for allowing her imagination to play spiteful tricks on her, Sera continued on past the Glassmakers guildhall. Such intellectual life as the community might boast centered around the red brick guildhall. Not all who attended meetings there were actually glaziers, glassblowers, or lensmakers, for the Glassmakers Lodge, of all the guilds, was the last repository of the old craft mysteries, the last to celebrate the ancient rituals in full knowledge of their philosophic and occult significance, and Men and dwarves and gnomes from all walks of life eagerly sought entry into the speculative branch of the Guild. Three times a year they marched through the town in their hiero-phantic robes and gorgeous glittering medals, bearing before them the enigmatic symbols of their order and chanting their mysterious creed. The rest of the year they hosted genteel little suppers and devoted themselves mainly to charitable works.

They also kept up a steady correspondence with other, more active, branches on two continents. It was through the good auspices of the Thornburg Glassmakers—and particularly of Jedidiah's patrons, Master Ule and Mr. Owlfeather—that Sera, Jed, and Elsie had been able to sail to the continent of Calliope and escape from their powerful enemies. Though Sera was strongly sensible of the great debt she owed to the Glassmakers—as kindly and respectable a collection of gentleman dilettantes as anyone could hope to meet—when she considered their misguided meddling in ancient mysteries, when she recalled how a similar dangerous spirit of inquiry had proved so ruinous to her grandfather, Gottfried Jenk . . . how ardently she wished that Jed had never joined them!

Arriving at Mr. Jonas's establishment, Sera rang the bell. The door was locked and the shutters latched, giving the normally welcoming shop a close and uncommunicative look. A moment later, Jed opened the door and ushered her inside, through the shop, and into the workroom at the back.

Sera sat down on the ladderback chair Jed offered her, sweeping an eager glance around the room. She had never been in Mr. Jonas's inner sanctum before, and she was naturally curious. Low shelves lined the room, crammed with books and papers and all manner of queer instruments which (alchemist's granddaughter though she was) Sera did not recognize. In the center of the room stood a great engine made of brass and blued steel: a complex thing of gears and pulleys and weights and pendulums; Sera could make neither head nor tail of it, though she remembered that Jed had said something about experiments with perpetual motion. A number of faded maps and diagrams were pinned to the plaster walls above the shelves, and a chart of the heavens had been painted on the ceiling. A window at the back of the room opened on a garden with a fountain.

Jed, who had answered the door in his shirt sleeves and corded silk waistcoat, slipped into his coat and straightened his neckcloth, assuming an air of great formality. Mr. Jonas came in through a side door, bearing the tea tray. Sera raised an inquiring eyebrow. With the presence of what could only be the gnome's best silver service, Jed's careful attention to his appearance, and the tingling air of suppressed excitement in the room, Sera began to believe that some extraordinary announcement was actually forthcoming.

"Miss Winter, I suppose, was unable to accompany you?" asked Mr. Jonas, edging around the machine in the center of the room and arranging the tea things on a low table.

Sammuel Digby Jonas, thought Sera, was a fine figure of a gnome. He had a broad, good-natured face framed by a handsome set of bristling red whiskers. Though standing rather less than three feet high, like most gnomes he possessed a great sense of his own dignity, as well as a magnificent pair of beautifully curved polished horns, which added immeasurably to his presence. Sera had never seen him but when he was dressed with quiet good taste—gnome fashion, mostly in dark colors, with a tall stove-pipe hat cunningly designed to fit over his horns when he went out—but he almost invariably went barefoot. His feet were long and broad, equipped with massive ivory-tinted claws—admirably suited for digging and tunneling—which rendered boots or shoes uncomfortable and unnecessary.

Sera offered Elsie's regrets, but the gnome waved them away. "It does not matter. Your brother—I suppose we must continue to call him your brother, even in private—pays such frequent visits to the Bullrush establishment, no doubt he has already acquainted her with some of the particulars."

"As to that," said Sera, "if you mean that Jed is courting Elsie, he seems to be going about it in the most desultory fashion imaginable! Though I doubt that it was to discuss Jed and his matrimonial intentions that you have invited me here so mysteriously today," she added, ignoring Jed's indignant glare, and calmly accepting a delicate teacup and a plate filled with sugar cakes from the gnome. "So I *wish* you would tell me, without further preamble, what all of this means."

"Very well, then," said Mr. Jonas, sitting down on a low stool, while Jed, rather huffily, deposited himself in a second ladderback chair. "Though just where I ought to begin . . . perhaps with Lord Skelbrooke and his daring theft of the Duchess's magic parchment—or rather, with the intense excitement of our friends in Thornburg when he first gave the document into their keeping. They recognized it immediately, of course, for the manuscript had once fallen into their hands, very briefly, many years before. They knew that the parchment was more than it seemed, that besides the simple talismanic spell of protection which all could see, it also concealed a certain ancient spell of *tremendous* magnitude, written in secret writing. Yet for all their efforts, no one found the means to bring that greater spell to light. But I believe you knew some of this history already?"

Despite herself, Sera felt a flicker of interest. "I did, but only a little. Pray continue."

"With the greatest pleasure," said the gnome, as he poured a cup of tea for himself. "Well . . . you are certainly acquainted with the manner in which Mr. Owlfeather and Master Ule chose to convey the parchment to Nova Imbria, for you yourself were instrumental there . . . but perhaps you do *not* know that all these past weeks I have been engaged—and young Jedidiah with me—in an attempt to render the invisible characters visible, and so uncover the secret spell."

"And a tedious long time we have been about it," put in Jed, ladling sugar into his own cup. He still remembered the old days, when money was short and sugar was dear, and it seemed he could never get enough sweets even in his new prosperity. "I suppose we tried every means known to Man, dwarf, or gnome, mostly without result. We examined the parchment by sunlight, by starlight, and by the light of the moon in all her phases. Then we bathed the parchment, successively, in vinegar, in wine, and in seawater . . . subjected it to heat and smoke. Growing more audacious, we treated it with salts and acids—but still without any luck. After that, we examined the parchment through a series of lenses of varying strength and composition: with clear glass and with tinted, with rock crystal and rosy quartz.

"It was then," said Jedidiah, pausing impressively, with the porcelain teacup half way to his lips, "it was then that Mr. Jonas conceived the idea of using magic ruby spectacles."

"Of course a pair of rubies large enough to be ground into lenses were very dear, oh yes, exceedingly expensive, and I was obliged to apply to the Guild for funds," the gnome acknowledged, as Sera's eyes opened wide in astonishment and she sat up a little straighter in her chair. "But what better device could one conceive to reveal secret writing? Every gemstone falls under the dominion of one of the Planetary Intelligences, and rubies, as we all know, are ruled by Sadrun . . . the Guardian of Secrets, the Master of All Things Hidden. I was only amazed that the idea had never occurred to anyone before.

"I obtained the rubies, at what cost you can easily imagine, ground them into lenses, and mounted them. After that . . . But you shall see the result for yourself," said Mr. Jonas.

At a nod from the gnome, Jedidiah put aside his cup. He produced a fragile-looking parchment and a pair of very odd spectacles, exhorting Sera to take a look at the document through the crimson-tinted lenses. Then he plunked down in the chair next to hers again.

"My goodness!" exclaimed Sera, catching her breath. As soon as she put on the spectacles, the hidden text and diagrams had instantly appeared. "It looks—it looks like a map!"

"It *is* a map," crowed Jed, craning his neck to look over her shoulder, like a big excited child. "But I'll wager you can't guess what map it is!"

Sera studied the document more closely. "I have not the least idea," she said, and waited politely for further enlightenment.

Mr. Jonas cleared his throat. "Those symbols: the moon and stars, and the writhing serpent, which have been visible all along but *now* appear to be imposed on those two large islands on the hidden map . . . have long been associated with the lost civilizations of Panterra and Evanthum. And see those two bits of land on either side? One is undoubtedly the isle of Imbria off the coast of Euterpe, and the other just as certainly a recognizable portion of the coast of Calliope. Yes," he said, as Sera glanced up, peering at him over the ruby spectacles, "we do believe that this map reveals the location of the two drowned island empires."

For all her reservations about the Glassmakers and their activities, Sera was suitably impressed. "But if the map is accurate, both Panterra and Evanthum were far larger than anyone previously supposed!" she exclaimed, straightening the eyeglasses and taking another look at the map. "Why, the Alantick Ocean is over two thousand miles across, and the Panterran archipelago (as I suppose we may call it) spans most of that distance. Not mere islands, then, the two largest bodies, but something more approaching continents!"

"That is so," said the gnome. "And yet not so surprising after all. Many old tales recall a terrible time of widespread destruction: of earthquakes, floods, tempests, throughout the world on a scale unimaginable, the sudden disappearance of many smaller islands, the emergence of Imbria and Mawbri out of the oceanic depths, the subsequent collapse of all civilization and a slow rebuilding. In short, disasters more in keeping with the death of two continents than of two insignificant islands.

"Also," Mr. Jonas continued, pointing a finger at the frail yellow parchment, as though he could see the spidery brown lines which marked out the dimensions of the map as plainly as Sera could see them herself, "you may note the proximity of Panterra and Calliope."

It required several minutes for Sera to absorb all of this. "But what a marvelous discovery," she said at last, bestowing a brilliant smile, first on the gnome, and then on Jedidiah. "This must prove of the greatest interest to scholars everywhere. I do congratulate you, Mr. Jonas . . . and you, too, Jed! You have accomplished something truly remarkable."

"Of far more than scholarly interest—" the gnome began, only to be interrupted by Jedidiah:

"That writing about the edge . . . those smaller diagrams . . . it's the spell we were looking for: a magic spell for raising the islands, for bringing them right up out of the ocean!"

Sera removed the ruby spectacles. Her delighted smile changed to one of patent disbelief. "My dear good Jed, you cannot be serious. To raise two drowned continents, to bring them up from the ocean floor by the means of—of magic . . . that is clearly impossible!"

"I don't see that," Jedidiah replied hotly, lapsing, as he sometimes did when extremely agitated, into his old rough way of speaking, "Not when everyone agrees, your scholars and your philosophers alike, that it was magic as *sunk* them islands. Yes, and the gentlemen of the Glassmakers Guild reckon it's altogether possible, which is why they've agreed to finance the enterprise for us."

Sera stared at him for several moments in speechless astonishment. Recovering her voice, she shifted her gaze to Mr. Jonas. "Do you mean to tell me, sir, that you actually intend to *attempt* this thing?"

"That is *precisely* what we intend to do," said the gnome.

3.

Which continues the Revelations of the Former.

"We *do* mean to attempt it," said Mr. Jonas, accepting the ruby spectacles and the parchment into his hands. "Or rather . . . not anything so ambitious as raising the two larger bodies. But you saw the smaller islands—most particularly the western-most isle? If the map is accurate, that must have been located less than a hundred miles off the Cordelian coast. According to all accounts, the Panterrans built a temple dedicated to the Evening Star on the western isle, and it is that temple, if any part of it still exists, that Jed and I most *particularly* wish to bring up out of the depths."

Jedidiah and the gnome exchanged a sparkling glance. "The ancient Panterrans and Evanthians, as you must know, were a race of magicians and philosophers," Mr. Jonas continued. "The wonders of their civilizations have never been equaled since! They knew how to catch the light of the moon or the sun in a lamp . . . invented sky-ships powered by magnetism, that they might sail among the clouds . . . built mighty celestial engines whose movements replicated the courses of all the stars and planets. According to some accounts, they knew the secret of the fabulous stone, Seramarias. And they inscribed all their secrets on marble tablets, which they sent to be guarded in the inner precincts of their temples. To gain such knowledge for ourselves . . . ah, Miss Thorn, that would be a great thing!"

"Yes, I quite see *that*," said Sera, her straight dark brows drawing together in a thoughtful frown. "And yet . . . and yet if I may say so, it sounds the most fantastic and impossible scheme!"

"Not so fantastic as you might think," the gnome replied earnestly. "To begin with, the ocean is surprisingly shallow throughout that area, with unexpected reefs and ridges—oh,

14

you must not suppose that the waters there are dangerous, only that the soundings are a bit queer, so far from the nearest land. It may be that none of the islands are sunk so deep as we had previously imagined. Also, the spell to raise them specifies the time of the full moon, when earth and sea enter into a restless state, and are highly disposed to divulge their secrets. Moreover, we shall do much more than recite magic words and perform magical passes. The parchment also describes, in great detail, an elaborate machine, apparently designed to make use of the magnetic attraction existing between the earth and the moon.

"You are a young female of superior education," Mr. Jonas added, with a deferential bow. "You do not subscribe to antiquated notions such as that which describes the moon as a fiery orb inhabited by salamanders, though many who call themselves scientists remain firmly convinced of the same. I need not explain to you, but only remind you, of the elliptical lunar orbit, and how the magnetic attraction I mentioned before naturally increases as Iune draws near the earth. We have proof of these things, not only in her apparent change in size, waxing visibly larger even as she grows rounder, but in the minor disasters, the high tides and the earth tremors, which her proximity invariably brings forth.

"What we hope to achieve, Miss Thorn, shall be accomplished not by magic only, but through a brilliant combination of scientific and magical principles!"

Yet Sera remained skeptical. "But if, as you inform me, the island in question is located near the coast of Cordelia—I am not a scientist—my acquaintance with natural philosophy is merely adequate," she said. "But it seems to me that your efforts might well occasion just such a terrible cataclysm as you have already described . . . if not throughout the world, at least sufficient to cause the people of Cordelia considerable trouble and grief!"

"I will not deny," said Mr. Jonas, "that some danger certainly exists, should we choose to act precipitously. Which is why we intend to proceed cautiously instead. We shall not raise the island all at once, but by easy stages over the course of perhaps two days, and even then, we do not mean to bring the entire island to the surface, but only to raise it so high that the central eminence (on which the temple stands) emerges from the water."

Sera made a last attempt to dissuade them. "Yes . . . But has it not occurred to you that the Duchess of Zar-Wildungen kept the parchment for—well, we don't know precisely *how* long she kept it, but perhaps for many years. And surely the Duchess possessed all the resources of wealth and influence necessary to mount just such an expedition as you plan. Therefore, if the spell is effective—which I am not at all prepared to allow— is it not highly probable that the Duchess has already done this thing before you, and claimed the secrets of Panterra and Evanthum all for herself?"

"Supposing that she knew the entire contents of the parch- ment—which *we* don't incline to allow—yes," countered Jed, recovering his grammar along with his eloquence. "We appre- hend that she knew the value of the document and something of its history, but there is no reason to believe that she knew, also, the secret of the ruby spectacles."

Sera shook her head stubbornly. Though she was willing to admit the sense of this, when it came to the wisdom of the enterprise itself, the probability of a successful conclu- sion . . . No, *that* she could by no means accept. However (she realized with a sinking sensation, and a heartfelt sigh), the attempt would undoubtedly be made, with or without her countenance.

The sun had set and a lazy crescent moon with silver horns rose over the water, as Jed escorted Sera back home along the mathematically precise streets. Whatever had ailed her earlier, the uncanny feeling that someone followed after her, that some nameless doom waited to pounce on her, had faded to a vague prickly uneasiness.

"It is now so late in the year," said Sera, as they walked through the gathering shadows. "I fail to see how you can possibly undertake this expedition of yours before Quickening. Do you intend to winter here in Lootie's Bay?"

Jedidiah shook his head. "The gentlemen of the Guild believe we can do the thing cheaper—*and* quieter—if Mr. Jonas and I arrive in Cordelia a season or two before we mean to set to work, make a push to establish ourselves in the community, then hire our ship and set sail when the time is right. Mr. Jonas has a friend there, a gentleman Glassmaker by the name of Mr. Herring, who lives in a little town right on the coast."

They crossed the square, passing the town lamplighters, a somber-looking pair in black coats and cocked hats, busily at work with their ladders and long sulphur-dipped matchsticks, lighting the lanthorns on all four sides of the square. Sera caught an unpleasant whiff of brimstone as she walked by.

"And have you settled it—you and Mr. Jonas between you, while you were settling everything else—that Elsie and *I* ought to accompany you on this remarkable expedition?"

Jedidiah grinned broadly. "Naturally, you and Elsie must come along for the adventure! Didn't we three solemnly vow to stay together, wherever the Fates took us? And the truth is," he added more soberly, "it's been preying on my mind: we have lived in this place much too long. It isn't wise and it isn't safe." From which Sera gathered that he, too, felt a strong sense that the pleasant little town was a trap closing in on them.

He glanced down at her with a questioning look. "You don't feel any obligation to stay on with the Mayor and his lady?"

"No indeed," said Sera. "And I do not imagine that Elsie will feel any obligation either. It was understood from the beginning, you know, that we should not stay here for long. But wherever we go," she added sternly, "Elsie and I must find some suitable employment. We will not live on your charity, nor will we allow the Glassmakers Guild to support us!"

They had arrived at the Bullrush mansion, and Sera paused at the foot of the marble steps, glaring up at him.

But Jed looked insufferably smug. "We guessed as much, Mr. Jonas and I, and indeed, we *have* arranged it. There's a school for young ladies in Hobb's Church, and they are looking for genteel young women of good education to serve as schoolmistresses. Mr. Herring will recommend you, and everything will be neatly settled."

"Well then," replied Sera, with an angry little laugh (for though this news they would soon leave Nova Imbria lifted a great weight from her heart, she was also rather miffed that Jedidiah should make so many plans without first consulting her or Elsie), "I see that everything has been most *masterfully* arranged for us, and we 'poor females' have nothing to do but meekly comply!"

4.

Which introduces an Agent, a letter, and a brief and inglorious History of Francis, Lord Skelbrooke.

The downstairs parlor was a cozy room, cluttered and a bit overdecorated—for the dwarf had never been born who could resist an opportunity to paint the lily. The walls were a pleasant jumble of gilded moldings, oil landscapes, peacock-feather fans, and silhouette portraits of three generations of Bullrush and Vole children, mounted behind glass in silver frames; and the room at large boasted a rather more than ordinary number of chairs, tables, chests, sofas, clocks, footstools, and lacquered fire screens, all jostling for elbow room.

On a sofa sandwiched between a bookshelf and a curio cabinet, Elsie shifted uncomfortably, desperately wondering *how* on earth she could politely rid herself of the lanky gentleman seated so close beside her.

The other guests had long since departed. Old Madam Bullrush lay fast asleep in her wing-back armchair, snoring gustily, not likely to wake again before supper. But Moses Tynsdale, the itinerant clergyman, Minister of the Gospel of the Immortal Fates, lingered on like a bad odor. For all his flawless manners, his dignified bearing, Elsie sensed something vaguely improper in the personal tone of the minister's conversation, the urgent, inquisitive nature of his questions.

It is almost as though he believes me guilty of some dreadful secret vice, which he expects me to confide in him! she thought indignantly. The feverish intensity of his dark gaze, an avid expression on his lean brown face, made Elsie want to shiver and shrink away, but he had already edged her into a corner of the sofa, and she had no place farther to go. *This man has an unquiet spirit. If his soul is sick, then how can he hope to minister to mine?* She felt a cold wash of relief when Mr. Tynsdale finally arose, begged her to convey his compliments to her friend Miss Thorn, bowed, and stalked out of the room.

Elsie moved out of her corner, smoothed out the ruffles of her white dimity gown, and unfolded the crumpled handkerchief she had crushed in one damp palm. She was not even certain what the man had said or done to fluster her so, or why she should feel so unaccountably violated.

Mr. Tynsdale is a fanatic, that I know. But why he keeps coming 'round here, as though this house were a perfect haven for sinners and apostates . . . that I do not know. Elsie jumped in her seat as a step sounded in the hall and the parlor door opened—but it was only Sera, returning from her afternoon call.

"My dear, you look positively rattled," said Sera, untying the ribbons of her bonnet and taking a seat on the sofa. She reached out to smooth Elsie's disheveled golden curls. Though no longer sickly, Elsie still retained a deceptive air of fragility that aroused all of Sera's protective instincts.

"I have been teased and bothered nearly to distraction," Elsie admitted. "But let us not talk of that. Tell me, if you please, what you learned today from Jedidiah and Mr. Jonas. No . . . I *don't* know," she added, in answer to Sera's inquiring look. "Jed has been dreadfully provoking, this last fortnight, with all sorts of hints and veiled promises, but he never said anything that made the least sense."

As nothing short of an earthquake or an explosion was likely to disturb the napping Granny Bullrush, Sera very readily told Elsie everything she knew, describing at length (and with a strong air of disapproval) the plans and arrangements already made by Jedidiah and the gnome. As she might have expected, the romantic aspects of the proposed undertaking so delighted Elsie that she clapped her hands and declared herself willing, should the need arise, to pack up her bags and depart on a moment's notice.

"But Sera," she asked, grown suddenly sober, "perhaps *you* are not so eager to resume our travels? After all, it has been more than a year since we left Thornburg, and Francis Skelbrooke—"

"—can find me in the one town quite as easily as another," Sera finished for her, a trifle crossly. Anger was better than self-pity, and she would *not* play the role of the abandoned maiden, no matter how much her heart ached. "That is, supposing he meant anything he said to me that night in Zar-Wildungen . . . and that he really does come looking for me."

She reached instinctively for the little bit of spiral sea-ivory set in gold, which she wore on a fine chain around her neck. The trinket had come to her eight weeks before—through what mysterious channels she could only guess—by way of the Glassmakers Guild. It had arrived in a little wooden box inscribed with her first name, and a card inside bore only the initials "F.S." Yet of the elusive Skelbrooke himself, or his present whereabouts, she had received no word.

"But I think he *will* come for you," Elsie insisted softly.

"Do you?" Sera spoke a little huskily. "But things never *do* go right for me . . . as we know quite well. But don't let it trouble you, my dear. I am twenty years old and a confirmed spinster. I may not be satisfied with my lot in life, but I can imagine much worse.

"And really, Elsie, you disappoint me," she added, speaking very low and gesturing toward the hall. The voices of Mistress Bullrush's arriving supper guests could be heard in the hall. "Lord Skelbrooke's name . . . along with our own names, our true relationships . . . our very reasons for being here, in the New World . . . these are not things we should mention aloud even among ourselves. We can never tell who may be in the house to overhear us!"

Alas for Sera, and alas for secrecy, those very names were already familiar to a recent visitor to the Bullrush mansion. In a modest bedchamber at the Sea-Horse Inn, a gentleman sat at a small desk of varnished maple, writing a letter by candlelight.

To the Most Gracious and Exalted Lady, Marella, Duchess of Zar-Wildungen, he wrote in a dashing hand.

> *I have good reason to Believe that I have at last Suc-ceeded in regard to that Inquiry which Madam has Entrusted to me. Two young Women, bearing a close resemblance to the Misses Seramarias and Elsie Vorder are currently Residing in the town of Lootie's Bay in the colony of Nova Imbria, under the assumed names (as I conceive) of Sera Thorn and Elisabett Winter. I shall*

*Write all that I know of these two Young Women, so
that the Gracious Lady may decide for Herself whether
or no I have Successfully located her Quarry . . .*

After describing his first meeting with the two young ladies,
the spy paused briefly and thoughtfully, then dipped his quill
pen once more into the standish, and continued on.

*. . . though I must Confess that I am baffled by one
Circumstance which I had not Anticipated, viz.: the
Existence of one Mister Thorn (as he calls himself), a
young man Posing before the Community as the brother of Sera Thorn. This Imposture (as I must suppose)
rendered particularly Convincing not so much by a Similarity of Stature and Complexion, but Most of all by the
Affectionate Disrespect displayed by both parties, each to
the other, which argues a Long but scarcely Lover-like
Intimacy between them. Perhaps Madam, being better
informed than Myself, knows of some Male Relation or
Foster Brother who might have Accompanied the young
Ladies on their Journey.*

The gentleman paused again, to trim the wick of the candle,
which had begun to flicker, and to take a sip of wine from a
cup at his elbow.

*These things Said, I shall turn to the Question which
the Gracious Lady addressed to me in her last letter,
viz.: my Previous Acquaintance with the poetical Lord
Skelbrooke. To answer fully, I must needs Reveal something of mine own history, and my close Involvement in
a terrible series of Events, which the Newspapers came
to call the Waxbridge Horror.*

*Six years ago, when quite a Young man, I had the
ill-fortune (though Great Good Fortune it seemed to me
at the time) to be admitted into a circle of Magicians, the
which were all Disciples of a certain Noblewoman who
appeared to be a White Sorceress of no Mean Ability.*

*To be brief: the Woman was not what she Seemed,
and indeed it was her Custom to gradually Introduce
the young Men of the Circle to one filthy and pernicious*

*Vice after another, until (her Disciples becoming by Slow
Degrees as Vicious and Degraded in their inclinations
as she was Herself) she deemed it time to Initiate her
followers, one by one, into the loathsome mysteries of
the Dark Arts. I, like many others who fell under the
Influence of this Gloriously Seductive creature, was
Deeply Infatuated, nor did it take me long to Succumb
to those Enticements which she offered me, and engage
in practices of the Utmost Depravity.*

*But to return to Francis Skelbrooke (a mere Mr.
Skelbrooke as he then was): he had come to the City
of Lundy, quite against the Wishes of his Noble Relations, to study the Science of Medicine, for he had a
great Desire to do Good and Minister to the Sick and
Suffering. He, also, joined our Circle, and fell in love
with the Woman.*

*I will spare the Gracious Lady the distressing Details,
and say only that the Sorceress was in the Habit of Using
young orphan Children in the course of her Perversions,
in a manner both bestial and cruel. These Unlawful practices at length coming to the Attention of the Authorities,
the Woman was unmasked and brought to Trial, and all
her Disciples with her. Only Mr. Skelbrooke (a late and
uninitiated member of our Circle) escaped prosecution.
As for the Woman, she was Quietly and Discreetly
executed, while we, her Accomplices, on Account of
our Youth and due to the Influence of certain Family
Connections (for we were none of us of Lowly birth),
being spared the full Rigor of the Law, were sentenced
to spend the Rest of our Days behind Prison bars.*

*How I escaped this Dismal Fate can be of no interest
to the Gracious Lady . . . suffice it to say that a great
deal of Gold changed hands, and my Departure was
effected at Dead of Night with the aid of a rope. I shall,
therefore, pass on to those Things which I know of Lord
Skelbrooke's subsequent Career.*

The gentleman paused in his writing, absently slipped one
hand around the wrist of the other, rubbing gently, as if he
could still feel the chafing of iron fetters. Then, with a sigh,
he dipped his pen in the ink and continued writing.

*Did I say that Francis Skelbrooke escaped Punishment?
Yet he was not entirely Spared neither. For learning
of the Part he had indirectly played in luring certain
Pitiful Urchins into her clutches . . . overcome by
Remorse . . . he was stricken by a Sweating Sickness
and a Brain Fever so Virulent they seemed likely to
Carry him Off. Due to the Devoted Nursing of an
Old Schoolfellow of his, a Mr. Hermes Budge, young
Skelbrooke did recover, but long remained in such a
pitifully Nervous State that his return to Reason for some
time remained Doubtful. I believe it was at this Period
that he first made use of the Sleep Dust, to which he
afterwards became Addicted.*

*As to those subsequent Activities of which Madam
entertains some Suspicion, I know nothing for Certain,
though I think it Entirely in Keeping with what I know of
His Lordship's Character, that he should Attempt some
form of General Restitution by indulging in just such
Heroic and Flamboyant behavior as the Gracious Lady
describes.*

*In light of the above, Madam might wish to ask: was
Francis Skelbrooke indeed cured—is he now as Sane
as he ever was? As one who has shared many of the
same Experiences, and Considering myself even at this
Late Date more than a little Mad, I can only say that I
entertain some Doubt. And if the Gracious Lady should
wish to ask further: do I then regard Lord Skelbrooke as a
Dangerous man, I should have to reply in the Affirmative.
It is always so with your Disillusioned Idealist.*

*In the hope that this somewhat Lengthy Epistle shall
find favor with the Duchess's Grace, I remain, Respectfully, ever hers to Command, &c., and Awaiting her
Further Orders . . .*

The spy heavily underlined the last phrase, then signed his
name with a flourish:

Euripides P. Hooke

5.

Which whisks the Reader across the Sea—a Proceeding which (let him be Warned) is like to become a Commonplace before our Tale is done.

The white road leading north between Katrinsberg and Ghyll ran broad and straight for league upon league. But a mile beyond Ghyll, where the vast resin-scented pine forests gave way to barren steppes, the road abruptly ended.

Indeed, there was little need for a road: few traveled beyond that point even during the warm seasons. And if the land was bleak, it was also flat. The soil stayed frozen for most of the year, as hard and as black as iron, so that even a light early snowfall (like that which had been sifting down for a day and a half) did not readily turn to slush. Until the first heavy snows fell, travel north on horseback or by sledge would remain comparatively easy.

The Duchess of Zar-Wildungen, of course, insisted on her comforts. Her reindeer-drawn sledge, a grand and gilded affair—boat-shaped, with a leaping lion as the figurehead—skimmed smoothly along on scarlet runners, while the lady reclined amidst furs and cushions, protected from the cold by a mantle of crimson velvet, powdered with snow, and a swansdown hood.

Keeping pace with the sledge rode Jarl Skogsrå, mounted on a fine, coal-black stallion. The stallion pranced and tossed his head, and the Jarl looked exceedingly debonair, resplendent in the scarlet and gold uniform of a Nordic cavalry officer, with a dark green cloak floating out behind him. But the third member of the party was less prepossessing: a sober young man in a brown wool greatcoat, a grey muffler, and a tricorn hat which had seen much use, he trailed a little behind the others, plodding along on an undistinguished but serviceable little mare.

The pale winter sun was dipping toward the horizon when the Duchess spoke up in her sweet, childlike voice. "How much farther to Skullgrimm's palace?"

The Jarl shrugged his shoulders under the green cloak. "Another eight or ten miles, perhaps. It is many years since I last came this way, and of course there are no landmarks to speak of."

The little Duchess sighed, her hands tightened on the crimson leather reins. "I had hoped to arrive before nightfall."

"That I should certainly advise," answered Skogsrå, with grim satisfaction. "At whatever cost to your team. Few Men travel in these parts—few living Men—and with good reason. At sunset, or a little thereafter, Skullgrimm releases his hounds."

A tiny frown appeared between the Duchess's well-shaped eyebrows. "But surely so long as we remain with you, Mr. von Eichstätt and I will be perfectly safe. You are first cousin to the King—"

The Jarl shook his head, a single sharp motion. "Skullgrimm's creatures heed no one but the King himself. Indeed, even His Majesty sometimes experiences difficulty in controlling them.

"They are certainly trained to recognize the scent of troll, and they will not molest *me*," he added, with a mocking little bow. "Your own scent, Gracious Lady, may trouble and confuse them, and so may save you. But as for the horses and the good doctor . . ." Skogsrå's smile was more a baring of his even white teeth. "For their sake, I should advise that we increase our pace."

The Troll King's stronghold appeared in the distance, a dark and sullen pile, completely surrounded by a fence of tall iron pickets, like the wall around a graveyard. The Duchess and her party arrived at the gate just as the sun slipped below the horizon. A discreet-looking serving-troll dressed in baggy knee-length breeches and an antiquated tunic with a wide white collar came to open the gate, and then close it with a clatter behind them.

There was no chance of this one masquerading as a Man, mused the Duchess, eyeing the troll as her sledge swept through the gate. No chance of imposing on credulous humanity as Skogsrå had done successfully for so many years. Though he presented a manlike appearance from the waist up, the legs below the flaring breeches undeniably marked the gatekeeper as a troll: they were spindly and bristled, ending in a pair of slotted trotters. In addition, he sported a long tufted tail like a cow.

"They are a little behind the fashions here," said Skogsrå, with a grimace.

"As I perceive," the Dutchess responded dryly. "About a century, I should say."

Two lean black mastiffs, red-eyed and oddly hairless, paced at the ends of long, heavy chains. As they passed the dogs, the horses whickered and shied, and the Duchess's reindeer rolled their eyes and might have bolted but for her firm grip on the reins. She had her hands full trying to control her team, until a groom appeared to take charge of them.

"At least," she said, "we have arrived in time to avoid a dangerous encounter with Skullgrimm's hounds."

The Jarl dismissed the mastiffs and all their ilk with a lordly sweep of the hand. "Those you see there are only His Majesty's *dogs* . . . had we met with his *hounds,* you would know the difference."

Poor Mr. von Eichstätt looked utterly miserable, his nose blue and his teeth chattering—whether because of the cold, the drooling black mastiffs, or a sinking realization that he had truly arrived in the midst of a settlement of trolls, it was impossible to tell. The Jarl dismounted first and assisted the Duchess out of her sledge.

"I fear that you will find Skullgrimm and his court very dull," said the Jarl. "They care for nothing here but their books and their sorceries. It is a failing, I regret to say, common among my race."

"But it is to consult your King on the subject of sorcery that I have come so far," said the Duchess, putting back her swansdown hood. "Sorcery—and revenge. But do tell me, my dear sir," she added sweetly, "how it happens that you yourself have overcome this 'failing' of your race?"

The Jarl made an airy gesture. "I have no time for such things. Besides, it is healthier so, for those who stand too near the throne. His Majesty surrounds himself with scholars and magicians (which is all the company that amuses him), but when any of his cousins show too great an interest, or too formidable an aptitude, Skullgrimm grows uneasy.

"It is not in the nature of trolls to hunger for the flesh of their own kind," added Skogsrå, "but Skullgrimm has been known to overcome his distaste, in order to make an example of an overambitious kinsman by killing and eating him. It was to avoid just such a doleful fate that your young friend Vodni (the merest collateral relation) found it necessary to absent himself from the court."

With von Eichstätt lagging a bit behind them—as if he dreaded to reach their final destination—they proceeded across the snowy yard to the palace. That was an ominous, frowning structure, many stories high, with weird-looking outcrops and overhangs and balconies sprouting out in unexpected places, and tall, twisted towers. A steep staircase winding up the side of the central pile led to a pair of heavy bronze doors.

The Duchess paused after a dozen steps, with her skirts in her hands and the velvet mantle trailing behind her. She stared up at the palace with wondering eyes: not polished stone, as it appeared from a distance, but some unknown dark wood; every visible surface had been covered with carvings—bizarre, dreamlike pictures that seemed to emerge out of the grain of the wood and not by any craft of knife or chisel. "I had no idea your people were capable of anything like this."

"They say that it took the demon slaves of my great ancestor—Hellgrind of the Golden Bristles—a single night to construct the entire castle," said Skogsrå. "But me . . . I think it is all superstition."

They mounted to the great double doors, where more troll servants came to greet them, and proceeded down a long, narrow corridor lit by smoking torches that flared into life as they approached, and just as mysteriously died as soon as they passed by. Another set of doors opened soundlessly before them. *Skullgrimm's vanity*, thought the Duchess, *squandering his sorcery to impress his guests. Skullgrimm's arrogance.*

Escorted by the Troll King's servants, the Duchess and her party passed through chamber after chamber, then mounted another twisting stair. This palace, mused the Duchess, betrayed the workings of a convoluted mind—if not the mind of the present occupant, at least of the ancestor who built it.

"They are all in black . . . all of the servants in black," whispered Skogsrå. "It would appear, then, that the King has lost another bride."

"Pray enlighten me, lest I make some dreadful blunder," the Duchess whispered back, putting her hand on his arm. "Is it Skullgrimm's *Queen* who has died?"

"His Queen, yes . . . but not a woman of his own race, as I suppose you mean," replied Skogsrå. "It was the same sort of marriage you meant me to contract with Elsie Vorder . . . a blood marriage."

The Duchess tilted her chin disdainfully. "It was Skullgrimm, then, who killed her? Full mourning, under those circumstances, seems a bit excessive."

The Jarl glared at her, curling his lip as though greatly offended. "Undoubtedly, she died when the royal thirst became too imperative, when His Majesty's demands upon her became too fatally taxing . . . that is not to say that her death did not arise as an accident, or that Skullgrimm does not feel her loss. Indeed, she cannot be long dead," Skogsrå added, "or he would have replaced her by now."

At last they came into a lofty wooden hall, lit by a great fire on an immense central hearth. Massive pine logs snapped and exploded, filling the air with a resinous fragrance. King Skullgrimm XII and his courtiers had gathered for supper around a long table draped in black linen, set with pewter, silver, crystal, and gold. In the shadowy chamber, the effect was rich but somber.

The Duchess studied the assembly with unconcealed curiosity. Many appeared to be so-called half trolls like Skogsrå, victims of some minor deformity, a hoof or a twisted limb, but a number displayed disfigurements fully as extravagant as the pig's trotters and tufted tail of the warden at the gate.

The Duchess's glance passed from one troll to another, a little bewildered by their variety: a haughty nobleman, who sat with goatlike feet tucked under his chair—when he spoke, a forked tongue flickered, serpent-like, between his lips . . . a lugubrious grey-skinned scholar, sporting a nose at least twelve inches long, which a servant was obliged to hold aside for him, whenever he lifted his cup . . . a voluptuous female, auburn-haired and rather attractive, with a sharp, vixenish face and pricked ears to match, vivaciously addressing her dinner companion, an elderly troll, distinguished by a fine set of snowy whiskers and an equally impressive pair of ivory tusks.

Skullgrimm himself sat at the head of the table, in a high-backed throne chair. He also wore mourning, deep sable velvet with a wide collar of immaculate point lace; his hair hung to his shoulders in dark golden lovelocks, each curl tied with a black satin ribbon. Handsome and dissipated, he bore a striking resemblance to his cousin the Jarl—until the Duchess chanced to notice the clumsy, bearlike paw resting on the arm of his chair, and a pair of short white horns that grew just above his ears.

"So . . . you arrive," said Skullgrimm, inclining his head as the Duchess and Skogsrå approached him. (Mr. von Eichstätt still hung back, attempting to efface himself behind the tiny figure of the Duchess.) This was not, perhaps, the most gracious of welcomes, but the King smiled as he spoke, revealing teeth as white and as even as the Jarl's own.

The Duchess sank to the floor in a deep curtsy and spoke a few graceful words, but Skullgrimm waved them aside, gesturing with his good hand. "You have come too late to join us . . . nor would you find our feast to your liking." Here, he directed a sly glance at the whey-faced, shrinking Mr. von Eichstätt. "A servant will show you to the rooms prepared for you, and a more suitable repast will be served to you there."

The Duchess had come a long way in order to do business with the King, but even she dared not gainsay the royal decree. So she resumed an upright posture, Skogsrå and the doctor each bowed—the Jarl gracefully, von Eichstätt stiffly—and they followed the indicated servant out of the hall.

The Duchess left the room seething, outraged by this apparent discourtesy, but she was somewhat mollified to discover that the bedchamber allotted to her was spacious, and luxurious in its way, with a white bearskin on the floor, woven hangings upon the wall, a roaring fire on the hearth, and a blanket of silky white furs cast carelessly across the bed. The maid-servant, too, who had been assigned to wait on the Duchess during her stay, appeared comely and decent in black wool and spotless white linen. The girl *looked* human enough, but whenever she moved, a rustling and a rasping sound issued from the modest skirts of her gown.

Mr. von Eichstätt bestowed only a cursory glance at his own bedchamber before hastening to wait on the Gracious Lady.

"Well, Doctor," said the Duchess. "Do you now regret the impulse of scientific curiosity that brought you so far?"

"By no means," he replied, with another clumsy bow (he was not usually nearly so awkward, but fear tended to stiffen his limbs). "If my manner seems odd to you, it is merely . . . excitement. I believe that I may do much good here."

"You may certainly benefit me, if Skullgrimm agrees to an exchange of favors," said the Duchess, as the serving-maid divested her of the heavy crimson mantle and swansdown hood, and arranged the skirts of her matching velvet gown. "But your motives, I collect, are rather more lofty."

A pair of trolls arrived shortly thereafter, bearing trays of food, which they arranged on a trestle table near the fire. "You will join me, of course," said the Duchess to the doctor. "And you, too, my dear Skogsrå," she added, as the Jarl appeared in the doorway and limped into the room.

In chairs hastily provided by the servants, the three sat down to dine. The main course proved to be a spiced stew of unknown origin, presented in a silvery tureen. Von Eichstätt declined a portion, and even the Duchess hesitated.

"You need not fear to taste it," smirked the Jarl. "The delicacy you are thinking of is far too hard come by in this part of the world, for Skullgrimm to waste it on unappreciative palates. The odds are, you will find this contains nothing more exotic than reindeer meat. The servants virtually live on it . . . though seldom so carefully prepared."

Nevertheless, the Duchess and the doctor chose to dine on bread and cheese that evening, and to wash down their meal with the bitter troll ale.

In the morning, Skullgrimm summoned the Duchess to wait on him in his library. "You had best begin by stating what object brings you here," said the King, indicating a chair for her to sit upon. "Your letter, announcing your imminent arrival, was . . . somewhat obscure."

The Duchess sank into the chair with a rustle of satin gown and silken petticoats. She had dressed, this morning, in pearl-grey taffeta and cobweb lace, the nearest thing to full mourning that she could contrive on short notice.

She looked very dainty and even deceptively frail, in that high dark room. Crimson velvet draperies covered the windows; towering bookshelves rose all the way up to the lofty ceiling. A ladder equipped with blunt brass hooks and a brass railing that ran all around the upper portion of the room were apparently intended for use by the servants in procuring the higher volumes for His Majesty's use. The only light came from a narrow slit between the curtains and a small, aromatic fire burning on an iron tripod beside Skullgrimm's chair.

"Your Majesty will perhaps recall a conversation we had, some three or four years past, when I had the privilege to meet you in Katrinsberg. You told me then," said the Duchess, folding her hands in her lap, "that the physical . . . traits . . . of your people weigh heavily on your mind, imposing as they do such a fearful obstacle to your 'wholesome intercourse' with the other races."

Those, indeed, had been Skullgrimm's words—though speaking privately afterwards, the Jarl had assured her that His Majesty's motives were not nearly so elevated. "*We have, as I must tell you, a marked aversion to our own deformities—particularly Skullgrimm, who is amazingly vain and selfish . . . yes, even for a troll. Were all or most of us born the same, I believe we should long since have accepted our peculiarities, even learned to regard them as marks of distinction. But since our misfortunes are so many and so varied, this does not occur. Nor are we a race known for tolerance and compassion. As a result, we find ourselves, almost without exception, the most repulsive beings on the face of the earth. Do not ask me how (this being so) we contrive to mate and bring forth new generations,*" Skogsrå had added distastefully, "*for it is not a subject that we care to discuss. Suffice to say that Skullgrimm wishes to cut a dashing and desirable figure . . . and cannot do so, even in the eyes of his own people.*"

Now the King leaned a bit forward in his chair, an expression of deep interest written on his face. "Am I to understand that you have found a way to cure my people of their disfigurements?"

"Not I, myself," said the Duchess. "But I bring with me the brilliant young doctor, Mr. Theophilus von Eichstätt. He caused a great stir in Wäldermark, at the Prince's College of

Chirurgeons, by removing the natural spurs from the legs of one rooster and successfully grafting them to the comb of another. I, myself, was privileged to see the results, and I beg leave to assure you that no trickery was involved."

By now, the Troll King leaned well forward in his chair. "Mr. von Eichstätt," continued the Duchess, "is confident that he can perform a similar operation on your behalf, substituting a perfectly formed human hand for your own . . . somewhat eccentric appendage. It would only be a matter, I suppose, of diverting a portion of meat from Your Majesty's table?

"Though I very much fear," she added, with a regretful shake of her head, "that nothing at all can be done about your horns— unless you would like them sawn off near the skull? Your hair would cover the—"

"I do not care so much about the horns," Skullgrimm interrupted her, making an impatient gesture with his hairy paw. "I wear a hat when I go out among Men. And here at court . . . I have been told they would be accounted quite handsome on a gnome."

He leaned back in his chair, appeared to be weighing the matter very carefully in his mind. "It is all very well, this talk of spurs and roosters," he said at last. "To graft tissue from one creature to another of the same species is one thing . . . but to mingle the flesh of the different races remains quite another matter."

The Duchess smoothed out her ruffles of cobweb lace, gifted the troll with her most enchanting smile. Even Skullgrimm felt the influence of that fairy glamour—a small, reluctant smile appeared on his handsome face.

"Am I not living proof that the flesh of different races may . . . mingle, as you put it?" *And equally proof of the folly of any such feat,* she added silently, though her dazzling smile in no way diminished. "They say, too, that of all the races, Man and troll are most nearly related. But indeed, even among totally different species the thing may be accomplished. And with Your Majesty's permission, we shall arrange a demonstration, one that must satisfy all your doubts."

The King made a steeple of his hands—the narrow-fingered perfect one and the grotesque paw. "I am interested, of course. But I do not believe that the Duchess of Zar-Wildungen comes all this way for the sole purpose of obliging me," he added shrewdly. "Tell me, then, what you expect *me* to do for *you*, in return for the services of your chirurgeon."

The Duchess made a tiny, fluttering gesture. "It is a small matter, really. I am told that Your Majesty, being an adept in the Dark Arts, has the power to create a simulacrum . . . an animate double to any sentient creature that walks the earth. Or was I misinformed?"

"You were not misinformed," said Skullgrimm, a frown creasing his brow. "Was it Haakon Skogsrå who told you this? I did not know he took so deep an interest in matters of sorcery."

"No, no," the Duchess hastened to assure him, remembering what the Jarl had said earlier: that Skullgrimm had a habit of devouring his more ambitious kinsmen. "It was Vodni, of course. Quite a clever fellow, young Vodni. His death was a sad loss. Skogsrå does not serve me nearly so well. His is not . . . not the very brightest of intellects, you know."

"You confirm my own opinion," said the King, his frown giving way to a smile of lazy amusement. "A handsome fellow, of course, and always a great favorite with the women. So very vain, he is, that even here, among his own kind, he does not remove his boots."

But then the King turned his thoughts to the matter of the simulacrum. "And so," he said, with a measuring gaze, "I have an idea you would like one of these doubles for your own use?"

"That is so," said the Duchess, striving to return his gaze with one that was wide-eyed and ingenuous. "I am a student of sorcery myself, but scarcely more than a dabbler. Indeed, I dabble in so many things! To create the simulacrum is quite beyond *my* poor art, yet I desire such a double for use in . . . in a little scheme of my own—I will not bore you with the details. That is what I should wish in return for Mr. von Eichstätt's services."

The Troll King laughed softly to himself. "That is something which I can easily provide you. Indeed, it were mere child's play for a sorcerer of my talents. Very well, arrange your demonstration. If I am satisfied with the results, perhaps I shall be disposed to grant your request."

6.

Wherein Mr. von Eichstätt tests his Resolve, and many Strange things are Accomplished.

Mr. von Eichstätt was a true Philosopher. Indeed, so great was his philosophy, it had brought him north to this present pass and enabled him to treat with trolls. He knew little—and concerned himself less—with the motives of his patroness, the Duchess; for the doctor, it was all scientific curiosity, and this unprecedented opportunity to conduct experiments which were strictly forbidden in his native land.

The trolls prepared an operating theatre for him, in a chamber behind the kitchens which had all the appearance of an abattoir, and there, two days following his arrival at the troll court, von Eichstätt performed an exceedingly delicate procedure, grafting a pair of human testicles which were brought to him on ice (*Never mind*, the doctor told himself, *how the organs were obtained . . . a small sacrifice in the service of science*), attaching them to the intestines of a live calf.

Then a fortnight passed, during which the doctor, the Duchess, and the King of the Trolls awaited the outcome. Needless to state, those two weeks passed uneasily for the young doctor, who displayed a queasy distrust of every bit of meat he was offered during that time. Nor could he repress a shudder when one of Skullgrimm's hairless black pets skulked into the room and rolled a sulphurous eye in his direction.

Even the Duchess, though possessed of a more sanguine temperament, felt a trifle uneasy. It seemed to her that Skullgrimm's courtiers often gazed at her with a speculative eye. She thought, perhaps, that some had a fancy to sample a dish of three-quarter fairy—for all they must know that her flesh, which contained six parts fire and air to every measure of earth and water, would hardly agree with them. The troll baroness with the foxy red ears was the worst of the lot; the creature

34

had an intolerable habit of running her tongue over her lips and smiling suggestively whenever the Duchess walked by.

At last the day arrived when Mr. von Eichstätt reopened the calf's abdomen to discover that the grafted testicles had, indeed, melded with the sturdy bovine tissue. Bloody and triumphant, the doctor looked up from the slaughtered calf to meet the Troll King's enigmatic gaze.

"Most impressive," said Skullgrimm.

But later, when the doctor had washed the blood and the noisome bodily fluids from his hands, slipped into his coat, and accompanied the Duchess from the abattoir to an audience chamber, His Majesty expressed some remaining reservations.

"There is a peculiarity of my people, which perhaps you do not know . . . we possess a certain regenerative ability, which is more a curse than a blessing. When one limb is amputated (whether by chance or as the result of some medical procedure), it often happens that *two* identical limbs grow back in its place."

"But of course we knew this," the Duchess replied airily. "And Mr. von Eichstätt has devised a method to combat that tendency."

The doctor cleared his throat nervously, took out a handkerchief, and mopped the moisture from his brow. "It is merely a matter of cutting off the extra limbs as they appear, and cauterizing the wound so they do not grow back again."

"Nevertheless," replied Skullgrimm, "you will give me a new hand, and we shall await the results, before I even consider granting the Duchess her request."

And so, the next day, yet another operation took place, during which von Eichstätt amputated the Troll King's hideous paw and grafted another hand, strong but beautiful, successfully in its place. (*Do not ask where it comes from,* the doctor had cautioned himself inwardly. *Does the stonemason ask whence comes his stone . . . the baker, his flour . . . the goldsmith, his gold . . . ?*)

A week later, His Majesty, well on his way to recovery, sent for the Duchess and Jarl Skogsrå. They found him in the library, standing by one of the windows, gazing pensively out across the frosty courtyard to the iron gates. He had exchanged his deep mourning for an antiquated suit of emerald velvet with a pair of puffed rhinegrave breeches, fringed and laced and adorned with primrose-colored ribbons, and his new hand had been bandaged in black silk. Except for the horns, he made quite a proper man.

"You know, of course, that to do as you request, I require a little blood from the creature you would have me duplicate."

"Of course," said the Duchess. "And I have come prepared." She reached into her reticule and produced a tiny bottle. "Here is a vial of Elsie Vorder's blood."

"The Gracious Lady is a miracle of resource," exclaimed the astonished Skogsrå. "How did she come by this?"

"Two years ago, when Elsie was bled for some trifling disorder, I instructed her physician—who was, as you may suppose, of my choosing and in my pay—to provide me with a small amount of Elsie's blood. Having no immediate use for the blood, yet refusing to discount the possibility that a use might someday present itself, I prudently kept this vial against some future need. It is hermetically sealed, as you can see, but I fear the blood has thickened over the course of time, despite all the spells I have worked to keep it liquid."

"It will serve," said the Troll King, turning on his heel. "You must follow me."

A door in a corner of the library opened on a narrow staircase, and the Duchess and Skogsrå followed Skullgrimm up two flights to a large chamber, which had been completely outfitted as a magician's laboratory, with copper vats and iron mortars, silver orreries, seals, wands, pentacles . . .

It was a strange and intriguing room, thought the Duchess. A pale green fire burned on the hearth, like to no fire the Duchess had ever seen before, undoubtedly sorcerous in origin. The laboratory boasted the usual stuffed crocodile, a collection of bones and skulls, a case of tiny, mummified animals, and something standing up in a corner, gazing back at her with glass eyes, which—heavens, it *was* . . . it could only be . . . a stuffed dwarf! There were also a great many shelves filled with books, some of them marked with the serpentine sign of the Scolos, and one enormous black volume, literally groaning with ancient secrets, which hung suspended over the fire, bound shut with massive chains.

The Duchess drew in her breath. "May the Powers preserve us. You actually own an agrippa!" An agrippa, as she well knew, was the rarest and most powerful of magic books, so powerful, in truth, that its very presence in any house must wreak havoc, unless its malice were restrained by bands of cold iron. The book shuddered in its chains and groaned more loudly than before when the Troll King walked by.

On a long table in the center of the room lay a life-sized clay figure, bearing a faint resemblance to the human female form. The Duchess eyed this simulacrum with a certain skepticism— the figure had been fashioned considerably cruder than she had anticipated. "And can you really animate this . . . this heap of clay? Will it truly become a convincing counterfeit of Miss Elsie Vorder?"

"I will," said Skullgrimm, "but the means to achieve that shall remain a secret. I must celebrate the rituals and chant the spells in strict privacy. Come to me again, tomorrow afternoon. You will know then the extent of my abilities."

At the appointed hour, the King's servants came to escort the Duchess and Skogsrå to His Majesty's somber bedchamber. There, seated in an ornamental chair of the by now familiar dark wood, was a demure figure costumed in a white gown and a gauzy veil.

With a flourish, Skullgrimm lifted the veil. The Duchess gasped. Incredible to think that graceful figure, those soft golden curls, that sweet fragile smile, could possibly belong to an artificial creation. "Amazing! Incredible. It is a perfect replica!" the Duchess exclaimed, clapping her hands together. "Does it speak?"

"It may, in time, learn to parrot certain phrases . . . but that is the most that you may expect," said Skullgrimm. "The blood you provided me—along with my spells—animates the monster, gives it the form that you see. But for the golem to retain this semblance of life, you must feed it daily, according to my instructions. You must provide the creature with—have you considered a name for the monster?" he interrupted himself. "It will be more docile and responsive if you give it a name."

"Her name is Cecile," said the Duchess, walking a full circle around the chair, the better to examine the Troll King's creation. "A pretty name, is it not?"

Skullgrimm nodded his approval. "Elsie . . . Cecile . . . they contain the same sounds. Yes, that is an excellent notion. It will serve to bind them more closely together.

"This . . . Cecile, then," he continued. "You must provide her with the viscera of living creatures every day. If you feed her by hand, again she will be more likely to obey you. The hearts of cold-blooded creatures, of fish or reptiles, will do at need, though the golem will then incline to be sluggish, and the hearts of mice and birds are better still. The fresher they are—as, for instance, if they should be torn directly from the breast of the living animal—the greater will be her degree of animation."

The Duchess shuddered distastefully. Though she was more than willing to sacrifice any number of tiny lives to feed the golem, she did balk at ripping out their hearts before they were dead.

"Ah well," said the King, recognizing her reluctance. "It is not an absolute necessity. You may kill them more gently first . . . by the use of spirits of mandragora, or by drowning them, or by any other method you prefer. You are not (I perceive) an artist like myself. You do not wish to do these things precisely as they ought to be done."

With smiles and many professions of gratitude, the Duchess took the simulacrum by the hand and coaxed it out of the room. The Jarl followed after her.

"Be ready to leave in some haste at sunrise," said the Duchess, very low, once they were out of earshot of Skullgrimm's servants.

The Jarl raised a painted eyebrow. "Why so hasty a retreat? Shall I notify Mr. von Eichstätt, or will you?"

"I do not intend to take the good Theophilus with me," said the Duchess. "He would only slow us down. Moreover, I am certain he would refuse to leave so soon. He will wish to remain, in order to monitor the King's recovery. But as for me . . . I do not wish to be in the palace, or anywhere in Skullgrimm's realm, when the flesh mutates and new paws continue to appear."

The Jarl registered extreme astonishment. "But is it not true that this can be prevented by cauterizing the wound as von Eichstätt has explained?"

"Well," the Duchess admitted, as they proceeded down the corridor, with the obedient golem in tow, "it is just possible— but I am inclined to think not. You are (of course) aware that no one knows *which* of the Nine Powers created the race of trolls, that many scholars believe your people only a mutation of the human race. Theophilus proceeds from the misconception (and I confess that I was unwilling to disabuse him of that notion) that the singular properties of troll regeneration, quite as much as troll deformities, arise from some fleshly disease that afflicts your race."

"And you believe otherwise?" whispered Skogsrå.

"I am perfectly convinced otherwise," said the lady. Her bedchamber door silently opened at her approach, and she led the docile "Cecile" across the threshold.

The demure maid-servant was in the room, tidying up the scattered petticoats, gloves, lace handkerchiefs, and silken hose with which the Duchess had littered her bedchamber. It was impossible to speak while the maid was present, so the Duchess dismissed her.

"I do not wish to insult you on this occasion, my dear Jarl," said the lady, as the door closed softly behind the departing troll. "But I believe that the odd characteristics of your race are entirely due to a spiritual disease.

"Back in Thornburg," she continued, "Mr. von Eichstätt's colleagues, putting his methods to use, might do much good among those innocent unfortunates who come by their deformities either by accident of birth or as the result of some injury or disease. But I believe that some disfiguring . . . taint . . . of black magic, in which your people have steeped themselves for hundreds of years, has worked itself into the very fabric of your flesh. You are the victims of a spiritual disease, and for *that* you are not likely to find any simple bodily remedy."

"But then," said the Jarl, wrinkling his brow, "but then, if Mr. von Eichstätt's theories should be proven false, it is altogether likely that the King will *eat* him. For myself, I regard that consequence of little importance, but I had thought the Gracious Lady cherished a certain degree of fondness for that young man."

"As I do," the Duchess answered, with such exaggerated sweetness that the Jarl experienced—as he had often experienced before—a sudden violent urge. Naturally, he stifled it.

All unaware of the tempestuous emotions she had aroused in his bosom, she maneuvered the golem into a corner of the room and left her standing there, out of the way. "But really, I do not anticipate such a doleful fate for such a clever young fellow as Theophilus. For one thing, his flesh is diseased. Oh yes, I assure you. You have observed his pallor, his nervous habits . . . not altogether due to his discomfort in these surroundings.

"Such is his scientific zeal, his devotion to his philosophy," the Duchess went on, as she took a seat in a chair by the fire, "that he has actually infected himself with syphilis, in order to observe the progress of the disease at first hand. He confided as much to me in an intimate moment—or one, at any rate, which threatened to become intimate—and for all I know, he may carry other loathsome afflictions as well. But the one should suffice to discourage Skullgrimm. I shall leave a letter for the King, acquainting him with that circumstance, for his own sake as much as the doctor's."

The Jarl shook his head doubtfully and continued to frown, but the Duchess went on blithely. "But even more than that, I have every confidence that Mr. von Eichstätt will be able to formulate a new theory and present it convincingly . . . and another theory, and still another, as proves necessary to appease the King and appeal to Skullgrimm's vanity . . . until—who knows?—he may actually stumble on the true solution, and ransom himself with a successful operation.

"It is just," said the lady, with a faint little shrug, "that I do not choose to linger here as the King's prisoner, until the day that Mr. von Eichstätt finally accomplishes that."

7.

Which carries us Back to the continent of Calliope.

It was a brisk, bright afternoon in the season of Frost, when the mail coach carrying Sera and her friends lurched down the coast road toward the town of Hobb's Church. The journey south had been a long and tedious one, as well as most odiously round-about—a necessary precaution to cover their tracks—and Sera, who sat crammed into a corner by the window, felt weary, rumpled, and crushed. For two days, she and Mr. Jonas had shared the forward seat with a matron in hoops and her excessively pretty and just as excessively silly sixteen-year-old daughter, and a constant stream of shrill, inconsequential chatter (thought Sera) was enough to induce the headache, even in someone who had not already suffered the discomforts of a fortnight's travel. Having endured a journey of just that duration herself, it was all she could do to stifle an impulse to give the girl a good shaking, and command her to hold her prattling tongue.

On the opposite seat, Elsie and Jed had fared slightly better, sharing the bench with a grim elderly tutor and his cowed little pupil. Sera pretended not to notice that Jed and Elsie, for the last hour, had been holding hands, under cover of Elsie's squirrel-skin muff.

The rhythm of the coach changed as dirt road gave way to cobblestones, and the diligence rumbled down Hobb's Church High Street. Sera lifted the curtain and peered out her window, hoping to get some sense of the town as she passed through.

It was a typical colonial settlement, built, like most coastal cities and villages, on rising ground; a stout seawall protected the town from the devastating lunar tides. It appeared to be a village mostly of full-sized men, and had more of the seaport about it than Lootie's Bay: sailors in blue coats walked the streets, with a rolling gait and gold rings in their ears; a dozen ships rode in the harbor, with white sails and red, and gaily painted figureheads; some of the merchants had even nailed up wooden figures over their doors, in place of shop signs.

The village green was located in the exact center of the town, and there on the square—nothing more, at this time of year, than a plot of frostbitten brown grass—the mail coach came to a halt. Sera, Elsie, Jed, and Mr. Jonas climbed out, and the coachman and the guard swung down from their perch. While the gentlemen attended to the luggage, and Elsie stuck her head back inside the coach, bidding the other passengers a polite, if insincere, farewell, Sera shook out her petticoats, retied her cloak strings, and glanced around her.

A marble statue of King Henry IX, late of Imbria, held court in the frosty square, with pigeons and screaming sea gulls as courtiers and sycophants. On the far side of the lawn stood a modest white church with a high steeple, and two wych-elms to shade it during the warm seasons. Beyond the church rose a brooding eminence . . . Spyglass Hill, according to Mr. Herring's letter, with the famous Deeping Caverns below, and the Old Seamen's Cemetery sprawled across the upper slopes.

"What a quaint little town," said Elsie. "All the crooked buildings . . . and I do think the figureheads mounted over the doors are terribly droll, don't you?"

Sera swept a dark apprehensive glance over the buildings clustered around the square: most did present an oddly tilted appearance, as though they were perched on sinking foundations. "Highly amusing . . . I only hope the whole place may not tumble down about our ears."

From the square to the home of Mr. Siegfried Herring was only a step. Things were managed differently here in the colonies, and the "gentlemen Glassmakers" (which was to say those members of the speculative branch of the Guild not in any way involved in the manufacture of glass) were not the noblemen and merchant princes who formed the Continental guilds. No, the Guild drew its members from among the ranks of honest tradesmen of every sort and description: coal merchants, peruke-makers, joiners, upholsterers, printers, booksellers, and the like. Mr. Herring made his living as a cabinetmaker, and he lived alone. He ushered his visitors into his cluttered little cottage near the harbor, with many expressions of pleasure and good-will.

"A bachelor establishment, as you can see. You, my dear Sammuel, and you, too, Mr. Thorn, are more than welcome to lodge with me here, but as for the ladies . . ." As he spoke, he removed a pile of books and papers, a pair of gloves, and a woolen muffler from one of the chairs and offered the seat to Elsie. " . . . as for you ladies, it is well we have already made more suitable arrangements."

Mr. Herring was a lean, lively little Man, long-limbed (for his size), and as agile as a monkey. His linen was immaculate, his coat and his waistcoat of the fashionable cut, and he wore a brown wig, marvelously curled and pomaded. In contrast to the state of his apartments, Mr. Herring displayed an inclination to be fussy about his appearance.

"I have reserved a private dining room at the Eclipse—a most respectable tavern—and we shall dine there at six," said Mr. Herring. "After that, I shall count myself privileged to drive the ladies out to the Academy. It is not much more than a mile."

They arrived at the Eclipse precisely on the hour. The landlord ushered them into a cozy private parlor, papered and paneled in rose and oak, and informed them that supper would be served in a quarter of an hour. In the meantime, Mr. Jonas took out some odd sketches he had made of the island-raising engine. Climbing up on a chair, he spread his papers out on the table, and proceeded to explain the remarkable device to Mr. Herring.

"Yes, yes," said the cabinetmaker, bobbing up and down in his excitement. "I see exactly what you mean. The bronze mirrors to capture the lunar rays . . . the magnets to draw the island up out of the depths . . . and, hmmmm, yes . . . a most *ingenious* system of gears!

"I can provide you with a workroom behind my shop, and all the wood you need to build a framework for the engine," he offered handsomely. "And I know just the man to cast the mirrors and provide the worm screws. But, my dear Sammuel, how on earth do you mean to *attune* the magnets?"

"We have some Panterran relics—in particular, a figurine cast in orichalcum, which may serve to produce a sympathetic vibration and so set up the necessary attraction," said Mr. Jonas.

All during this discourse, Sera stood warming her hands by the fire, listening to Mr. Jonas with growing astonishment. At last, she had to speak. "Such nonsense," she said, under her breath, to Elsie, "I never heard in all my life. Or rather . . . I *have*, but never hoped to hear the like again!"

Jedidiah, who chanced to overhear her, crossed the room, scowling ferociously. "Yes, but it's true," said Sera, her eyes kindling. "You remember Dr. Mirabolo and the 'healing properties' of his magnetic tub. He never *healed* anyone, with his horrid animal magnetism, only sent a parcel of foolish women with imaginary ailments into hysterical convulsions . . . and frightened poor Elsie so badly she was virtually prostrated." She glared a challenge at him. "You said yourself, Jed, that the fellow sounded like a dreadful quack!"

"That," said Jed, with withering dignity, "has nothing to do with the present instance. The healing properties of magnetized waters have yet to be proven, but any fool knows that magnets *attract things!*"

Sera opened her mouth to retort, but thought better of the impulse and held her peace. She was in no mood for one of Jed's painstaking lectures on "natural affinities" and "lesser luminaries" and "the first entity of metals" . . . as though he could overcome her skepticism by explaining things slowly and carefully. As though I were a child or an imbecile, she thought.

But now the landlord and his wife were entering the room, and dinner was about to be served. Mr. Jonas rolled up his plans and put them back in his coat pocket, and Mr. Herring invited his guests to take seats around the table. They all made a good meal on pork pie, clam chowder, corn bread, and ale, then strolled back through the lamplit streets to Mr. Herring's cottage, the three gentlemen discoursing learnedly on pumps and flywheels, balances, valves, and verge escarpments.

Along the way, they passed a clocktower, about a block from the square: a tall brick building with a most decided tilt. The clocks on all four faces had stopped, each at a different hour. "Indeed," said Mr. Herring, following Sera's glance and rightly interpreting her troubled expression. "The structure is so dangerous that no one dares to venture inside and reset the mechanism."

Jedidiah then asked if the town was built on unstable ground . . . was the area prone, as many coastal regions were, to flooding and earth tremors at the full of the moon?

"We believe that our sinking foundations result from extensive tunneling on the part of hobgoblins," replied Mr. Herring. "The local breed is very large and active. No, you have nothing to fear, ladies. They are not at all vicious, only amazingly destructive. Indeed, at one time, we considered them rather an amusing novelty, they are such queer and cunning creatures. In a whimsical moment, the town fathers even named the village after them. But now they cause us a great deal of trouble. Besides their eternal tunneling, they are the most dreadful thieving little rascals you can imagine. Nothing very large, mostly bright trinkets of pinchbeck and paste, which people are inclined to leave carelessly around, and bits of velvet or lace . . . needles and pins . . . they seem to collect these things like—well, rather like magpies are attracted to anything that glitters. Efforts have been made to exterminate the vermin, but—unfortunately—the community is not united on how to deal with them."

He lowered his voice, though there was no one on the street to overhear him. "Some few residents of the town, misled by the creatures' size and appearance, have conceived the fantastic notion that the hobs are actually Rational Beings. Yes, sentient creatures like you and me! An outrageous proposition, of course. But on those grounds, they insist that our methods are much too harsh.

"But really," he added, with a smile, as they entered the cottage gate, "you have just arrived in town, and it is too soon for you to trouble your heads over this bitter debate."

It was now growing late, so the cabinetmaker hitched up his horses, and he and the other gentlemen loaded Elsie's and Sera's baggage into the gig. "The school is located between here and the marsh," said Mr. Herring, lighting the carriage lanthorns, as Jedidiah assisted first Sera and then Elsie up into the open carriage.

"I'll come by tomorrow and see how you like the place," Jed promised Elsie, giving her hand a comforting squeeze before he relinquished it.

"*Are* we so near the marsh?" asked Sera, making room for the cabinetmaker on the narrow seat. "That hardly seems a healthy climate for children to grow in."

"The climate in these parts is wholesome enough, and the children grow rosy and healthy." Mr. Herring took up the reins and spoke to his horses, and the gig started off at a smart clip. "It is, perhaps, not the ideal location for a school, but Miss Jamaica Barebones, the headmistress, has maintained Mothgreen Academy quite successfully for more than fifty years. One cannot blame the *climate* because Miss Barebones finds it difficult to hire and to keep schoolmistresses," he added, as they drove down a dark country lane. "It is— I hope neither of you young ladies suffers from a nervous disposition?" he interrupted himself. "The house . . . they say the house is haunted."

"Stuff and nonsense!" sniffed Sera, though her skin crawled and the hair at the back of her neck stood up just the same. She had far more experience of ghosts than she cared to admit. She did not believe in spectres because she *would* not—past encounters quite to the contrary. Why, the existence of disembodied spirits would be an offense against Reason, a violation of every sensible, orderly principle that Sera held dear—she was not about to encourage the ramshackle creatures by allowing them a speck of credence!

But Elsie, more tolerant, found the prospect delightful. "How exceedingly romantic. That is . . ." She paused doubtfully. "I hope the ghost is not a malignant spirit, or a mischievous one?"

"Not at all," replied Mr. Herring. "Rather a sad one, I should say. By all accounts it is the spirit of old Izrael Barebones, who owned the house before. He was a scholar and an antiquarian, most respectable, for all that he did entertain some odd ideas. Yet, he apparently died with some grave sin on his conscience . . . or perhaps just in possession of some knowledge he is desperate to communicate. He has been endeavoring to do so, without success, for some fifty years now.

"It is not because of any gross misbehavior on the part of the ghost that the previous ladies left the Academy," he added. "It is merely that *elderly* spinsters (as so often take posts of that nature) incline to take the presence of even the most well bred spectre sadly amiss. But it is far otherwise with Miss Jamaica Barebones and the other old ladies now in residence. They are all of a mystical bent, and just as eager to converse with the ghost as he is to communicate with them."

Sera said nothing more, only sat very stiff and erect, and kept her concern to herself. A town undermined by tunneling hobgoblins . . . a school unhealthily located in the vicinity of a bog—sure to be a breeding ground for stinging insects, to say nothing of miasmal airs . . . a school, moreover, said to be haunted by a lugubrious spirit and run by a lady with the fanciful (not to say lurid) name of Jamaica Barebones. No, Sera could not help but entertain serious misgivings as the brisk little gig continued down the road, nor prevent herself from wishing, most heartily, that she and Elsie were safely back in the sane and sensible little town of Lootie's Bay!

Though the night was overcast and most awfully dark out in the country away from the lights of the town, the road ran so smooth and straight, the carriage lamps sufficed to bring them safely to the gates of Mothgreen Academy. They drove past the gates and down a short drive between stunted fruit trees lit with hanging lanthorns, and soon came up before the house.

Outwardly, the building had a respectable appearance, at least by lamplight: two stories high and an attic with dormer windows, two wings built of fieldstone and mortar, and a fine stucco façade at the front, with delicately molded figures of flowers and urns. With candlelight spilling out of a half dozen windows, the house presented a warm and welcoming aspect as the gig drew up in front, and the young ladies and Mr. Herring mounted the steps to the door.

A gangling youth in a cotton smock—evidently the gardener and man of all work—opened the door and took charge of their baggage. "Miss Barebones is in the parlor. You can find your own way, I reckon, Mr. Herring, sir?"

"Indeed I can," said Mr. Herring affably. "Do not trouble yourself, Nathaniel."

Miss Barebones arose immediately from her seat by the fire and came to greet them at the parlor door. A fine, fresh, bustling old lady, dressed with taste and propriety, she looked as ordinary and respectable as the house itself.

Mr. Herring pulled up chairs near the fire for Sera and Elsie, declared that he could not stay—no, not even for a minute—as he had guests of his own, and departed forthwith. While Miss Barebones escorted him to the front door, Sera and Elsie took advantage of her absence to examine their surroundings rather more thoroughly than strict good manners might otherwise have allowed.

There were chintz curtains at the windows, and a collection of fine china arranged on a mahogany sideboard. Yet the parlor otherwise had something of a masculine air, as though old Mr. Barebones, if not actually haunting the place, had at least impressed his personality on the room. There was a fireplace made up of blue and white tiles, with a pair of brass firedogs—firedogs, indeed, for they had been cast in the semblance of two rather belligerent pugs—guarding the hearth. Books in covers of calf and vellum, an antique hourglass, and a porcelain pagoda graced the mantel, and a display of ancient weapons was arranged on one paneled wall. But more than these masculine appointments, more than the dark, heavy furnishings, was the *odor* of the room, an atmosphere of snuff or pipe tobacco pervading the chamber, though it could hardly be that Miss Barebones or the other ladies indulged in the vice themselves.

The headmistress soon returned. Taking a seat on a horsehair sofa, she acquainted Sera and Elsie with their manifold duties. Mothgreen Academy offered instruction in the areas of history, mathematics, geography, poetry, composition, painting, fine needlework, religion, deportment . . . "There are only the five of us to do it all, you know, besides the servants, and we turn out young ladies who are completely educated, not only in the classical mode, but also in household management."

"It sounds very agreeable . . . very sensible," said Sera, her initial prejudices beginning to fade. Through an open double door at one end of the room, she caught reassuring glimpses of her future pupils: a long procession of well-scrubbed little girls in calico wrappers proceeding down the hall, and from there (presumably) to the upper regions of the house.

"They have just had their supper of bread and milk," said Miss Barebones. "And it is now time for bed."

"They look rather sweet," said Elsie. And Sera could not but agree.

The other two schoolmistresses, both impoverished gentlewomen of indeterminate age, entered the parlor soon after. Miss Eglantine was tall, spare, and severe-looking; Miss Fitch was a faded individual who struck Sera as silly but harmless.

"You appear to be healthy and hardy young women . . . I can only hope that your nerves are good," Miss Eglantine announced in ominous tones.

Miss Fitch tittered and fluttered her eyes. "Oh, Rosabelle, pray do not speak so! You will frighten them away on their first night."

"By the Nine Powers! Who said anything to frighten them away?" Miss Eglantine wanted to know. "It is you who will put ideas into their heads."

The headmistress personally escorted Sera and Elsie upstairs to their rooms, lighting the way with a candle. "I do hope that Uncle Izrael does not disturb either of you during the night," she said matter-of-factly, as they climbed the stairs to the top floor—quite as though a resident apparition were the most natural thing in the world. "He does sometimes get restless when there are new people in the house."

Sera (still reeling from this declaration) felt only a little reassured to discover that her attic bedchamber was directly next door to Elsie's. But the rooms were neat and well aired, each with a dormer window and a view of the rose garden below.

"Some of your pupils—the younger girls—are just down the hall," said Miss Barebones, lighting the candle on Sera's nightstand and turning to go. She paused on the threshold. "Some of them can be quite lively . . . they do not easily settle down to sleep at night. But you must be very firm with them. Should anyone come knocking at your door, you must just send her away."

Sera and Elsie helped each other to unpack their baggage, moving from one room to the other. Then Sera took up her candle, kissed Elsie good night, and returned to her own bedchamber.

A sharp rapping on her bedchamber door woke Sera from a deep, dreamless slumber. Her first impulse was to ignore it, in the hope that whoever had knocked would grow discouraged and go away. But then the rapping grew louder, more insistent, and someone rattled the doorknob.

Sera climbed wearily out of bed, wrapped herself in a shawl she had draped over a bedpost, felt her way in the dark to the door, and threw it open.

Only a dim oil lamp hanging from a beam near the top of the stairs lighted the corridor. Sera took a tentative step across the threshold, and then another. Except for herself, the hall was empty. But that being so . . . She thought she must have heard any footsteps retreating across the bare floorboards, a creaking of hinges if one of the doors down the hall had opened and closed—it was impossible to move silently in these elderly houses. Sera shivered a little, standing there in her nightgown in the shadowy corridor, barefoot and puzzled.

Behind her, the bedchamber door suddenly slammed shut. Sera jumped, gasped, and clutched at her shawl. Then she laughed, a trifle breathlessly, and scolded herself for reacting so foolishly.

"Only a draught," she said aloud, with only the tiniest tremor in her voice. But when she put her hand on the knob and turned it, she found that the door refused to open. Rattle the handle and shake the door as she might, it simply would not budge.

Sera ground her teeth, a surge of irritation banishing her fear. She had a strong mind to tell Uncle Izrael Barebones what she thought of him, but it was beneath her dignity to speak with imaginary spectres. *Whoever it was,* she thought, *I'll not give him or her the satisfaction!*

And with that resolution, she straightened her spine and lifted her chin, and proceeded down the hall to Elsie's bedchamber, where she climbed silently into bed beside her sleeping cousin, and spent a very long, and very restless, night.

8.

Which reunites the Reader with a certain Elusive gentleman.

It was the thirty-first day of the season of Frost, a short ten days
'til the turn of the year, and grim winter held sway over vast
stretches of Euterpe. But in Zammarco, the picturesque city of
canals and bridges, the weather remained mild: frosty nights
and mornings, and cool, bright, sunny afternoons. It was that
time of the year known as the Winter Carnival, when the walk-
ways and plazas were crowded with pedlars, open-air puppet
theatres, strolling musicians, and masked revelers, when the
gondolas and pleasure barges along the canals had been freshly
painted and gilded, and decorated with ribbons and banners.

But the city-state of Zammarco was traditionally a city of
masks and intrigue—not only during Carnival. An aristocracy
masquerading as a republic, Zammarco was ruled by a heredi-
tary senate; and the Senate, in turn, labored under the domi-
nation of a conclave of powerful families—from whose ranks,
invariably, rose the most powerful figure of all: the President of
the Senate, or Oligarch, as he was more commonly called. The
Senate as a whole, and the Conclave in particular, had earned
a reputation for ruthless methods, a brutal efficiency enforcing
its edicts: on the senatorial payroll, at any given time, were
dozens of spies and paid informants, poisoners, torturers, and
bully swordsmen.

The Most Exalted and Equable Republic remained, exclusively, a city of full-sized Men. Dwarves and gnomes might
come there to visit or to conduct business, but an edict forbade
them to settle within the city. The good citizens of Zammarco
were rampant xenophobes—this did not, however, prevent
them from keeping black-skinned slaves.

The Oligarch lived, at the Republic's expense, in a lavish
residence on the lagoon, a great ornate building (it was never

51

called a palace) with a prison and a number of public offices attached.

To the Residence at nightfall, on the day in question, came a slight foreign gentleman, who entered not by the principal gate on the lagoon, but by a small "secret" entrance at the back. *Sir Simon Blood* was the name that he whispered at a wrought-iron grillwork, and a door swung open to admit him.

His appearance was dapper if somewhat somber, considering the time of year. He wore his hair loose in a tumble of powdery white curls about his shoulders, and was dressed all in black, even to the falling lace at his throat and his wrists. His very eyes were a sober grey, his skin so fair it was almost white, and the only bit of color about his person was a tiny crimson patch, heart-shaped, that he wore under one eye. He carried an ebony cane, adorned with black tassels.

The rugged-looking individual who opened the door led Sir Simon through a maze of marble halls and corridors. He lifted a tapestry to reveal a hidden door, knocked three times, and whispered a few words. The door opened soundlessly.

At his escort's invitation, Sir Simon passed through, into a vast gilded and frescoed chamber. His guide did not follow him in, and the door snapped shut, as silently as it had opened.

Sir Simon shook out his ruffles, glanced casually around him. But that casual glance was remarkably comprehensive; he had trained himself to notice the most minute details. At one end of the chamber, upon a sort of stepped dais, stood a gathering of perhaps a dozen aristocrats robed in senatorial red. They were grouped around a low marble seat and an old man in a ponderous black wig and purple robes, so bent that his head nearly touched his knees.

"You may approach," said a haughty voice. Since his eyes had been momentarily elsewhere, Sir Simon could not tell who had spoken. He walked gracefully toward the dais, removed his hat, made them a prodigiously elegant bow, and waited politely for further instructions.

These came from the man in purple, evidently the Oligarch, speaking in a harsh and rusty voice, who ordered him to state his business. "It is to be a denunciation, I suppose?"

"Indeed," said Sir Simon, in his pleasantly accented voice. "I am employed, as you may know, by the government of Imbria, to investigate the white-slave trade. In the course of my investigations, I have taken a keen interest in one group of scoundrels in particular, who conduct their vicious traffic in human flesh in all the great cities of Euterpe. Since arriving in The Most Exalted and Equable Republic, I have identified one of the principal master-minds behind the whole dreadful operation as a certain Count Azimet, resident in this city."

There was a stir of excitement among the senators. "You have proof of this?" asked the Oligarch.

Sir Simon bowed low once more. "Not any compelling proof, not as yet. But I had been informed . . . That is, I understood that the correct procedure in Zammarco was to lay information with the authorities and the Senate would conduct its own investigation."

"Such information generally comes to us through one of our own citizens," said the sneering voice, and this time Sir Simon located the source: a proud, pale, ascetic aristocrat in a black wig. "We do not usually welcome the interference of foreigners."

Sir Simon assumed an air of gentle, almost wistful apology. "I beg your pardon. I had supposed, since I was admitted here, that my friend Baron Onda had already presented my credentials. If you wish, I will— "

"Ah, to be sure," the haughty senator interrupted him. "Our trusty Baron Onda—*not* in any way connected with the government of Imbria, but a longtime votary of the Glassmakers— has acquainted us with some of your more colorful exploits. We apprehend that you are not even a constable or a thief-taker, but, in fact, a paid assassin!"

Sir Simon delicately removed an imaginary piece of lint from one dark sleeve. He needed time to compose himself. Though he cherished few illusions about his calling, the senator's words struck him most forcibly as an insult—particularly coming from a member of a body notoriously addicted to the use of the strappado and garrote.

"I am a gentleman of independent means, and though my activities are, to some extent, sponsored . . . by the Imbrian government, or the Glassmakers Guild, or some other body altogether—it can scarcely matter to you . . . it is not to murder people that they employ me," he replied steadily, though a tiny muscle twitched at the corner of his mouth, and his eyebrows met in a hard line.

The frozen hauteur of the senator's face grew considerably more pronounced. "I stand corrected. These many deaths for which, according to Baron Onda, you are responsible . . . they were merely a matter of personal inclination? The—what should I say?—the restless high-jinks of impetuous youth?"

Sir Simon clenched one small, white (and surprisingly capable-looking) hand. How he might have replied remained unknown, for the Oligarch made an imperious gesture, indicating that this discussion held no interest for him.

"You are correct in supposing that, in general, a single denunciation is sufficient to set the wheels of justice into motion," the Oligarch said in his creaking voice, nodding his heavy head. "Nor are you the first to question the source of Count Azimet's really quite extraordinary wealth. Many of our aristocrats, myself and my colleagues included, disapprove of his lavish . . . some might say decadent . . . style of living. Yet he is undoubtedly a man of power and influence, and rather more to the point: a member of one of our senatorial families. Under these circumstances, you must appreciate the need for more solid evidence.

"If you should choose to continue your investigation and obtain that evidence, you may address us once more. In the meantime," said the Oligarch, "you may leave the same way that you came."

Though far from satisfied, Sir Simon had no choice but to bow once more, murmur a few words of gratitude for the Oligarch's kind indulgence, and withdraw by the same door he had entered. He found his rugged escort waiting on the other side to show him the way out.

Puzzling over the question of just how to obtain the necessary evidence, how to ingratiate himself with the Count and so gain his confidence (or at least access to his private papers), Sir Simon was at first too preoccupied to notice the hasty footsteps that followed him down the corridor—not until the one who came hurrying in pursuit had almost caught up to him. Then he whirled around with his hand on the knob of his cane, prepared to pull out the concealed blade . . .

Recognizing the elegant figure in red as a member of the secret conclave he had just addressed, Sir Simon did not draw his sword. Instead, he bowed his head. "I have not the honor . . . ?"

"Don Balthazar Onda. Perhaps my cousin has mentioned me."

"Ah yes," said Sir Simon, studying the senator's features. The face within the heavy chestnut wig did bear a strong familial resemblance to Baron Onda's own. And his friend had mentioned a kinsman in the powerful inner circle, a man who possessed a greater zeal for justice than any of his fellow senators, a man who might, for that reason, be regarded as a possible ally.

At a motion from the aristocrat, Sir Simon's escort withdrew, leaving the senator to lead the way out of the Residence. "You are personally acquainted with Count Azimet, Sir Simon?"

"Only by reputation."

"Then I will perform the introduction," said Don Balthazar, as they proceeded down the corridor. "I have been invited to an entertainment at the Count's palace two nights hence. You shall go, too, as my guest. And also, if you will permit me, I give you a word of advice. The Count is ruled by two obsessions: his love of luxury and his collection of curiosities. If you wish to win his favor and his confidence, you cannot do better than to bring him some rare gift to capture his fancy. Is it possible that you can contrive something on such short notice?"

A smile flashed in Sir Simon's eyes as he made the senator a very pretty obeisance. "I am known for my contrivances. And as for your offer of an introduction: I accept with pleasure and a keen sense of obligation."

"I am pleased to be able to offer you my services," said Don Balthazar, with a bow fully as elegant as Sir Simon's own.

The following afternoon found Sir Simon twenty miles from Zammarco, in the country of Spagne, at the rural estate of a certain noble and wealthy dwarf. The gatekeeper recognized him at once—for he had been a recent and welcome visitor at the villa. Sir Simon turned his horse over to a groom, crossed the statuary garden with a light step, and mounted the shallow stone steps to the front door. He gained immediate entry to the house and from there into the master's study.

"My good friend," said the dwarf, rising from his chair to greet Sir Simon, with an expression of friendly concern written plain on his broad face. "I am delighted to see you, of course . . . but so soon? Was our lodge brother, Onda, unable to provide the aid that we expected?"

"Baron Onda and his kinsman have been very kind. But I come to ask you a great favor," said Sir Simon, removing his plumed tricorn, dropping his silver-handled riding whip on a table, and taking a seat opposite his host. "I must ask for the loan—perhaps the gift—of the Chalazian triptych."

And he proceeded to explain the circumstances of his upcoming introduction to Count Azimet, as well as Don Balthazar's advice. The dwarf declared himself entirely willing to loan the valuable artifact. "So many innocent lives ruined . . . what is the phrase you so often use? 'The rape of innocence,' yes. And I, too, wish to do my part in combating those wicked men."

"I hope to be able to return the triptych unharmed, but I can make no guarantee," said Sir Simon.

His host laughed softly, as though the matter were of supreme indifference. "It is, after all, only an object, and this collection of mine merely an amusing pastime. It is true that I would not *sell* my prize to another collector, not for all the money in the world, but to *give* it away, in such a good cause, that is another matter entirely." He sent a trusted servant down to the vault where he kept his treasures.

With many expressions of gratitude, Sir Simon accepted the ivory altarpiece, most beautifully carved with images of the Seven Fates, the Nine Seasons, and, in a glory at the center, the Father Creator. Then he took his leave of the good old dwarf.

The next evening, the night of Count Azimet's entertainment, Sir Simon was back in the city of canals. He had arranged to meet Don Balthazar on the steps of the cathedral and ride to the palace in the senator's gondola.

Sir Simon had dressed very carefully for the occasion, still in black, but this time with touches of silver. Silver, also, were the ribbons that tied back his hair, and he wore a diamond brooch at his throat. In one hand, he carried a velvet half-mask, in the other, a black satin bag containing the Chalazian triptych. Don Balthazar came late, leaving Sir Simon to stand outside the cathedral and watch the bustling world of Zammarco pass by.

An intriguing place, this city of Zammarco, with its golden domes, deteriorating palaces, ancient churches, and cyclopean statuary. The dress of the inhabitants was equally exotic. The men wore old-fashioned full-bottomed wigs, or their own hair tied back in clustering ringlets hanging almost to the waist. They loved bright colors, and the full cut of their coats and breeches, as well as the fabrics they favored, showed an Oriental influence. The women, for the most part, dressed very discreetly in sober colors, but the hems of their gowns (which they wore over great hoops) barely reached their ankles. They never left home without covering their heads—and sometimes their faces as well—with filmy scarves and lacy veils, except during Carnival, when many went masked.

"My dear Sir Simon," said Don Balthazar, as the foreigner stepped into his scarlet and purple gondola. "It appears that someone is spying on you. That man over there . . . he was watching you intently as I approached. But as soon as I hailed you, he conceived an elaborate interest in that puppet show by the steps. I mention the matter because he cannot possibly be one of *our* spies—they would never be so clumsy!"

Sir Simon maintained a bland expression. "A tall fellow with a pronounced stoop? Or perhaps a little man dressed as a common sailor?"

"It is a little man wearing dark spectacles and a cocked hat."

Sir Simon's shoulders shook with suppressed laughter. "I had thought he had entirely abandoned that 'disguise' in favor of the other. You must not allow him or his stoop-shouldered friend to worry you. They are merely agents of a certain great lady in Marstadtt, and they follow me wherever I go. Indeed, I hardly regard them any more, for they never inconvenience me in any way. I believe they have been assigned in the hope I may eventually lead them to . . . something the lady has lost and wishes to regain." And he seated himself, quite nonchalantly, on a velvet-cushioned bench beside the senator.

"You understand," said Don Balthazar, lowering his voice, so as not to be overheard by the gondolier, "that if you succeed in capturing Count Azimet's interest, he will undoubtedly make inquiries concerning your background."

"You may rest easy on that head," said Sir Simon. "I have been *Sir Simon Blood* for some time now, and during that time, my activities under that name have all been consistent with that character. Even if his spies should approach my faithful watchdogs . . . they may know me by another name, but I doubt they can tell the Count anything which will fail to reassure him that I am exactly as I shall present myself."

"And that will be?"

Sir Simon inclined his carefully powdered head. "As a liar, a cheat, a gamester, and a thief."

Don Balthazar gave a surprised little laugh, as if slightly taken aback by his protégé's effrontery. "By the Sacred Powers! You seem to have nerve and enough to spare for this daring enterprise."

Outwardly, Count Azimet's palace was typical of the fading grandeur that characterized the city. Damp spots disfigured the stone façade, the golden dome of the roof had a tarnished look, and all the cornices, friezes, statues, and columns were cracked or chipped. Two gargantuan figures, wrought in marble, flanked the door: a man and a woman nobly attired, with wreaths of olive branches encircling their brows.

A dusky Oranian slave admitted the senator and his guest. Within the palace, it was all light and color, with great mirrors and immense hanging chandeliers, and frescoes upon the walls. Donning their masks, Sir Simon and Don Balthazar followed a crowd of costumed revelers down a long bright corridor and up a crystal staircase to an equally brilliant ballroom, where Count Azimet held court.

Sir Simon had expected a big man—rumor had prepared him for that. By all he had heard of the Count's greed, his decadent and self-indulgent style of living, he had come to expect a gross slug of a man, wallowing in silken luxury. Nothing had prepared him for the reality.

Count Azimet was enormous. Even seated, he was impressive; standing, he could not be less than eight feet high. But if he was big, he was also beautifully formed, with a trim, powerful body and exceedingly regular features. Though dressed in the height of Continental fashion, in pale blue satin and foaming white lace, nothing about him suggested the fop. His heavy-lidded eyes were a particularly piercing shade of cerulean blue, and he had a broad, good-humored smile which seemed to indicate that he found the world a very amusing place.

Don Balthazar made the necessary introduction, then tactfully drifted away.

"If the Count would be so gracious as to grant me a private audience later in the evening," said Sir Simon, "I believe he may find it well worth his while."

The Count lifted his quizzing glass, regarded the dapper little man with mock dismay. "Is it possible that the good senator has unwittingly introduced a petitioner into my home . . . or are you merely a common tradesman? You certainly do not have that appearance."

Sir Simon doffed his mask. "Don Balthazar is certainly unaware of my purpose in coming here. I regret infinitely that I was obliged to impose on him. And yes, I am a tradesman of sorts . . . though by no means a common one."

Count Azimet studied him with dawning amusement. "Well, well, you intrigue me . . . a little. I will send a servant to fetch you, when (and if) I am ready to speak with you."

Sir Simon bowed and withdrew.

He spent the next four hours sipping an emerald-green Spagnish wine, breathing in fumes of hashish—which smoldered in pots or on brass tripods in every room he entered—nibbling on a variety of highly sweetened seasonal confections, and watching the brilliant entertainments which the Count had arranged for his guests. The company was preparing to sit down to a second lavish supper when Sir Simon felt a light, respectful touch on his elbow.

A little Oranian page-boy in an enormous turban touched his head to Sir Simon's hand and announced that he had been sent to escort "the pretty little foreign gentleman" to a private meeting with the Count.

Count Azimet received him in a gilded chamber off of the ballroom, lounging against a particularly ornate marble mantelpiece. Though Sir Simon thought he had been prepared for the sight of Count Azimet standing, this was not the case. The man was a veritable giant.

Without any preamble, Sir Simon presented the Chalazian triptych, counting on the altarpiece to make a strong impression. The Count examined the ivory ornament carefully, then shot him an alert, suspicious glance.

"You did not come by this honestly. I know who this comes from, and also that he would never sell it."

Sir Simon bowed a courteous acknowledgement. "You are entirely correct. I admit quite frankly that I stole it, in the hope of impressing the Count and obtaining his gracious patronage. If you recognize the object, then you undoubtedly know how carefully it was guarded—I daresay, to any man less talented than myself, those obstacles would have been insurmountable."

Count Azimet cocked his head, with a look of rather more than polite interest, and Sir Simon felt encouraged to go on. "With all due modesty, I present myself as the Prince of Thieves . . . beyond all others, I excel at my profession. Yet few men can afford to purchase my services, for the items I steal are often so valuable that even wealthy men cannot dream of owning them. Still, I require an occupation, an object for my life . . . what remains, then, for the Prince of Thieves but to seek employment with the very Emperor of Collectors?

"Moreover," said Sir Simon, "I am a man of vast and varied talents: there is little that I cannot or will not do if the payment is high enough. Perhaps, therefore, you may know of other ways in which I could serve you."

This somewhat long-winded (and utterly conscienceless) speech seemed to appeal to the Count. "But yes, it is possible that I might find some employment for you. The triptych—a gift, I assume?—certainly provides an effective introduction. But I never discuss business during Carnival. It is a long-standing policy of mine." The big man made a show of polishing his quizzing glass with a bit of silk. "I take it that you plan an extended stay in Zammarco?"

"I expect to remain another fortnight, at least. Longer, if it should serve the Count's pleasure."

"Then I insist that you join me here as my houseguest. We may then further our acquaintance over the next few days, and after the New Year . . ." The Count smiled graciously. "Perhaps then we can make an arrangement, you and I."

Though fully cognizant that this sudden and gratifying invitation could only be prompted by the Count's desire to keep him under observation, while sending out the necessary spies and agents to look into his background, Sir Simon was perfectly content to accept. "The Count is kindness itself. I confess myself . . . overwhelmed by his generosity."

"Oh, I am not, by nature, a generous man," said Azimet, continuing to smile urbanely. "And so I must warn you: if you should happen to succumb to the temptation to steal anything from *me*—no matter how valueless—my vengeance will follow you to the ends of the earth."

9.

In which Sir Simon experiences an Unexpected encounter.

The next day, Sir Simon moved his simple belongings into Count Azimet's palace. He took a circuitous route from his previous lodgings, first walking, then riding in a gondola, in order to give the stoop-shouldered man the slip. This he did for his own amusement only, because he knew it would not take his two bloodhounds long to learn his present whereabouts—yet he liked to think that the Duchess's minions were earning their pay.

It is a wicked age we live in, mused Sir Simon, as he settled into the spacious apartments the Count had assigned him. Even he, adventurer that he was (and, perforce, accustomed to a certain amount of intrigue and deception), could not but shake his head at the intricate complications of his present situation: he was spying on Count Azimet; agents of the Count were, undoubtedly, rushing from one end of Euterpe to the other, gathering information about him; the spies deployed by the Duchess continued to dog his footsteps—and there could be little doubt that agents of the Senate were spying on every single one of them.

In the days that followed, Sir Simon spent an hour or two each day in the company of his host, who seemed to find his conversation amusing, at least in small doses. Otherwise, he roamed through the palace freely—though he had a strong impression, the whole time, that Count Azimet's servants kept a close watch on the Count's silver and other small objects of value whenever "the pretty little foreign gentleman" came into a room.

As for the Count's famous collection of curiosities, that proved, in some sense, a disappointment. So vast was the Count's pride in his curios, apparently, that he kept them

61

perpetually on display. Many piqued Sir Simon's interest, but on the whole, he had been privileged to view far more impressive private collections in Wäldermark and Imbria. The real fascination lay in the methods the Count employed to guard his treasures, the traps and the poisons and the magical protections. Many of these *were* exceedingly rare and of incalculable worth. Sir Simon wondered if it appealed to Count Azimet's sense of humor to place an antique vase, worth perhaps a thousand pounds sterling, inside a ring of magical fire generated by a golden circlet, worth ten times as much.

But therein also lay a great source of frustration. Sir Simon intended to gain access to Count Azimet's secret letters and papers, which ought to contain documentary evidence of the aristocrat's involvement in the white slave trade—and perhaps of the import and export of other forms of contraband as well. These papers he had originally hoped to locate by *first* detecting such magical safeguards as the Count used to protect and conceal them.

And indeed, among so many other guests, amidst all the revelry which began each night promptly at sunset, Sir Simon moved easily about the house, investigating with pendulums and magnets and the other devices he brought with him. Unfortunately (and here, perhaps, the Count's true cunning was more fully revealed), Sir Simon's pendulums and talismans continually led him astray: the presence of so many impenetrable crystal domes, flaming pedestals, and magically sensitive poisoned needles, guarding the aristocrat's collection of curios, proved too confusing.

How to locate a single strong source of magic, when magically operated devices might be found in practically every room?

"I have something of the utmost interest to show you," drawled Count Azimet, one afternoon. "It is not something I display to casual visitors, but I fancy it may intrigue you." He led Sir Simon out onto a marble terrace, overlooking a small enclosed courtyard.

Down in the faded winter garden below, an old man (a humble-looking individual in a worn suit of clothes and a battered tricorn) sat on a stone bench by a reflecting pool, watching the antics of an exquisite little female not more than eighteen inches tall. The tiny creature—Sir Simon could not, at this distance, determine whether she was a child or a woman—

danced about the garden, among the withered vines and the crumbling statues and the moldering remains of an ancient gazebo, apparently intent on some private game of her own. The old man looked on with a benign smile.

"Another of your curiosities?" asked Sir Simon, staring at the little female with uncommon interest. Too small to be dwarf, fairy, troll, or human, but too daintily formed for a gnome or a hobgoblin, it was impossible to guess at her race. Her coloring, too, was odd, though not unattractive: her skin had a faint golden cast, and her long silky hair a tint of green. It seemed to Sir Simon that she moved about the garden with something more than mortal grace.

"More than a curio . . . she is entirely a mystery," said the Count. The marble balustrade did not even reach his knees, but he was able to sit down on the railing with his legs negligently crossed, and look perfectly comfortable in doing so. "The old man—her keeper—claims to be her father . . . though that, of course, is clearly impossible. I found him in dire straits: more ragged than he appears now, and half starved. Would you believe it? He actually kept this so-called daughter of his in a wicker cage, like an animal or a tame bird."

Sir Simon stood up a little straighter, as if, by doing so, he might better see the hunched figure down by the pond. "He mistreated her, then?"

"I should not say mistreated her," said the Count, following her every movement with his eyes, a strange smile quirking his lips. "For I apprehend that he wished principally to shield her. He had no desire to make a freak show of pretty Eirena. One must honor his delicacy, of course. Such a dainty creature can only be . . . enjoyed . . . by a true connoisseur, would you not say?"

Sir Simon eyed him suspiciously, not certain how he ought to reply—not certain, even, what perverse form the Count's "enjoyment" of the little female might take. Rape seemed a physical impossibility, considering their relative sizes, but something hungry in Azimet's expression as he watched Eirena dance around the garden made Sir Simon feel queasy.

"The old man is a foreigner," added the Count. "He cannot speak any language but the northern tongue, and that most barbarously. Not from your own homeland, I should think, but a native of Wäldermark, by his accent."

"Indeed," said Sir Simon casually, to conceal his suddenly burning interest. "I visited that principality some years
back . . . in the province of Marstadtt . . . or perhaps Wie-
marchen." He pretended a vague confusion. "I had no idea
that they grew the females so small there."

The Count's eyes glinted at this pleasantry. "Nowhere in
the world, so far as I have been able to ascertain. It appears
that Eirena is utterly unique."

He might have said more, but just then one of his black
Oranian slaves appeared, announcing that the Oligarch had
come to call.

"You will excuse me," said the Count, rising to his feet.
"My interview with the Oligarch is not likely to be a pleasant
one, and I would prefer to conduct it privately."

After the Count withdrew, Sir Simon remained for a long
time, leaning with his hands on the marble balustrade, contemplating the oddly matched pair in the garden below. Then, with
a sudden decision, he descended the stairs and approached the
gnarled pigtailed figure by the pool.

"Mr. Braun, your servant," said Sir Simon, in their common
language. The old man gave a visible start and rolled a panicky
eye. "I beg your pardon . . . do I have the name wrong?"

"You've the name aright," said the old fellow heavily. "No
need to beg my pardon. It was just sommat in the way you
said it . . . made me think maybe we'd met afore."

"I cannot claim a previous acquaintance," said Sir Simon.
"And yet I feel as though I do know you. Your young kinsman,
Jedidiah, is a most particular friend of mine."

The old man began to quiver, to cast uneasy glances around
the garden. "Who . . . who was it as sent you?" he whispered
hoarsely.

Sir Simon smiled reassuringly. "The Glassmakers sent
me . . . but not in search of you," he said gently—so kindly
and gently that the Count, had he heard him, would have been
surprised. Indeed, his entire manner had altered, as though one
man had left the terrace and another man arrived in his place
down in the garden. "Mere chance brings us here together—or
perhaps I should say: the inscrutable work of the Fates. You
have nothing to fear from me. I wish you only well."

Caleb Braun digested that for a moment. "My grandnevvy
Jed—you said you knew him?" he asked eagerly. "Whatever

become of Jedidiah? I've worried about that boy, but there weren't no way . . . no safe way anyways—"

"Exactly," said Sir Simon. "But Jed, I have reason to suppose, is a good safe distance from those who might harm him. As for yourself, Mr. Braun . . . I beg you will forgive me for speaking plainly, but my affection for your young kinsman motivates me. I know that you have an extremely dangerous enemy in the person of Thomas Kelly, but I wonder if you appreciate that you have, in some sense, merely escaped the frying pan to enter the fire. Count Azimet is every bit as dangerous as the sorcerer Kelly."

"I know that well enough," said Caleb. "But the Count has taken a fancy to my little daughter, and at least for now, we've got his favor. If we got powerful enemies, it stands to reason we need a powerful man, like the Count is, to protect us."

As if in response to her "father's" unease, the dainty creature had abandoned her game, and wrapping her arms around Caleb's knees, she rubbed her tiny face up against his legs.

Sir Simon took a snuffbox out of his waistcoat pocket—the box was a fanciful receptacle, cunningly fashioned in the form of a ram's horn, wrought in silver. He opened the lid at the broad end and took out a pinch of snuff, eyeing the old man with a great deal of exasperation. The presence of Jedidiah's granduncle in Zammarco (still more, the totally unexpected existence of little Eirena) brought complications he had hardly reckoned for.

Sir Simon inhaled, sneezed, and dusted off his fingers. It would be nearly impossible to save a man who had no desire to accept his protection. He could only hope that he would be able to arrange things, to spare his friend's old uncle the full force of the coming catastrophe.

During the frustrating days that followed, days which Sir Simon devoted to more futile investigations, he found many opportunities to speak privately with Caleb Braun, to improve his acquaintance with the mysterious Eirena. *She* had taken a liking to him, and came running whenever she spotted him, but the old man remained adamant, for all Sir Simon's repeated warnings and persuasions.

"I appeal to you as Eirena's father," said Sir Simon, on one such occasion, going down on one knee beside the tiny creature, reaching into his pocket, and bringing out a silver ring which he slipped on her wrist like a bracelet—he had fallen into the habit of buying small gifts for her. Eirena rewarded him with an enchanting smile. "I cannot believe that any man would wish to place his daughter under the protection of . . . of a voluptuary like Count Azimet."

"Aye," said Caleb, maddeningly calm. "I know all that, the Count and his nasty habits. But you can be sure I make precious certain she don't witness none of his lewd ways. *She's* beyond his reach, anyway," the old man concluded.

About this—though his imagination continued to balk—Sir Simon entertained some uncomfortable doubts. But Caleb repeated the old argument: they were safer here at Azimet's palace . . . no, he could not be convinced to take Eirena elsewhere, even if such a thing were possible.

Uncertain how far the old man's loyalty to the Count extended, afraid he had said too much already, Sir Simon did not dare to tell him: should his own mission here prove successful, the Count's protection would no longer hold.

It was not that Sir Simon troubled himself so much over Caleb Braun and his probable fate—he would scarcely break his heart over the stubbornness of one misguided old man— but Eirena was another matter.

Even on closer acquaintance, he could not fathom the origin of the tiny creature, nor begin to guess at her age. Though formed like a little woman, she apparently could not speak, and there was a freshness about her, a childlike quality, that Sir Simon found oddly moving.

As the days dragged by, Sir Simon gave more and more thought to Eirena and her plight. What her fate must be . . . in the event his investigations proved successful, and she was confiscated by the State along with the Count's other, less animate property . . . he did not like to think. That she *would* be regarded as property—perhaps even put on display as a freak of nature—was highly probable. Her inability to speak or otherwise clearly communicate must relegate her to the status of brute beast . . . at least in the Exalted Republic of Zammarco. And while it was one thing—faintly distasteful—for Eirena to be viewed by Count Azimet and his favored guests, the thought of a public exhibition struck Sir Simon as patently obscene.

If forced to it, I shall simply kidnap her, he finally decided.

The New Year passed in a blaze of glory, a multi-colored swirl of activity. On the eve of the holiday, on the night known as Sundark, preparations began a little before midnight. In every house, every shop, every church, every palace in the city, lanthorns were shuttered, candles, lamps, and fires quenched. Then, precisely at midnight, the bells in all the churches rang out at once, announcing the advent of Sunreturn. Then men carrying rekindled torches, boys carrying colored lanthorns, ran through the city until sunrise while the bells continued to peal.

At Count Azimet's palace, the entertainment continued well past sunrise, with comedies, tragedies, and impromptu operas performed by a troupe of traveling players.

A little before noon, the Count sent for Sir Simon, by way of the Oranian page-boy. The small black youth bowed so low that his outsized turban almost touched his toes, as he relayed Count Azimet's message.

"It is time we had a little talk," said the aristocrat, sitting propped up by pillows in his enormous four poster bed. At Azimet's command, two naked black girls who had shared his bed crawled out from between the covers, gathered up their skimpy costumes, and went off to perform their ordinary duties in the kitchen.

"I did not know, Sir Simon," said the Count, watching him closely, "that you numbered kidnapping among your many accomplishments."

Sir Simon stared at him, in obvious bewilderment. "You affect surprise—well, I will tell you: my spies have been . . . talking, *most* persuasively . . . with agents of the Duchess of Zar-Wildungen," the Count added helpfully.

"Ah . . . that little matter," said Sir Simon, thinking quickly. "But yes, I was employed, some while back, to spirit away two young women in whom the Duchess took a certain interest. I do not know why that should surprise you."

"It does not," said Count Azimet. "But I am somewhat puzzled to learn that the Duchess's agents continue to dog your footsteps, as if expecting you to lead them to the young women in question. Or can it be—in the course of your duties— that you chanced to form a sentimental attachment to either of the ladies?"

A tiny frown appeared between Sir Simon's shapely eye-brows, his nostrils expanded. "Ah . . ." he said. "We will not speak of that, if you please."

Count Azimet burst out laughing. "Now you *have* surprised me. Can it possibly be, my friend, that you are a man of honorable principles?"

"When it pleases me· to be so," retorted Sir Simon. "And when it does not hamper me. But I can assure you: I am not, in general, inclined to be sentimental about females."

The Count leaned back against his pillows. "Or anything else, Sir Simon?"

"Or anything else," said Sir Simon, smoothing out a minute wrinkle on the sleeve of his coat. "I wonder that you should ask. Could it possibly be, Count Azimet, that your spies have uncovered a single instance of moral integrity on my part?"

"Not at all," said Azimet, his eyes crinkling at the corners. "You seem to be a man without a single redeeming feature—for which reason, I am much inclined to employ you, at the first opportunity."

Sir Simon sketched a bow. "You relieve my mind," he said.

But of course the Count had not relieved his mind at all. Sir Simon realized that his time was growing perilously short. Once Count Azimet sent him off on some larcenous mission, he would cease to enjoy free run of the palace, and his investigations must end.

It was solely due to a fortunate accident the next afternoon that Sir Simon stumbled on the solution to his problem—and in the last place where he had expected to find it.

He had just entered the salon adjoining the ballroom, the same gilded chamber where Count Azimet had received him on that first night. As he approached the marvelously ornate fireplace, he felt a blaze of energy at his breast. Something had activated the lead talisman dedicated to Sadrun, which he wore on a ribbon around his neck between his black cambric shirt and brocaded waistcoat.

Concealing his surprise, Sir Simon turned with his blandest smile to answer a question the Count had just addressed to him. Yet all the while, his mind continued to spin busily.

For the past fortnight, he had expected to find some secret closet, some sliding panel, in one of the rooms where only the Count, his intimates, and his most trusted servants had access. That the hiding place should open on so public a chamber as this one . . . that was astounding. And yet, in some sense, the very publicity of its location provided a safeguard.

Sir Simon listened with one ear while Azimet recounted some amorous exploit. During the day, he thought, he could never examine the fireplace and the wall around it, for fear of interruption. By night, it would be risky to come downstairs, where he had no business to be, now that the holiday revels had ended. For if the Count's servants should discover him at his work and overpower him . . . Sir Simon impatiently dismissed that thought from his mind. He must simply see to it that he was *not* caught in the act.

That night in his bedchamber, when the palace was dark and quiet, Sir Simon prepared for his mission of stealth. He slipped a loaded pistol with a chased silver stock into his belt, a slender stiletto up one black sleeve. He knew full well that discovery meant the failure of his mission, but still he might hope to elude capture if he went armed. In his pockets, and sewn into the lining of his coat and his black and silver waistcoat, and even in the hollow three-inch heels of his shoes, he always kept other useful items as well. Sir Simon preferred to be prepared for any eventuality.

Unfortunately, a need to move quickly and silently meant that he must leave his shoes behind. He twisted the heels, one after the other, and the fuses and tiny bottles of explosives dropped into his hands. He disposed these, as conveniently as possible, elsewhere on his person.

Absentmindedly, he reached into his coat pocket, drew forth a small gold box with an inlay of pearl and ivory. Flipping open the lid, he took a pinch of the fine crystalline powder that he kept inside. Then, realizing what he was about, he shook his head, dusted off his fingertips, and closed the box.

He needed to be alert tonight, aware of every sound and movement. Even a tiny pinch of the Sleep Dust would rob him of that sharp edge. Without the drug, his senses would be painfully keen, his lungs would burn, his heart would race, and his pulse become tumultuous, but that extra keenness might well save his life. And many hours must pass before his failure to take the drug would begin to debilitate him.

Light-footed and agile in his stocking feet, he made it from his room on the third floor all the way to the salon off the ballroom without any serious incident—though once he was forced to dodge behind a marble statue, to avoid being seen by the Oranian page, and once slide under a low table, to avoid an encounter with one of the white-skinned servants.

He closed the double doors behind him, took out a reel of unspun cotton, which he proceeded to lay against the crack at the bottom. Then he paced his way in the dark across the room, found the candles he had observed earlier on the mantelpiece, lit them, and began his search.

Using his lead talisman as a pendulum, dangling it on the ribbon and observing its movements, he located the sliding panel beside the fireplace. But this would be no ordinary secret panel—not for Count Azimet. A panel operated by an elaborate mechanism, a devious combination of mechanics and magic, this Sir Simon wholly expected. It was the magic, of course, that had activated the pendulum.

Sir Simon knew he must proceed with the utmost caution. Any small mistake in operating the mechanism would either set off an alarm or else spring some deadly trap. Yet the more ingenious devices of this sort were invariably the work of gnomes—and gnomes were devoted to mathematical and philosophical puzzles.

He took down one of the candles, drew back a pace, the better to observe the surface of the wall, which had been painted with a lurid fresco depicting the last days of the Imperial court at Evanthum. It was a little-known fact (which Sir Simon knew quite well) that gnome traps and alarms always contained in their design a series of clues which the canny observer might actually decipher, and so learn to work the mechanism.

Sir Simon proved to be a canny observer. The fresco, he realized, offered several clues, and it was also useful to carry (as he did) a compendium of favorite gnomic theorums and equations around in his head. In half an hour, he had deciphered the puzzle, made a touch here and a touch there, twisted an ornamental molding attached to the mantel, waited breathlessly for some trap to spring, in the event that he had made some slight mistake in the sequence—

Then the secret panel slid aside, revealing . . . not the hidden cupboard he had been expecting . . . but a room about half the size of the salon. Sir Simon ground his teeth, disgusted by his own stupidity. Had he thought to make a thorough investigation of this part of the palace, he must have noticed, long before this, a disparity between the dimensions of the salon and the sizes of all the surrounding chambers.

But he had no time to waste on useless self-reproach. Picking up the candle he had placed on the floor behind him, he stepped through the panel and entered the room beyond. What he saw there amazed and dazzled him, a treasure trove beyond compare, a library of rare and ancient volumes, and a museum of diabolical artifacts.

Sir Simon left the secret room convinced of one thing, at least: he had finally succeeded in providing a noose large enough to encompass Count Azimet's neck.

10.

In which Sir Simon is obliged to face the Bitter Truth.

A sleepy Don Balthazar Onda, sporting the turban he always wore to bed at night and clad in a rich brocade dressing gown, received his unexpected visitor in his study. "You choose a late hour in which to call, my friend," he said, yawning and not best pleased by this nocturnal intrusion.

"A thousand pardons," said Sir Simon, though he did not sound in the least apologetic. "But I have uncovered a plot of such magnitude . . . it seemed best to bring the matter immediately to your attention."

For a moment, Don Balthazar had the unnerving sensation that a perfect stranger was staring at him out of Sir Simon's eyes. The thought was a fleeting one, swiftly banished by the import of Sir Simon's words. He removed his turban, ran his fingers through the short hair necessitated by his heavy senatorial wig, and sat down behind his desk. "You have obtained the evidence you sought? But this is splendid, my very dear sir! However," he added, with a wry smile, "I do not think that a call on the Oligarch and the other gentlemen of the Conclave would be advisable at this hour."

Sir Simon dropped down into a chair, though none had been offered him. "I have evidence, but not such that I could carry it here with me. I believe that you—and some other witness whom the senators would be inclined to credit—ought to view these things exactly as I found them," he said wearily. "And the crime is rather more serious than we had thought. A crime—if not more reprehensible than the one you know of—at least more likely to cause a stir of indignation among the noble senators.

"I accuse Count Azimet of black Witchcraft, and treason against the State."

Don Balthazar, who had been leaning forward with his elbows on the desk, now stiffened in his chair. "That is a serious accusation!" He considered for a moment. "My cousin the Baron may consent to accompany me . . . but where do you mean to take us?"

Sir Simon shifted uneasily in his seat. "To Count Azimet's palace. But I do not know, as yet, how I shall go about smuggling the two of you inside, at an hour when our activities are unlikely to attract the Count's notice."

Don Balthazar shrugged his shoulders and spread his hands wide. "That is no problem. I can gain access, unannounced, to Count Azimet's palace anytime that I wish. Would tonight be too soon? No? Then I will arrange it."

Now it was Sir Simon's turn to sit up, rigid and suspicious in his chair. "And just precisely how—if I may ask—do you propose to accomplish this?"

Don Balthazar grinned at him. "The Senate has spies and informants within Count Azimet's household, paid agents to do our bidding. You affect surprise, but surely you expected no less? We keep spies in all the great households. And it is no use any of us trying to weed them out, for new ones must always come to take their place.

"Yes," he added, in answer to Sir Simon's inquiring glance, "even in this house, there are those among the servants who regularly report all my activities to the Oligarch. And though I do not know, for certain, which ones are spies, I naturally entertain my suspicions."

From that point on, things moved swiftly—far too swiftly for Sir Simon's comfort. An hour later, he and Don Balthazar spoke with the Baron; two hours and a number of bribes later ("Even our agents must be paid to take these risks," said Don Balthazar), they stood in the Count's gilded salon, facing the secret panel.

While Don Balthazar and his cousin guarded the salon door with loaded pistols, Sir Simon disarmed a small explosive device which he had previously contrived with some fuses and mercuric fulminate—lest anyone entering the secret room during his absence should encounter evidence of his intrusion. With the bomb now harmless and the way made clear, Sir Simon led the two aristocrats into the hidden chamber.

Don Balthazar paused on the threshold, glancing around him in bewildered amazement. The museum-like room contained Count Azimet's *true* collection, curios more valuable than anything he kept on public display. But not for their value only did Azimet keep these things hidden, for here were the diabolical books and the fiendish tools of a black magician.

Sir Simon drew the senator's attention to the far end of the chamber, and a little gilded stage, the size of a puppet theatre. Indeed, at first, the aristocrat mistook it for an ordinary puppet show, until his cousin the Baron lifted up one of the elaborately dressed and exquisitely modeled little marionettes, this one garbed in senatorial red, and held it out for him to inspect.

Then Don Balthazar drew a deep, indignant breath. "Infamous!" he said. "Count Azimet's wickedness passes all bounds."

Sunrise found Sir Simon and the two aristocrats back in Don Balthazar's study, where the senator filled out a warrant for Count Azimet's arrest. "Believe me," he told Sir Simon, still fuming with indignation, "justice will certainly be done."

Sir Simon did believe him, for among the "poppets" on Count Azimet's stage were figures bearing the strongest resemblance to people Don Balthazar knew: the Oligarch and all the senators of the Conclave . . . and among them Don Balthazar himself. The senator was profoundly shaken by the idea that Count Azimet could use that puppet—perhaps had already used it on some previous occasion—to influence his actions.

"If you will pardon one question before I go," said Sir Simon, leaning up against the door, as though no longer capable of bearing his own weight. His pulse was racing, his limbs trembling, and if he did not soon take a large dose of the Sleep Dust, he would be in a sad case indeed. Yet it had all gone so easily tonight, his success had come so swiftly and almost unexpectedly, that he only now began to entertain second thoughts, to contemplate the consequences of his own actions. "The Count's servants . . . they will all be arrested and questioned?"

"But naturally," said Don Balthazar. "Yes, even our agents . . . arrested and questioned. Though only those who appear to know more than they are telling will be put to the torture. We know our business here, and you need not fear that the innocent will suffer.

"In any case," he added offhandedly, "they are most of them Oranian slaves, of little account."

He went back to his warrant, but glancing up a minute later and observing Sir Simon still leaning against the wall with his face so white and hard, such a savage hostility in his eyes, the senator felt moved to add: "If there is one among the white-skinned servants to whom you feel obliged, one that you would spare some inconvenience, I advise you to spirit him away before the Senate takes official action. You have, perhaps, two hours. But do not get any ideas about helping one of the Oranians. You could not possibly smuggle him out of the city. We have very strict laws about the transport of slaves."

Sir Simon rubbed his aching forehead. He knew that this was so, yet still he wished to at least spare the little black page, who, being smaller than any of the others, might be more easily disguised. Beyond that . . . beyond that, he must just content himself with rescuing Caleb and Eirena. In fact, removing Eirena—if it had not been so already—had advanced to paramount importance. If even a man like Don Balthazar could speak so casually of torturing Oranian slaves (who, if they were dark-skinned, at least were full-sized men), one could hardly expect the xenophobic Zammarcans to extend any gentler treatment to a creature as exotic as Eirena.

But at least now it would be possible to insure Caleb's cooperation. Before leading Don Balthazar and Baron Onda to the secret room, Sir Simon had removed two of the puppets, and carried them now in his coat pocket. One was a dapper little man, dressed all in black and silver, the other, a grizzled old fellow with a pigtail, carrying in his arms a much smaller female figure.

Sir Simon calculated swiftly. He need only take Caleb, Eirena, and the page-boy out of Zammarco and as far as the villa, where he might leave them to the protection of the kindly old dwarf. "Then, with your permission," he said coldly, "I will take my leave."

"By all means," said Don Balthazar graciously. "But Sir Simon . . ." The foreigner paused on the threshold. "Sir Simon, in addition to putting an end to that most pernicious traffic in human flesh, as you originally intended, you have also performed a great and valuable service to the Republic, almost certainly saving the lives of a noble body of men. Baron Aquilar misspoke when he called you an assassin. You are a most heroical gentleman."

"You are kind to say so," murmured Sir Simon. But for himself, he was not so certain.

He had not, of course, really put an end to the white-slave trade—no, the kidnapping and export of young men and women to Eastern harems and brothels would undoubtedly continue . . . though, lacking Count Azimet's direction, on a greatly reduced scale. And his thoughts still lingered with those Oranian slaves and the fate he most probably—in his zeal and willful blindness!—had visited upon them. The cruel torture and possible death of perhaps a dozen guiltless Oranians, in exchange for the lives of as many Zammarcan senators? That did not appear to him in quite such a favorable light as it must, perforce, appear to Don Balthazar.

"I beg you to convey my profoundest compliments to your colleague Baron Aquilar," said Sir Simon, with a self-mocking little bow. "Pray tell him that he has not mistaken me at all. I am really not much better than the assassin he named me."

11.

Hobb's Church, as Mr. Herring informed Jed and Mr. Jonas, was too small to merit a Guildhall of its own, so he offered to take them to visit their fellow Glassmakers in the town of Moonstone, south of the marsh. "I fancy," said Mr. Herring, "you will find their papers of particular interest and will want to spend a day or two exploring the archives." Since Jed and the gnome were at loose ends, waiting for the turn of the season to begin constructing their machine, they readily accepted his invitation.

The Guildhall at Moonstone was an eccentric structure, a haphazard building, part timber, part brick, and part stone. The interior was a maze of chambers and corridors: smoking rooms, libraries, dining halls, sanctuaries where the guildsmen performed their rituals, wardrobes where they kept their ceremonial garments, a museum of sorts (whose principal treasures were some odd bits of glass, three bolts of fossil lightning, some potsherds, a mermaid's tooth, and half a dozen flea-ridden hunting trophies), and many more great echoing chambers that had seen no use for years. Some few of the members even lodged there, in private apartments at the back of the building. The archives mentioned by Mr. Herring reposed in two dusty little rooms: shelves crammed with antique scrolls and crumbling yellow manuscripts, cabinets and trunks and boxes filled to overflowing with deeds and letters and documents—everything from sermons to ballad sheets.

Jedidiah and Mr. Jonas spent a long industrious afternoon rummaging through the archives, making several intriguing discoveries along the way. There was *An Inquiry into the Optickal Properties of Balthorian Crystals,* which Mr. Jonas pounced on gleefully. And Jed conceived an awful fascination, leafing through a manuscript *On the Antiquity of Blood Sacrifice*. Nor could either resist a document which purported to outline the precise methods for making artificial jewels "of the Very Finest quality" out of common window glass. They spent an hour or two reading that one, turn and turn about, first Jed reading aloud while Sammuel Jonas dug through a box of deeds and legal documents; then Mr. Jonas read awhile, while Jed skimmed through the contents of a trunk of letters. Pleased with the treasures they had so far uncovered, they determined to come again the next day.

However interesting, it had been thirsty work, and the light none too good. So, on the second day, they brought an oil lamp with them, a bottle of port wine, and two goblets. But today it was all very dull: sermons and land grants, some ancient accounts, marriage certificates, and the like. It seemed, Jedidiah thought indignantly, that the magistrates of Moonstone, the Town Council, and the church all sent their trashy old papers to be stored in the Guildhall archives.

Then he picked up a yellowing tract and began to leaf through it. The first several pages were missing, and the manuscript began in the middle of a sentence. It ended that way, too, as if the final pages were missing as well. But the name of the author and the subject of the tract, writ very small in faded ink at the top of each page, attracted Jed's attention, causing his pulse to quicken: *Iz. Barebones: Being a Discourse on Panterran artifacts, Recently Discovered in the New World.*

Jed poured himself another glass of port, sat down on a trunk by the oil lamp, and began to read. The more he read, the more elated he became, the more convinced that the subject of Izrael Barebones's essay was an ancient ruin "*built in the Panterran style,*" which was apparently located somewhere in the vicinity of Mothgreen Hall. "See here," said Jed to Mr. Jonas. "Just you take a look at this!"

The gnome took the papers and scanned through them quickly. "My dear Jedidiah!" he cried with kindling excitement. "This would appear to support the map. And now that I think about it . . . I do remember stories of ruined structures—far too complex to be the work of the aboriginal mound-folk—that early settlers discovered on this continent. And I remember, also, that I once read a paper . . . it may have been the work of this Mr. Barebones . . . advancing a theory of Panterran settlements in the New World. How dull of me not to recall any of this when we discovered the map!"

Mr. Jonas continued to glance through the papers. "How I should like to examine these ruins. We could learn . . . well, there is no telling what we might learn! But I find no indication of *where* Mr. Barebones found them—or what befell any of the artifacts he discovered there afterwards. We must ask Siegfried Herring and the other gentlemen what they know of these ruins. But in the meantime"—Mr. Jonas removed his coat and dusted off his hands, as if now he was prepared to begin digging in earnest—"we must try to find the missing pages."

They searched until late that night, then went back home and asked Mr. Herring what he knew about Mr. Barebones and his theory of Panterran settlements in the New World. "Oh, that . . ." said Mr. Herring, after only a cursory glance at the papers. "Yes, I do seem to remember some fantastic utterings. Old Izrael had a habit of raving on and on, and no one really listened to him. I fear that eccentricity rather runs in that family," he added, with a whimsical smile. "My dear Sammuel, you should not regard this account as a true record . . . as likely as not, it was only a romance Mr. Barebones dreamed up for his own amusement."

Nevertheless, Jed and the gnome returned to the archives the next day, and the day after that, and proceeded to turn out the contents of both rooms, examining every letter, every manuscript, every legal document in the archives—without success. It seemed that the missing pages had either been lost for good . . . or else carelessly destroyed.

On Fridays, Sera spent the morning with her youngest scholars, teaching them history, geography, and deportment. Meanwhile, the oldest girls were down in the kitchen with Miss Barebones and the cook, learning to bake bread, to boil a rose-leaf pudding, or prepare an elegant repast of lobsters and syllabub; or else they were in the stillroom, learning to make jellies, cordials, and syrups. Many of these girls came of extremely wealthy families and would never again cook another meal after leaving the Academy. However, it was a maxim of Miss Barebones that "*it is always well to know more than your servants.*"

After dinner at one o'clock, the little girls went downstairs for singing lessons (with a master who rode over from the music school), and the big ones came up to Sera's schoolroom to be educated in mathematics—though it frequently occurred that these unfortunate maidens received a lesson in household management as well: Miss Thorn had a tendency to set them knotty problems involving accounts and the use of household ledgers.

Fortunately for Sera, these older pupils of fifteen and sixteen required little supervision. She had only to teach them a brief lesson, assign them some problems to work on, and then she was free to spend the rest of the afternoon as she liked.

On this particular Friday, the morning brought a brief flurry of snow, but the clouds passed and the wind dropped a little after noon. It was only (thought Sera) a mile from Mothgreen Academy to the town, and the road would be clear, except in a very few spots. If she and Elsie dressed warmly, the walk would not be too cold or too difficult—and then, there was a good possibility that Jed would drive them back, if he could borrow Mr. Herring's team and sledge.

Sera left her pupils hard at work and went down the hall to the upstairs sitting room, where Elsie and the "middle" girls—pupils between the ages of ten and twelve—occupied themselves with a number of pretty tasks. One girl embroidered a sampler, another worked on a quilt, four others engaged in artistic pursuits: cutting out silhouettes, painting a landscape, gluing dried leaves between two sheets of translucent parchment to make a decorative fire screen. Lively red-headed Luella Battersby (who could rarely hold still for more than five minutes except when she had her little snub nose in a book) read aloud to the others from a book of poetry.

"You can ask Mary Partridge to watch them until supper," said Sera. Mary Partridge was the parlor maid, the middle-aged daughter of a local fisherman. "I want you to come into town with me. Most of my stockings defy mending, and I broke several teeth off my tortoiseshell comb."

Elsie shook her head in a disapproving way, as though she wanted to say—but could not, while the girls were listening—that Sera would not keep spoiling her combs if she would just learn to curb her impatience and not drag her comb through her dark curls in such a reckless manner. However, she was more than willing to summon Mary Partridge, and walk with Sera into the town. "Only, you know, we shall have to ask Miss Barebones first."

"I hardly think there will be any trouble about that," said Sera.

The day was cold but sunny, as they left the house and began their mile-long walk into town. Their breath made big white puffy clouds in the frosty air, but between their heavy boots and flannel petticoats, their woolen gowns and hooded cloaks, their mittens and squirrel-skin muffs, they managed to keep warm enough.

Though Sera had only visited Hobb's Church perhaps half a dozen times, mostly on Sundays, she felt a growing fondness for the town. The cobblestone streets were always swept clean, the housewives and merchants were amiable folk, the sailors and fishermen rough but respectful; and the Church of Seven Fates was a cozy old church, presided over by a benign old vicar with the entirely appropriate name of Benjamin Bliss. And if the sight of so many tilted and crooked buildings still made Sera vaguely uneasy . . . well, she had since learned that not so much as a chicken coop had come crashing down, and was forced to conclude that the rest of the buildings were probably safe.

Skirting the frosty lower slopes of Spyglass Hill, Sera and Elsie entered the town. On the village green, a knot of people had gathered around the statue of old King Henry at the center of the square. A fire-and-brimstone preacher had appropriated the base of the statue for use as a pulpit, and proceeded to harangue the crowd with an open-air sermon. The two girls stopped to watch and listen.

The minister was a tall, lean man, wearing a low-crowned beaver hat with a wide brim, which shadowed most of his face. It seemed he must be an impressive speaker—his entire audience had a conscience-stricken look, and some of the ladies were actually in tears, as if he had brought them all, suddenly and forcibly, to a painful awareness of their own iniquity.

But as for Elsie, she did not care for the sermon, or for the preacher—no, not at all, he expressed himself so violently! And when he removed his hat and began to wave it about for emphasis, she and Sera gave a simultaneous gasp of surprise.

"I do believe that is the Reverend Moses Tynsdale, from Lootie's Bay," said Sera, the color rising in her cheeks.

Elsie tugged at her sleeve. "Yes, I think it is. But do let us go, Sera. If we move on at once, he may not recognize us."

Much to her dismay, Sera refused to budge. "He has already recognized us—see how he nods his head in greeting. It would look very odd if we left before he finished, without even saying how-do-you-do." But the truth was, Sera found the itinerant clergyman's fiery rhetoric strangely thrilling, and she had no wish to move on. "We must not behave as though we have anything to hide, you know."

The sermon over, the crowd dispersed, and Mr. Tynsdale descended from his perch. He made a curt bow to Elsie, and accepted, with stiff gallantry, the hand that Sera held out to him.

"An unexpected pleasure, Miss Thorn. I knew, of course, that you and your brother and Miss Winter left Lootie's Bay, but I had received an impression . . . yes, I am convinced that I heard something to the effect . . . that you would be visiting friends to the north. Had I thought to find you here in Cordelia, I might have made inquiries, and paid you a visit long before this."

Elsie blushed, but Sera flashed him a smile. "Indeed, reverend sir, but you know that gossip is often inaccurate. Had you thought to ask *us* where we were bound, you might have learned our destination. But now that we *have* met: perhaps you will be good enough to call on us at Mothgreen Academy. Shall we say Sunday . . . after the morning service?"

Mr. Tynsdale declared that it would be his pleasure, excused himself, bowed, and strode off in the direction of the Eclipse, with the skirts of his long coat flapping like the wings of some great crow.

"But why did you ask him to call on us?" wailed Elsie, as soon as the preacher was out of earshot. "You do not—my dear, you cannot *like* Mr. Tynsdale? I think he is the most odious man!"

Sera paused to think before she spoke. "No, I do not precisely *like* him," she said deliberately. "But Mr. Tynsdale interests me. He speaks with such passion about vice and degradation, that it seems he must know everything about them. And yet, to all appearances, he is the very pattern of moral rectitude. I do not think him an agreeable man, yet I must confess that he exerts a certain fascination. Also, when he preaches, there is an intensity, a wildness in his glance, that reminds me—" Sera put her hand up to the little bit of sea-ivory at her throat. "I believe if I became better acquainted with him I might learn . . ." She shook her head, gave an odd little laugh. "What that wild look *means*—and how it originates—that is what I might possibly discover."

They continued on across the green, but stopped again when a cheerful voice hailed them. "It's Jed," Elsie said breathlessly, glancing about her with a look of pleasure.

It was Jed, emerging from the tavern, rosy-cheeked and hearty in a rough brown overcoat and a wide-brimmed beaver hat not unlike Mr. Tynsdale's, though Jed's had a sweeping plume. He saluted Sera on one cheek in a brotherly fashion, accepted the warm little hand that Elsie removed from her muff, and kissed it—taking rather longer about the process than was absolutely necessary.

Then he fell into step beside them, and accompanied the young ladies on all their errands, only waiting with Elsie outside Mistress Morgan's shop while Sera went in to buy two pairs of dark stockings.

By the time they completed their business the light had faded, and the streets were practically deserted. They headed for Mr. Herring's cottage, to borrow his team and sledge. With no one near to overhear their conversation, Sera quizzed Jed about his and Mr. Jonas's recent activities.

"We've made the acquaintance of an old sea-dog, a Captain Hornbeam," said Jedidiah enthusiastically. "He owns his own ship, a little rebuilt merchant frigate—the *Otter*, she's called—and she seems to be precisely what we need for our enterprise come Quickening."

He then went on to tell them all about his discovery at the Guildhall, the fascinating document written by the late Izrael Barebones.

At mention of the Mothgreen Academy spectre, Sera gave a forced laugh. "Please, I do not wish to hear anything more about Uncle Izrael. I am quite out of patience with old Mr. Barebones—or should be, if I believed he was really haunting the Academy! You have no idea what queer behavior he inspires in Miss Barebones and her whole deluded circle of ladies from the town. If it is not spirit raising, it is tea-leaf reading . . . if it is not tea-leaf reading, it is some other nonsense. They even speak of holding a Dumb Supper. Not only is it a great waste of time, I believe it sets a bad example for the girls, who are all at an impressionable age. Luella Battersby, for instance, is a most high-strung and excitable child, and I am convinced it is all this talk of ghosts that keeps her awake and roaming through the house at all hours of the night."

"Luella Battersby is simply growing much too quickly," said Elsie. "I was just as restless and excitable at her age . . . though not nearly so naughty. That was the very thing that convinced poor Mama that I suffered some nervous complaint, if not some dreadful physical malady."

"Be that as it may," said Sera, with a curling lip, "I do not understand why the mothers of these girls allow their daughters to be exposed to this nonsense."

Elsie gave a humorous shrug. "So many of them were pupils at the Academy in their time . . . or so the girls tell me. I think everyone is accustomed to Miss Barebones and her odd obsessions. By now, her eccentricities have become something of a local institution." She smiled wistfully up at Jedidiah. "I think it is sad more than anything else. Those poor old dears . . . desperately attempting to talk to Mr. Barebones— and he, apparently, just as eager to communicate with them, at least if one goes by all his midnight rappings and moanings (which you have heard as well as I have, Sera, for all you like to pretend that the little girls are responsible!)—and yet, somehow, they are none of them able to pierce the veil. For all the *burning* interest in—in ghosts and spectres displayed by Miss Barebones and her cronies, they none of them possess the ability to speak with spirits."

They had reached the gate outside Mr. Herring's cottage. Holding the gate open for the ladies to pass through, Jed glanced at Sera with a quizzical gleam in his eye. "It is an odd thing, you refusing to countenance a belief in spirits, when you very nearly died by the hand of a dead man back in Thornburg."

Sera bit her lip. "*I* don't know that he was a dead man. I know nothing of the sort. He certainly seemed lively enough to me!"

"But *I* know that he was dead, and you might take my word for it," Jed insisted, with a reminiscent shudder, as they climbed the steps to Mr. Herring's porch. "I saw him there in his coffin, with his eyes sewn shut. Lying there so still and cold, that at first I took him for a wax figure. I thought . . . Well, it hardly matters what all I thought, but I will tell you this: it never even occurred to me that he might rise up out of his casket and walk about as he did!"

12.

Containing two Brief Scenes.

Even by the dim, distant light of the street lamps flaring at the foot of the hill, the bookshop had a deserted look. Ivy covered the walls, overhanging windows and doors, and the cracked diamond panes wore a coating of dust so thick they were almost opaque.

The housebreaker surveyed the building by a single ray from a covered lanthorn. He knew better than to try the door, which had been locked for many seasons, nor did he attempt to force an entrance, for all that he carried an iron crowbar with him, clutched in one powerful hand. Instead, he crept around by the side, down a narrow passage between buildings, straight to the place where a broken pane allowed him to reach inside, unfasten a latch, and then lift the window sash and crawl through.

Once inside, he rotated the metal covering on his lanthorn, permitting more light to spill out. The shop smelled of dust and mildew: the books crammed into the dark wooden shelves, aisle upon aisle, were all rotting away. The cracked window panes had allowed river damps to seep into the building and work their damage for more than a year.

The burly housebreaker spared only a contemptuous glance for the moldering books on the ground floor. He walked past a moon-faced grandfather clock at the foot of the stairs, climbed a steep flight, pushed open a door, and entered a room as dusty and cluttered with shelves and books as the one below. Laying aside his crowbar, he set swiftly to work rifling through the contents of a shelf.

This was but one of many nocturnal visits that Peter Schütz had paid the bookshop; he had been making these methodical searches for many seasons now, though at infrequent intervals. He never dared to come, for instance, when the moon was

86

bright and full, when all Nature existed in a state of agitation, and the people of Thornburg were likely to be wakeful . . . and watchful . . . and perhaps to take notice of his stealthy incursions.

He came only when Iune was dark, at dead of night, when the neighbors were (or ought to be) peacefully asleep in their beds. In this manner, working only for an hour or two at a time, he had spent the last year making a thorough search of the shop on the ground floor, and a cursory search of this floor and of the living quarters up in the attic.

Pausing in his labors, he stepped back, lanthorn in hand, to examine an ancient oak wardrobe. A great brass padlock hung on the face of the cabinet, which seemed to promise *something* of value, if not precisely the something he had been employed to discover. True enough, his search had been fruitless and discouraging up until now, yielding not so much as a scrap of silver plate or a hoard of copper pennies. Only the laboratory downstairs behind the shop contained anything of value, but how to dispose of such odd bits and pieces of equipment he had no idea.

A board creaked somewhere down below; a cold draught passed through the room. A superstitious man might have taken fright—if any place had the appearance of a haunted house, it was the bookshop—but Peter Schütz stuck doggedly to his task. He knew these old houses always creaked and settled at night.

Setting his lanthorn down on the floor beside the wardrobe, he took up his crowbar and pried open the door, breaking the rusty hinges in the process. A swift glance sufficed to tell him that the oak cabinet did not contain the priceless old books he was looking for. It contained old papers: deeds and documents with heavy wax seals, bundles of letters tied up with fraying string. He sifted through a sheaf of papers in a half-hearted way . . . until he discovered a little wooden box buried at the back of the cabinet. That, thought the housebreaker, his fingers curling around his crowbar, looked considerably more promising.

The box was locked as well, but Schütz had no difficulty breaking the trumpery little padlock. Inside, he found two wrinkled bank notes and a handful of silver coins. *Not bleeding much,* he reflected, as he pocketed the money, but it was a little something to supplement the modest wages paid by his employer.

So softly did the frock-coated figure enter the room, that at first Schütz failed to notice the intrusion. But when a board creaked directly behind him, the housebreaker looked up with a start, to see a stoop-shouldered old man with a curiously waxen face bearing down on him. Reacting instantly, Schütz reached for a long knife he carried tucked into his belt.

But the newcomer moved with surprising speed and agility, stopping Schütz with the cold clasp of a steely hand around his wrist, and an equally powerful grip on his shoulder. The knife dropped from suddenly slackened fingers, and a queer numbing sensation stole up the housebreaker's arm.

"I could kill you, if I wished to do so." The old man spoke with a faint accent. Schütz flinched away from the glance of his dull, dark eyes. They had . . . they had a curiously glazed appearance, like the eyes of a corpse. "I shall not do so, however, if you answer my questions—if you do not try anything foolish."

The housebreaker nodded sullenly.

"You have been here before. Who sent you, and what do you look for?"

Schütz made an evasive reply. He gasped as the grip of those icy fingers tightened on his arm. His head started to spin, and his lungs to labor in a futile attempt to take in enough air. In a sudden panic, Schütz realized that he was really dying—by some unnatural means the old man was actually sucking the life right out of him—and he could not even struggle.

But then, just before Schütz lost consciousness, the fingers around his wrist relaxed, the pressure on his shoulder lightened. "I suppose your loyalty is admirable in its way. And after all, I stand to gain nothing by killing you . . . and you might even be of some small service."

For a moment, the old man appeared to consider. "Go back to your master," he said. "Go back and arrange a meeting. I believe that he and I may prove mutually useful."

The next afternoon, a large, heavy-laden coach, liberally decorated with gilt and armorial bearings, came rumbling through the Great North Gate and into the town of Thornburg.

The Duchess lifted a curtain and peeked out the window,

watching, with a somewhat listless eye, the rows of houses passing by. "Well, it is a fine thing to be home again," she said to her companion on the seat opposite. "I do not wish to offend you, but I must say . . . I did not care for your King or his court."

Jarl Skogsrå took no offense. "Skullgrimm's court possesses few attractions," he acknowledged. He yawned behind his hand. "And yet . . . did not the Gracious Lady accomplish all that she meant to?"

Skogsrå nodded at the silent golden-haired figure sitting beside him. "She grows rather pale and listless, our Cecile. Perhaps she ought to be fed as soon as we arrive."

The Duchess could not repress a shudder. "You must see to her needs, my dear sir. I weary of the task—and indeed, I think it far better suited to *you*."

The Jarl gave the faintest of shrugs. He crossed his legs, the better to display his gleaming, military-style boots. "It is all the same to me. But really, I find your reluctance, your profound distaste, utterly inexplicable. The creatures we feed the monster are sound and healthy, their flesh is perfectly clean and wholesome. And you . . . why, you partake of meat every day—if not the flesh of mice, at least of birds and other small animals—and all without a single qualm."

"Yes," said the Duchess rather pettishly. "But I do not butcher the creatures myself, nor dress the meat afterwards!"

The Jarl smiled mockingly. "I will admit that the task is somewhat beneath your dignity. Though why you should be so squeamish . . . the Gracious Lady is, in effect, a hypocrite. It is living among these Men and dwarves, one supposes."

"Anything you like," said the Duchess, putting a hand to her forehead. The rattling of the berlin, the many trials attendant on a long journey, were beginning to tell on her. A brief visit along the way, to the Wichtelberg in Zar-Wildungen, had offered little in the way of rest or ease. The old Duke was ailing . . . Well, he had been ill for years, really, growing steadily more frail, more disordered in his mind . . . but now it seemed that he might soon be gone, her good old husband of so many years. He was half her age, in truth, but these humans aged so swiftly, already he was senile and fading, though not much more than ninety.

The Duchess swept a hand across her eyes. She would have

stayed to nurse him, but there was nothing she could do for him . . . and most of the time, he scarcely recognized her.

"I do hope," she said, in a very small voice, "that I shall find everyone well at home!"

The coach drew up before the ancient Zar-Wildungen mansion. Skogsrå gathered up his gloves and his hat. No sooner had the footman opened the door and let down the steps than the Duchess was out of the berlin and climbing the cracked marble steps to the house, too impatient to wait for the Jarl's assistance. She left it to Skogsrå to veil the golem and help her out of the coach.

The footman ran on ahead of the Duchess and lifted the heavy iron knocker on one of the doors. But the servants had heard the berlin arrive and were already hastening to fling the double doors wide and welcome the Gracious Lady home. There was a flurry of movement, a skittering across the floor, and a small body flung itself against the Duchess's skirts.

She bent down to scoop up the tiny indigo ape and cuddle him in her arms. "He looks well cared for, that I must own," she said to her portly dwarf butler. "My Sebastian did not pine for me while I was gone?"

"How could one tell?" said Skogsrå, with heavy scorn, as he led the simulacrum up the steps and into the marble entry hall. "That monkey is lugubrious by nature."

The Duchess cast him a sour glance over Sebastian's head. "Attend to Cecile, my dear Jarl . . . feed her and put her away, where she will come to no harm. Then attend me upstairs in my sitting room."

The Duchess's own apartments, quite in contrast to the faded splendor of the other rooms, had been recently decorated all in rose and cream, with scenes of pretty rustic lovers in attitudes either amorous or comical painted on the walls and ceiling. By the time that Skogsrå arrived she had changed from her traveling dress into a loose negligee of pink satin, and was comfortably seated, quite at her ease, upon a fragile loveseat covered in cream brocade. The ape, Sebastian, perched on the back of the sofa, and a great many letters and scented note-cards lay scattered across the seat and on the Duchess's lap.

She scarcely noticed Skogsrå's arrival, absorbed as she was in that history of Lord Skelbrooke which Euripides Hooke had taken such pains to lay out for her. But then, returning to the business at hand, she reread all the pages of his letter concerning Sera and Elsie Vorder.

"And so . . ." she told the troll triumphantly, " . . . our young friends may be found in Nova Imbria—and the inestimable Mr. Hooke, of all my spies, picked up the scent and followed them there! I told you, did I not, that he was the cleverest man I know?"

"I had thought the unfortunate Mr. von Eichstätt—possibly, by now, the late Mr. von Eichstätt—merited that distinction," said the Jarl, sitting down, as she indicated, on a gilt chair with an embroidered seat. He, too, had taken the time to change his attire, from the uniform which became him so well, to a coat of shimmering silver satin, pearl-grey smallclothes, and a waistcoat of corded silk. In addition, he carried a very pretty fan of painted chickenskin. "And I suppose—but of course, why else did the Gracious Lady go to all the trouble to obtain the monster, Cecile?—I suppose that we, no sooner home, shall embark on our travels once more?"

"Indeed we shall," said the Duchess. "Or rather," she amended, with a sudden impatient gesture, "not just immediately, but as soon as may be. A crossing at this time of year would be too dangerous. And I have business to attend to first . . . Arrangements, so many arrangements to be made, before I can travel such a distance."

With which pronouncement, she rose from the sofa and seated herself at an ornamental little writing desk, where she composed a number of letters over the next hour and a half. The Jarl, left with no better occupation than to wave his fan gently to and fro, eventually picked up a book which the Duchess kept by the loveseat and leafed through the pages. It chanced to be a book of poems, in a visionary, alchemical mode, and when he glanced at the inscription on the flyleaf, he received something of a shock.

He looked up to find the Duchess staring at him, with a bitter smile on her lips. "You astound me, sir. Do you find those verses to your taste?"

"Not at all," said Skogsrå, putting the book aside. "They are much too flowery. But I must confess that you have surprised *me*. I should not have thought you still had a value for Skelbrooke's gift."

"Should you not?" The Duchess continued to smile mechanically. "But I have a warm heart, my dear Skogsrå, and once I bestow my affections, I cannot so easily withdraw them."

Skogsrå cocked an inquiring eyebrow. "Do I understand, then, that you intend to spare Skelbrooke when you ruin the others?"

The Duchess suddenly looked very much older. "No," she said, in a husky voice, "no, I would not spare him. Not if I loved him twice so well. I wonder that you do not realize by now . . . My motives have nothing to do with loving or hating."

She was just sealing the last of her letters when the butler stalked in to announce a visitor. "He *would* insist on speaking to the Gracious Lady herself, though he came by the tradesmen's entrance," said the butler, looking down his nose in an imperious way that he had (no easy feat for a dwarf). "And I must say, a more rough and villainous individual—"

"His name, my good Mugwort, his name?" the Duchess asked impatiently. This being provided, she surprised the dwarf by ordering him to escort her unsavory visitor to the morning room downstairs. "I shall meet him there presently. No, Lord Skogsrå, you need not accompany me," she added, as the Jarl made a move to abandon his chair. "I wish to speak to the fellow privately."

She rose slowly, picked up Sebastian, and left the room. Taking the opportunity afforded by her absence, the Jarl limped over to her writing desk to see what he could learn from her correspondence.

The letter she had received from Hooke had been carelessly tossed to one side. Skogsrå picked it up and read all the way through with considerable interest. The other letters that she had already opened seemed mostly to be social invitations, or else concerned her endless and endlessly tiresome (or so thought the troll) charitable concerns. It never ceased to amaze him that a woman so ruthless and forceful as the Duchess should also labor under this grotesque compulsion to waste her substance on dirty beggars and unwanted children. His interest flagging, he continued to sift half-heartedly through the letters the Duchess had written and sealed, examining the direction on each. Most of the names were unknown to him, but the one he recognized caused him a tiny jolt of surprise: Lady Ursula Vizbeck.

The Jarl folded his hands and stared thoughtfully up at the ceiling. He had believed that Lady Ursula Vizbeck (*née* Bowker, then Borgmann—for her disgracefully married and expeditiously executed highwayman husband) was feuding with the Duchess.

But the more he thought about it, the more it baffled him. He could not for the life of him begin to guess what part the audacious Lady Ursula could possibly play in the Duchess's schemes.

13.

Wherein things Begin to go Awry in Hobb's Church.

Siegfried Herring was a master cabinetmaker. He maintained a shop at the foot of Spyglass Hill, where he and his two 'prentices practiced their craft. In addition to beautiful furniture of walnut, maple, and oak, Mr. Herring also sold brooms and walking sticks, every sort of lathe-turned goods, and (according to the sign out front) "fine Women's hats: Leghorn—horsehair—Beaver—and chip straw."

He had also, generously, allotted a comfortable cubbyhole to Mr. Jonas, that the gnome might conduct a little business grinding and polishing lenses. The nearest lensgrinder lived as far distant as Moonstone and had more than enough custom to last him all the year long; he would not mind at all (said the Moonstone spectacle-maker), if Mr. Jonas cared to set himself up in a small way.

Rather more significantly, a large shed was attached at the back of the shop. Very cold and draughty it was during winter, but now that the season of Thaw was upon them, and the Festival of Quickening no more than five weeks away, Jedidiah and the gnome took possession of the shed. There, they began to construct the elaborate mechanism with which they hoped to raise the island temple.

Slowly, the machine began to take form: first a solid framework of oak, then a complicated assembly of metallic gears, wheels, pulleys, and weights.

"Do you think . . . do you think, Mr. Jonas, that this enterprise of ours is like to make us men of great wealth and position?" Jed asked diffidently, on the day they mounted two great bronze mirrors on the machine.

"If we are successful, this enterprise will bring us treasure of incalculable worth," replied the gnome. "But naturally, it

94

will then be our task to see that everything falls into the proper hands—not to *sell* that treasure for gold. As for position: that we may well achieve. We shall be, you know, the two greatest authorities on the Panterran civilization alive in the world today, and the prestige of that should be considerable."

"I rather fancied as much," said Jed, with such a sigh of deep-felt discouragement that Mr. Jonas was moved to inquire sympathetically:

"Do you truly believe you must acquire a large fortune before you can persuade Miss Winter to marry you?"

Jedidiah set his jaw stubbornly. "I can't persuade her if I don't ever ask—and I *won't* ask, not until I have something more to offer her than all I possess now."

Mr. Jonas walked across the room, picked up one of the coils of silvered glass that were supposed to conduct the power of the lunar rays from the mirrors to the magnets. "I had no idea," he said dryly, "that Miss Winter's motives were like to prove so mercenary."

Jed flashed the gnome a swift indignant look. "I think you must know they are nothing of the sort," he said, with a heightened color. "But you don't know the life she led, back in Thornburg. Her father had a great house—bigger and grander than anything you ever saw in Lootie's Bay or Hobb's Church. Elsie never set foot out of the house without Sera and one of the servants to escort her, and she had nothing to do all day long but to pay visits and go to balls, and tea parties, and picnics, and to the theatre, and . . . Well, mostly she did none of those things because she was seldom well, but—"

"But there, I believe, you miss the point entirely," said Mr. Jonas. "*I* have never seen Miss Winter but when she was in excellent health and spirits, and it appears to me that the life she leads *now* suits her admirably."

Jed smiled with an obvious effort. "It may do for now, but eventually she'll tire of it and want all the things that she had before. And her family, too—they would never receive me!" He picked up a cloth and began furiously polishing one of the mirrors. "By the Nine Powers, *they* know my disgraceful origins, if nobody here does. And how could I possibly divide Elsie from her parents?"

Mr. Jonas began to screw the coil into place. "But it seems

to me, my dear Jedidiah, that Elsie and her parents are already divided . . . by two thousand miles of ocean, which is a formidable barrier, you must admit. Nor—pardon me, I know I have no right to interfere in your affairs, but I am very fond of you, my boy!—nor does Miss Winter appear to repine. Was she much attached to her parents?"

Jed shook his head with a sharp motion. "I can't say. It wouldn't be proper for me to ask her. That is . . . Her mother was not a pleasant woman, and her father never cared a rap for anything but his own comfort, but I daresay that Elsie *was* fond of them. Someday, she may wish to go back, and someday, it may be safe to do so. But she can't go home if she is bound to me, and if I've no fortune to offset my deplorable lack of birth and breeding. For me to marry Elsie under the circumstances . . ." Jed gave a savage little laugh, then balled up one hand into a fist and pounded it against a wooden beam. " . . . that would be just the sort of trashy, no-account behavior her parents would expect of a lowborn rascal like me!"

"Your sentiments do you honor," said Mr. Jonas. "Nevertheless—"

The walls of the shed began to creak and shake. A powerful shudder ran through the more sturdy structure to which it was attached.

"Earthquake?" said Jed, still breathing heavily, as he held on to the wooden framework of the machine for support.

"I should not be surprised. The moon is full in two days, and I believe there will also be an eclipse. The natural world is in a state of flux," said Mr. Jonas calmly. His big broad feet lent him a marvelous stability and proved quite useful at moments like this.

However, it developed that the tremor was rather more localized—had been confined to the one building, to be precise.

"Burn and blister those wretched hobgoblins!" exclaimed Mr. Herring, coming out to the shed in his apron, to see if all was well. "This entire town is crumbling at the foundations, and it is all their doing! Yes . . . not only do they continue to tunnel, but they have taken to gnawing on the timbers as well. And their thefts have grown quite out of bounds! A lady of my acquaintance says that she has only to leave a spool of thread, a feather fan, a lace cap, lying about, and it will be missing the next day." Mr. Herring gave a snort of disgust. "One can scarcely keep *all* one's possessions under lock and key!"

"Have you tried setting traps?" Mr. Jonas inquired helpfully. Quite oblivious to the continued creaking of the building, he began to test the system of weights and pulleys that was meant to move the mirrors and keep them in constant alignment with the moon.

"We have," said Mr. Herring, wildly disarranging his precious brown wig, so great was his agitation. "Some of them quite ingenious, but the hobs are so cunning, they almost invariably find a way to take the bait without tripping the mechanism."

"In Marstadt, we just slaughtered the vermin on sight," Jed offered, with a certain bloodthirsty relish. The sport of hobsticking enjoyed considerable popularity among the young men who lived along the river Lunn. "Of course," he added, a trifle apologetically, "no one minds that, because the hobgoblins there are such nasty, vicious things . . ."

"Yes," said Mr. Herring. "But we hardly ever *do* catch sight of them here, they are so swift and sly. Nor do they swarm or run mad at the full of the moon, as they sometimes do elsewhere.

"We have tried pouring poison and lowering gunpowder charges down their holes," he added, with another despairing clutch at his wig. "One imagines that does kill some of them, though of course we never see the bodies. But it doesn't kill *enough* of them, and still the destruction continues!"

In the parlor at Mothgreen Academy, the ladies were entertaining. Or rather, *Sera* was attempting to entertain Mr. Tynsdale, while Elsie practiced on the harpsichord in the next room, and Miss Barebones, Miss Eglantine, and Miss Fitch played three-handed cribbage, using a queer old pack of cards of Yndean origin, and a scrimshaw board with ivory pegs. As they played, the three elderly ladies discussed among themselves the most recent activities of the Academy Ghost.

A small fire burned on the hearth, between the pugnacious brass firedogs, but the room, as always, smelled not of woodsmoke, but of snuff.

Sera sat on the horsehair sofa, feeling unusually fine in a splendid new gown of straw-colored satin with deep ruffles of lace on the sleeves and the corsage. But she also felt somewhat flushed and harassed, forced as she was to divert the preacher's attention from all this talk of "Uncle Izrael," by keeping up a constant flow of sensible conversation. Every now and again she glanced through the double doors to the next room, where Elsie doggedly continued to play one sprightly tune after another—but there was no expecting any support from Elsie. She did not like Mr. Tynsdale, was clearly dismayed by his frequent visits; nor did she feel in the least equipped to discuss religion under the clergyman's burning regard.

"A quaint old book . . . did you never read it, sir? Dr. Cornelius advanced a theory that the primitive Church in assigning the origin of the various beasts and all the races of Rational Beings, each to one of the Nine Powers, actually followed the tenets of an older religion, originating in . . ." Sera continued on valiantly, for over an hour. When the tea tray arrived, Elsie abandoned her harpsichord to pour out the tea and pass around biscuits and scones, but she left the discussion to Sera and Mr. Tynsdale.

"Indeed, it is an arresting theory, but if I may say so, Miss Thorn, I wonder at your kinsman exposing a young woman like yourself to such patently heretical . . . and you are still, after all, of tender years . . ." Mr. Tynsdale continued to keep up his end of the conversation, with a porcelain teacup in one hand and a dish of apple fritters in the other.

Sera gave an indignant gasp and replied with some vehemence. Accepting the cup that Elsie offered her, she balanced both teacup and saucer on an arm of the sofa.

"With all due respect," said Mr. Tynsdale, "it has been my experience that young females—"

Sera, in the act of raising her teacup to her lips, chanced to look down into the bowl of the cup. What she saw there caused her to start violently. The cup slipped out of her fingers and landed in her lap, splashing the straw-colored satin with hot tea, and scattering wet brown tea leaves across her skirt. With an effort, she recovered her composure.

"How—how remarkably clumsy of me," she said, scrubbing desperately at her skirt with Elsie's handkerchief. "I really must learn not to express myself with such heat—it inevitably leads to some utterly graceless act. If you will excuse me, sir, I will go upstairs and make myself presentable."

She was out of the room in an instant, and Elsie followed a moment later. Elsie caught up with her on the stairs. "Sera, you *saw* something in that teacup . . . was it a message from Uncle Izrael? There is no use pretending otherwise, for I saw how you jumped when you looked in the cup. And I do wish that you would confide in me. Uncle Izrael *has* been trying to tell you something, hasn't he?"

Sera continued on up the stairs to the attic, with Elsie right behind her. "I thought, just for a moment, that I saw a word spelled out in the tea leaves . . . but really, I only imagined it. Why should Mr. Barebones . . . or—or anyone send me a message like 'catacombs'? It makes no sense at all," said Sera, pausing for a moment to lean up against the balustrade. Truth to tell, she felt a little weak about the knees. "It *must* have been my imagination! I am not usually suggestible, as you know, but with all this talk of tea-leaf reading and table tipping! My dearest Elsie, do not tell me that you are beginning to *believe* in such nonsense?"

"I don't know why I should not," countered Elsie, with an unusual spark of defiance. "Jedidiah says that *he* believes it. Yes, and he says that you used to believe it, too, when you were younger. You used to see things in teacups and mirrors. At the time, he says, he was the skeptical one, but now that he knows . . . well, the things that he knows, about sidereal spirits and sublunar astral essences, he is convinced you have a natural talent which may actually enable you to speak with spirits. And only think, Sera," she added coaxingly, "perhaps Uncle Izrael Barebones has something of vital importance to tell you."

Sera swept her a contemptuous curtsy. She had no idea what sublunar astral essences might be, and she doubted that either her cousin or Jed was perfectly clear on the subject. "My dear Elsie, I will tell *you* that nobody ever learned anything in the least agreeable speaking with spirits. On the contrary! When I was young and believed in such things, it seemed I was always entertaining some morbid fancy. I cannot begin to tell you how wretchedly unpleasant it all was. That being so, I have nothing at all to say to Uncle Izrael, and I fervently hope that he has nothing to say to me!"

But when she had climbed the stairs and entered her bed-chamber, when she had changed her silk gown for a simpler one of white cambric, she chanced to notice a ragged old volume which *someone* had placed on her bed, in the middle of the patchwork quilt. Sera glared down at it with angry apprehension. She did not recall seeing the book there two hours past, when she came upstairs to change into the straw-colored gown. And all this time, the girls had been playing quiet games or strolling among the budding fruit trees down in the garden, under the watchful eyes of Mary Partridge. Then who could possibly . . . ?

She took up the book gingerly, handling it with extreme distaste; for the cover, besides being frayed, was quite appallingly dirty as well—not dusty, as a volume must be if left too long on a table or bookshelf, but covered with fresh earth as though it had lately been buried in the ground.

When she dropped the book on a little table beside her bed, the cover fell open. On an impulse, Sera leaned forward, the better to see the name written in faded red ink upon the flyleaf: *Izrael Falconer Barebones.*

Sera stood there with her hand on her heart and the grue running cold up and down her spine. "It must—it *must* have been one of the children, who brought it up before as a prank, and . . . and I simply did not notice it."

But she knew very well that the book had not been there the last time she came upstairs. If she had not seen it, she must certainly have *smelled* it, for it filled the room with the dark, gritty odor of garden mold.

14.

Perhaps the Shortest chapter in the Book.

South of Thornburg, at the mouth of the river Lunn, stood the seaport of Ilben, a breezy little town of white-washed buildings with blue slate roofs, built on the verge of a broad mudflat. A vast network of piers and boardwalks beginning at the seawall led out from the town to the harbor.

The twenty-ninth day of the season of Thaw, a fair but blustery day, discovered the Duchess, along with Jarl Skogsrå and Sebastian the ape (trailing behind on a jeweled leash), strolling on one of the weathered boardwalks. The big merchantman the *Waxing Moon*, a great wallowing vessel with parchment-colored sails, waited at the end of the pier to carry them off to the New World.

With them, as mute as ever, obedient as always—within her limited range—came Skullgrimm's artificial creation, heavily veiled. It would not do, the Duchess had said, so near the town of Elsie's birth, for the monster to be noticed and recognized by any intimate of the Vorder family. Accordingly, they had swathed her in yards of black tulle.

As they proceeded up the gangplank the Duchess continually glanced around her, thinking to find a familiar face on the wharf, or waiting for her on shipboard.

"Perhaps he has changed his mind," said Skogsrå, though he, too, directed a glance over his shoulder. "I confess that I would not be disappointed if he had. I do not like this new traveling companion of ours. He brings with him the odor of the grave . . . an atmosphere of things long buried that should not have come to light." The troll shuddered distastefully. "He fairly reeks of corruption."

The Duchess lifted her own light veil, which was attached to an exceedingly becoming bonnet. She gave a tiny sigh. "I

101

quite agree with you. And yet he may prove to be a valuable ally. Also . . ." she added, in a low, intense voice, "in return for our aid in recovering those books of his, he has vowed to perform what Jenk the alchemist promised but did not deliver: the creation of a living homunculus, a small, perfect child for me to call my own. I have waited so many years to become a happy mother," she added wistfully. "I believe I would do almost anything to reach that fortunate state."

"If so," said the Jarl, in that provokingly prosaic way that he had, "the Gracious Lady might just as well adopt a child."

The Duchess shook her head emphatically. "I had something of the sort in mind when I sought to become Elsie Vorder's godmother . . . and you see what trouble came of that. I was passed over, insulted, most brutally offended! I shall not try anything on *that* order again, I can assure you."

Though Skogsrå walked arm in arm with the simulacrum, and the monster followed docilely wherever he went, she now began to drag her feet, to lag a step behind him. "She is losing animation, she requires to be fed," said the Jarl.

"We can hardly feed her up here on the deck, for all the world to see," said the Duchess, making a face. "I shall go with you below, to your cabin."

In the Jarl's cabin, the Duchess sat on the edge of his bunk, and the blue ape squatted down at her feet. Skogsrå took out a cage full of white mice from among his luggage, removed two of them, killed each one by the simple expedient of breaking its neck, and proceeded to slit them open with a little knife. Watching him do these things, the golem became restless, even agitated, making inarticulate whimpering sounds deep in her throat.

The Jarl took up one of the warm, bleeding mouse hearts and delicately placed it between the monster's rosy lips.

"Indeed, you amaze me," said the Duchess, taking a little lace-edged handkerchief scented with civet and vetivert out of her reticule and waving it under her nose. "You display such solicitude for the creature, you treat her . . . so gently. You almost seem fond of her."

"It is a sort of game that I like to play," replied the Jarl, with a mutinous glance. "A harmless fancy I choose to entertain, that our Cecile is a creature like myself, that her eagerness at moments like this is a reflection of my own hunger, my own obsession. I am entitled to my amusements, am I not?

"And she is . . . a pretty plaything," he added, so low that the Duchess could not be certain whether he spoke to himself or to her. "Far more attractive than any troll woman would be."

The Duchess was shocked, and more than slightly revolted. "My dear Jarl, I fear you have conceived some unwholesome attachment. But you must realize that the monster is not really alive, that she is no more, really, than an animated doll!"

"I am in no danger of forgetting that," retorted the Jarl, as he washed his bloody hands in a basin of water. "Indeed, how could I? Did I not see the clay figure from which Skullgrimm created her? Nor am I so stupid, so gullible, as the Gracious Lady likes to pretend."

He led the simulacrum over to a corner of the cabin and left her standing there.

"But we trolls . . . we are a lonely race," he went on, in a sudden burst of confidence. "We do not even like each other very much, as you know. So why should I not grow a little . . . fond . . . of this Cecile, even make a pet of her, as you have made a favorite of the ape Sebastian?"

The Duchess bristled up, for the comparison offended her. She took the little ape up into her lap. "If you continue to spout such disgusting nonsense, I shall have to take steps to save you from this . . . yes, this monstrous attachment," she said, smoothing Sebastian's long indigo fur. "I shall have to take charge of Cecile myself—which I confess I am loath to do—or, better still, turn her over to Mr. Kelly.

"Why should I not?" she asked rhetorically. "I should think them a most compatible match, for they *are* creatures of much the same sort. They are both more dead than alive."

Skogsrå glared at her, as he picked up the cage and put it inside a small cupboard built into the wall above his bunk. "The Gracious Lady amuses herself at my expense. But it shall not be. If I am to continue to lend myself to your schemes, I am at least entitled to this one indulgence."

The Duchess raised an eyebrow. This show of spirit was unlike the Jarl, whose occasional rebellious flashes more often came out in the form of subtle, petty revenges, and not in open defiance.

"Oh, very well . . . why not?" she said, with a languid gesture. "It costs me nothing, after all. And if it affords you some twisted satisfaction, why should I not indulge you?"

The Jarl smiled, showing his teeth. "The Gracious Lady is all generosity."

15.

On the shores of Lake Valentina, in the mountainous little principality of Schwannstein, clustered many fine inns, hotels, and guest houses. The jewel-like lake, the rugged alpine scenery . . . these brought artists and nature lovers from all parts of Euterpe. In addition, Lake Valentina was located on one of the principal routes through the Alps. There was one quaint inn in particular, a frosted gingerbread chalet overlooking the sapphire lake, that was a favorite stopping place for traveling nobility.

One such visitor, who had stopped for nearly a fortnight, was a certain Imbrian gentleman of eccentric habits, for he came and went at all odd hours of the day and night, and apparently traveled without a valet—a surprising omission on the part of so obviously fashionable a gentleman. Other visitors found him polite but distant, absorbed in his own affairs, though neither they nor the innkeeper nor the inn servants ever learned what that business might be; however, the boy who polished the boots (who was known to have a lurid imagination) declared that he had detected about the elegant little gentleman a strong whiff of gunpowder, on more than one occasion.

The gentleman strolled into the inn at ten o'clock one morning—very prettily attired he was, in rose velvet and creamy lace, his satin waistcoat embroidered with a pattern of morning-glories worked in palest blue—as immaculate as ever, for all he had been out the entire night. He caused a stir by sending for the innkeeper and demanding his reckoning: "For my visit, regrettably, has come to an end." The innkeeper experienced a pang of considerable disappointment; since nothing had been said about the length of his visit, all had assumed the Imbrian gentleman would stay for the season. But as there was no help for it, the innkeeper produced the bill.

The gentleman went upstairs to pack his baggage. The boot boy came up half an hour later, to find him just fastening the last of his bags.

"I shall not need your assistance, as you can see, though you are really most obliging," said the gentleman, dusting off his fingers with a handkerchief, as though he found the business of packing his belongings rather dirty work.

"Begging your pardon, Mr. Carstares, sir," said the youth. "These letters come for you yesterday, when you was out."

Mr. Carstares daintily accepted the letters. Both were, indeed, addressed to him, one in a hand that he knew. "You are very good. The coach arrives at noon, does it not? You may come in another hour to take down my bags."

The boy bobbed his head respectfully and withdrew. Mr. Carstares opened one of the missives and took it over by the open window in order to read it. The letter was written in the Glassmakers code, and it came from the dwarf Trithemius Ave. Mr. Carstares skimmed down to the last paragraph:

> *Caleb Braun and Eirena do very Well, and I expect them to Stay with me for some little Time. The page-boy is even Now on his way to Orania. As for Count Azimet, as far as the Zammarcans are concerned, he simply Vanished—it is Often the way in the Equable Republic—but Baron Onda assures me that his Cousin witnessed the Execution, and there can be no Doubt that the Villain is Dead. Two of his Oranians—under what Duress one can only Imagine—admitted Complicity in the Count's treasonous Schemes, and were drowned in the Lagoon. What became of the others Baron Onda does not say— however, I think you may Congratulate yourself for having the Foresight to remove the Boy. As one of Azimet's favorites, I believe it Would have gone Hard with him, and he might even now be lying at the Bottom of the Lagoon with those other Unfortunates.*

Mr. Carstares crumpled the letter with one convulsive movement and cast it into the fireplace. He crossed the room in three swift steps and flung himself down into a chair. A parade of conflicting emotions passed over his face, as the many personalities inhabiting the one body contended for dominance. Then a shudder ran through his wiry frame, the small white hands clenched and unclenched . . . and the elegant Mr. Carstares emerged once more.

He reached into a waistcoat pocket and drew out his box of Sleep Dust, took a generous pinch, and inhaled. Then he remembered the other letter, which he had stuffed into his coat pocket.

This missive, also, was written in code, a personal cipher known only to himself and to one other.

> *My very dear Francis . . . or Should I say Robin or Simon?* [wrote Hermes Budge]. *I have recently received Word from our Friends in Thornburg, to the Effect that a Certain Great Lady (along with her constant Companion, a gentleman of Unnatural Appetites) sets Sail this very day for Nova Imbria. I am persuaded that this News . . .*

Mr. Carstares read the entire letter through twice, with mixed emotions, though nothing on the order of his previous reaction. The brain storm having passed, he was, for a time, in complete control.

He had feared, for several days now, that something of the sort was in the wind, ever since *his* constant companions, the Duchess's bloodhounds, disappeared. Taken altogether, it could mean only one thing: the Duchess had picked up some clue as to the whereabouts of Sera Vorder and her cousin Elsie, and had gone to the New World in pursuit of them.

Yet as bad as that was, he also felt a surge of relief. He had been delaying his own voyage to Nova Imbria, for something more than a year, lest the Duchess or her agents follow him there. But to go looking for Sera *after* Marella had picked up her trail . . . that was another matter entirely. Mr. Carstares heaved a deep sigh. Whatever else might come of it, this news set him free to follow his heart.

However, there was one small item of business back in Thornburg that he meant to attend to first.

Seven days later, a fresh-faced youth dressed like a country squire was seen to hesitate on the doorstep of a certain notorious establishment on the banks of the Lunn. The house was a high-class brothel, known as the Sultan's Jewelbox, and those who observed the country-bred youth could not suppress smiles of amusement: it was obvious the place exerted a strong attraction, equally obvious that he entertained panicky second thoughts.

In the end, however, lubricity (or perhaps just curiosity) evidently triumphed over the dictates of conscience. The young squire squared his shoulders and entered the house of ill-repute.

A painted boy with rings in his ears greeted him at the door, begging the gentleman to state his pleasure. The young squire replied, with a burning blush, that he was invited to the supper upstairs.

"Second floor, at the back of the house," said the boy, adding, with an ugly smirk, "But if you're wanting a girl for later, you'd best make the arrangements now."

The visitor blushed more painfully than before, and stammered a reply: that he had not yet reached a decision on that score. The boy declared that he was perfectly free to suit himself, and gestured toward the stairs.

It was fortunate the boy had elected to remain at his post by the door, for after the young gentleman climbed the first two flights he continued on up the stairs for two flights more.

Moving softly, he passed by the door at the top of the steps, and went on to the end of the corridor, where another door opened on a set of newly decorated luxurious rooms: the private apartments of the proprietor, one Mr. Jagst.

Finding those rooms unoccupied—as might be expected so early in the evening—and noting with approval how the intervening floors removed these apartments from the rowdy merriment in the house below, the young gentleman made a few trifling arrangements, set a comfortable chair against the wall near the door by which he had entered, and sat down to wait.

More than an hour passed before the door opened and Mr. Jagst strolled into the room. He had closed the door behind him and advanced halfway across the chamber when a tiny sound, a soft click, caught his attention. He wheeled around to confront his unexpected visitor.

He did not immediately recognize this intruder lounging so idly in the gilded chair, for many seasons had passed since their last meeting, and that, of necessity, had been rather brief.

However, he had no difficulty identifying the object in the visitor's hand: it was undoubtedly a cocked pistol. Mr. Jagst's complexion tended more toward the sallow than the ruddy, but he rapidly lost what little color he possessed.

"Lord Skelbrooke . . . it *is* Lord Skelbrooke?" said the pimp.

The young squire—no longer so very young, as he had miraculously acquired some seven or eight years since entering the room—smiled a singularly disquieting smile. "Indeed, Mr. Jagst. You find me here intact, and precisely as my Creator made me."

Mr. Jagst cleared his throat uneasily. "This matter of castration . . . that was suggested to me, you know, by the manner in which you threatened Lord Krogan."

Lord Skelbrooke's glance hardened, his grip on the silver-chased pistol tightened. "And the hot iron which you applied to the soles of my feet? What—if one might inquire—what suggested that to you?"

"A matter of expedience," said Mr. Jagst, "I feel certain your lordship will understand the necessity."

His lordship continued to smile awfully. "You will pardon me if a certain prejudice prevents me from doing so." He gestured with the pistol. "You will find a weapon, loaded and primed, on that very pretty lacquered table behind you. It is the mate of the one you see in my hand."

Mr. Jagst slithered around behind the table, wiped his forehead with the back of his hand. "You mean to challenge me to a duel, then?"

"I do," said Skelbrooke, rising slowly from his seat. "I suppose that even a cur like you deserves his chance."

The pimp eyed the pistol on the lacquered tabletop with evident distaste. He cleared his throat again. "I must tell you, if you cherish any illusions of fair play, that you have me at a complete disadvantage."

"You can hardly expect me to take your word for that," Skelbrooke replied coldly. "Besides, neither am I a crack shot. I have a habit of shooting at close range."

Mr. Jagst smiled weakly. "But supposing . . ." He took a step toward the table. " . . . supposing I refused your challenge?"

"Then I would kill you anyway. I said you deserve your

chance, but having offered and been refused, I would have no compunction about murdering you out of hand. My own wrongs are as nothing," said his lordship with a hardening glance, "but you have caused much misery in this world. When I think of the scores of innocent youths and maidens you have kidnapped and condemned to lives of misery and degradation—"

Without warning, Mr. Jagst reached for the pistol, leveled, aimed, and fired. Lord Skelbrooke fired in the same instant.

Skelbrooke's shot whizzed past Jagst's ear, but the pimp had chosen the easier target. The ball took Skelbrooke in the shoulder, causing him to stagger back with a cry and collapse in the chair by the door.

"As I suspected, you are a liar," his lordship said weakly, as a spreading wetness soaked through his coat, staining the wool a dark red.

"As I did *not* suspect, you told the truth," gloated Jagst, dropping the spent pistol on the table with a thud. "You are certainly not a crack shot." Grown marvelously steady for a man who had so recently quaked in his shoes, he moved toward the door to summon his minions.

"Regrettably, I am not," murmured Skelbrooke, the chameleon, reaching with his good hand into his pocket. "Which is precisely why I always carry a second pistol with me." And the hand emerged holding a large-barreled specimen, with which he coolly proceeded to blast the astonished Mr. Jagst between the eyes at point-blank range.

Outside the apothecary shop on Blue Phoenix Lane—a street so narrow that the overhanging stories of the ancient buildings to either side made a kind of dim tunnel between—a hanging green lanthorn cast a welcoming glow at all hours of the day and night.

It was very late indeed when the little owl-eyed apothecary, Mistress Sancreedi, fresh from a mission of mercy, trudged up the lane between the hovering buildings and paused outside her door, fumbling in the basket she carried until she found a large brass key. But the door, she suddenly realized with a start, already stood cracked open, and when she checked the lock, she saw that it had been battered and broken with some heavy object, like a rock or an iron bar.

Mistress Sancreedi hesitated. But she was too old now and

too set in her ways, she told herself sternly, to experience a failure of nerve. Very slowly, she pushed the door aside; very cautiously, she entered the shop. A single candle, placed on the counter, illuminated the room: the shelves crammed full of bottles and boxes and jars and pots, the strings of poppy heads and bundled herbs hanging from the beamed ceiling, the big cauldron by the fireplace, in which she had last boiled a batch of rose-scented soap . . .

A fragrance of rose petals lingered on the air. She put her basket down on the counter, behind a row of large jars filled variously with lemon drops, linseed, yarrow, and horehound, and picked up the candle.

A faint voice called to her from the next room, the little kitchen where she cooked her own meals and brewed up some of her simples. Taking the candle with her, and gathering up her skirts in one hand, she hurried into the kitchen, gave a soft cry of distress as she recognized the blood-stained figure slumped in a chair beside the hearth.

"Francis Skelbrooke . . . my poor boy! What has happened to you?"

"A pistol ball in the shoulder . . . not likely to prove fatal . . . and I already staunched the flow of blood. But to remove the ball myself"—Lord Skelbrooke smiled weakly "that heroical effort is quite beyond me."

"As I should think so indeed," said the little white-haired woman, putting the candle down on the table. Removing her hat and her woolen shawl, she immediately set briskly to work, helping him to remove his coat, examining his wound, which was uglier than he had led her to believe, and bringing in the basket containing her lancets and bandages.

Then she brought him a tumbler full of brandy. "Drink all of this down. I am like to cause you considerable pain."

His lordship obliged. She was silent after that, intent on her task, removing the ball, which was buried rather deep, stopping a new flow of blood, dusting the wound with basilicum powder, and finally bandaging the shoulder, neatly and deftly, with several yards of lint. Skelbrooke endured it all with a white face and his teeth set tight, but he slumped a little lower in the chair when she had finished.

"I suppose, unless you were carried here," she said, "that you can walk?"

"With your assistance . . . I believe that I may." She slipped an arm around his waist and supported him up a short flight of stairs to her bedchamber, where she helped him to lower himself down on the bed.

"If you would be so good . . . There is a little box, a little pearl and gold box in a pocket of my coat . . ." he said, just above a whisper.

Mistress Sancreedi left the room and came back a few minutes later with his blood-stained coat. But when she opened the box and recognized the fine crystalline powder, she favored him with a sharp, disapproving look. "You carry the powder with you . . . you are addicted to the Dust?"

But this was not the appropriate moment for a lecture. So she put a large pinch of the drug in the palm of her hand, slipped her other arm under his shoulder, and lifted him up that he might inhale the fine powder.

"I thank you," he said, lying back against the bed, with a gasp. "I will rest easier now."

When he awoke the next morning—or perhaps it was the next afternoon—she was sitting in a rocking chair beside the bed. A faint light from the street crept in through a window, and a lighted oil lamp hung from the ceiling. In the circle of golden lamplight the tiny apothecary looked almost translucent—and considerably more frail than he remembered her.

"I wonder if it would be dreadfully impertinent for me to inquire how old you actually are?" he asked, with the faintest of smiles.

Mistress Sancreedi showed no surprise at being addressed by a man she had supposed asleep. "It is . . . but I will answer you anyway." She folded her beautiful white hands in the lap of her ancient velvet gown. "I am approaching my second century. I hope you will now say that you are astonished to hear it."

He laughed softly. "You do not look it . . . but I am not surprised. You are the most ethereal creature I have met in my life—even more so than the Duchess."

She continued to regard him with that benign look. "Yes, we hybrids are an unpredictable lot. Marella Carleon is three-quarters fay, and I only half . . . yet I bear the more visible marks of our shared heritage. Then again, there are others who bear no resemblance to fairies at all—or to Men, either, poor monsters! There are certain qualities, however, not so easily remarked, though unmistakable when one knows to look for them . . ."

His lordship flung up his hand, as if imploring her not to go on, but the lady continued anyway, in her low, sweet voice. "You *shall* hear me, Francis. My poor boy, I know very well that you received a wound six years back . . . far worse than the hurt which brought you here last night, for that earlier one was a psychic wound and infinitely deeper. Since then—"

"I deplore the necessity of contradicting you," his lordship interrupted, "but it was not *I* who suffered six years ago, not—not in any extraordinary way. Others, more innocent, suffered most horribly due to my criminal weakness, and for that—"

"Pardon me," said Mistress Sancreedi, "but I only meant to say: I believe that you were unhappy long before that. Not so miserably unhappy as you are now, but a man at peace with himself would have been able, to some extent, to excuse his own mistakes, would scarcely have taken so deep a blow to his self-esteem. And Francis, if you wish to be well again, you must finally recognize the nature of your complaint."

His lordship made a wry face. "Since you would have it so, madam, pray tell me the nature of my complaint."

"It is a complaint which Marella Carleon—and to a lesser extent myself—knows very well," said Mistress Sancreedi, stretching out a hand to give his good arm a comforting pressure. "Come, Francis, you know what I would tell you, but you refuse to believe it. Can it be that you carry a prejudice against my kind?"

Skelbrooke frowned and shook his head. "I am not a bigot, but . . ." One hand plucked uneasily at the covers. "I should like to think that someday I might be . . . whole. But if this thing you would tell me should chance to be true, then I never shall be, shall I?"

Mistress Sancreedi made a hopeless gesture. "Perhaps we should speak of this later, when you are feeling stronger. Instead, I shall attempt to say something reassuring. The ball did strike the bone, but only just, and you are not like to be permanently disabled. But perhaps I need not tell you that."

He smiled ruefully up at her. "I am not in the habit of sustaining these wounds quite so often as you seem to suppose, dear lady." He struggled to sit up, and she left her rocking chair to rearrange the pillows under his head and shoulders.

"I was alluding, of course, to the years you spent studying medicine in Lundy," she said. She draped a grey wool shawl across her shoulders and settled back into her chair. "You may tell me, now, who it was that shot you, and under what circumstances."

"I fought a duel with . . . with a man who had once done me a great wrong."

She heaved a great sigh, as though some weight had been lifted from her mind. "It was a fair fight, then? You are not—not like to be taken up by the Watch?"

"It is unlikely that I will be taken up by the Watch. My enemy is dead, and no one knows that it was I who called on him last night." His lordship winced as he changed position on the bed. "I regret to say that it was . . . was not entirely a fair fight. I believe I neglected to mention that I had two pistols to his one."

He could see that he had shocked her—and very likely disappointed her as well—though she struggled to conceal the extent of her dismay. "Two pistols to his one? And what kind of behavior is that, pray tell!"

He looked up at her with a hurt, wistful smile. "Not the behavior of a gentleman—a man of honor—certainly. Though that was how I originally meant to conduct myself," he said quietly. "A deed worthy of an assassin, I should say."

The old woman shook her head disapprovingly, but her voice remained gentle. "An assassin . . . I see. And is that what you are, Francis Love Skelbrooke—is that how you intend to go on? I seem to recall a time when your ambitions were far more noble than that."

His lordship shaded his eyes, as if to protect them from the light. "It is rather late for me . . . now . . . to consider changing my occupation. I very much fear that I am no longer fit for any better work."

16.

Wherein Jedidiah and Mr. Jonas experience a Delay, and Sera begins to feel Persecuted.

The season of Thaw had nearly passed, and the days hastened on toward the Festival of Quickening. In the countryside surrounding Hobb's Church, the first green shoots of crocus and snowdrops pushed their heads above the soil, fuzzy catkins began to appear on the branches of birch trees, and red-gold buds virtually exploded on a stand of horse chestnuts outside the gates of Mothgreen Academy. In the town itself, flocks of migrating robins joined the sea gulls and pigeons feeding on the square; and the wych-elms shading the little white church were suddenly covered with tiny wine-colored blossoms.

Meanwhile, everyone began to prepare for the coming holiday. Girls made wreaths of twigs, straw, and bits of red yarn—meant to resemble bird's nests—which they hung over the doors of their homes or attached to the crowns of their bonnets. Housewives boiled eggs and baked tiny seedcakes. And their men climbed up to the roofs and took down all the weathercocks, which, painted in fresh bright colors and decorated with ribbons, they would put back in place on the eve of the holiday.

In Hobb's Church, the Festival began at daybreak with a bonfire (fed by nine different kinds of wood) on a barren stretch of ground just outside the town. That same afternoon, a pole was erected on the green, and the dancing went on for hours. But in Moonstone the events were rather more colorful, with processions by all the guilds, and a particularly impressive ceremonial at the center of the town, conducted by the Glassmakers of both villages.

A great wicker house had been previously erected, like a gigantic birdcage, and a multitude of artificial birds made of cloth and bright feathers was perched inside. At noon the Glassmakers emerged from their hall, in their most splendid robes and their powdered wigs, bearing on their shoulders enormous wicker beasts adorned with flowers and colorful ribbons, which they carried through the crowded streets to the center of the town, and deposited as offerings in the house of branches. The antiquity of the ceremony was known to all: in a wicked and violent era, midway between the fall of Panterra and the present enlightened age, the birds and the beasts had been living creatures, a sacrifice of blood and bone to terrible pagan gods. Some who observed today could not repress a shudder, thinking of that ancient horror, and of the shrieks and the stench when the cage was ignited and all the poor animals burned to death.

But now it was very different. The Glassmakers had soaked their creations in essential oils, and when the wicker house burned, the flames leaped up in lovely jewel-like colors and filled the air with the scent of flowers.

The holiday over, the citizens of both towns settled down to their usual pursuits. It was therefore to the most sober and hardworking of communities that Moses Tynsdale returned, two days after the Festival, from a journey of several weeks' duration.

He rode into Hobb's Church just after sunset, left his horse at a public stable, and started toward the respectable boarding house run by a decent old dwarf where he maintained a set of rooms. The lamps already burned on every corner, but in between there was only pale moonlight to illuminate his way. Crossing Gooseberry Lane, he met Jedidiah Thorn and Mr. Jonas.

"Reverend Tynsdale, sir. We believed we had seen the last of you," said Jedidiah, amiably enough, but with a sparkling hostility in his glance. The clergyman wondered, with contemptuous amusement, if young Thorn actually deluded himself that his frequent pastoral visits to the Academy were motivated by a desire to court either of the young schoolmistresses.

Tynsdale bowed solemnly. "I have been out to the western settlements. They are rough folk, but godly. I believe that my talents may be put to better use here in Cordelia."

They exchanged a few polite insincerities, then the youth

and gnome bowed, and continued on their way. Tynsdale watched them go, with something like a sneer on his face. They made a singularly ill-assorted pair: young Thorn so tall and broad, and the short, squat figure of the gnome stumping along beside him. They did not appear to notice when Tynsdale fell in behind them, and, keeping to the shadows as much as possible and moving with a soft step, followed silently after them.

They disappeared inside the Eclipse. Tynsdale waited a moment or two before entering the tavern. Once inside, he lingered in the shadows near the door, sweeping the room with his brilliant glance, until he spotted his quarry seated in an inglenook at the back of the common room, well removed from the other tables. They were deep in conversation with an old man in a rough coat and a cloth cap which marked him as a sailor.

Tynsdale experienced a moment of doubt. He had supposed that young Thorn and his female relations were settled in Cordelia, at least for another season or two. If they were not, if they planned a sea voyage, at this of all times . . .

The clergyman insinuated his way up to the bar, procured a mug of porter, moved a three-legged oak stool, and sat down on it just around the corner from the alcove, where he could hear most of the low-voiced conversation.

"Them repairs to the *Otter* is taking longer than I *inticipated*," the old salt was saying. "Nor it ain't been easy to recruit just the sort of crew you're asking for." He dropped his voice still lower, and Tynsdale had to lean toward the inglenook in order to hear him. " . . . and off we go without no cargo to speak of, to an unknown destination, and no explanation a-tall as to what's it all about . . . naturally, the men got questions. I hope the gentlemen won't take no insult if I speak out plain. We're honest seamen in these parts, and we don't want no part of piracy or privateering. Yes, and the trustier hands, which are inclined to keep quiet and discreet like you asked . . . why, they're just the ones as got to ask the most questions afore they sign on."

"I can assure you, Captain Hornbeam, that we contemplate nothing of the sort," said Mr. Jonas. "We propose an honest enterprise, though we mean to keep it secret. The merchandise that we mean to obtain . . . Well, you must understand that our . . . competitors . . . are not at all scrupulous men and might use any information they could obtain to our serious disadvantage. It is often so in trade, you know."

"That may be," said Captain Hornbeam. "Well . . . I know it's often so, and I'll pass your assurances on to the men. But what about that machine of yours you mean to bring on board? I can't make head nor tail of it, what you showed me, and the men won't understand it neither. What they don't understand, they're likely to suspicion. You might say we sailors is a superstitious lot, but there it is: we're mindful of our luck!"

Mr. Jonas cleared his throat. "Perhaps you, Jedidiah, could address the Captain's concerns. I should tell you, Captain Hornbeam, that Mr. Thorn at one time lived among fishermen and seafaring men and had a most particular acquaintance with— with the tides and the elements. Would you, Jedidiah, consider our device to be unlucky?"

"*Was* you a sailor, Mr. Thorn?" asked the Captain. Tynsdale cocked his head, listening for the reply; this was certainly the first that *he* had heard of it.

"I worked on a boat . . . on a river . . . not far from the sea," Jedidiah said carefully. "I've a fair degree of familiarity with sailors' superstitions, and entertain the very highest respect for the sagacity of seamen like yourself. You may accept my personal assurance that the magnetic device we mean to bring on board will in no way interfere with the luck of the crew."

Captain Hornbeam hemmed and hawed, but when young Thorn had regaled him with half a dozen stories, all of them bearing the ring of authenticity, current among "the sailors of the town where I was born," the Captain accepted his credentials, allowed himself satisfied, and said that he would speak with the men and attempt to reassure them.

The Captain then rose and took his leave. Moses Tynsdale, who did not wish to be recognized by Jedidiah or Mr. Jonas— particularly in the act of lurking around the corner—concluded that the time had arrived for him to depart, and left the tavern somewhat precipitously.

"All these delays," said Jedidiah to Mr. Jonas, as they left the Eclipse and proceeded down a lamplit lane in the direction of Mr. Herring's cottage. "If we remain here too long, Sera and Elsie will grow fretful, they will want to move on. Indeed, we *ought* to move on, for the safety of all concerned. That is the only way that we can continue to elude the Duchess.

"*I* ought certainly to resume my travels," he added remorsefully. "I promised Mr. Owlfeather I would keep traveling and that I would send back word, from time to time, telling him all I had learned about the manufacture of glass and porcelain in the New World. It's been a year and more already, and I've scarcely learned anything."

"My dear Jedidiah," said Mr. Jonas, as they went in at the cottage gate and climbed the steps, "if he knew what we have discovered, your Mr. Owlfeather must agree that what you do here to assist me is so highly instrumental to the Guild—and therefore, indirectly, to Mr. Owlfeather—that it far outweighs anything he asked you to do before you left Thornburg."

"Aye, maybe," said Jed, standing in the moonlight before the door, shifting uncomfortably from one foot to the other. He wanted desperately to stay and see the whole thing out, to satisfy the lively curiosity aroused by the map and the secret writing. For a long minute, that intense desire to remain warred with a miserably guilty sense that he ought to move on.

"I believe you are right, sir," he said at last. "If the need should arise, we can always send Elsie and Sera on ahead. But my place, at least for now, must be with you."

At Mothgreen Hall Sera prepared for bed, in a highly unsettled state of mind. Efforts by the ghostly Izrael Barebones— or *someone*—to establish some form of contact had begun to amount to virtual persecution.

She covered her looking glass with a scrap of cloth, lest any more mysterious handwriting appear; she dusted the latest sprinkling of garden soil (or grave dust, as Miss Barebones continued to call it) off of her quilt; and looked under her pillow to see what offering Uncle Izrael had been pleased to bestow on her tonight. With a grimace, she removed a handful of damp tea leaves and tossed them out the window.

If ever I discover which of the children is responsible for all this . . . ! Privately, Sera suspected the energetic Luella Battersby and her mischievous friend Patience Armitage, but she had a strong sense of justice and was therefore reluctant to accuse either girl without any proof.

Someone tapped softly, the door opened, and Elsie tiptoed

into the room in her white flannel nightgown. Then she stopped and gazed down at the floor when her bare feet touched the grit on the boards.

"Oh, my poor Sera . . . not more *dirt*?" she exclaimed— softly, so as not to disturb the children sleeping just down the hall. "I do wish that Uncle Izrael were more tidy in his habits!"

Sera eyed her warily. "I suppose you find this vastly amusing. Perhaps if we changed rooms for the night and you were the one to wake up in the morning with dust and gravel in your bed . . . or else snuff scattered between your sheets . . . !"

"Well, we can try that, if you like, but I doubt it would do any good," said Elsie, sitting down on the foot of the bed. "And really, you know, it is to some extent your own fault. Uncle Izrael was content to ply you with old books and gloves and other agreeable items, until you took to *burning* all of his offerings.

"Now what is this?" she innocently asked, bending down and scooping something up off the floor.

It was an ancient pocket watch with a gold ormolu cover. Elsie turned the watch over and read aloud the name inscribed on the case. "*Izrael Falconer Barebones*. In your place, I would not have it melted down," she said, with dancing eyes. "For undoubtedly it is a valuable family heirloom, and Miss Barebones would be mortally offended."

Sera deposited herself on the bed beside Elsie, flouncing a little to spread out her petticoats. "Did you come in here merely to gloat over my misfortunes?"

Elsie laughed merrily. "You are a little melodramatic, are you not? I'm sure that if you had any genuine misfortunes, I should be the last to gloat. No," she said, growing suddenly sober. "I have come for another reason entirely."

She thought for a moment, and then asked wistfully, "Sera . . . do you think that Jed will *ever* ask me to marry him?"

"No," Sera replied bluntly. "I don't believe that he ever will. Not . . ." she added hastily, for Elsie was so obviously distressed, " . . . *not* that he doesn't love you nearly to distraction, for I am certain that he does! It is just that Jed is too ridiculously humble and modest to put himself forward." Sera hesitated, knotting her fingers in her lap. "The real question, my dear, is how much *you* love Jed."

Elsie blinked at her indignantly. "Oh, Sera . . . need you *ask*? I always liked Jed better than any of the gentlemen I knew. Because—because all of them were so very affected, and Jed was always so beautifully natural . . . so big, and warm, and kindhearted.

"You remember, Sera, for you despised those men yourself!" said Elsie, warming to her theme. "They cared for nothing but the cut of their coats and the polish on their boots and their frivolous pleasures and—" Elsie stopped, clapped her hand to her mouth. "Dear Sera," she said penitently. "You know I did not mean Lord Skelbrooke. Of course he was always beautifully dressed and such lovely manners . . . but there were so many *other* things that he . . ."

"Yes indeed," said Sera tartly. "Like cozening the Duchess and stealing her parchment, and running from one end of Euterpe to the other on his mysterious errands—which even his friend Mr. Budge could not but deplore—and imposing on people under any variety of false names. Believe me Elsie, Elsie, whatever it was that recommended Lord Skelbrooke to my affections, it was never his virtue!"

"Well then," said Elsie reasonably. "What did recommend him to your affections?"

"I am sure I don't know," said Sera, unfolding her hands and staring down at them. Then she shrugged and gave an irritated little laugh. "Most likely a revolt against Reason, for I cannot think of any other excuse for falling in love with him! But we were speaking of you and Jed. If you *do* love him, you had better tell him so and ask him to marry you. You'll never marry him else!"

"Oh . . ." said Elsie, turning pink at the thought. "I don't think that I could ever do that. That would be so dreadfully forward and immodest on *my* part. I fear that Jed would be very much shocked."

"In all probability he would be," Sera agreed. "For with all his other virtues, he can also be most abominably straight-laced . . . Well, I suppose that he has to be, to make up for his humble upbringing, and the years he spent dragging bodies out of the river and living on grave offerings when he was so very poor. But if he is shocked, he will soon get over it. And he loves you far too well to think ill of you—even for an instant."

She took Elsie by the hand and gave it a comforting squeeze. "I believe, my dear, that you must eventually decide what really matters to you: marrying Jed . . . or preserving your maiden modesty."

17.

Wherein many Curious matters are Brought to Light.

The elaborate device over which Jedidiah and Sammuel Jonas had labored for so many weeks now stood complete: a wonder to those few who had been privileged to view it, a bafflement to all but Jed and the gnome. It was an impressive structure with its bronze mirrors, lead weights, ashwood and blued-steel gears, immense magnets, and shimmering coils of silvered glass. A system of disks made of zinc and silver, sandwiched between layers of felt soaked in brine, created a mysterious electrical charge when connected by a copper wire, and more wires conducted that charge to the mirrors, and from there to the magnets. Hoses made of waxed canvas and a complicated system of brass tubing carried a fluid embryonated sulphur (an "animating principle") to all parts of the machine. But Jed and the gnome had also found the time to add some decorative touches: brass gargoyles on all four corners, great clawed iron feet that also lent the oak framework stability, and at the top, a weathervane in the form of a winged Fate, cast in pewter.

In light of Captain Hornbeam's difficulties getting his ship together and signing up a likely crew, it was not possible to sail, as originally planned, before the next full moon. So Jed and Mr. Jonas, at distinctly loose ends, looked around them for some other means to productively pass their time.

"We might try to search out Mr. Izrael Barebones's Panterran ruins," Jed suggested one day. "He described them in such detail, I cannot believe it was all a romance! No use asking Mr. Herring or any of the other Glassmakers, for we've questioned them again and again. But *somebody*, somewhere in the town, ought to recognize the spot."

Accordingly, they armed themselves with some sketches and diagrams they had made from Mr. Barebones's careful descrip-

123

tions, and went about the town, displaying the sketches and asking questions, making a particular effort to seek out all the oldest citizens. Visits to half a dozen elderly ladies on the first day yielded only the most discouraging results. Jed and the gnome fairly sloshed with all of the tea they had been obliged to consume, but the ladies knew nothing at all about Panterran ruins or artifacts. But on the second day they stopped to talk with an ancient farrier, who sat out on a bench in front of his grandson's forge, where he could enjoy the afternoon sunshine and also a keep a sharp eye on the activities of all his neighbors.

He listened as Jed read from the Barebones papers, allowed Mr. Jonas to show him the sketches, then scratched his head and declared: "Sounds to me as though you're talking about them fancy floors in the old chapel on the hill."

"The old chapel? I was not aware . . . ?" said Mr. Jonas.

"The chapel up to the sailor's cemetery on Spyglass Hill," said the farrier. "The roof fell in during the great quake—when was that?—it must a been sixty years ago, and the sea come up over the wall 'til we thought the whole blamed town would drownt. I don't reckon there's many alive now, excepting some of them dwarfs the other side of town, as was alive *then* . . . and what business has dwarves with ships and seafaring men?"

Jed and the gnome exchanged an eager glance, but Mr. Jonas only replied, calmly and politely, that he wondered as much himself. But to return to the chapel . . . ?

The farrier took a long-stemmed clay pipe out of his coat pocket and stuck it between his teeth. "I was up to the chapel when I was just a lad . . . ten, twelve years old . . . when a sailor uncle of mine died and was buried on the hill. A mighty fine service it was, too, and I remember how I admired them pictures on the floor. Oh yes, they was lovely. I asked my granddad how it was they could afford them pretty tile floors— what do you call 'em? . . . mosaics, yes, I believe I heard that word afore—I asked how they could afford them pretty *mosaic* floors, a little church like that, and the congregation just simple folks."

"And how did your grandfather reply?" Mr. Jonas prompted him, with just the barest tinge of impatience, when he showed no signs of continuing.

The farrier shifted about on his bench. "Granddad said them

floors was a pagan relic . . . up and left there by them heathen savages as used to live here. And sailors being more than half heathen (as the saying goes)—them and their superstitions—he reckoned they didn't see no harm making use of them elegant floors when they built their chapel."

He smoked for a while, with a meditative look on his weathered face. "I don't know about them other things you asked about, though . . . just them pretty floors up on the hill," he said at last.

But he had said quite enough to fire Jed and Mr. Jonas with a strong desire to see the amazing floors for themselves. "They may be buried deep, under all that rubble at the top of the hill, and we may have to do as much lifting as digging," said Mr. Jonas. "Perhaps we ought to hire some laborers to assist us."

The very next morning they climbed up the hill to the old graveyard, accompanied by two able-bodied workmen carrying picks and shovels. Jed had dressed for the occasion in dark breeches, a pair of high boots, and a worn blue coat, which, along with his customary brown pigtail, gave him a distinctly nautical air. Altogether he looked a sprucer version of the old Jedidiah, who used to work on the river Lunn with his Uncle Caleb, before the dwarves took him up and made him into a gentleman. Over one shoulder he carried a spade.

Mr. Jonas, too, had donned an old suit of clothes, but he walked barefoot and carried a picnic basket instead of a spade. His broad feet with their formidable talons were beautifully designed for digging.

They had no difficulty locating the ruins of the chapel and set straight to work excavating. It was a hard, dirty, backbreaking labor, and it lasted for several days before they were able to uncover even a very small corner of mosaic floor.

The workmen stepped back while Mr. Jonas stooped down and brushed off the last of the loose dirt, and then washed off the tiles with a scrub brush and some soapy water. It was only a bit of border, a design of gold stars and fiery-headed silver comets on a rich blue background, but Jed was fairly flabbergasted by the astonishing brilliant colors.

"Indeed," said the imperturbable Mr. Jonas. "Remarkably well preserved, considering these tiles may be as much as three thousand years old. But really, the Panterrans and the Evanthians were capable of the most amazing things. We

know they were a race of great magicians and philosophers—
the Panterrans tending more toward Chemeia and natural philosophy, as the Evanthians devoted themselves principally
to vile sorceries. Our own Glassmakers and Spagyric alche-
mists have built their entire traditions on the merest scraps
and gleanings from the ancient Panterran mysteries—while
the Scolectics and the Mezztopholeean brotherhoods claim to
model their degraded rituals after the demonic rites of dark
Evanthum."

Highly elated by this discovery, they continued digging. In
the meantime, their activities caused a flurry of comment down
in the town. And when word reached Mothgreen Academy,
Miss Jamaica Barebones was most particularly intrigued, for
that lady could always be counted upon to take a lively interest in anything even remotely connected with her late Uncle
Izrael.

Now it happened that Tuesdays at the Academy were usually devoted to religious instruction (Sera and Miss Eglantine,
acting in concert), tatting and knitted lace (Elsie and the headmistress), and foreign languages (Miss Fitch), but on the Monday night, Miss Barebones declared that this Tuesday would be
a holiday of sorts.

"We shall take a picnic lunch up to the graveyard—it should
prove educational viewing the ruins, and I daresay that the girls
will benefit quite as much as we will. And then we shall spend
the afternoon walking on the beach, collecting seashells and
starfish . . . we have been rather neglecting our natural philosophy, I am afraid."

So they packed up the necessary supplies in a goat cart and
set out on foot for Spyglass Hill at eleven o'clock in the morning. By the time they all arrived at the foot of the hill the girls
wanted their luncheon. So they sat down then and there and
ate their picnic in the grass. Then they trudged up the slope
for a look at the excavation.

When Miss Barebones caught sight of the border of stars
and comets, she was virtually overcome. "Yes, yes, I remember that Uncle Izrael once described to me something of the
sort," she said, sitting down on a pile of old stones and timbers,
uncorking her salts, and taking a reviving whiff of *sal volatile*.
She was no longer young, and though the walk into town was
tolerable, her climb up the hill had been rather debilitating.

"At the time, of course," she went on, "I did not perfectly understand *what* he was talking about, for I am afraid that poor dear Uncle Izrael inclined to become somewhat obscure, not to say incoherent, about any subject that *truly* interested him. That was one reason why people neglected to take him seriously."

Jed did the honors, explaining that the picture they had so far uncovered appeared to be a map of the heavens. "But what is this?" asked Sera, pointing to a fanciful figure which seemed to be some kind of gondola fitted up with an enormous pair of feathered wings, sailing along among the planets and the clouds.

"A Panterran sky-ship," said Jed very importantly. "Or so we believe. And see this over here . . . ?" He indicated another picture, this one of a great moon-colored globe, caught in a net and attached to a basket which *appeared* to be some sort of conveyance filled with gleeful Panterran pleasure-seekers, heading for the outer planets. "A hot-air balloon!"

Sera and Elsie exchanged a glance of pure astonishment. "But could they really ascend to such rarefied heights?" asked Sera.

"So it would appear," said Mr. Jonas, with a twinkle. "Though perhaps we should make allowances for a certain amount of artistic exaggeration."

But as might be expected, a section of tile floor about two yards square could not hold the attention of the young girls for long. They soon grew impatient to go down to the beach, which was now exposed by a low tide. Miss Eglantine and Miss Fitch offered to shepherd the girls down to the shore, so that Sera, Elsie, and Miss Barebones could observe the continued excavation.

"But you must not allow any of them to go into the Deeping Caves, you know," Miss Barebones cautioned the two elderly schoolmistresses. "It is very easy to get lost down there, and the caverns become fearfully dangerous after the tide comes in. A number of people have drowned there. And do, *do* keep an especially close eye on Luella and Patience," she added.

"Trust me for that," said Miss Eglantine grimly, and Luella and Patience tried to look suitably demure. So the matter was arranged to everyone's satisfaction, and Miss Eglantine, Miss Fitch, and the girls departed.

The men continued on for another hour, digging, moving

stones and bricks and timbers, and scraping away the dirt. Then the workers decided to take a breather.

"If you like," said Jed to Elsie, as he wiped his hands clean on a scrap of old cloth and slipped into his coat, "we could go for a little stroll through the graveyard. There are a number of curious old headstones, and you might find some of the inscriptions amusing."

"I should like that very much," said Elsie, with a quickening pulse, for it was not often, anymore, that she and Jed went walking together.

They started off through the graveyard, with Elsie's arm tucked into Jed's. Sera and Miss Barebones were also interested in reading the inscriptions, but they wandered off in the direction of the sea, their skirts and their ribbons fluttering in the breeze off the water, discreetly allowing the young couple a few private moments.

Though still early in the year, the grass already grew long and green among the gravestones, and wild flowers were just beginning to appear: daisies and dandelions, clover and trumpet vine. The graveyard, decided Elsie, provided as pretty a spot for a proposal of marriage as any that she could imagine. She was conscious, too, that she appeared to advantage, in a gown of pale Yndian cotton tucked up behind to display a flowered petticoat, and a particularly fetching bonnet trimmed with pink silk roses—and though she was not a vain girl, it did rather serve to boost her confidence, this knowledge that she was looking her best.

"Jedidiah," she said, summoning up her courage to make a declaration. "Jed . . . we have been acquainted any time these seven years. For which reason, I feel certain you will forgive the familiarity, considering what old friends we are . . ." She stopped, suddenly out of breath, and had to compose herself before she could go on. She did not find it easy, because Jed was looking down at her with a look of painful inquiry that disconcerted her very much. "What I meant to say . . . Jed . . . is that I hope you will not be shocked if—if I speak quite frankly—

"—oh dear heavens!" she interrupted herself. "What is that lying over there beside the gravestone?"

Jed dropped Elsie's arm, followed her pointing finger. He took a step nearer, and went down on one knee to more closely examine a tiny figure, thin-limbed and naked, that lay huddled up against a marble slab. It appeared to be a young hobgoblin, and it was fast asleep.

Jed stood up again and spoke in Elsie's ear, so as not to awaken the hob: "Do you want me to go back and bring a shovel to kill it?"

"Oh no, I beg you will do nothing of the sort," said Elsie, clutching at his arm, as if to prevent him. "Do you not see the tiny claws on its feet and the cunning little horns . . . except for the scales, it looks very much like a baby gnome. I could not *bear* to have you kill it."

The hobgoblin, perhaps aroused by her voice, started to make feeble movements. It made a futile attempt to raise its head, crept a few feet, and then collapsed again in a pitiful heap of misshapen limbs. "Someone has injured the poor little thing! Sera . . . Miss Barebones . . . do come and see what we have found," Elsie called softly.

The two ladies hurried through the tall grass. "May the Powers preserve us!" said Miss Barebones, taking a step backward at the sight of the hob.

But Sera sat right down in the grass beside the tiny huddled creature. "We mustn't let the workmen see, or one of them may try to kill it. I've never seen a *live* hobgoblin before, but I am sure that this one ought not to look so *very* green. See how it trembles and moans. It must be ill or injured."

"If we just walk on and leave it here, it will die anyway," said Jed. "Slower and more cruel than a blow to the head with a shovel. And don't, I beg of you, get any wild ideas about taking it home and nursing it back to health," he added sternly. "You wouldn't know how to go about it, for one thing. And if word spread—as it certainly would—that you were harboring the creature, half the town would be outraged!"

Sera's eyes kindled and her bosom heaved. "I am sure we ought not to allow the opinion of 'half the town' (and not the best people either) to prevent us from doing what we know to be right," she said scornfully. "It would be most horrid cruel to abandon the poor thing . . . and as for killing it!"

Yet she had to admit that healing the hobgoblin was quite beyond her powers. "After all, one knows so little about them. Why, if we tried to feed it, or give it any medicine, we would poison the poor creature, as likely as not."

Instinctively, she put a hand on the necklace at her throat, suddenly wishing for Francis Skelbrooke, *wanting* him there beside her as she had not allowed herself to want him all the long, slow seasons since their last meeting. He might not know how to feed the hobgoblin, either, but at least he knew something of wounds and sicknesses, and despite what she had told Elsie, he did possess one saving virtue: his compassion for the young, the pitiful, and the helpless, which was apparently boundless.

"We must do something," said Elsie, wringing her hands.

"Certainly, we must," agreed Miss Barebones, wringing her own. Everyone, even Jed, looked to Sera for a solution.

Sera thought hard, cudgeling her brain for the right solution. "Well then . . . there is a hob-hole behind the clocktower— at least, there was one on Sunday, and we must hope that no one has filled it in since. I suppose we could take the creature there, after the workmen go home to supper . . . lower it down in our picnic basket . . . and leave it in the tunnel for its own kind to find. It might have some chance of living, that way. At least . . . if hobgoblins *do* take care of their own."

By this time, Mr. Jonas and the workmen had returned to their labors. Jed should have joined them, but he could not abandon the ladies in the midst of such a thorny dilemma. He took a deep breath, which he released slowly, staring up at the sky.

"If we pick it up and try to move it," he said at last, "it's more than likely to bite."

"No, they do *not* bite," said Miss Barebones decidedly. "That is: I never heard that anyone in Hobb's Church or in Moonstone was ever bitten by a hobgoblin."

"I know of many people, back home in . . . back home where my sister and I were born, who were bitten by hob-goblins," said Jed, with a frown. "These native hobs may be more docile, as you suppose . . . or maybe it's just that no one in this part of the world has ever tried to handle one."

Miss Barebones gave her skirts an impatient twitch. "But yes, I think that I *have* heard of some such thing. Uncle Izrael always took a great interest in the creatures. It was he, you know, who put forth the idea that they are indeed Rational Beings and ought not to be treated as vermin.

"That was a long time before the tunneling became so bad

and people started putting gunpowder and poison down their holes," she added, with a sigh. "The hobs were shy in those days, but not so elusive as they are now, and it was sometimes possible to catch and tame one. Not that anyone else wanted to try . . . but Uncle Izrael, I believe, kept several. He had a theory that hobgoblins had developed a language of their own, and he was attempting to learn that language, just before he died.

"You don't suppose," she added, on a sudden inspiration, "that Uncle Izrael wishes to communicate something he has learned about the nature of hobgoblins?"

Sera, for one, did not think anything of the sort. And she was far more concerned, just at the moment, about the plight of the young creature that lay quivering in the grass beside her. "It does not *look* as if it could do any real damage . . . it is much too weak and ill. And even if it should bite—well, hob bites are only mildly poisonous and we know very well how to treat them: rosewater and oil of clove."

"Aye, easy for you to say—since I'm the one you'll likely expect to pick up the nasty beast and carry it," Jed grumbled, under his breath. Yet he, too, felt a stirring of compassion when he looked down on the wretched little figure.

Eventually, they persuaded him to consent to Sera's plan. By that time, the workmen had picked up their tools and were heading down the hill, and Mr. Jonas went along with them to pay their wages.

Then the little girls came swarming up from the beach, bare-headed and windblown, but looking quite pleased with themselves and the seashells, bits of moss, and brightly colored pebbles they carried in their hats. "I suppose I ought to go home with Rosabelle, Sophia, and the children," said Miss Barebones. "It will seem very odd if I do not, and I feel sure I can trust the rest of you to do what needs to be done."

Jed escorted her down the hill and came back a short while later with the empty picnic basket. The hob had apparently fallen asleep, but it woke when Jed wrapped it up in Sera's shawl and shoved it into the basket. The creature struggled in his grasp and clawed at him with its tiny feet, but made no attempt to bite him.

"Now we must wait a bit; it won't be dark for another hour. We don't want anyone to see what we are about," said Jed, nursing his scratches. "I hope their claws aren't so poisonous as their bite," he added crossly. "Rosewater and oil of clove, you said?"

Sera, shivering a little in the rising wind without her shawl, nodded wearily. "I'll go down and purchase some now, if you like."

At nightfall, they carried the covered basket into town, procured a rope from Mr. Herring's shop (Mr. Jonas, when applied to, had lent them his key), and lowered the basket, hobgoblin and all, down the hole by the clocktower. Then they went off to the Eclipse for a light supper.

When they returned to the spot an hour later and Jed hauled up the basket, he could immediately tell, by the lighter weight, that the baby hob had either succeeded in crawling out or been carried away by other hobgoblins.

"Anyway," said Sera bleakly, as they gazed down the hole, "we did all that we possibly could."

18.

Which discovers Lord Skelbrooke upon the High Seas.

The good ship *Elephant,* two days out of Ilben, plowed through the waves with a strong wind behind her. As the day was fine, most of the passengers were strolling on the deck, taking full advantage of clear weather and the invigorating qualities of salt air.

Among these passengers were that bold beauty Lady Ursula Vizbeck and her callow young husband. The lady wore a picture hat and carried a parasol; her lord affected a scarlet coat trimmed with gold braid, and a bicorn hat with a striped cockade, which (or so he fondly imagined) lent him something of the appearance of a visiting admiral. Lady Ursula yawned and glanced around her, with a great affectation of languid boredom . . . until her gaze chanced to rest on a vastly elegant gentleman in mouse-colored velvet, who paced the deck with one arm immobilized in a black silk sling.

"My *dear* Lord Skelbrooke," the lady exclaimed. "We had no idea that we should find *you* on board."

Lord Skelbrooke favored her with a startled, suspicious glance. But he quickly recovered, smiled urbanely, and made a very pretty bow—for a man with one arm confined. "There is no way that you could have known. My departure from Marstadtt was, of necessity, attended by a certain degree of secrecy. I am convinced that I need not tell *you,* Lady Ursula, to what lengths one must go in order to escape the importunities of indignant tradesmen." He bowed again. "I beg you will aid me in this innocent deception, by addressing me hereafter as Mr. Hawkins."

"But of course," said the lady, fluttering her dark lashes in a fascinating way that she had. "It is shocking, is it not, how

dreadfully *forward* these tradesmen have become? We, our-
selves, are not precisely in *embarrassed* circumstances (though
I know too well the humiliations that attend on poverty). But
it *has* become advisable, just recently, for Lord Vizbeck and
I to leave the Continent and travel to the New World, where,
I am told, one may live quite *cheaply*."

"Indeed, we have been contemplating that action for some
time," added Lord Vizbeck. "But Lady Ursula could not make
up her mind to do it. Every time that I broached the subject,
she found some reason to delay our departure. And then, quite
suddenly, she one day announced that she had already booked
our passage."

The lady smiled coyly, slipped her hand through the crook
of Lord Skelbrooke's good arm, and fell into step beside him.
"Ah well . . . I am, after all, the most *capricious* creature on
the face of the earth."

Skelbrooke tactfully refrained from any remark. He knew
Lady Ursula to be vain, selfish, and governed by her passions,
but capricious—never! Past experience had taught him that the
lady always knew exactly what she wanted, and went about
getting it in the most expeditious, not to say ruthless, manner
possible.

But there was a great deal more along the same lines: the
lady endowing herself with any number of pretty, foolish
faults which she did not, in fact, possess; all the while casting
languishing glances upon the unresponsive Skelbrooke. My
lord began to suspect that Lady Ursula assumed the butterfly
pose for his benefit, under the erroneous assumption that he
would find it attractive.

It was the prelude, no doubt, to a light flirtation or even to an
affair, most likely with an eye to making her husband jealous.
That it could mean anything other than that never occurred to
him—such things were common enough in the Social Circles
they both inhabited.

The next days were trying ones, as Lady Ursula continued
to endeavor to beguile her journey with an agreeable flirtation, and Lord Skelbrooke endeavored, just as earnestly, to
avoid anything of the kind. He did not admire the lady, was
on his way (he hoped) to a meeting with the one woman who
did excite his love and admiration, and he had no desire to

inflict the pleasant, if somewhat gullible, Lord Vizbeck with the agonizing pangs of jealousy which Lady Ursula seemed so eager to induce.

Accordingly, he spent as much of the next week and a half as he possibly could bear confined to his cabin, going up on deck generally in the early morning, before Lady Ursula abandoned her bed, and sometimes late at night.

But when word reached him one afternoon that a herd of whales had been spotted in the distance, he threw caution to the winds and hastened above to try and get a glimpse of these seagoing behemoths.

Less than a glimpse, only a sort of haze of darker blue upon the horizon, was all that he could see from the rail. "Here, sir, you'll see better with this," said the boatswain, handing him a spyglass. "They'll never come too close, not they! They're wary of whalers, you see, and wonderful intelligent."

"I thank you," said Skelbrooke, flashing a smile as he accepted the telescope. "Yes, I know something of their habits and their migrations, but to actually see them . . . that I account a rare privilege!"

By leveling the spyglass on the horizon and adjusting the lenses (he had lately abandoned his sling), he brought one of the migrating monsters into sharp focus. He drew in a deep breath. Though he had seen pictures—woodcuts and tinted prints—nothing had prepared him for the magnificent reality: the shining metallic plates and jewel-like eye; the ornate, rather heraldic, fins and tail; and the water sprouting and steaming like a fountain from the blowhole—it must have been fifteen feet high!

"Truly a marvel," said his lordship, passing back the spyglass once he had looked his fill. He stayed a while longer to exchange seastories with the boatswain, and then started back toward his cabin before Lady Ursula should catch wind of him.

But as he approached the hatch, one of the sailors staggered past, stumbled, and fell in an awkward heap at Skelbrooke's feet.

"Drunk, I shouldn't wonder," sniffed one of the other passengers, who chanced to be sauntering by.

Skelbrooke knelt down to feel the unconscious sailor's pulse, to put a hand on his brow. "Not drunk but dangerously ill, I think. This man has a raging fever. Someone should summon the doctor."

The ship's physician arrived a few minutes later, examined the sailor more carefully, and made a grim diagnosis. "The Yellow Pox . . . there can be little doubt of it. As you can see, the pustules already begin to appear." He turned to his lordship, with an anxious frown. "As you have already placed yourself at some risk, sir, perhaps you will assist me in carrying this man to a private cabin? The disease is highly contagious and, I regret to say, too often fatal."

"I know something of the disease," said Skelbrooke. With the assistance of two of the stricken sailor's cabin mates, they carried the fellow down below and made him as comfortable as possible in a cabin adjoining the doctor's quarters.

The next days were tense ones for all on board. One after another, the closest associates of the first sailor came down with the Yellow Pox; then two passengers contracted the disease. A panic swept through the vessel. The other passengers, with few exceptions, demanded a share of supplies and holed up in their cabins to avoid exposure; the Captain and what remained of his crew (reeking of camphor, which was said to fight contagion) carried on the best that they could; and the doctor and Francis Skelbrooke exhausted themselves tending to those already stricken.

The doctor, as Skelbrooke soon learned, was an old school physician, firmly convinced of the sovereign virtues of bloodletting and purging, no matter what the disease, and he treated his patients with frogs' spawn and toads' tongues ("most efficacious against a spotted fever") so long as his supply lasted.

"If I might claim a moment of your time," said his lordship, with a troubled look, one day as he watched the physician open a vein. "I believe I told you that I studied at the Hospital of the Holy Powers in Lundy . . . Mr. Hay was one of my professors. He always contended that, while cupping is certainly effective in ridding the body of poisonous vapors, it is *not* indicated when the patient has already entered a moribund condition. Moreover, the use of purges in the presence of dehydration brought on by a high fever . . ."

But the doctor, scorning these revolutionary theories, preferred to stick with the tried and true. He continued on with his lancets, his cups, and his leeches; continued to force loathsome potions down the throats of his patients. Skelbrooke, though he wished to help, could not lend himself to either practice, not in good conscience. But barley water, that most ancient of simples, which the doctor had the cook make up in quantity, was soothing, relieved the raging thirst of those stricken, and perhaps provided a modicum of nourishment.

So Skelbrooke carried on, administering barley water and dispensing pinches of his own Sleep Dust to those in a delirium, cleaning the blood and the vomit and the feces from the beds and garments of those patients whom the doctor had purged, and rubbing on an ointment which the cook had boiled up for him in a large pot, out of ingredients present in the galley.

"If you mean to prevent this woman from scarring," said the doctor scornfully, standing blood-stained and weary in a doorway to watch him, "you would have to wrap her in yellow flannel and allow her to sweat the disease out through the pores of her skin. But we haven't the flannel . . . at least, not in the necessary quantity . . . and you would do much better to assist me in saving her life, rather than minister to her vanity."

"I beg your pardon," Skelbrooke replied with the greatest civility—unshaven, unwashed, and stinking as he was. "I mean only to spare her the terrible itching, and by relieving that hideous discomfort, perhaps allow her a little more rest. Even you must agree that sleep is Nature's best medicine."

The next day, the doctor collapsed in the passageway below the hatch. The Captain summoned Skelbrooke to attend him.

"The Yellow Pox . . . it's taken him, too," announced the Captain, not waiting for his lordship's diagnosis. "There's two men died, and two men and a lady near it, and the others likely doomed." He ordered a strict quarantine, which was to say: all those who had contracted the disease were herded or carried down to the hold, and left there, with scant food and provisions, to die.

"There is nothing more that can be done for them," said the Captain, and gave instructions to seal the hold.

"With your permission," said his lordship, watching these procedures with hollow eyes. "I would like to attend them down in the hold. I may be able to preserve *some* of them . . . and if anyone still standing is likely to carry the disease, it is certainly I."

But the Captain refused. He was not a hard man, not without compassion, but he was exhausted after many sleepless nights, terrified of the disease, and he knew nothing better to do. "You go down there, you're as good as dead, Mr. Hawkins. Take to your cabin, like them others . . . that way, you come down with the disease, there'll be no harm to the rest of us. You done your best, all this time—though it was no task for a gentleman like you—and we're mighty grateful. We'll see that you're well provisioned."

Skelbrooke wiped his forehead with the sleeve of his filthy and sweat-stained shirt. He had once been forcibly confined, injured and ill, in the hold of a ship, an experience he was not eager to repeat. "Nevertheless, I would prefer to take my chances down in the hold, where I might actually do some good," he insisted.

"I do not wish to speak ill of the doctor," he added, with a tightening around the mouth. "But . . . he was somewhat conservative in his methods. I may, just possibly, be able to help where he could not. But if I should fail . . . at least there will be someone on hand to ease the final agonies of the dying."

Though highly disposed to argue the point, the Captain finally allowed Skelbrooke his way, even providing more food and water, more blankets and mattresses, than he had first intended. While these were lowered into the hold, his lordship returned to his cabin and brought out a small chest containing several vials of the Sleep Dust.

Then he went down into the dark hold with his patients and ministered to them as best he knew how, while two of the sailors nailed the grating shut, sealing him in.

19.

In which Things continue to go Ill in Hobb's Church.

The little town was in an uproar. Buildings continued to creak and settle as the earth beneath them shifted, to the great dismay and discomfort of the inhabitants. Glassware and porcelain, falling from shelves, shattered on the floor; mirrors and picture frames, descending precipitously, cracked beyond repair; doors and window sashes jammed shut; in one house, burning oil splashed out of a lamp which had been carelessly filled, and started a small fire; and in another house, a similar disaster was but narrowly averted when a flaming log rolled out of a grate only to be stopped with a pair of tongs and cast back into the fireplace. It was like living in a state of perpetual earthquake.

Then one terrible night, the bells in the clocktower rang out for the first time in years, as the entire structure shuddered, swayed, and collapsed, burying two men under an avalanche of falling bricks.

Shocked by these sudden deaths, a committee of angry citizens organized the next day, vowing to destroy the tunneling hobgoblins once and for all. Many schemes were contemplated, but none that could be immediately put into effect. Meanwhile, other citizens, acting in the general hysteria, started digging tunnels of their own, in an effort to get at the hobs, or shooting pistols down existing hob-holes. Someone even organized a bucket brigade from the town pump to the hole by the clocktower, hoping to drown the creatures out . . . an utterly futile effort, for the hole led to tunnels so deep and extensive it was doubtful that a single hobgoblin so much as got his feet wet.

None of this commotion reached Mothgreen Hall, and only vague rumors of the measures taken. The ladies did not learn any more until the Sunday, when they herded their little flock down the road and into the town for the morning service.

Very sweet and demure the girls looked, too, walking into town in two long lines, all dressed alike in their white muslin gowns, with pastel sashes and wide chip-straw bonnets over lacy caps, with twenty pairs of yellow-gloved hands clasped properly over their prayerbooks. As soon as Miss Barebones caught sight of the restless and agitated crowd gathered in the streets, she turned the girls right around again, and she, Miss Eglantine, and Miss Fitch marched the girls back to the Academy.

But Sera and Elsie remained in town, joining a large crowd outside the Church of Seven Fates, and listening to Moses Tynsdale hold forth with another of his open-air sermons. Strangely enough, the wild-eyed clergyman expounded the view that it was not the *hobgoblins* who were responsible for the present calamitous state of affairs.

"No, by the Nine Powers, no!" he ranted, as Sera and Elsie drew nearer, the better to hear him. "It is the wickedness of the people which brings down the wrath of the Father Creator! And if you continue in your evil ways, he will continue to send his Divine Messengers to chastise you!"

Many people hung their heads and shuffled their feet, suddenly conscious of their secret sins. And Tynsdale continued to rail at them. They were vain (said the preacher), they were corrupt. The citizens of Hobb's Church were wallowing—yes! wallowing—in their own greed and luxury, and they made a mockery of everything sacred.

"Well, really, I cannot agree with any of that," Elsie said in Sera's ear. "The people who live here in Hobb's Church are hardly what *I* should call wicked. If Mr. Tynsdale wishes to see vanity, corruption, greed, and luxury, he has only to visit any large city or town across the sea and observe the manners of Fashionable Society. The people *here* are godly enough."

"Yes," said Jed, coming up behind her. "But according to men like Preacher Tynsdale, it's the good folk He always comes down on the hardest. He just leaves the wicked to dig their own graves."

Elsie rewarded him with the faintest of smiles. Her face had lost all of its pretty natural color, and her eyes were dull and heavy. Jed shot Sera an inquiring glance, but Sera responded with a curt shake of her head. For the last ten days Elsie had been unable to sleep at night, only dropping off for a restless hour or two in the early morning, or for a brief nap in the afternoon. And she had conceived a sudden, inexplicable fear of the dark. Sera, who had devoted the better part of her youth to nursing Elsie, in the bad old days when her cousin was nearly always ill, felt considerably more frightened than she liked to admit.

As Elsie seemed absorbed in the sermon, Sera took the opportunity to draw Jedidiah aside. "She has been so well and strong for nearly two years now," Sera whispered urgently. "I cannot think what has caused this apparent relapse."

"Maybe it's the ghost," Jedidiah suggested, also very low. "Perhaps Uncle Izrael has left off plaguing you and started tormenting poor Elsie instead."

"Uncle Izrael is just as particular in his attentions as he ever was, thank you very much," hissed Sera. "He spends so much time following me about, I am persuaded he has no time for Elsie! Besides, she isn't a bit afraid of Uncle Izrael— or who-ever is really behind all of that nonsense—she always finds his activities vastly diverting. Or at least . . . she used to laugh at them before she became so ill and nervous."

Elsie, catching the sound of her own name, glanced briefly their way. Jed motioned Sera away from the church, and they both moved out toward the statue at the center of the green.

"It's a funny thing, but we seem to have acquired our own ghost, over at Mr. Herring's," said Jed. "He's not given to rapping and moaning like your Uncle Izrael, but he does move things about . . . and not the sort of things that hob-goblins like, either. So far, only some books up in my room, but—"

"Books?" said Sera, with a twinge of apprehension. "What books?"

Jedidiah spoke even lower. "The books we brought with us from Thornburg: the books from the coffin."

Sera took him by the arm and pulled him farther from the crowd, so that they could speak more freely. "Jed, there are too many queer things happening here. I fear that Mr. Tynsdale is in some sense right. There is some—some unwholesome influence at work in Hobb's Church. And it really is time that we moved on.

"Oh, we can't go immediately, of course," she added, in response to Jedidiah's dark look. "For Elsie and I to leave the Academy without finishing the term would be utterly wicked, after all of Miss Barebones's kindness. But when the term ends . . ."

"After that, you and Elsie must certainly go," Jed agreed, with a troubled frown. "I am certain we can find friends of the Guild to take you in . . . somewhere. But as for me: Sera, my place is here with Mr. Jonas. The map . . . the island . . . You must see that I am obliged to stay on. It's not as though your Duchess is likely to come looking for me . . . why, I'd wager you any amount she doesn't even know that I exist."

Sera gaped at him, utterly aghast. "And so we are to go off, Elsie and I, to some unknown destination, all by ourselves? Well . . . you know that I was against bringing you along in the first place, uprooting you in such a dreadful fashion, when you were doing so well back in Thornburg. But once that was settled, once we all found ourselves in a foreign land, we agreed—indeed we *vowed*—to stay together, for mutual comfort and protection, until we could all go home again.

"I don't know why I need remind you of this," she continued huffily. "For I am sure that you remember it as well as I do. And here is poor Elsie on the verge of a decline. Jedidiah! You don't mean to throw poor Elsie over, all for the sake of your wretched map and your imaginary island?"

Jedidiah hung his head. "It ain't . . . it isn't a matter of—of throwing her over. Sera, I know I've done wrong allowing Elsie to learn to care for me, when there's no way on earth . . ." His big hands knotted into fists. "I think it might be better if Elsie and I were apart for a time, if we neither spoke nor wrote. Otherwise, we might be tempted to do something . . . rash."

"Well," said Sera, with an indignant sniff. "If by 'something rash' you mean getting married, I see no reason why you should not—except, perhaps, for a deal of false pride, and . . . yes, the fact that you and Elsie are still very young. But are you really concerned to do the right and honorable thing by Elsie— or just looking for an excuse to stay in Cordelia? I wish you would look me straight in the eye, Jedidiah, and not hang your head, as though—as though you had something to hide."

Jed, obligingly, met her gaze straight on. And it was then, for the first time in many weeks, that she really looked at him, studied his face as she had not done before. What she saw there disturbed her profoundly.

Because Jed had changed. The brown eyes were just as candid as ever, but they burned a little brighter, and the rest of his face . . . that was different, too, though Sera could not say precisely how. Perhaps it was only a matter of expression, a sort of restless eagerness which had never been there before.

"Jed . . ." said Sera, with a sudden horrible premonition. "Jed . . . what is it, really, that you hope to find on that island?"

"Not the thing that you are thinking," said Jedidiah. "I've no wish to follow in your grandfather's footsteps . . . nor yet my Uncle Caleb's! I've not fallen prey to a lust for the stone Seramarias—or any other alchemical folly. That I can promise you!"

"Perhaps not," said Sera, with a hard little smile. "But perhaps you have fallen prey to an obsession every bit as dangerous, conceived a desire every bit as impossible, as our wretched family curse!

"You have the very same look that my grandfather had, there at the end," she added bitterly, "when he and your Uncle Caleb were conducting their dreadful experiments with dead bodies and things, behind the bookshop. And I wish you would stop and think what you are doing, Jed . . . before you allow your obsession to destroy you, too!"

20.

In which the Reader is encouraged to Contemplate matters of Medicine, Reformation, and Justice.

Francis Skelbrooke left the dark and stinking hold, more than a fortnight after he entered it, blinking a little in the brilliant sunlight, pale and unsteady from care and exhaustion, but in tolerably good spirits. Nearly half of his patients had survived, including the doctor; he had suffered only a mild attack of the disease himself; and it was apparent that the Yellow Pox had finally run its course.

He could not, of course, be certain that he had personally saved a one of them. There had been so little that he could do for any of his patients, and those who had not already died by the time that he took charge were likely to be those with the stronger constitutions. Yet perhaps he *had* saved some of them, just by being there to pour water down their throats and keep them alive while Nature did the rest.

After seeing all of his convalescents comfortably disposed in upper cabins he went on deck, still dirty and disheveled as he was, and listened and watched solemnly while the Captain read a brief service for the dead, and one makeshift wooden coffin after another was consigned to the deep. Tired as he was, it seemed that he ought to be there.

But then he felt free to go down to his own cabin, where he inhaled a larger dose of the Sleep Dust than he had allowed himself in weeks, threw himself down on his bunk, and slept for a day and a half.

He awoke, considerably refreshed, stuck his head out into the passageway, and demanded hot water from a passing sailor. A big basin of hot water arrived soon after, carried in by Lord Vizbeck's valet, who also came armed with scented soap, a sharp razor, and a message from Lord Vizbeck. Lady Ursula had begged her lord to send Mr. Hawkins her compliments.

She did not think she would meet him again before they landed. Her constitution was not a strong one, and she feared some lingering contagion. Lord Vizbeck, however, would be pleased to receive Mr. Hawkins in his cabin, that very evening, for a celebratory glass of wine.

Bathed, shaved, barbered, and clad in clean linen, his lordship felt more himself. He put on a suit of lilac taffeta, a plumed tricorn, black stockings, and a pair of shoes with rhinestone buckles, and went up on deck for his first untroubled breath of air in three weeks.

He had entered the hold resigned to die—it had not been possible to do the deed without first accepting the virtual inevitability of his own death—and had emerged into the light and the air in some sense reborn. Standing by the rail, gazing out across the dancing blue water, it seemed an appropriate occasion for examining his past life.

Not all of his adventures were pleasant to recall. Many, in retrospect, struck him as shameful—for in order to bring down dangerous men, he had been forced to adopt some of their methods: lying and cheating his way into their confidence; deceiving the innocent, as well the guilty; yes . . . he had even stooped to assassination—nor had only the wicked suffered. When . . . he asked himself, with a sudden surge of self-hatred . . . when did the Vigilante, the self-appointed agent of vengeance, cease to be an instrument of Justice, and become just another embodiment of the forces of Evil—become, in effect, the very thing he most loathed and despised? And once a man crossed over that line . . . what chance had he, then, of redemption?

Skelbrooke turned away from the rail, trudged back to his cabin, still turning these dark and troubling questions over in his mind. How clear and how pure, by contrast (he thought), had been his original ambition: to become a physician, to heal the sick and succor the helpless. One memory burned brightly in his mind, a certain conversation he had with Sera Vorder, two years back, during which she had exclaimed, *"But I think you would have made a very good doctor!"*

Not that Society at large would applaud his decision, if he resumed once more that compassionate course—no more than his own family had applauded, all those years past, when he left the family estate and went off to Lundy to study medicine.

A wealthy nobleman in the role of physician . . . that was a shocking anomaly, almost more shocking than his present calling. But as for Sera Vorder . . .

He had a strong presentiment that he stood more chance of winning her heart if he came to her hat in hand as a humble physician than if he swooped down and carried her off in the flamboyant style appropriate to a noble assassin.

Many hundreds of miles distant, at Mothgreen Academy, Sera *was* wishing for a reputable physician, though not with any intention of marrying him. Elsie's health had continued to fail, and Sera thought more and more about engaging the services of some reputable doctor. Yet the wrong sort of doctors had done Elsie so much harm in the past, that Sera hesitated, unwilling to consult with just *any* physician.

"The doctor in Moonstone is highly respected," Miss Barebones offered when Sera asked her. "He is not one of your young men with all sorts of startling new notions, nor yet again an old man whose treatments are hopelessly antiquated. He is just what I would call comfortably middle-aged."

To take Elsie to visit this Dr. Bell now became Sera's ambition. After much coaxing, she finally gained Elsie's consent, wrote for an appointment with the good doctor (at an hour when lessons were over), and convinced Mr. Herring to drive herself and Elsie into Moonstone.

The day was sunny but cool, with a breeze blowing in from the sea. Elsie sat in Mr. Herring's gig, bundled up in innumerable shawls and scarves, which she had donned at Sera's insistence. Though she shivered in the gentle breeze, two spots of hot color burned in her cheeks.

The ride was not a long or arduous one. Elsie had little to say and Sera was much occupied with her own thoughts, but the cabinetmaker endeavored to keep up a cheerful flow of conversation as they bowled along through the green countryside, along the wide loop of road swinging east to avoid the marsh, and finally into the larger town.

On the Moonstone High Street they passed a gloomy coach, a grand but funereal-looking brougham draped with great swathes of heavy black crêpe. As they drove past, Sera thought she saw one of the sable curtains move, as if someone inside were peeking out, though it was impossible to catch a glimpse of either the interior of the brougham or its occupants. "My goodness, who can it be?" asked Sera, with an involuntary shiver. "That coach looks so much like a hearse that as we drove by, I almost believed that I caught a whiff of—of embalming fluid."

"I should suppose it was the widow woman and her brother, who recently let Stillwater Hall, out on the marsh," said Mr. Herring, smiling at what he supposed was a pleasantry. "She rarely comes into town, they say, and always most lugubriously veiled. No one has seen anything of her brother, though she has mentioned him more than once."

As Mr. Herring pulled up before the doctor's big house, Sera put the coach and its mysterious owner out of her mind. Mr. Herring helped Elsie down from the carriage, and Sera ushered her into the surgery.

Dr. Bell exactly matched Miss Barebones's description: stout, fatherly, and comfortably middle-aged, with a gently solicitous manner that Sera found soothing. He examined Elsie carefully and asked a great many questions. Then, deeming Sera the elder and the more responsible, he took her aside for a few private words.

"I find nothing specifically wrong with your friend, yet she is certainly very ill. It would appear to be a nervous condition . . . perhaps a touch of brain fever. Despite what we like to pretend," said Dr. Bell, "we really know so very little about the causes of human suffering. We can mend broken bodies, but as for the diseases which afflict them . . ."

Though Sera was naturally charmed to meet with an honest physician, after all of the dreadful quacks who had attended Elsie in the past, this was scarcely reassuring.

"I shall prescribe her a tonic of catmint, meadowsweet, and marigold, to strengthen her blood, a good plain diet to improve her constitution . . . these will treat the symptoms, though not the disease," said Dr. Bell. "Beyond that: allow her no time to brood on whatever is troubling her. If her daily tasks are not too strenuous, see that she continues them. And I believe you said you were contemplating a journey? That is out of the question. In her present nervous state, she requires the constant reassurance of familiar surroundings."

Perceiving much good sense in this prescription, Sera could not argue with any of it—for all the doctor had put an end to her plans to remove Elsie from Hobb's Church at the first opportunity.

"What did you and the doctor talk of—that I was not permitted to hear?" said Elsie, as they climbed back into the gig.

"We are to stay at Mothgreen Academy for another season at least," said Sera briskly, as she tucked a lap robe around the invalid. There was no use repining over something that could not be helped.

"I am glad," said Elsie, with a weary little sigh. "I am so tired of moving about. It was all very exciting and adventurous when I was well, but now that I feel so tired and nervous . . . Sera, do not think me quite a coward, but—but I wish we could just settle somewhere and stay there for a long time."

They rode out of the town without again encountering the ominous-looking coach, but as they traveled back down the road skirting the fens, Sera suddenly remembered the gloomy brougham.

"It's a crazy old place, Stillwater Hall," said Mr. Herring, in answer to Sera's question. "An unhealthy situation, some might say, and the house, which has stood untenanted these sixteen years, exists in a largely ruinous state . . . falling apart from damp and neglect."

"Then why would anyone wish to live there?" Sera asked indignantly.

"A desire for seclusion, I should imagine. The place is so isolated and the road so difficult, it is enough to discourage unwanted visitors. And the woman is recently widowed, after all. She may find her surroundings congenial."

But to Sera, it all sounded so dank and depressing, she could not repress a shudder.

Even as Sera and Elsie discussed the new owner of Stillwater Hall, they were the subject of discussion between the occupants of the big black broughham. The coach had turned off the main track and was traveling down the difficult road to Stillwater Hall, a road so rutted and muddy that the Duchess and her new accomplice, Thomas Kelly, were jostled and bounced in a disagreeable fashion, highly injurious to their dignity. But a satisfying glimpse which they had both gained of Elsie as she passed by had set off a comfortable train of conversation, which served to beguile the journey.

"The young woman certainly looked ill," said Kelly, with the coldest of smiles.

"Yes indeed," the Duchess agreed cheerfully. A veil and an auburn wig lay on the seat beside her, and her own pale curls hung loose about her shoulders. But she still wore a pair of high wooden pattens which she always slipped on before visiting the town, in order to disguise her tiny stature.

As they had penetrated so far into the marsh that it was unlikely they should be seen or recognized, the Duchess drew back the curtains. "It is the proximity of her double that drains the life from her. And poor Skogsrå is ecstatic: the weaker Elsie grows, the livelier becomes the monster. He is convinced that the grotesque sounds she makes now are actually attempts at speech.

"I do not think," she added, with a thoughtful frown, as she settled back in her seat, "that Skogsrå quite realizes that this pleasant state of affairs cannot long continue. When Elsie Vorder dies, his sweet Cecile must perish along with her."

Kelly made a steeple of his hands and rested his chin on them. "I must confess that *I* do not understand why you have adopted this elaborate scheme of revenge," he said. "You are a woman of means . . . why not hire a man to pose as a high-wayman and shoot both of the young women dead? It would be the surer road to revenge, and I make no doubt that . . . Mr. Hooke, for instance . . . would gladly accept the task, or any similar commission."

The Duchess tilted her chin disdainfully. "Indeed, you do not understand, for you know nothing of the intricacies of fairy justice. A gnome might understand," she added thoughtfully. "But not, I suppose, a creature like you."

The muscles on Kelly's face stiffened into a smile. "You astound me. I had no idea that the race of gnomes was inclined to practice the art of revenge."

"They do not, of course," said the Duchess, with a ful-minating glance. "Gnomes pride themselves on their dignity, but they haven't a shred of what *I* would call pride. However, they do build tricks and traps, and sell them to Men and to dwarves. Very complex their traps are, too, but there is always at least one way out. Gnomes believe in fair play, and so do Fees and Farisees, and a proper scheme of revenge in the grand fairy tradition must be as intricately crafted as a gnome's trap."

The Duchess wrapped a pale coil of hair around one finger. "My victims, you see, must participate in their own destruction . . . I may lure them in, trick them, even resort to coercion, but I cannot stoop to physical force. It isn't enough to merely ruin them . . . No, I must *outwit* them as well, prove myself superior. In that way, I gain a moral advantage."

"And this moral advantage . . ." said Kelly, with that same stiff smile, like the rictus on the face of a corpse. "That will make you . . . happy, I suppose?"

"Happy?" said the Duchess, forcing a laugh, and Kelly wondered why she should look so surprised. "I do not know if it will make me happy . . . but at least it should serve to satisfy me."

21.

In which "Absent Friends" prove not so absent after all.

On the thirty-second day of the season of Leaves, Sammuel Jonas received a message from Captain Hornbeam, requesting a meeting at the Eclipse. Naturally, the gnome and Jedidiah were highly elated, expecting the news would be good. They arrived at the tavern a good half hour ahead of time, and waited impatiently for the old seaman to arrive.

Nor did Captain Hornbeam disappoint them, when he finally turned up. "The *Otter*'s shipshape and ready to sail anytime you say, gentlemen. And I've hired us the trustiest and most experienced crew on the whole blamed Cordelia coast!"

"Excellent," said Mr. Jonas. "The moon will be full in another fortnight. Allow us a week to make the final arrangements, and then we will sail." And with matters thus favorably arranged, they toasted their venture with tankards of ale, and then Jed and the gnome returned to the cottage for a good night's rest.

But the next morning, when they entered the shed behind Mr. Herring's shop, a dismaying sight met their eyes. "D-------n! It's naught but a heap of splinters," cried Jed, turning deathly pale as he surveyed the ruins of the complex machine he and Mr. Jonas had so carefully constructed.

Mr. Jonas picked up a gear and a convoluted piece of copper wire. "This was no accident . . . someone has utterly and mischievously destroyed our creation. But who—or rather more to the point, why?"

But Siegfried Herring, when they called him in to view the damage, had a ready answer. "Hobgoblins!" he said, wrinkling his nose. The room reeked of embryonated sulphur. "Who else could it possibly be?"

"But surely not," said Mr. Jonas, ruefully examining a piece

of waxed canvas hose which had either been chewed or else
clumsily hacked apart. "Surely the creatures have never been
given to wanton destruction. All the damage they have done
before was merely the unfortunate result of their incessant
tunneling and gnawing."

Mr. Herring bit his thumb, thinking intently. "With all the
hob traps one sees in town these days, perhaps they thought
the device was meant for their destruction."

"*Thought?*" asked Jed in a harsh voice, and he and Mr. Jonas
exchanged a horrified glance. Mr. Herring had the grace to
blush, right up to his pomaded wig—for had he not proclaimed
from the beginning, most vociferously, that the hobgoblins
could not possibly be Rational Beings and therefore ought to
be classified and treated as vermin?

Mr. Jonas was shocked to the core of his honest being. "If
even you are willing to credit the hobs not only with cognitive
thought but also with a fair degree of foresight . . ." he said,
sitting down abruptly on a stool, " . . . then surely you must
realize that the complete extermination of the species would
be nothing less—my good Siegfried!—nothing less than geno-
cide."

Indeed, the three races, Man, dwarf, and gnome, had lived
together so long and harmoniously (and the other races apart,
but more or less peacefully) only because an absolute prohib-
ition existed, forbidding any action that could possibly be con-
strued as the systematic destruction of one race by any other.
To violate that principle was unthinkable . . . obscene!

"You are quite right," said the shame-faced Mr. Herring. "I
did wrong to accuse the hobs of this at least. They could have
no reason to destroy your machine."

But however the damage had occurred, without the device,
it would be impossible for Mr. Jonas and Jed to carry forth
their plan.

"We cannot hope to build another like it in the week . . .
no, the six days remaining us," said Mr. Jonas, sifting sadly
through a pile of glass and splintered oak. "It will take another
fortnight at the least, working as swiftly as we can, for some
of the calibrations are extremely delicate—to say nothing of
reharmonizing the magnets. And then we shall have to wait
another full cycle of the moon!"

* * *

A pleasant flutter of anticipation pervaded Mothgreen Academy, for Miss Jamaica Barebones was at long last arranging the promised Dumb Supper. All the mystical old ladies of the town had received their gilt-edged invitations, and all of them had accepted. Miss Barebones meant to serve them a veritable feast: "For it would not be correct to do the thing cheaply or meanly, you know! Our otherworldly guests would be vastly offended."

This pleasant anticipation did not, of course, extend to Sera, who viewed the preparations with mounting horror, convinced that the affair could only exert an unwholesome effect on poor Elsie. But Miss Barebones would not allow anything of the sort. "How could it harm her indeed—the more so, as *you* have convinced her that she ought not even attend?

"Besides that," the headmistress continued, with determined optimism, "if Elsie is troubled by night-terrors, we may hope to induce some more friendly spirits to assist us in banishing them."

Just as though, Sera thought, with a shiver of disgust, as she went upstairs to her classroom, *a man like Izrael Barebones (how dreadfully evocative the name!), decent and respectable when he was alive, is likely to lose all sense of propriety now that he is dead, and appear before a congregation of aging spinsters without even the ordinary concealment of his corporeal vesture!* The very thought of speaking with spirits made Sera turn cold.

Rather worse, Miss Barebones's arrangements strongly reminded Sera of that shocking travesty of a wedding feast which she and Elsie had both attended back in Thornburg, with Lady Ursula Bowker as the bride and a dreadful wax effigy, representing the lady's recently executed husband, doing honors as the groom.

Fortunately, both Sera and Elsie had a number of wholesome and sensible tasks to occupy them in the meantime. This afternoon it was a lesson in deportment, which they taught together in a big sunny chamber on the second floor.

But the little girls evinced more interest in the coming Supper than in their afternoon lessons. "I do think it's hard that we haven't been invited," said Luella Battersby, as she balanced a book on her head—an exercise meant to improve her posture. "I am sure we should all of us welcome the opportunity to eat an elegant supper with a gentlemanly spook or two."

Her friend Patience Armitage fervently agreed. "Uncle Izrael is no good at all. All *he* ever does is moan and rap and move things about . . . and follow Miss Thorn wherever she goes. I think he is sweet on her!"

Strangely enough, it did not fall to Sera to punish this shocking piece of impertinence. Before she could say a word, Elsie had already descended on Patience and Luella in an uncharacteristic fury, her face suffused with a burning blush, and banished the two girls to their separate bedchambers for the rest of the afternoon.

On the night of the Dumb Supper, Sera and Elsie tucked their charges into bed at an unusually early hour. Then Sera left Elsie in her bedchamber with a novel and a pot of tea to occupy her, and went into her own room to change her dress.

Naturally, Sera had not wished to attend the Supper, had fully intended to decline the invitation. But Miss Barebones, Miss Eglantine, and Miss Fitch were all so pressing. "Because Uncle Izrael has taken such an interest in you," twittered Miss Fitch. "And we have a much greater chance of success if you are there."

Which is just as much as to say: If I am not *there, and nothing happens (which of course must be the case) . . . why then, they will all just blame it on* me *and resolve to repeat the whole foolish exercise at some later date,* thought Sera.

At the appointed hour, she reluctantly entered the dining room. The table was set with the very best china, silver, and crystal: places for Miss Barebones, Miss Eglantine, Miss Fitch, and Sera; places for all the old ladies from the town; an elegant setting at the head of the table awaited Uncle Izrael, and a number of other settings and empty chairs had been designated for "the spirits of absent friends, whether on earth or in heaven."

The ladies came into the room, all very fine in their rustling gowns of satin or taffeta, scenting the air with perfumes and pomade; Miss Eglantine and Miss Fitch had even powdered their hair. No one spoke after they entered, but, at a mute signal from Miss Barebones, they all took seats. Much to Sera's dismay, Elsie slipped into the room and sat down along with the others.

Sera scowled most horribly and shook her head. Elsie mouthed an apology, but kept her seat. Meanwhile, Miss Barebones took a pinch of salt and solemnly dropped it onto the plate in front of her, another pinch for the empty plate beside her, then passed the salt cellar on to the next lady. Shivering with excitement, one by one, the other ladies repeated the gesture. When the salt cellar came to her place, Sera gritted her teeth and imitated the rest.

There followed a great deal more: a ritual breaking of bread, an elaborate ceremony over the wine . . . then Miss Barebones, moving with hierophantic dignity, uncovered the first of many covered dishes, and the actual feast began.

Never before had Sera been in a room full of so many people and eaten so quiet a meal. There was no sound but the muted clank of silver on china, the soft gurgling of wine poured from a bottle into a crystal goblet, the rattle of a silver lid replaced on a chafing dish. The meal consisted of several courses: beef, lamb, fish, and fowl, with pies, stewed vegetables, jellies, and conserves on the side. But nothing much out of the way happened, until the dessert course of boiled pudding arrived.

The long table, which was made of solid oak, suddenly tipped wildly from side to side, causing the dishes to slide back and forth, as it lurched and then righted itself. A brisk sound of tapping came up through the floorboards. Someone stifled a gasp; there was a strangled exclamation of horror. But the old ladies remained mindful that silence was required and nobody said a single word—though all exchanged glances of triumph or dismay.

Then Miss Barebones jumped up from her chair, flung out a trembling hand, and Sera, like the rest, looked in the direction she pointed. A very old and very beautiful, but hitherto perfectly ordinary, gilded mirror hung suspended above the sideboard; on the surface of that mirror, a dim, clouded image was slowly forming. Everyone watched, in wide-eyed excitement, as the image grew . . . until a blood-curdling shriek from Elsie drew all eyes her way.

In the chair beside Elsie, a misty figure of a man could be plainly seen, which gradually became more solid, taking on clear and recognizable features. Or rather, Sera (with the blood pounding in her temples and her breath coming swiftly) most *certainly* recognized the phantom, and Elsie must have done so as well, for she leaped out of her chair, took two stumbling steps, and then crumbled to the floor in a dead faint. The figure of a man began to fade.

In the general commotion that followed, chairs fell over, candles were extinguished, and the invited guests all fled the room. Only Miss Barebones and the redoubtable Miss Eglantine remained, to help Sera carry Elsie out the door.

An hour later, lying on her own bed up in the attic, with a damp cloth on her forehead and a shawl spread over her like a blanket, a tearful Elsie said to Sera: "You recognized him, too. It was Jarl Skogsrå. And it cannot have been any kind of a trick, because nobody here knows anything about him . . . not anyone but you and I."

"No, it can't have been a trick." Sera sank down on the bed beside her. "But what it means I do not know. Unless . . . unless Jarl Skogsrå is dead, and has come to haunt you. Having witnessed that scene down below," she added bitterly, "I suppose I must now admit that such things are possible.

"What a disheartening thing it is, to be sure," she added, with an angry laugh, "to discover that what you have always known—but would not for the world believe in—should be true after all!"

"No, he isn't dead," sighed Elsie, her face very white against the pillows. "Miss Barebones said spirits of absent friends, living or dead, did she not?"

Sera considered that with a frown. "But living *or* dead, Haakon Skogsrå is no friend of yours . . . or mine."

"Yes, but he . . . he *was* very nearly my husband," Elsie faltered. "We stood together before the altar, the ceremony had already begun. Sera . . . do you think that I and Lord Skogsrå were . . . were somehow *joined* together, in a form of spiritual wedlock?"

"Surely not," Sera insisted. "We interrupted the wedding long before anything like that might have happened." But then, with a keen look at Elsie, she added, "Why do you ask? My dear . . . is there something you have failed to tell me?"

Elsie protested, but after considerable coaxing she finally disclosed that she had been experiencing "the strangest dreams at night." Dreams of a faceless man who entered her bedchamber and whispered endearments in her ear, who kissed her and caressed her with great tenderness . . .

"—like a demon lover," Elsie blushingly disclosed. "I was ashamed and afraid at first . . . though it was only a dream . . . but then I came to *long* for his presence. Only perhaps it wasn't a dream after all, and I . . . I have been— Sera, what have I been *doing*?" she asked, her eyes opening wide in horror.

"It must have been a dream!" said Sera. Anything else would be altogether shocking and she would not believe such a thing of innocent Elsie. "Not an ordinary, natural dream, perhaps, but . . . oh, Elsie, you must have *known* the difference if it had not been a dream. Someone has been inflicting you with these—these wicked hallucinations.

"But whatever else it means," she added, springing to her feet, "it must also mean that Skogsrå and the Duchess are in Hobb's Church looking for us . . . or somewhere very near. And that being so: we are no longer safe. We must not wait another day, but must leave this place immediately—whatever Dr. Bell might say."

But Elsie insisted that to remove from the vicinity would accomplish nothing. "Because . . . if I am somehow spiritually bound to Haakon Skogsrå—as I must be, if he is able to reach out from a distance and touch me that way—then where on earth could I possibly be safe?"

22.

Wherein Mr. Carstares is much Offended.

The Glassmakers Guild in Hollifax—a country town of moderate size, some two hundred miles to the north of Hobb's Church—was a group of gentlemanly, congenial souls, who, not content with thrice-annual festivities at the local guildhall, had a habit of gathering in force in their own homes, at least once in every fortnight.

They were met, one particular evening, in the library of an elegant town house belonging to a certain wealthy Mr. Alcock, when their host introduced a brother Glassmaker from across the sea. "Gentlemen, I present to you: Mr. Carstares."

The newcomer removed his hat and bowed very low. As visitors from Euterpe were comparatively rare, the gentlemen gathered eagerly around, in order to make his acquaintance. But this Mr. Carstares scarcely presented a particularly Continental appearance: he wore his fair hair unpowdered and uncurled except for a slight natural wave; his face was innocent of patches; and though undoubtedly a gentleman, he was very plainly dressed.

"I have come to Hollifax," said Mr. Carstares, replacing his simple tricorn, "in search of certain young friends who might have settled in the area. They would have arrived bearing references from the Glassmakers Guild in Thornburg-on-the-Lunn—and may or may not have come here under their own names: Mr. Jedidiah Braun, and the Misses Seramarias and Elsie Vorder."

The gentleman Glassmakers all shook their heads, expressed their regrets. No such persons had appeared in Hollifax, no combination of two young ladies and a youth bearing references had sought the Guild's protection.

"But stay a bit . . ." said Mr. Alcock, cocking his head.

"The one name does put me in mind of something. Now, what was it?"

"It was the box," said another gentleman, taking snuff for himself and offering a pinch to Mr. Carstares. "Last year, was it not—during the season of Ripening?"

"Ah yes," said Mr. Alcock. "That was it, indeed. A little box like a jewel box, sir, with the legend 'Seramarias' writ in gold upon the lid—as it might be a lady's name, rather than the mythical Stone of great price. We were instructed to pass it on from lodge to lodge, until it should finally come into the proper hands."

Mr. Carstares paused, with the snuff between his thumb and his forefinger. "I am acquainted with the box. It was I who sent it. But do you know what became of the box . . . do you know if it ever came into the young lady's hands?"

"We sent the box to Philodendria, where it apparently did *not* find her, for it came back to us again, almost immediately," said Mr. Alcock. "It went to Birch Corners after that, with much the same result, though it took longer to return. After that . . . let me see—" Mr. Alcock thought for a time.

"Lootie's Bay," the gentleman with the snuffbox prompted him. "We sent it on to Lootie's Bay."

"Indeed," said Mr. Alcock, nodding his head. "We did send it on to Lootie's Bay. And we never saw it again after that."

Mr. Carstares inhaled his pinch of snuff, sneezed into a large, plain handkerchief, and put it back in his coat pocket. "It is possible, then, that the young lady received my gift in Lootie's Bay?" he asked.

"It is *possible* that the young lady was there to claim it," said Mr. Alcock. "Also possible that Mr. Bullrush merely sent the box on to another lodge. Still, you might do worse than go there and ask. And I will give you a letter for the Mayor, if you like."

The mail coach between Philodendria, to the south, and Lootie's Bay, in the north, did not arrive in Hollifax until the next morning. Rather than spend the remainder of the day at the inn where he was lodged, the visitor decided to beguile the rest of the afternoon with a leisurely stroll through the shady streets of the town.

As he sauntered down Oakapple Lane, he was surprised to

hear his name called out in a familiar voice. Turning, he saw a tall, auburn-haired beauty, in deer-colored satin and a wide leghorn hat, just descending from a sedan chair.

"Dear Lord Skelbrooke—or should I say Mr. *Hawkins* . . . how charmingly unexpected!" gushed Lady Ursula.

His lordship gritted his teeth, replied politely that it certainly was, and bowed over the hand she extended to him. He did not think it worth his while to inform her that he was now using the name of Carstares. "Is it possible, madam, that you and Lord Vizbeck have settled in this very town?"

"Indeed yes," she replied, with a great play of dark eyelashes. "And you, sir, have you . . . ?"

"Alas, no," said Skelbrooke, with such gallantry as he could muster. "I remain for a few days only."

"Then what a fortunate chance that we happened to meet. It does almost seem—does it not—that the Fates conspire to bring us together?" she asked, with a smile that contrived to be coy and flirtatious, both at the same time. His lordship replied only with a silent bow.

As the lady made no move to do so, and the bearers seemed to expect it, Skelbrooke was obliged to pay for her chair. Then Lady Ursula linked her arm familiarly through his, and they proceeded down the street.

"Do you know? I almost did not recognize you, you look so very different," she said, eyeing him seductively. "Yet I must say that this austere style rather suits you. I had always thought of you as quite a little man, but now you appear . . . well, certainly not any *taller,* but so—so very substantial!"

Skelbrooke thought nostalgically of the latter days of their voyage, when Lady Ursula's continuing fear of contagion had spared him her company. Today, however, he was well and truly caught, and what he was to do with her, he really did not know.

He had no wish to escort her home—even if he had an inkling where that might be—for fear she would invite him in. Nor did he dare to invite her up to his own room at the inn— the Fates alone knew what that might lead to! In the end, he made the best that he could of a bad situation, by taking her to an open-air café by the park in the center of town, and sitting down with her at a little table with a flowered cloth.

Over cakes and chocolate, Lady Ursula waxed sentimental.

"I wonder when either of us shall see Thornburg again?" she said, with a sigh and a pensive smile. "But you know, it seems that many of our acquaintances have emigrated recently. You will never guess whom I met with, just the other day."

My lord, in the act of raising a cup of chocolate to his lips, begged her to continue.

"Miss Sera and Miss Elsie Vorder . . . yes indeed! And that *was* a great surprise, for I remember the scandal when they both disappeared, and no one had *any* idea where they had gone. I might add that they did not seem at all pleased to meet me."

Skelbrooke put down his cup so suddenly that the chocolate spilled out on the flowered cloth. "And where was this, Lady Ursula?" he asked, determinedly casual. "Not here in Hollifax?"

"Oh no," said the lady, crumbling a sugared biscuit on her plate. "I was visiting friends in Cordelia, in a quaint little village called Hobb's Church. I must say, the young ladies both looked well and prosperous enough, which was also surprising. I had heard that one or the other of them had eloped with some horrid young ruffian who worked on the river." Skelbrooke stiffened and his eyes dilated, but the Lady continued on, apparently oblivious. "Though why *both* of them should run off with him—well, if true, it is really very shocking!"

"Indeed," said his lordship coldly. He took out his pocket watch—an elaborate affair, about the size and shape of a hen's egg—and ostentatiously checked the time. "If such a thing *were* true, it would be shocking. But rumor so often lies. I fancy you are thinking of Miss Sera's foster brother, a respectable youth who at one time did have some professional connection with the river—and a most particular friend of mine."

Lady Ursula smiled sweetly. "Then it seems that my news is no news at all, for you already know everything about it."

"No," said Skelbrooke, in a voice still tinged with ice. "I did not know where they were living, but of this much I am certain . . ." He snapped the case of his timepiece decisively shut. "Wherever they are and whoever they may be with, Miss Sera and Miss Elsie Vorder will undoubtedly conduct themselves like the perfect ladies they are!"

23.

Wherein Mothgreen Academy suffers an Invasion.

At Mothgreen Hall, Miss Barebones and her cohorts were as pleased as they were baffled by the success of their Dumb Supper, for none of their previous attempts to communicate with the spirit world had ever yielded such spectacular results . . . or indeed, any noticeable results at all.

"I am convinced that you have a natural gift," the headmistress told Sera. "You must play a part in all our spirit-raisings, after this."

"I beg your pardon, but I certainly shall not!" said Sera, and rather rudely stamped out of the room.

Yet one favorable result had occurred. Elsie confided to Sera that her phantom lover had ceased to woo her. She slept better at night and her health improved slightly, though her color remained poor and she had little appetite.

With the end of the term on the last day of the season, the little girls went home for an eight-week holiday. The house was strangely peaceful for two days, until a sudden invasion—not by ghosts or school girls, but apparently by hobgoblins.

Far more disturbing than Uncle Izrael's knockings and rappings were sounds of movement within the walls, a pattering of tiny feet across the roof all night . . . and Nathaniel, the boy who worked in the garden, discovered a hob-hole under a rosebush . . . at least, it had once been a rosebush, covered with salmon-pink flowers, but the branches were all chewed off short, nearly down to the ground.

And things began to disappear, things for which Uncle Izrael could have no possible use: a tablecloth, a velvet drape, a lace-trimmed pillowcase. Miss Barebones concluded that the hobs had tunneled all the way from the town, a distance of nearly a mile!

"Perhaps, after all, most of the 'ghostly manifestations' that plagued us from the beginning were nothing more than the tricks of hobgoblins," Elsie suggested doubtfully. The ladies had gathered in the garden to view the hole and the violated rosebush. Rose petals and green leaves lay scattered all over the ground, as though the hobs had no interest in anything but the wood.

"If that is so, and they were here from the very start, why should they suddenly become more active now?" asked Sera, with a puzzled frown.

"Why should we suddenly become infested in any case?" asked Miss Fitch, drawing in her drab skirts, as though she suspected they were in imminent danger of being snatched away. "And I never heard before that hobgoblins were housedwellers, or lived inside the walls."

"It must come of all the digging and poisoning and explosions in the town . . . the creatures have run mad with fright," Miss Barebones suggested, shaking her head. "Perhaps they come here because they feel safer. We did rescue that little one, you know: Miss Thorn, Miss Winter, and I. Or perhaps some of them remember Uncle Izrael's kindness and have come here for sanctuary."

"Mr. Barebones has been dead for fifty years," Sera felt obliged to point out. She bent down and scooped up a handful of rose petals, allowed them to sift through her fingers and drift slowly to the ground. "Do hobgoblins live that long?"

Miss Barebones heaved a sigh. "It hardly seems likely. But perhaps they tell stories about him—oh dear, that would argue a degree of intelligence on their part, wouldn't it? And to think that people are exterminating them!"

"Why they have come here is quite beside the point," Miss Eglantine said sternly. "The question is: what do we intend to do about them?"

"But I don't think that it *is* beside the point," Miss Barebones protested, as they headed back toward the house. "If the poor creatures have conceived a trust of us, if they come here for refuge, it seems terribly heartless to—"

"I am sure we should all feel compassion at the sight of a rat caught in a trap," Miss Eglantine interrupted, in her decided way. "Or a poor little mouse in the claws of a cat. Under those circumstances, any one of us might feel, as you did, inclined to rescue the creature. But if the house should afterwards be infested by rats and mice as a result, I doubt we should be so wrong-headed as to welcome them to stay."

They continued their discussion over breakfast in the parlor. Miss Barebones steadfastly declared that she would have no traps or poisons at Mothgreen Hall. "Though if anyone chooses to buy a cat to keep in her own room—to guard the sanctity of her bedchamber—she may feel quite free to do so."

"For my part," said Miss Eglantine, "I shall buy *two* cats."

Meanwhile, in the town, people remained divided on how to deal with the hobgoblin problem—for despite the invasion of Mothgreen Hall, goblin activity still continued to plague the town. But in Hobb's Church, the very harshest methods were under discussion.

Traps . . . poisons . . . explosions, all had been tried and proven ineffective. So an army of stoats was imported and released down all existing hob-holes. As no weasel ever emerged, folks were forced to assume that the hobs, though disinclined to attack their larger persecutors, had bloodily disposed of the invading stoats. Even some of the more compassionate citizens, who had first counciled moderation, no longer did so. But there remained a large faction, whipped up by the hectoring of Moses Tynsdale, who continued to proclaim loudly that the depredations of the hobgoblins were a clear demonstration of divine displeasure. These folks held loud revival meetings which lasted most of the night, called for the abolition of any establishment selling gin or spirits within the town, and the removal of all sinful luxuries—such as velvet cushions and prayer stools—from the church.

Loud arguments broke out at the Eclipse . . . two fist-fights between sailors and a number of duels between gentlemen were but narrowly averted. Then word spread (no one knew who began the story) that the ladies at the Academy were actually "harboring the nasty little creatures."

When Sera came into town on an errand, a boy threw a rock at her, then disappeared down an alley, and she could hear people muttering angrily after her as she continued her walk down the cobblestone street. It seemed to Sera that even the very figureheads nailed up above the doors in place of shop signs eyed her with open hostility. She tied the broad yellow ribbons of her chip straw more firmly under her chin, drew on her gloves with a defiant air, and marched down the lane with a firm step.

Unfortunately for Sera's dignity, it soon developed that the children of Hobb's Church were at war among themselves, quite as much as the adults. Rounding a corner, she was horrified to encounter Luella Battersby actually engaged in a most hoydenish scuffle with a crowd of small boys. Heedless of her gown, her bonnet, and her gloves, Sera dove into their midst, restraining Luella with one hand, and using the other to lift a naughty little gnome up by the seat of his breeches.

While she was thus occupied, Sera chanced to look around her for some possible ally among the goggling spectators, and met the eyes of a fair-haired gentleman who stood watching her efforts with apparent appreciation. With a jolt of surprise, she recognized Francis Skelbrooke.

Eventually, Sera sent the boys packing. Then she took a handkerchief out of her reticule and proceeded to scrub the dirt from Luella's face. She looked up at Lord Skelbrooke's approach, her cheeks very hot and her eyes very bright, struggling to reclaim what dignity she could.

Little wonder she had been so startled, for he was very conservatively dressed, in a sage-green coat, buff-colored small clothes, and a soft felt hat cocked up into a "shovel" brim. He and Sera had never met but when he was powdered and patched, attired in rustling satins and cascading lace. And she was not even certain, now that she thought about it, whether she had previously known the color of his hair.

He took off his hat and made a sweeping bow. "What a delightful circumstance, Miss . . . I beg your pardon, my wretched memory! I do not seem to recall your name, though *you* I remember very well indeed."

"Sera Thorn," she said, for the benefit of Luella and the staring neighbors, as she stripped off her ruined gloves and offered him one of her hands. *How like Lord Skelbrooke, when he finally arrives,* thought Sera, *to discover me in the midst of such an awkward situation!*

And considering his passionate declarations at their last meeting, and all of the time that had elapsed between . . . that he could greet her now so coolly and with such perfect composure—that was perfectly outrageous!

"Of course . . . Miss Thorn," he murmured, and Sera was somewhat mollified to feel his hand tremble, ever so slightly, as their fingers touched and he raised her hand to his lips.

"It is a pleasure to see you again, Lord—"

"It is just plain Robin Carstares," he interjected smoothly, still retaining her hand. "No . . . you need not apologize. As I recall, when we met before, my father was commonly supposed to be on his deathbed and I had every expectation of succeeding to his title. Fortunately, he recovered, and it seems likely that many more years will pass before you may address me as Lord . . . Wyvernwood."

"Mr. Carstares, yes," said Sera, between her teeth. She wondered if he made up these facile prevarications as he went along, or whether he practiced them in advance. Regaining possession of her hand, she added, "Perhaps you will be good enough to walk with me. I have so much to tell you!"

"I am entirely at your disposal," said his lordship.

With a continued exchange of false pleasantries, they escorted Luella home, then started down the long, deserted country road toward Mothgreen Academy. It was a warm, balmy day, the air scented with grass and apple blossoms. Suddenly, Skelbrooke surprised her by blurting out: "I suppose it is a bit premature for me to ask you to marry me?"

Sera stopped dead in the middle of the road. She experienced considerable difficulty catching her breath. "Premature?" she managed, when she was able to speak again. "My dear Lord . . . my dear Mr. Carstares, it has been almost two years since we last met, and in all that time—"

"It has been far longer than that," he said. "It has been . . . an eternity."

And he immediately began a long explanation: why he had not come looking for her at once, how he had followed the Duchess to the New World and subsequently lost track of her. "Nor was it so easy to find you as I had originally hoped," he continued earnestly, as they resumed their progress down the road. "Indeed, I should not have done so as soon as I did, were it not for Lady Ursula."

"Lady Ursula?" said Sera, who was beginning to feel she had experienced enough shocks for any one day. "Lady Ursula *Bowker*? But what had she to do with it?"

A tiny frown marred his lordship's alabaster brow. "It was Lady Ursula—now married to Lord Vizbeck—who told me she met you here in Hobb's Church."

"She did no such thing," said Sera. "That is . . . she may have been here, for all I know, but she certainly never spoke to me!

"And I rather fancy she was *not* here," Sera added thoughtfully. "For she could not do so—could not visit anyplace, you know—without causing a stir among the male inhabitants."

Lady Ursula, besides being strikingly beautiful, did have a way of making her presence felt, as Lord Skelbrooke must be the first to admit. His frown darkened. "Then I am at a loss to discover why she should pretend that she *was* here. Unless . . . it is possible, I suppose, that Lady Ursula is in the Duchess's pay and was sent to lure me here."

He continued to turn the matter over in his mind, walking along with his hands clasped behind him and his gaze fixed on the road. "Yet, if so, it was clumsily done! She must have known that you would deny seeing her. And whatever else she may be, Lady Ursula is no fool."

Only one solution came to mind. "Well, it may be that the Duchess employed her to spy on me and to convey the information, but has not succeeded in buying her entire loyalty," he guessed. "Not a mistake, then, but a friendly warning, meant to alert us to some danger."

"Yes," said Sera, lifting her skirts an inch or two, as the road led them up a slight incline. By now, she was perfectly composed, and proud of herself for being so. "There is little, I believe, that Lady Ursula would not do for money . . . But she has no reason, that I know of, to wish Elsie or I any serious harm."

Lord Skelbrooke glanced up, smiling faintly. "I fear that the lady has some small reason to be cross with me." Yet it occurred to him that perhaps Lady Ursula had been no more attracted to him than he was to her—that her attempts to flirt with him had been only a method of getting close, without revealing her true intentions. This was a blow to his vanity, to be sure, but one from which he must soon recover.

"It may be," said Skelbrooke, "that the Duchess, having better information, has arrived in Cordelia before me, and that it serves her purpose to gather us all here together."

"I have reason to believe that the Duchess and Jarl Skogsrå are certainly somewhere not very distant," said Sera, wincing slightly, for she knew that an argument was coming.

Now it was his lordship's turn to stop, this time in the shade of a spreading oak tree. "If that is so, you and Miss Elsie must make haste to leave Cordelia as soon as possible!"

But Sera explained about Elsie's dream, the ghostly Jarl, and the conclusions that she and Elsie had subsequently drawn. "It seems that there is no place Elsie and I can go that the Duchess and Skogsrå cannot follow her," said Sera, as they continued their leisurely progress toward Mothgreen Hall. "And to tell you the truth, sir," she added defiantly, over his sudden vociferous protest, "though it seemed an excellent plan when we left Thornburg, we are not inclined to go on traveling for the rest of our lives."

Sera was a little surprised to hear those words come out of her mouth. Up until now, she had always forced herself to take the practical view, had refused to listen to the promptings of her heart.

"If we must, eventually, face the Duchess," she added, a trifle crossly, for it was really too much that he should suddenly appear after all this time and suppose that he could instantly take charge. "I believe we had far better stand our ground here, where Elsie and I have friends, and the Duchess does not."

Though Skelbrooke endeavored to convince Sera otherwise, he was eventually forced to realize the futility. "But then, at least, you must allow me to caution you," he said gravely, as they paused outside the gates of Mothgreen Academy. "You must go nowhere alone. Do not so much as step across your threshold without some trusty friend to accompany you . . . preferably some gentleman friend, like Jed or myself.

"I wonder," he added, opening one side of the wrought-iron gate and standing aside for Sera to pass through, "if you would mind very much should I claim kinship with you—or perhaps, more convincingly, with Miss Elsie—and invite myself for an extended visit at the Hall?"

"You are very welcome to do so," said Sera, leading the way down the tree-lined drive. "That is," she added with a blush, "I do not believe that Miss Barebones would have any great objection. And perhaps Elsie would find your presence reassuring."

"And for yourself?" he asked, with a look of earnest inquiry. "Should you welcome me, as well?"

Sera refused to meet that disturbing grey-eyed gaze. "I, also, would find some comfort in a gentleman's protection, just at this time."

"I see," said Skelbrooke, sounding disappointed. "Why then . . . if I can serve you, in even so small a way, I am naturally pleased to do so."

24.

Which finds Discord reigning at Stillwater Hall.

Stillwater Hall, though once a very fine house, was now dilapidated and damp. The lions at the gate had a shapeless appearance, rendered nearly featureless by a covering of moist green moss. Willows, laurels, and dark yew trees lined the drive, forming a dense wall of untamed foliage. And the porch, as well as the nine steps leading up to it, was slick with more of the same green moss. Though the builders had displayed a degree of foresight in erecting walls of grey stone, wooden floors and a shingle roof suffered in the damp, as did windowsills, doors, and thresholds; and it seemed that every metal fixture in the house was either stained blood-red with rust or blue-green with verdigris.

In a great gloomy chamber, made even darker and more dismal by rotting purple draperies over the windows—a room so vast and chilly that a roaring fire on the hearth did little to warm it, and three branches of candles were insufficient to light it—in that mournful chamber sat the Duchess and Thomas Kelly, resting in high-backed ebonwood chairs, whiling away the long hours between sunset and bedtime.

"Why do you delay?" said the Duchess, with an angry shake of her head. "Have I not provided you with a laboratory and all the equipment you could possibly need? At great expense, I might add—the more so, because the whole had to be done with the utmost secrecy. Yet despite this, you ignore our agreement, you do nothing at all toward the creation of a living homunculus."

"We had an agreement," said Kelly, his waxy skin glowing faintly by candlelight. "I would help you to exact your revenge, I would also create for you the homunculus . . . but you would assist me to regain my books. I have, I believe, been of some material use to you in arranging the former . . . and I do not see why I should do anything more, until I have received due payment for services already rendered."

The Duchess regarded him narrowly. "I wonder . . ." she said. "Yes, I begin to wonder whether or not you do carry the formula about in your head—as you have been at such pains to convince me. Or is it, perhaps, that you require the books before you can even begin?"

Kelly made a motion with one gaunt hand. "I know all that I need to know," he said.

Yet the Duchess continued to eye him suspiciously. If Kelly was *unable* to proceed without his books, if he had not learned the formula by heart . . . then what *good* was Kelly without the books—and what particular use (for that matter) once she had obtained them?

Not a scrap of use in the world, she decided, her lips tightening in a hard line. *Because if I have the formula and all the equipment, I can work the spells myself.*

Kelly moved uneasily in his chair, as if he guessed what direction her thoughts were tending. "You are suddenly most impatient . . . oddly impatient for a woman who commissioned the destruction of the machine made by Jedidiah Braun and the gnome Sammuel Jonas. Had you not done so, we might have discovered its purpose long since. But you are so intent on your petty revenge, on gathering together all the actors in your little drama . . ."

"I have more on my mind, at present, than my petty revenge—as you are pleased to call it." With an angry little flounce, the Duchess rose from her chair and drifted toward the fire. A creature made primarily of the elements flame and air, she could tolerate the occasional river damps of Thornburg, but the perpetual humidity of this moist climate caused her severe discomfort. "And I have a very good idea what the machine is for. As I believe *you* have as well, for all you might wish to pretend ignorance," she said over her shoulder. "I wish to see the device in operation, but that I cannot do if the parties involved load up their machine and sail off for unknown parts. That is why I ordered the engine destroyed—so that I might have ample time to make arrangements of my own, before the machine is whisked away."

"But then, in the meantime," said Kelly impatiently, "why

not send Mr. Hooke to steal my books? Those books are more to me than you imagine. They and I are bound by the Fates . . . united by the strongest magics."

"In which case," said the Duchess sweetly, "you may easily wait a bit longer to recover them, knowing as you do that they must return to you eventually. What is a week or two . . . indeed, what is a year or a decade, to such as you and I?"

She turned her back to the fire. "And I do not wish to tip my hand too soon . . . do not wish my young friends to suspect that either you or I may be found in Cordelia." She narrowed her eyes. "Indeed, my good sir, indeed I must warn you. Do not do anything to hinder me in my aims, or I may decide to continue on without your assistance."

The Duchess swept out of the room, but Thomas Kelly remained motionless in his chair. He was wondering what the Duchess would do if she realized how much he needed those books. Though his mind continued to work with the same cold precision, though he remembered with great clarity his ruling purpose, he retained only fragments of memories of most of his former life—and not one of the formulas he had known before had survived the transition from life to death, and half way back again. To make matters worse, his body was finally beginning to rot, to slowly decompose . . . a process he did not know how to effectively halt, except through the knowledge contained in those volumes—or in some repository of an *older* tradition. Therefore (unknown to the Duchess), he had already tried to exert his power over the books in order to bring them back to him . . . an attempt which had not only failed, but may have announced his presence to those who now possessed them.

And he was wondering . . . what the Duchess would do if she knew just how much he had already guessed about the machine at Mr. Herring's—and how that marvelous engine fell in so neatly with his own schemes and ambitions.

The next afternoon, Thomas Kelly paid a visit to Jarl Skogsrå in the troll's draughty bedchamber. The room boasted a large fireplace, but the hearth was bare, as though Skogsrå had lacked the energy to bring in the wood, lacked even the energy to hunt up a servant and command that service—as he apparently lacked the energy now to rise from his seat in a wing chair, or to offer his visitor the other chair.

Kelly took the chair anyway, which happened to stand by the empty fireplace.

These last weeks had not been kind to Skogsrå. He had lost the sleek, well-fed look which had formerly characterized him. But it was more than that, thought Kelly, wondering what diseases trolls might suffer from. Clad only in his breeches and a stained cambric shirt, with his brassy hair hanging lank and dark around his shoulders, Skogsrå looked tired and ill, as well as disheveled.

Kelly noted, with mild interest, that the monster Cecile, standing motionless in a corner, was in a similar state of undress. "Do you bed with her, I wonder?"

"It is no business of yours what I do with her," the troll replied sullenly. His shifted his position slightly, causing the unwieldy hoof at the end of his leg to scrape along the floorboards. It was a clear sign that something was seriously wrong, when Skogsrå no longer sought to conceal his disfigurement from Kelly's eyes.

"I ask merely out of intellectual curiosity," said the magician, with the smile that sat ill on his cadaverous face. "I suppose that the creature has her physical attractions . . . But even for a troll, I had thought that something more was required."

The Jarl stared at his hands. "She is stupid, Cecile, she is dull and placid . . . but me, I am no longer young. They say that our races, Man and troll, were once the same. It often happens among your kind, I think, that a male of my years forms just such an attachment . . . for a pretty young woman with a placid temper and negligible intelligence."

"That may be so," said Kelly, his lips twitching scornfully. "Indeed, I did not entirely understand these things when I was fully alive, and now . . ." He folded his hands in his lap. "I apprehend, at least, that you have some value for the monster. And perhaps . . . perhaps you do not know that when Elsie Vorder dies, her double will die also."

The Jarl stiffened. "I do not believe you. Why should I believe you? The Duchess says nothing of this."

"If you do not believe what I tell you, you must work out the logic for yourself. If you are capable of doing so," said Kelly. "You know that the golem obtains life by sharing Miss Vorder's essence. They are, in some sense, the same person."

The troll appeared to consider, sitting there with his head cocked to one side. "Yes," he said at last. "That would explain . . . certain recent experiences of mine."

"In that case, you must comprehend that when Elsie Vorder dies, the monster will return to its former state: a featureless thing of inanimate clay. Naturally," the sorcerer added carelessly, "it can be reanimated again, in a similar manner, using blood from another source. But then it must assume an entirely new aspect. And that . . . that would not satisfy you so well, I think."

"No," said the Jarl, shifting ponderously in his chair. "That would not satisfy me. I wish to keep her exactly as she is. But perhaps you will tell me: what do you expect me to do about this? You must expect something, or you would not have come here."

Kelly gestured in the direction of the mute figure standing in the corner. "You might take your Cecile and flee with her. Then Elsie Vorder would grow strong and healthy again, the Duchess would have to find another means to lure the unfortunate girl into her trap, and Cecile would be safe . . . at least for a time."

"I might do that, yes," Skogsrå said dully. "But that, alas, would require more enterprise than I seem to possess. Once . . . once the audacity of such a venture would have appealed to me. But now I have no strength. I am not getting enough blood, I think."

Kelly raised a skeptical eyebrow. "I have seen you consume enormous quantities of flesh and blood."

The Jarl shook his head sadly. "Beef and pork and lamb—it is not the same. It is not invigorating enough. But the Duchess does not allow me to make use of the young women in Moonstone or Hobb's Church. She fears it might lead to comment."

Kelly sneered at him. "You are superstitious, I regret to say. It cannot possibly matter to you where the blood comes from."

The troll made a feeble motion. "You think so? But what, after all, do you know about it? I suppose you account yourself wise, but you are not of my race. I know what I need: a woman in whom the life force runs strong and passionate, a woman who will go through the rituals with me. It has been too long since I took a bride."

Again Kelly stretched his thin blue lips in a sneer. "Well, well, you are a pitiful creature altogether. But perhaps . . . perhaps if you are too weak and cowardly to defy the Duchess, I might be able to arrange something for you."

The sorcerer leaned back in his chair. All his movements were so small and somehow lifeless, it was easy for those who knew him to remember that he was virtually an animated corpse. "I might be willing to help you to a bride. Providing, that is, that you promised to afterwards find the energy to take the golem and escape with her."

The troll stared at him with a certain dim suspicion. "And why would you do this? What prompts this generous impulse?"

"My own self-interest," replied Kelly. "I believe that the Duchess now considers me expendable . . . if not absolutely a thorn in her side. For my part, I wish to continue our association, at least for a time. And the Duchess must have someone to serve her. If you are gone, then my value increases, and the Duchess will be less inclined to dispose of me . . . as ruthlessly as she plans to dispose of your Cecile."

But the troll remained suspicious. "But why should you fear the Duchess . . . you who are virtually invincible, who can kill with a single touch? Why do you not . . . dispose of *her*?"

"I may yet be driven to do so," Kelly replied coldly. "But, as I told you, I wish to continue our association for some time to come. I believe the Duchess may be of considerable use to me.

"Also," he added, "like the monster Cecile, I can partake of the essence of others—which, in my case, does confer the power to kill with a touch. But a vessel can only contain so much—then, too, there is the strength of the container to be considered. I am stronger, in some ways, than when I was mortal. I am impervious to fire, poison, and most forms of injury, but still this human frame has its limitations. The Duchess, however, for all her apparent fragility, is made of matter at once stronger and more subtle. I will tamper with her only if I am forced to."

Skogsrå continued to stare at him with dull, discouraged eyes. "I do not understand you."

Kelly rose from his chair, stood looking down at the troll with ill-concealed contempt. "When I drained Gottfried Jenk of his last remaining years, I found the draught invigorating.

And those few weeks or seasons that I gained from this grand-daughter Sera, when I had her in my grasp, they had a similarly beneficial effect. But the Duchess . . ."

Kelly twitched a careless shoulder. " . . . it is hard to tell with these hybrids how long they may live. The lady might, in the natural course of things, be expected to continue on . . . perhaps for another two centuries. And were I to attempt to compass her entire life-span in a single draught, it might be more than this human vessel could contain without shattering."

25.

In which the course of True Love does not run Smooth.

Though Sera was willing to present Lord Skelbrooke to the community at large under any name he might care to assume, she refused to impose on Miss Barebones. Moreover, she thought it time and past time to make a clean breast of things by telling the headmistress her own name, Elsie's name, and their present circumstances.

It might be (Sera told herself) that Miss Barebones would cast them both out—she would certainly be within her rights to do so. In that case, they would just have to find a new place to live, someplace where they would *not* abuse the hospitality of their hostess with lies and deceptions.

But of course Sera need not have worried; Miss Barebones expressed only interested sympathy. "You must stay here as long as you wish, and use what names you please," said Miss Barebones. "And to think you have been here using false names all this time—how very romantic that is! As to any danger that may involve the rest of us . . . well, that hardly seems likely, but it is good of you to warn me."

As for Skelbrooke, she took to him at once, charmed by his well-bred air and his fine manners. To the other ladies, Miss Fitch and Miss Eglantine, Elsie introduced him as her cousin, Mr. Carstares.

"*Doctor* Carstares . . . I am a practicing physician, you know," his lordship corrected her, with a mischievous gleam in his eye. "Finding myself in the vicinity of Hobb's Church and learning from Miss Thorn that my cousin suffers some mysterious malady, I at once resolved to make an extended visit to Mothgreen Hall, in order to observe her condition."

In no time at all, he had won over Miss Eglantine and Miss Fitch, as thoroughly as he had won Miss Barebones. Both ladies were pleased to have a physician on the premises—especially one who took such a flattering interest in all their complaints, real or imaginary.

"I wonder that you are not ashamed of yourself, the way you go on here," Sera scolded him, as they walked in the garden the next afternoon.

"But my dear Miss Thorn, I believe you once told me that I made a mistake when I abandoned the practice of medicine," said his lordship, choosing to misunderstand her. "I recall that you expressed yourself rather forcibly on the subject."

Sera drew in her breath sharply. "I am sure that I never said or did anything half so impertinent," she said indignantly. "Though perhaps I did say that you would make a good doctor."

"Indeed, I think those were your very words—what an admirable memory you have, Miss Thorn! And so I have it in mind to do just that," said his lordship. "I had very nearly completed my course of study when I left the University, you know, and I had extensive practical experience at the Hospital of the Holy Powers. There are many practicing physicians less qualified to do so than I."

They stopped beneath a leafy grape arbor. "I should, eventually, like to spend another year or two assisting some professor of medicine," he added, "but that must wait on more pressing matters. For now, I shall stay in Cordelia and . . . Sera, will you take me to visit Jedidiah tomorrow? I am most particularly interested in this machine he is building. Also . . . there are one or two things I must tell him."

As they ambled down a flagstone path, his lordship launched into a brief description of his adventures in Zammarco and his encounters with Caleb Braun and the mysterious Eirena.

"Caleb Braun's *daughter*?" said Sera, with a disbelieving smile. "But that hardly seems . . . Perhaps you can tell me, sir, who the child's mother is supposed to have been!"

"It would appear," said Skelbrooke, "that she *has* no mother and never had. Sera, I beg your pardon, for I believe you will not like to hear this. Nevertheless, I think you ought to be told. Before I left the Continent, my friend Trithemius Ave finally convinced Caleb to divulge his secret (which I had already begun to suspect) and admit that Eirena—far from being born in the usual way—is in fact a homunculus, created in the laboratory by your grandfather and Caleb Braun, using arcane materials and an ordinary mandrake root.

"No doubt," added his lordship, "you will now tell me that the thing is impossible."

"On the contrary," Sera said, with a troubled frown. "You forget that my grandfather played a dominant role in my education. I do believe that such things *may* be done . . . sometimes. The question is: whether they *ought* to be. And even if—if the end result should be reckoned harmless . . . considering the cost and the high probability of ruinous failure . . . whether the attempt should even be made.

"But you . . . you have actually seen the creature," she said. "Are you quite, *quite* convinced that Caleb spoke the truth?"

"I am," he said, with a deep bow. "For once the idea had entered my mind, everything I knew of Eirena supported the notion. Perhaps you, too, remember something about those last days at your grandfather's bookshop . . . ?"

Sera considered for some time, a frown knitting her brows and her dark eyes distant. "Yes . . ." she said reluctantly. "Yes, I do remember—oh, things that made no sense at the time! A tiny shroud, and a word let fall by Caleb Braun . . .

"But if this incredible thing should happen to be true," she added, "then Eirena must—in some sense—be my *grandfather's* child as much as Caleb's."

Skelbrooke cleared his throat, spent a moment adjusting the plain bands at his wrist. "As to that . . . I would prefer to spare you the specific details, but the circumstances surrounding Eirena's creation were such . . . In short, she can claim kinship with Caleb and Jed, but none at all with you!"

They continued their stroll side by side, through the scented pathways, between beds of flowering lavender, rosemary, and bee-balm. Sera was very quiet, for Skelbrooke had given her much to think about. But when they came to a low gate and passed through it to the orchard, she suddenly asked: "Speaking as a physician, sir . . . do you tell me this thing is possible?"

"Speaking as a *physician,* Miss Thorn, I should have to say no. But speaking as a magician and a Glassmaker," said Skelbrooke, "I am utterly convinced of it."

"As a magician . . ." Sera's eyes went darker still. "But of course you must be. You are deep in the councils of the Guild, are you not?"

He suddenly caught her in his arms, robbing her, for a moment, of breath. Though surprised and considerably ruffled, she made no move to extricate herself. "Dear Sera," he said, grown suddenly very earnest. "I cannot say that is a part of my life I could easily or instantly abandon. But if you would prefer to be . . . not a magician's wife, but the wife of an ordinary physician, I can only promise that I would *strive* to be—"

Unfortunately, at that very interesting moment, Miss Fitch appeared at the end of the path, and Skelbrooke was forced to relinquish his hold. Blushing furiously, Sera stepped out of his arms. Though nothing more could be said on the subject, Sera's softened expression gave her suitor reason to hope.

But later that evening, after supper, when his lordship and the ladies went into the parlor—the old ladies and Elsie to sit down and play a game of whist, and Skelbrooke to assume a negligent pose by the fireplace, with one elbow on the mantelpiece, the better to observe Sera as she mended a pair of gloves—my lord made a serious blunder. In reaching for his snuffbox, he brought out the box of Sleep Dust instead.

Instantly realizing his error, he snapped the lid shut. But Sera had already recognized the little gold box with its inlay of pearl and ivory, identified the fine crystalline powder, and was unable to disguise her chagrin. He saw that she had long since realized all the implications of his immunity to the Dust. With a faint blush, he put the box back in his pocket.

It did not seem a propitious hour to continue their conversation from the garden.

Tired and out of sorts, confused by her own tumultuous emotions, Sera went up to her bedchamber early, ostensibly to make certain that her gown and her bonnet were in perfect order for church on the morrow.

Her temper grew worse when she could not find the little necklace of sea-ivory and gold, which she had removed the day before—on what perverse impulse she was not quite certain . . . perhaps lest his lordship should suppose he could take her for granted—and had not remembered to put on again this morning. She thought she had put it away, very carefully in a drawer . . . was firmly convinced that she had closed the drawer immediately afterwards . . . but rifle through her gloves, her handkerchiefs, and her stockings as she might, the necklace was not to be found.

Sera stood back from the chest of drawers, trying to remember. Perhaps she had placed it in another drawer? That hardly seemed likely; her memory for these things was always very good. Nevertheless, she searched through the other drawers, through every chest and cabinet in her room, even—growing a little frantic—through Elsie's room as well, in case the necklace had been accidentally transferred when Elsie borrowed a lace scarf or a pair of gloves . . . all without success.

With tears of frustration stinging her eyes, Sera sat down hard on the edge of Elsie's bed. Had hobgoblins taken her necklace for the sake of its glittering gold? But hobgoblins did not open drawers or cabinets. They only took what people left lying carelessly about, as though they actually felt compunction about stealing what others treasured. That was why Sera had taken such care to put the necklace away in a drawer.

She clasped her hands together. Hobgoblins did not *open* drawers, but perhaps they might take something from a drawer that was already standing open? *Had* she left the drawer open, earlier in the day, when extracting some item? She certainly did not remember doing so, but perhaps in some moment of distraction, when the ivory charm was no longer on her mind . . .

One thing was certain, Sera thought miserably. If the hobs had taken her necklace . . . Skelbrooke's gift . . . it was irredeemably lost.

26.

In which Jed and Mr. Jonas receive Visitors, both Welcome and otherwise.

In the workshop behind Mr. Herring's establishment, Jed and Mr. Jonas were hard at work, busily reconstructing their fabulous machine. They had worked so industriously these last few days, they had very nearly completed their task. Nor had any further damage occurred to set them back, possibly (they thought) because Mr. Jonas had rigged a trap over the door, and they set it to spring on any intruder each night before they went home.

When someone rapped briskly on the door at the front of the shop, Jedidiah and the gnome exchanged a puzzled glance. They had not expected company, and Mr. Herring, naturally, possessed his own key. But Jed put down his hammer and his nails and went off to answer the door, coming back a few moments later, very warm and indignant, followed by Moses Tynsdale.

Mr. Jonas greeted this intrusion with a frown—an expression rarely seen on his broad, good-natured face. In combination with his curving horns, the effect was surprisingly formidable.

"He insists—*most* vociferously—that he won't go home without gaining a look at the 'infernal' machine we are building here," Jed briefly explained.

When not in the midst of some violent harangue, the clergyman always conducted himself with perfect formality, and this occasion was no different. "Indeed," he said, with a stiff bow and a dark glance. "And a fiendish mechanism it looks to be."

Jed leaned against a wall and folded his arms across his chest, as though it were necessary to confine those big active limbs of his in order to prevent them from taking violent action. But

Mr. Jonas went back to calibrating the delicate instruments on the machine.

"If that is how it appears to you, I beg leave to tell you: you are greatly mistaken," the gnome replied dryly. "You might call it, rather, a celestial engine."

Tynsdale paced a circle around the machine, continuing to fix it with a brooding eye. His nostrils dilated as he caught a whiff of brimstone. "I apprehend that it has some connection with the pagan ruins up on the hill?"

"There is some tenuous connection," replied Mr. Jonas, measuring the distance between two of the magnets. "And we are not unearthing a pagan ruin on Spyglass Hill, but the remains of a chapel dedicated to the worship of the Nine Seasons."

"I stand corrected," said the Reverend Tynsdale, coming to a halt. He clasped his hands behind his back and stood rocking back and forth from heel to toe. "And perhaps you will also be so obliging as to explain to me just what precisely you intend to do with this device."

At this, Jedidiah could no longer contain his outrage. "Burn and blister him! He has no right to come here and question us this way, curse his impudence! *He's* not the vicar, and *we're* not obliged to answer his questions."

"No more we are," said Mr. Jonas. "Though I must suppose that his calling in some sense justifies his curiosity—at least in his own mind. The device is harmless, Mr. Tynsdale, you may accept my assurance of that. As to its precise function . . . I shall not trouble you with an explanation, for it is very complex and you would not understand the half of it.

"And I must beg your indulgence," he added, with a stiff little bow of his own. "Mr. Thorn and I were just finishing up. The hour is late and we are eager for our beds. So if you would be so kind . . . ?"

Mr. Tynsdale stalked out in high dudgeon, and Jedidiah went after him to bolt the door.

When Jed came back into the shed, he found Mr. Jonas sitting on a stool beside the device, surveying his handiwork with a thoughtful frown.

"Word is leaking out," said Jed, thrusting his hands into his pockets. "Our activities are hardly a secret anymore. And we may be called to account yet. I wish I had held my tongue, or at least contrived to be more polite. The temper of the town is not very pleasant, these days, with all the fuss and bother over hobgoblins, and we have seen how successfully this fellow Tynsdale is able to stir up a mob."

"Nevertheless," said Mr. Jonas, "until we are called to account for our actions publically—which we may still avoid, yet—we must maintain such secrecy as we are able. It would not do to trumpet our intentions before the whole world."

Sera walked into church the next morning, on Francis Skelbrooke's arm. As usual, his lordship succeeded in charming everyone he met—and as it developed, there were a great many who attended early morning service at the little white Church of Seven Fates, who were eager to make the acquaintance of such an elegant gentleman.

Sera had to admit that he looked very fine, in a suit of primrose satin, with a malacca walking stick carried in one hand, and a tricorn hat with a feather panache. His hair was immaculately powdered, he was delicately scented with bergamot and neroli, and he had placed one tiny patch, in the shape of a five-pointed star, under one eye.

Beside him, Sera felt very dowdy and countrified, in her cherry-striped poplin and chip-straw hat.

After church, Sera took him up past the gravestones to the top of Spyglass Hill, that he might view the floors of the ruined chapel. Most of the rubble had been cleared away, and the tiles beneath were all scrubbed clean. Besides the border of stars and comets, the gilded boats and balloons full of interplanetary travelers, they had uncovered a seascape filled with strange plants and fantastic aquatic creatures, some of them (so said Mr. Jonas) not natural creatures at all, but certain to be mechanical in origin.

Lord Skelbrooke took a pair of scissor eyeglasses out of his pocket and examined a picture—it appeared to be a silver-plated whale equipped with wheels and portholes—which (according to Mr. Jonas) could only be meant for an underwater vehicle.

"Dear me," said his lordship, quirking an eyebrow. "I cannot imagine how anyone ever mistook these for the work of savages!"

Sera regarded him with a puzzled frown. Along with his fine clothes, his hair powder, and his scent, he had also regained something of his old affected manner. As had happened so often before, Sera did not quite know what she ought to make of him.

They left the cemetery, walked down the hill, and started across the green, on their way to Mr. Herring's cottage to meet with Jed and Mr. Jonas. As on most Sundays, Moses Tynsdale held forth in his customary spot, at the base of the statue of Henry IX. The rector of Seven Fates, the mild and saintly Mr. Bliss, steadfastly refused to share his pulpit with the rabble-rousing Tynsdale.

As they drew near the marble statue, Skelbrooke suddenly stiffened. "That man, Miss Thorn . . . do you know him?"

"Why, yes," said Sera, wondering why he should speak so sharply, stare at the clergyman so fiercely. "That is the Reverend Moses Tynsdale . . . the itinerant preacher."

His lordship continued to frown. "His name is not Tynsdale, it is Hooke," he said grimly. "He *was*, I believe, at one time a clergyman, but no sooner ordained than defrocked. He is not at all a proper person for you to associate with."

Sera smiled disbelievingly. "Because he is here pretending to be someone he is not?" She lowered her voice. "But it seems we all use assumed names these days . . . it has become the merest commonplace. Perhaps he—like the rest of us is trying to hide himself."

His lordship took her firmly by the arm and led her down a street—in quite the wrong direction as it happened, but Sera was not paying attention, either, being most forcibly struck by this masterful attitude, which she liked rather better than his earlier pose of lazy elegance.

"Considering what bad odor he was in with the authorities, when last we met, I can readily imagine that he wishes to hide himself," fumed Skelbrooke. "Indeed, I am astonished to find him so brown and healthy—I should have expected something along the lines of a prison pallor. For which reason, I repeat, he is a very dangerous man, and not a proper person for you to know!"

Sera refrained from the obvious retort. Instead, she asked curiously, "You are well acquainted, then, with this Hooke or Tynsdale?"

"There was a time, to my sorrow, when we were intimately acquainted," Skelbrooke replied brusquely.

"But you are not . . . by any chance . . . united by ties of blood?"

His lordship was plainly startled at being compared to the swarthy Tynsdale. "By the sacred Powers, no! Do you mean to tell me that you perceive some resemblance?"

"Not . . . any similarity of feature or figure," said Sera slowly. "But sometimes . . . one of expression."

Skelbrooke's grip on her arm had not slackened. "Euripides Hooke and I once shared some remarkably painful experiences. It was not a time in my life that I care to remember. One supposes these experiences leave their mark."

His mood lightened considerably when Mr. Jonas and Jedidiah took him off to their workshop to view their engine. He examined the device through his eyeglasses, plainly delighted by it. And he asked a great many questions—questions which Jed and the gnome were more than happy to answer, thinking it natural that his lordship should take a proprietary interest in the whole enterprise . . . after all, it had been Skelbrooke himself who first stole the Duchess's parchment and turned it over to the Glassmakers.

Afterwards, walking back to Mothgreen Hall, Sera asked if he intended to sail with Jed and Mr. Jonas on their "treasure-hunting expedition."

"I most certainly do," said his lordship. "But surely . . . That is, I understood that you and Miss Elsie were to come along as well."

"Yes," said Sera, with a sigh, "I fancy we did promise something of the sort."

My lord was thoughtful and silent for a time after that. "You do not like the enterprise," he said at last. "That is not to be wondered at, considering your family history. I believe that you would rather dismiss these matters as errant nonsense than risk animating your own interest by examining them dispassionately," he guessed shrewdly. "Again not to be wondered at. But if I may say so, and without any wish to offend, perhaps your grandfather was not very wise in the *manner* in which he approached the mysteries."

It was a sultry day, and Sera removed her gloves, stripping them off and jamming them impatiently into her reticule. "My grandfather . . . whatever success he may have enjoyed at the end, with the creation of the homunculus . . . my grandfather not only wasted his entire substance—a modest but comfortable fortune—in a quest for the mythical stone Seramarias, but it also seems likely that his sudden death came as the direct result of a lifetime pursuit of hidden knowledge. Nevertheless, he was not a young man, and he had seen a good deal of life and the world! I wonder if you are really so very much wiser than he was?"

Lord Skelbrooke inclined his carefully powdered head. "Your grandfather was a secretive man, too proud to take the advice of other men, men who had already successfully traveled that same dangerous path he meant to follow."

Sera was silent, remembering how Mr. Budge had told her once that Lord Skelbrooke was also a proud and secretive man.

"No, I cannot claim to be wiser than your grandfather was," his lordship continued, as the road led them through a shady copse of birch trees. "But I do, occasionally, rely on the advice of friends who *do* have that wisdom . . . men like Mr. Owlfeather, Mr. Jonas, and Master Ule.

"And as for wasting my substance . . . with all due modesty, there is nothing at all moderate about my own fortune. I should have to be quite spectacularly foolish in order to waste the half of it. If you marry me, Sera, I can safely promise that you will never want for anything."

Sera's color fluctuated from red to white. It was an annoying habit he had, continually declaring that he was willing to marry her, but never actually *proposing* straight out. And she finally remembered why she had once disliked him. She did not find it agreeable, this dreadful, pulse-pounding, heart-fluttering state that he always induced in her (*Like the girl in some overwritten romance,* thought Sera) . . . or anyway, she knew that she *shouldn't* enjoy it, and that was much the same.

"And whatever gave you the idea . . . Mr. Carstares . . . that I wished to marry a wealthy man?"

The road led them out into the sunshine again. "Well, in any case, I believe you are far too sensible to think of marrying a man who was likely to ruin himself. I wish to reassure you on that point. And I do not think you would actually *dislike* being a baron's lady and living a life of ease. I own a fine old country estate, back in Imbria, and also a house in Lundy."

Sera flashed him a look of anxious inquiry. Truly, he was such a bundle of contradictions, she had difficulty trusting him. "I had thought the plan was to take up your studies once more and practice medicine on the continent of Calliope."

"Indeed yes, for a time. And then afterwards to return home and raise a family on my ancestral estates . . . providing that plan meets with your approval."

"And your present . . ." Sera hesitated, wound the strings of her reticule tightly around her fingers. "I suppose one might call it an occupation . . . do you plan to continue that as well?"

"By no means," said Skelbrooke. "I rather think that I have abandoned that trade already."

Sera sighed deeply. "Yet you do still carry the Sleep Dust with you."

His lordship refused to meet her eyes. "I do not carry it for the sole purpose of rendering my adversaries instantly unconscious. And it is . . . really quite a harmless vice."

"Yes, I believe it is always so, with those who pursue these destructive habits," Sera said, with a bitter smile. "They always strive to convince themselves that it is no great matter."

27.

Wherein the Duchess suffers a Bereavement, and Jarl Skogsrå makes Wedding Plans.

At Stillwater Hall, the Duchess struggled valiantly to maintain those niceties of existence she had known in Thornburg and at the Wichtelberg in Zar-Wildungen. And a struggle it was: not only did the situation of the house militate against her, but all the servants she had hired in Moonstone were slovenly and lazy. No decent housekeeper, butler, or chamber maid could be possibly induced to set foot in an establishment as damp and ramshackle as Stillwater Hall.

Nevertheless, the Duchess did her best. She slept late each morning, drank a cup of chocolate at noon, played with Sebastian for about an hour, then dressed (with the aid of the maid-servant she brought with her from Wäldermark) and descended the stairs to the gloomy drawing room sometime after two o'clock.

Today, she found a fire already burning on the hearth, evidence that someone had come down before her. The lazy servants never bothered to kindle a fire or draw the curtains except in the presence of direct and immediate instructions. She found a handful of letters on the drawing room desk and carried them over to a broken-down velvet sofa near the fire.

She was still reading the first of these letters when Thomas Kelly walked in. "How vexing this is!" she said, without looking up, though she waved him toward a chair. "Captain Kassien writes of considerable difficulty outfitting the ship as I have requested. That seems odd, for my instructions were simple and clear. I fear that one of us will have to go up to Turtle Bay and speak with him, and discover exactly what the problem may be."

Now, Kelly might have told her that no problem existed—that the letter was, in fact, a forgery—but of course he did not do so. Nor did he imagine that Captain Kassien would disabuse her, by denying all knowledge of the letter when the Duchess confronted him. The sorcerer knew (as the Gracious Lady did not) that the good Captain was addicted to the bottle, and did not always *remember* everything he had or had not done.

"I daresay I shall have to go myself," she added, tossing the letter aside. "I cannot trust poor Skogsrå to handle the matter . . . he is not good for much just now. Mr. Hooke is otherwise occupied, and as for you—well, you do not seem to have *much* to occupy you after all, but nevertheless . . ."

"It is true that other people do not find my presence . . . reassuring," said Kelly. "Indeed, they tend to grow uneasy whenever I am near. Yes, you had best attend to the matter personally."

The Duchess picked up another letter and slit it open with a tiny knife. She had only read a line or two when she cried out in distress. She continued reading, right on to the end, and then took out a dainty lace handkerchief and wiped her eyes. Kelly was interested to note that her mouth trembled and genuine tears sparkled on her cheeks. Such a display of emotion, he had imagined, was quite beyond the Duchess's sensibilities.

"The Duke is dead . . . to think that he has been dead all these weeks . . . and without knowing anything about it, I have been a widow in very truth," she said. "How I shall miss him!"

Kelly raised a skeptical eyebrow. "Miss him? But perhaps I labor under some misapprehension: you and the Duke have lived apart these ten years and more, have you not?"

The Duchess made a tiny gesture. "Ten years . . . what is that? I visited him as often as I possibly could. And before that, when he had his health . . . we lived together quite—quite amicably for forty years. Yes, we were married for half a century! None of my other husbands lasted nearly so long," she added, with a mournful shake of her head, "though the Duke was not a young man when I married him."

She looked at Kelly with a touch of defiance amidst her grief. "I was devoted to him, you know, for all my infidelities."

Kelly was not inclined to argue, for the point really did not interest him. "And what will you do now?"

The Duchess put up a little white hand to wipe a tear from her cheek. "I am not quite certain. The house in Thornburg is mine, and my solicitor informs me that the Duke left me a considerable sum of money. But the Wichtelberg and the bulk of his estate must go to that dreadful nephew of his. I never did like that young fool, and he is rather an old fool now—so I cannot suppose I will be asked to live with him. The lawyers will handle the details . . . and perhaps I shall not return to Wäldermark at all."

She smiled tremulously. "I have never lived so long in one place before—people do become so curious when one does not *age,* and though my fairy blood is not a well-kept secret, I have never cared to have my origins generally known. But I need not decide anything at once. I must have time to think. This is really a dreadful blow . . ."

A tear dripped down her nose and fell in her lap. "One thing I do know: I shall not marry again. They do not last long enough, these poor fragile humans, and I could never be happy with a full-blooded fairy . . . they are so stiff and stern and careful of their dignity, they can spend days poring over their musty old rituals or studying their tiresome genealogies!"

The sorcerer was not entirely certain what form of comfort she expected. But she seemed to expect something, so he made such effort as he was able. "You might, one supposes—after a suitable period of mourning, and if you find living alone intolerable—you might marry one of your own sort."

The Duchess looked up at him, her eyes still shining with tears. "My dear Mr. Kelly, there is none like me—not in all the world. We hybrids are each unique. No, I fear that I must grow accustomed to living alone."

She put up her handkerchief and blew her nose, a surprisingly prosaic gesture. "I may begin my new life by settling here in the colonies. Or perhaps go back to the northern counties of Imbria, where I was born. There can be no one there now who could possibly remember me. Yes, I shall go home, at least for a while," she said, with a sudden decision.

"Once all debts are settled, once I have prosecuted my rightful vengeance, then I can begin anew, at peace with all the world."

Skogsrå came downstairs to join them for dinner an hour later; he lurched across the vast dining hall, his limp more pronounced than ever. He had finally dressed himself, in crimson velvet and point lace, with an enormous gold brooch at his throat; he had even made some attempt to dress his hair in the old way, with the golden lovelocks hanging down to his shoulders; but he lacked his usual meticulous elegance, and his boots needed polishing. He bowed to the Duchess, inclined his head in the direction of Thomas Kelly, and took a seat at the far end of the long table.

One of the sullen and dirty servants from Moonstone brought in a covered dish and thumped it down on the table before him. The troll removed the lid, eyeing distastefully a massive portion of nearly raw beef. Yet once he set to work, the shoulder rapidly disappeared.

Kelly ate very little—a small piece of bread and a sip of port or canary wine was all that he ever required. However, he was lacing that wine now with natron and balsam, to slow down the process of decomposition. The Duchess scarcely touched the food on her plate, and soon withdrew, with the indigo ape trailing behind her, leaving the two gentlemen to share the port and whatever masculine confidences that might occur to them.

"The Duchess leaves for Turtle Bay in a day or two," said Kelly. "Her journey there and back again, as well as any business she may transact along the way, will keep her away for a week at the least."

The Jarl brightened. "You have arranged this?"

"I have," said Kelly, uncorking the flask in which he kept the natron, and pouring a little into his cup. "Though by good fortune, a second letter arrived today, quite unexpectedly, informing the lady that the Duke of Zar-Wildungen is dead."

Skogsrå stared into his wineglass. "That would explain why the Gracious Lady appears distraught. A merciful release, some might say, but not likely to appear so to the Duchess. I believe she was greatly attached to him."

"So she informs me," Kelly said coldly, glancing down the length of the table with those hard, dull eyes of his. "It could not have happened at a better time. Not only does the Duchess remove herself on account of the letter that *I* arranged to be sent to her . . . but her grief may conveniently distract her for some time to come. When she returns to find you and your monster gone, she may lack the energy for an immediate pursuit."

"That is so," said Skogsrå, pouring another glass of port for himself. He spent a moment in pleasant contemplation of his approaching nuptials: the service . . . the gown . . . the minister. Then he bowed to the sorcerer. "But you are arranging this—it is for you to say how we shall proceed from here."

"First, you must select your bride," said Kelly. "For that, it will be necessary to go into Moonstone. I hope the effort is not beyond you?"

"I have already selected my bride," said the troll, smiling for the first time in days. "And she does not live in Moonstone."

28.

In which Sera accepts a Most Pressing invitation.

The hobgoblin furor, set off by the collapsing clocktower, gradually died, and life in Hobb's Church (despite Mr. Tynsdale's efforts to the contrary) slowly returned to its customary placid course . . . until the arrival of a traveling musical consort caused a brief flurry of interest among the more genteel inhabitants, who forthwith planned a series of "cultural" evenings, to be held at the church.

To the first of these events, Miss Barebones and the ladies at Mothgreen Academy were most particularly invited—an olive branch, perhaps, on the part of those citizens who had treated them badly during the recent troubles.

Of course they all of them planned to attend—but Elsie suffered a dizzy spell in the morning, spent the afternoon lying down in her bedchamber with a throbbing headache, and though she felt better by suppertime, reluctantly decided that she had much better spend the evening at home. Quite naturally, Dr. Carstares was delegated to remain at her side in case of a relapse.

And so he deserves, presenting himself as the sympathetic physician on every possible occasion! thought Sera. But it proved unfortunate for Elsie as well. Had there not been a doctor in the household, Jed might have been asked to stand guard, and they might have spent a pleasant evening together in the parlor, chaperoned by the chamber maid and the garden boy. As it was, Sera sent a note to Jedidiah, informing him that she, Miss Barebones, Miss Eglantine, and Miss Fitch required an escort into town, and could he oblige . . . ?

Then she went upstairs to change into the newly repaired straw-colored satin. She had been forced to rip an entire panel out of the skirt and replace it with a fresh length of fabric . . .

194

but the dress looked very well. Particularly combined with a pair of lace gloves, a cameo brooch, and a wide-brimmed hat of black straw, tied with pale yellow ribbons. All that was wanting to complete the outfit, Sera thought with a pang, was her missing sea-ivory necklace.

She experienced a pang of another sort when she went downstairs and his lordship held up his scissor lorgnette to examine her gown. "Magnificent, Miss Thorn! I quite envy your brother the privilege of escorting you. Would that I might go in his place!"

Jedidiah arrived in plenty of time, driving a borrowed carriage. Jed also appeared to advantage in a suit of bottle-green velvet, quite the gentleman indeed, with his brown hair lightly powdered and a black satin ribbon at the end of his pigtail.

Jed took Sera aside for a private word and showed her a pistol and a long knife that he carried. "Merciful heavens," said Sera, with one hand on her heart, eyeing the pistol mistrustfully. She knew perfectly well that Jed was handy with a knife. "I suppose you intend to defend me from the Duchess if the need should arise. But have you any idea how to use that—that dreadful object?"

"I have," said Jed, with a wide grin. "It is a gentleman's weapon, you know, and I have been acquiring the habits of a gentleman. Also," he added, "I've a loaded fowling piece under the seat of the carriage."

"Well," said Sera, pluming her feathers a bit, "you must suit yourself. But I have noticed that Lord Skelbrooke, for all his cautions, never sees fit to arm himself when he and I go out for a walk."

"No, he does not," agreed Jed, with an even broader grin. "That is . . . if you don't count the twelve-inch blade concealed in his walking stick, the stiletto stickpin in his cravat, the two or three small pistols he carries about his person, and the explosive pocket watch!"

Which at least provided some method to his lordship's overpowering finery—and perhaps (thought Sera) he was not quite so vain as he might appear.

"He sounds a perfect walking arsenal," she said. "I perceive that my own precautions have been quite unnecessary." And she opened her reticule to reveal a scimitar-shaped letter-opener she had culled from Uncle Izrael's effects.

Jedidiah gave her an amused glance. "Do you plan to *stab* somebody with that piddling little thing?"

"I do," said Sera, with a challenging light in her eyes. "Do you imagine that I lack the nerve?"

As it developed, neither guns, nor explosives, nor letter-openers were required during the ride into town. They arrived in Hobb's Church quite safely, and Jed helped the four ladies to descend from the carriage.

The weather had turned exceptionally warm, and all the doors of the church stood wide open, in the hopes of attracting any evening breeze. For all that, the church was stifling when they entered. Most of the seats were already filled, obliging Jed and the Mothgreen ladies to take separate pews.

The first entertainment on the program was the traveling string quartet, playing music in the pastoral mode. Sera sat with her hands in her lap, listening with deep appreciation. But half an hour later, when Madame Castiglione from the music school stepped up to the platform to sing operatic arias, the church had grown so unbearably hot that Sera could not resist slipping out for a breath of fresh air.

It was the fault of the straw-colored gown, of course—why had she foolishly dressed in silk, instead of muslin or cambric like most of the other women? She had planned to impress Lord Skelbrooke, of course, before she had learned he would stay behind . . . and this was what came of her wicked vanity. For all that, she refused to sit meekly in a pew the whole evening long, to be boiled in her silken gown.

Sera glanced longingly in the direction of Spyglass Hill, for it seemed to her that it must be breezier, and therefore cooler, up on the heights. If she dared to venture so far into the dark alone . . .

It was then that something small and furtive, moving about in the shadows, caught her attention. There was a second skittering, about a dozen yards from the place where she stood, and a scratching on one of the rooftops—it seemed that the square was alive with hobgoblins!

Sera felt a tug at her skirt. Looking down, she was greatly astonished to see a young hobgoblin clinging to her skirt with a tiny clawed hand, staring back up at her with what could only be described as a pleading gaze.

Really, thought Sera, the creature appeared so harmless and forlorn, she could hardly view its actions as threatening. With a glance back over her shoulder, to make certain that no one observed her, Sera stooped down to speak to the hobgoblin.

"I daresay that you cannot understand a word I say . . . but I must tell you, you risk yourself quite foolishly here. Go back to your tunnel with all haste, before somebody sees you and sends a stoat or—or a nasty little terrier after you."

But the hobgoblin continued to pull at Sera's skirt and make tiny, incoherent noises, as if anxious to communicate.

"My good creature," hissed Sera, taking several steps away from the church. "I do not speak a word of your language . . . that is, supposing that Mr. Barebones was not mistaken, and you do *have* a language. But whatever it is you mean to tell me—"

Just then, another hobgoblin stepped out of the shadows, dangling a chain and a little ivory-colored object, which it waved back and forth in a tantalizing way . . . and then loped off in the direction of the hill.

"You wretched little thief!" exclaimed Sera, recognizing her missing necklace. Lifting her skirts, she immediately gave chase.

Halfway up Spyglass Hill, her usual good sense returned to her. It was ridiculous to suppose that she could catch the hobgoblin and wrestle her necklace out of its grasp . . . dangerous to be running about at night, all on her own. Sera paused to catch her breath and consider the situation. The hobgoblin ran on ahead for a moment, seemed to notice that she no longer followed, and then stopped, too.

Only a small and tremulous moon shone in the sky. But the night was clear and a thousand brilliant burning stars provided sufficient light for Sera to make out the hobgoblin's scaly face and form, as it perched on a gravestone and continued to dangle her necklace. It *might* be the very same hob that she and the others had rescued . . . or again it might not. One knew so little of hobgoblins and their distinguishing features.

But it did not appear to be at all vicious . . . or even particularly mischievous, for all that it continued to hold up the precious necklace in such a teasing manner.

"You mean to lead me up the hill . . . madness to follow, for it might well be a trap," said Sera. Yet any idea that the Hobb's

Church goblins and the Duchess of Zar-Wildungen could possibly be in league was so utterly fantastic . . . "Very well, you horrid little beast. I do want that ivory charm back, and if that means taking a look at whatever it is that you want to show me, then so it must be."

And perhaps some other little hob had been injured . . . or was otherwise in distress. Perhaps these others had come to her seeking her aid. Sera gathered up her full skirts and petticoats and proceeded purposefully up the hill.

The hobgoblin led her through the grass between the gravestones, all the way to the windy summit and the ruined chapel. Sera gave a gasp of astonishment, for a section of floor was missing. A large stone slab to which the tiles were cemented had been simply lifted and moved aside, revealing a set of stone steps, which apparently led down into the heart of the hill.

"Did Jedidiah and Mr. Jonas discover this?" she asked herself aloud. "No, I think not, for I should know if they had. Jed could hardly have kept the news to himself. But what a remarkable discovery—I wonder where it leads? It would be folly to descend . . . yet how intriguing the prospect!"

The hobgoblin had ducked into the hole, then skittered out again, an exercise the creature repeated again and again, evidently meaning her to take the hint and follow the steps down into the earth.

Sera was still hesitating, with one foot on the top step, when Jed finally caught up with her. Huffing and puffing—for he had run up the hill without pausing to catch his breath—he scowled at her ferociously. A full minute passed before he regained enough breath to begin to scold her.

"Of all the hare-brained . . . Whatever possessed you, I'd like to know, to leave the concert? As soon as I seen you was missing . . . I went out into the square. And when I couldn't find you there, I reckoned the Duchess had sent someone along to whisk you away . . . 'til I chanced to look up and seen you here, silhouetted against the stars, like . . ."

"Jed," Sera flashed back at him, "I wonder if it is possible for you to scold me without lapsing into some dreadful river dialect? I really think you—"

"Lucky for *you*," said Jed, continuing on exactly as before, "you wasn't spirited away. Lucky for me, because how on this earth was I to explain, to Elsie and his lordship, how I ever come to let you run off? You wanted a walk in the air, you should've asked me to come with you."

"Yes, I suppose I should have. But I never meant to venture even a dozen feet from the door," said Sera. And she proceeded to explain to him, over the chirping of perhaps dozens of goblins down in the hole, exactly what had occurred. "This is evidently a passage leading down into the caverns. I am not afraid to follow, but—"

"—but you're a d--n sight too sensible, praise the Powers, to go down into the caves without so much as a candle to light your way," Jed finished for her. He considered for a moment, shifting from one foot to the other, and back again. "I suppose I could go home, fetch a lanthorn and a rope, while you stay here to . . . No, I can't. I can't leave you here alone."

"I won't be alone," said Sera, gesturing toward the dark hole. "There seems to be a tunnel full of hobgoblins down below, and I do believe they are favorably disposed.

"No, do not show them your pistol . . . you might frighten them off," she protested, as Jed reached inside his coat, meaning to offer her the weapon. "They have been shot at and stoned and exploded so often. Besides—you know that I haven't the least idea how to handle a pistol. Just hurry, Jedidiah! It is growing quite late. And it would be dreadful if the hobs grew discouraged and simply disappeared without showing us any thing!"

Jedidiah returned, perhaps a quarter of an hour later, bearing a length of rope, two lanthorns, and a piece of chalk. To Sera, of course, it seemed he had kept her waiting for ages.

"Hope they don't mind if I make a few marks as we go along. We don't want to get lost . . . supposing these steps really *do* go down to the Deeping Caverns," Jed puffed, for he had run both going and coming.

"Whatever you wish," said Sera, giving his arm an impatient shake. "Only let us not stand here talking, but light the lanthorns at once!" For the chattering and scrabbling down in the hole had ceased, and Sera was afraid the hobgoblins had deserted her.

Jed handed her a lighted lanthorn and then lit one for himself. Then they both made haste to descend the stairs, stumbling a little in their eagerness. Part way down, they found a pair of hobs huddled together on a narrow landing, waiting to lead them farther.

The steps were not only damp but crumbling at the edge, making it necessary to take each one carefully. The stairs went down and down for several flights, and then ended at a great iron door, set into a stone archway.

Sera drew a sharp breath. "I suppose it must be a tomb. What else, indeed, could those who built the original temple have meant it for?"

"I don't know," said Jed, lifting his lanthorn high, in order to illuminate the whole of the mysterious portal. "But as wet as it is down here . . . you would think after nigh onto two thousand years, the door would be eaten by rust. There's a spell on this iron, I'll wager.

"I suppose," he added, with a sigh and a sideways glance, "there's no use telling you this is no proper adventure for a young lady? No use offering to take you home, and come back later with Mr. Jonas and Lord Skelbrooke?"

"Not the least good in the world, I thank you very much!" said Sera, with a toss of her head. "I mean to see this all the way through."

The door stood open about six inches, just enough for the hobs to pass through, but it was necessary for Jed to shove it a bit further, in order to make room for himself and Sera.

They stepped through into a lofty chamber, evidently a natural cavern much enlarged and modified. It was undoubtedly a tomb, and by no means a primitive one. All the stalactites and stalagmites had been carved to form stylized pillars . . . a series of marble vaults, very ornate, lined the original walls . . . and down the center of the chamber marched a procession of onyx catafalques, some with the bones still lying in state. A second arch appeared to lead into another similar chamber.

"Catacombs!" said Jed, with a kindling eye. "And unless I am mistaken, the very same Panterran ruins that old Mr. Barebones described in his paper. I guess he wasn't such a crank as the people in these parts are inclined to believe."

"But why didn't he ever *show* this place to anyone?" Sera wondered, as they strolled through the chamber, examining the mysterious letters and the figures carved in high relief along the walls. The Panterrans had dressed in a surprisingly modern fashion: swallow-tail coats and long, tight breeches for the men . . . wide skirts and startling low necklines for the women, entirely exposing their breasts . . . and great preposterous hats and wigs for both sexes. "If he had done so," said Sera, "surely no one would have dared to doubt him then."

"It may be these caverns lead into the hobgoblins' tunnels," said Jed. "In that case, he didn't want people to come poking about and disturbing the hobs. He did have a fondness for the creatures, you know."

"As well he might," breathed Sera. She stopped where she stood, clutching at Jed's arm. "Jedidiah! The hobgoblins knew we took an interest in the ruins, and they led us to this place on purpose. They must . . . oh, they must be more intelligent than people generally suppose.

"But how are we to prove that to the people up above?" she asked, the light dying from her eyes. "Who will believe that we didn't stumble on this place by accident, and then convince ourselves that the hobgoblins meant us to find it?"

"I don't know," said Jed. "But it appears the hobs may have something in mind. See over there by that archway . . . it looks like we haven't yet seen everything they mean to show us."

Indeed, the two goblins who had already escorted them so far were now jumping about impatiently and gesturing wildly.

"Jed . . ." gasped Sera. She had been too occupied, up until now, with the treacherous steps and the wonders of the tomb to take a good look at the hobgoblins escorting her. "Jed . . . it looks like one of them wears . . . yes, one of them sports a grotesque little garment—a kind of a coat, I think! I never heard yet that hobgoblins were inclined to dress themselves."

"Neither did I," said Jed, "but we already know these native hobs are different from the kind back home."

"Very true," said Sera, continuing to clutch at his arm, so great was her excitement. "And it seems to be that we may be about to discover just exactly how different they are!"

29.

In which our Story continues in a Subterranean vein.

Jed and Sera followed their queer hobgoblin escorts through one branching chamber after another, until they came to a tunnel, so low and so narrow, it could hardly be meant for full-sized Men. Sera had only to lower her head, but Jedidiah, being so much taller, had to bend over at the waist in order to enter, and he continued on thereafter with a pronounced stoop.

The wide skirts of Sera's gown brushed the sides of the passage as she walked, and the hem kept catching on projecting roots and sharp-edged rocks. *It will be little more than a filthy rag, by the time that I come out of here*, she thought, with a sigh. It did seem that the silk gown was doomed to destruction, one way or the other.

Tunnel after narrow tunnel, chamber after chamber, opened off that wider way. Most of the chambers were dark, but in every tunnel Sera saw tiny woven hanging baskets, stuffed with a phosphorescent green moss, which lent a dim illumination. The goblins were artisans, she realized, and these crude little lanthorns bore witness to their craft.

"If hobs can see in the dark like cats and dwarves—as I suppose they must—I daresay these passages seem bright enough to them," she said, pausing for Jed to catch up with her.

She directed her lanthorn into the nearest chamber. On shelves and niches all around that room were nests of straw and woven twigs. A sort of drowsy twittering, that rose to an irritated chattering, seemed to indicate she had inadvertently disturbed the sleeping inhabitants. Sera withdrew her lanthorn, and she and Jed continued on, following their hobgoblin hosts.

Somewhere, a long way off, Sera heard a roaring and a booming, like the rush of mighty waters. It came to her then that these tunnels must indeed open into the Deeping Caves, and what she heard now was the rush of an incoming tide echoing and reechoing through cavernous chambers. But as the tunnel led gradually downward, the roar of the waters faded.

Sera soon grew weary, walking with her head down and her neck bent lest she brush against the rocky ceiling, but she said nothing—imagining how very much worse it must be for Jed, following behind half in a crouch. "For the Fates' sake," she heard him say, "if you get too tired or you want to go back, just say the word."

Just as though, Sera thought indignantly, she were some frail and fading female. "Thank you," she said, "but I shall do very well . . . unless the tunnel gets lower. If that happens . . . well, I don't see how I can possibly manage to crawl along at any great rate, hampered by all these petticoats."

As they walked on, it seemed to Sera that there was some plan or design to the branching tunnels, the many small adjoining chambers, and though the plan itself continued to elude her, a faint sense of pattern and form took hold of her mind. A dwarf or a gnome might comprehend the plan . . . as it would also take a dwarf or a gnome (Sera thought) to appreciate the full magnitude of the hobgoblins' labors.

"There must be hundreds of tunnels here under the hill, and if they extend from here, under the entire town. There must be thousands of hobgoblins, perhaps tens of thousands of hobs," she exclaimed. "May the Fates preserve us! For all their accommodations strike us as primitive, I believe we are traveling now through a great hobgoblin city. But how do they contrive to live down here? They can't survive solely on rats and mice and moles . . . nor the little bits of food they may scavenge up above—not such a multitude of them."

"We know these tunnels open on the sea—we could smell the saltwater a short time back," Jed said behind her. "They may eat fish . . . and the roots of plants and trees up closer to the surface. Though, still, that hardly seems enough." Jed had also been considering the matter, as they went along. "Sera, I have it! They eat old wood. It's not casual mischief that leads them to gnaw at the posts in the foundations of the buildings up above."

"If they eat wood," said Sera, panting a bit, for they had come such a long way already and the hobgoblins set a rapid pace, "why don't they steal footstools and walking sticks, instead of the frippery items that so strongly appeal to them. I believe I know . . . they *do* eat live rosebushes when they can get them, but as for old wood: I think they eat termites and wood worms (as Oranian savages sometimes do) and they gnaw the posts to get at them."

At long last, the tunnel opened into a high-ceilinged chamber. With a great sigh, Sera assumed an upright posture and glanced around her. An extraordinary sight met her eyes, rendering her momentarily speechless—as Jed was also affected, when he came out of the tunnel and unbent with a groan of relief.

This chamber was vast—on an altogether grander scale than the caverns up above, and illuminated by torches and bonfires. Amazingly, it resembled nothing so much as a crowded marketplace . . . aisle upon aisle of stalls and shops made up of twigs and twisted roots, and a great multitude of chattering hobgoblins running about from place to place, conducting their business.

Sera's eyes grew wider and wider as she attempted to take it all in. There were stalls displaying more of the basket lanthorns, while others were heaped with the glowing green moss. Sera spotted a goblin selling crude wooden bowls, and another hawking mats (blankets? rugs?) made of plaited straw and colorful bits of thread and yarn. There were stalls offering shells, and hobgoblins selling feathers, and shops displaying shining trinkets—evidently stolen from the town up above. There was one stall, less pleasant to behold, in the manner of a goblin butcher shop, with rats and mice and small birds (and something that looked suspiciously like a skinned weasel) hanging from the twiggy rafters like so many plucked fowl or sides of beef. In an adjoining booth, an old she-goblin hawked tiny garments sewn from the skins of moles and ground squirrels.

And by now it was abundantly clear that the hobs *had* taken to dressing themselves, after their own fashion. About a third still ran about naked, but the rest wore anything from a single garment to an entire velvet gown or satin suit—all very gaudy and fine, adorned as they were with ribbons and feathers and laces, with beads and silver chains and bits of gold braid. Strange, even fantastical apparel, these garments of the hobs, though Sera fancied she saw some resemblance to the styles worn by Men and gnomes and dwarves.

Eventually, she recovered her power of speech. "Jed, if we had any reservations before, there can be no doubt now that the hobs are truly Rational creatures!"

"Yes . . . but they haven't acquired any *genuine* sense of decency—or half of them wouldn't be running about buck naked," Jed replied, over the excited chatter of their hobgoblin escorts, who kept leaping about at their feet, pointing and gesturing, as though to call attention to the many excellent qualities of their goblin goods.

"No, they cannot have any inherent modesty," said Sera, still looking about her; there was so much to see, she could not have seen it all had she explored the market for days. "But I believe that a love of—of ornamentation is one of the traits that distinguish the sentient races from the beasts. What do the Glassmakers say, Jedidiah?"

"Aye . . . I believe I've heard something like that. And something I do remember: dwarves and Men and gnomes, they're the Artisan Races—united by the common delight they take in the work of their own hands. It seems we share that with these hobs as well," said Jedidiah.

But then he added: "These creatures may have attained a dim rationality, but if they had any *sense* at all, then why did they build their city here—under the town—and not out in open country where they could live unmolested?"

"Because . . . because they somehow feel attracted to us," said Sera. "You see how they copy our clothes and ape our manners." Indeed there was a group of hobs, male and female, who seemed to have got up some sort of a quadrille in the center of the market, and were dancing gaily to some silent measure. "Jed, I believe they have been *changing* . . . perhaps slowly at first, down all the ages, but more rapidly during the last several decades. And the more civilized they become—why, the more they feel drawn to us, despite the danger."

They never knew how long they spent in the hobgoblin market, exploring the shops, examining the offerings of the goblin craftsmen. Jed had a watch, but forgot to consult it until the end, and then he was horrified to discover the hour hand pointing to midnight. "They'll be in a rare taking up above . . . certain the worst has befallen us both," he said, replacing the watch in his satin waistcoat. He slipped his coil of rope back over his arm and shoulder, then picked up his lanthorn again and took Sera by the hand.

"Yes," she said, with a weary sigh. "I suppose we had better go back now. You did mark the way that we came?"

"I did," said Jed, as they started back toward the tunnel. "And took note of every turn as well."

This time, Jedidiah led the way, while Sera followed behind. It was slower and harder going uphill, and by now they were both exhausted. Jed's green velvet coat had a rumpled look; he had scuffed his shoes, and one brass buckle was missing— a fortunate find for some lucky hobgoblin. As for Sera, the hem of her gown was tattered and dusty, the dress was beyond repair—yet she accounted that as nothing, for she now wore the sea-ivory necklace safe around her throat, where she meant it to stay forever. The goblin who had lured her into the caverns with it had returned the charm, with a grand flourish and a very creditable attempt at a bow.

"We must tell the people up above," said Sera. "We must bring some of them—those we can trust—down here to see the goblin city for themselves. Mr. Jonas, and Miss Barebones, and the vicar. They will understand what it all means. And perhaps—perhaps if somebody makes a real effort to communicate with the creatures . . . there *must* be some way that we can continue to live side by side, without causing each other so much trouble and grief!"

"If we *could* speak to them," Jed replied morosely, for as weary as he was he could not help taking a grim view of matters, "there is no guarantee that we could then convince them to leave off their chewing and their digging and their thieving ways—nor that our people would like them any better, once they knew the truth. We don't mix much with fairies, or selkies, or kobolds, you know . . . we display an unconquerable prejudice against trolls and giants, for all they are as intelligent (or near as intelligent) as we are."

"Fairies and selkies and kobolds and the like cherish their own concerns, far removed from ours," said Sera, trudging along with her head down. "It would not make sense for us to mix with them, or they with us. And as for giants and trolls— really, Jed, they *eat* people, as you very well know. Whereas these creatures are only . . . only destructive and, I regret to say, rather light-fingered."

"But there you have it," said Jed. "Honest citizens don't feel much sympathy for 'thieving rascals,' not even their own kind. If people up above learn of this hobgoblin city, if folks accept that the hobs are Rational Beings, then they may come down here, some fine day, with their guns and their hobstickers, round up a dozen or more hobgoblins dressed up in stolen finery—and string them up like so many pickpockets or housebreakers, as an example to the rest!"

By now, they had reached the catacombs again and could walk upright, side by side.

"Very true," said Sera. "Yes, they might do something like that. So we must be very careful whom we tell, just at first. But Jed," she added very earnestly, "if the Power that created these creatures intended them to grow in wisdom and in stature until they grew fit to live as companions to Men and dwarves and gnomes . . . then surely it would be *sinful* on our part—now that we know so much about them—not to make every effort to effect an accommodation."

"I won't argue religion with you," said Jed, stifling a yawn. "The more so because I am half way inclined to agree with you.

"And it seems we *have* been chosen, by the hobs themselves, to act as their emissaries to the world up above," he added thoughtfully. "I guess we are, in some sense, obligated to carry the word. But we won't be very popular, you know, not with all the folks who have been preaching extermination!"

But the word "preaching" set Sera to thinking. "You know, Jedidiah," she said, as they emerged from the hole at the top of the hill and came out into the starry, windy night, "I believe there may be a number of people who will be much *inclined* to listen to everything we have to say . . . thanks to the ranting and the theological posturing of that mountebank—Hooke, or Tynsdale, or whatever his name is—who may have inadvertently prepared the way for us.

"Yes," said Sera, with a dawning smile. "We may be able to turn his sermonizing to very good account!"

30.

In which Moses Tynsdale plays the Villain.

Too exhausted to tell the half of what they had learned, Jed and Sera put the whole narrative off until the next day, when their friends gathered together in the parlor at Mothgreen Hall. As Jed had predicted, their story produced varying reactions. Mr. Jonas, Miss Barebones, and the Reverend Mr. Bliss—who had been treated, along with Lord Skelbrooke and Elsie, to the whole tale—proved both sympathetic and eager to learn more. A night-time visit to the hobgoblin city easily convinced these kindly souls to espouse the hobs' cause. Others, like Mr. Herring and the gentlemen of the Guild, who received a less complete narrative a day later, had reservations, but allowed that the matter certainly bore further examination.

Many strange stories began to circulate through the town, but at least the Guild members proved discreet, and Jed's and Sera's names did not circulate with them. Moses Tynsdale was in his element, making all that he could of the situation—on what mischievous impulse, Skelbrooke could scarcely imagine—but on the whole, and as Sera predicted, his efforts did the "Hobgoblin Party" more good than harm. What the end result of all this might be, no one could tell, for it was too large an issue to be settled overnight, but Sera and Jed, in private consultation, agreed that the situation looked promising.

"It was just so simple to call the hobgoblins 'vermin' and treat them accordingly," said Sera. "But now that we have forced the good citizens of Hobb's Church to really *think*, they will keep *on* thinking and asking questions until they finally reach the truth."

Of course, Sera came in for a good deal of scolding at Mothgreen Hall. Miss Barebones held the minority viewpoint: "Miss Thorn and her brother were perfectly safe the entire time, for Uncle Izrael was undoubtedly with them. And now that we have discovered his secret, dear Uncle Izrael can rest in peace." And perhaps she was right: the Academy was so surprisingly quiet in the days that followed that it began to look like the ghost (and the goblins as well) had finally been laid. But Elsie was very much shocked by all the risks that Sera had taken—and said so, in no uncertain terms—while Francis Skelbrooke said less, but made his displeasure more keenly felt, by the quiet intensity of the few words he spoke.

"I cannot think you perfectly understand the danger in which you now stand," said his lordship, very white about the lips. "Or you would never have been guilty of such foolhardy behavior."

"I *do* understand the danger," Sera retorted, "but really, I cannot spend my whole life in . . . in such restricted circumstances . . . for fear that the Duchess or her minions may come upon me, anytime that I happen to step out-of-doors for a breath of fresh air."

"No one wishes to make you a prisoner—certainly not I," said Skelbrooke. "I know you are accustomed to a certain amount of freedom—more so, I fancy, than a young lady more conventionally educated would have enjoyed. But with Jedidiah and myself both eager to serve as your escort, you have no need to venture out on your own."

Out of consideration for his feelings—even more, out of a concern for Elsie, who was again very poorly—Sera kept to the house for several days, never venturing farther than the garden, alone or in company. Though Friday was Midyear's Day, she did not elect to go into town to view the festivities, and Sunday she continued to stick to her kindly resolutions, by staying home from church.

In the afternoon she was extremely vexed when Jed arrived to beg a private word with his lordship, and he and Skelbrooke went out into the garden, leaving her alone in the parlor. *As though they can better protect me by keeping me in the dark,* thought Sera. *As though I were just a child!*

But in fact, the subject under discussion under the fruit trees was one which neither gentleman could possibly have broached while Sera herself was present.

Jed began by clearing his throat impressively, as though about to deliver a carefully rehearsed speech—as indeed he was, though the speech was of the briefest.

"My lord," he said. "Since I am now acting—acting in the

capacity of Sera's brother, I believe that it is my duty to ask you just exactly what your intentions may be."

Skelbrooke smiled sweetly. He had been expecting something of the sort for some little time now. "Why, I intend to marry, Sera, of course," he said easily. "Did she never tell you so?"

Jed shrugged. "I heard something to that effect—not from Sera," he admitted cautiously. "And it set me to wondering, because . . . Well, the truth is, somebody told me once, a long time ago, that you didn't like women. Worse! That you held the entire sex in contempt."

"Ah," said Skelbrooke, contemplating the highly polished buckles on his shoes. "You had that from Hermes Budge, I think. Indeed, there *was* a period in my life when my sentiments were exactly as you have described. I should tell you, Jedidiah, that when I was your age, I fell briefly under the influence of a very wicked woman. For some time after that (I believe that I was not in my right mind) I regarded women as the source of all evil."

He glanced up sharply, looking Jed directly in the eye. "But I am not blind, I am not a fool. It did not take me long to perceive that women are as often victims as victimizers in this world . . . rather more often, I should say. I have tried very hard since then to make up for my earlier prejudice. Though even so," he continued, "a long time passed before I was willing to put myself in any woman's power by falling in love with her."

Jedidiah frowned at the dapper little figure pacing beside him. "And which, would you say, is Sera?" he asked bluntly. "Victim or victimizer?"

Skelbrooke shook his head. "I know that Sera, on account of her poverty, sometimes regards herself as the victim of circumstances, but she is so strong and courageous, that she must eventually overcome all obstacles . . . At the same time, her essential honesty, her generosity of spirit, must always prevent her from preying on those weaker than she is." His lordship smiled brilliantly. "Sera is neither victim nor victimizer. That is, I believe, her principal grace."

Jedidiah returned the smile, a trifle reluctantly. "It appears that you understand her very well, that you see her with a fair degree of clarity. But—"

"—but *you*," said Skelbrooke, "wish that Sera might also achieve such clarity in her estimation of me. Fear not, Jedidiah, she will not marry me until she does! Sera loves a challenge, but she abhors a mystery."

By Monday, Sera had become so restless in her confinement that frustration finally overcame her desire to spare those who loved her unnecessary worry. Moreover, the time was rapidly approaching when they would all pack up and set sail on the *Otter*. Easily convincing herself that she could not depart on that or any voyage without the necessities of human existence, Sera declared that she must and would go into town.

Naturally, Lord Skelbrooke insisted that he accompany her, insisted, too, that they take the gig, which had arrived an hour earlier with Jedidiah when he came to pay a call on Elsie. It appeared that Jed's resolution to part with Elsie had not stood the test of time . . . or, at least: had not served to conquer his very real concern about her failing health.

"I suppose you imagine I am like to be run down by a mail coach or a diligence if I should so much as set my foot down in the road," said Sera, holding herself very stiff and defiant. But she allowed Skelbrooke to help her up into the light carriage, and silently arranged her feet so as not to bump against Jed's antique fowling piece, under the seat.

"You will be so good as to direct me toward whichever shops you prefer to visit," said his lordship, as they entered the town.

Sera (who really had no place particular in mind) cast about for a minute before she remembered something that she needed to buy. "I should like to visit Mistress Morgan's establishment first, if you please. I am in dreadful want of hairpins, and I simply cannot set sail without them."

"Of course," said his lordship, amiably enough, "one quite understands the burning necessity."

It was only as he held the door of the shop open for Sera to enter and she passed under the mermaid figurehead that she realized her mistake. Besides hairpins, ribbons, and laces, Mistress Morgan also sold silk stockings, garters, and other intimate feminine trifles—it was not an establishment often frequented by the male sex, and certainly not one which a young lady might wish to enter in the company of a gentleman.

Sera blushed, but swiftly decided that a hasty retreat would only make matters infinitely worse. While his lordship folded his arms, leaned up against a counter, and proceeded to entertain a number of very pleasant fantasies, Sera purchased her hairpins, declined to examine any of Mistress Morgan's other intriguing wares, and swept out of the shop. Skelbrooke was mightily amused by her discomfort and had the poor taste to show it.

"And where next, Miss Thorn?" he asked cheerfully, tipping his hat. "I daresay there is someplace in town where you can purchase pomade and hair powder . . . and I am reliably informed that gloves and lace mittens are to be found at Madame Rush's."

Sera did her best to crush his impertinence. "I thank you, Mr. Carstares, but of course I shall be needing none of those things. I do, however, wish to visit Mr. Jakobson's bookshop. I have the desire for some improving literature."

"But naturally, Miss Thorn," his lordship replied sweetly, "I myself refuse to embark on any voyage without a full philosophic library on board." And Sera eyed him suspiciously, wondering what imp of mischief currently animated him.

They were strolling down the street after their visit to the bookshop when Sera called out in surprise. "Mr. Carstares . . . how extraordinary! Is not that Elsie walking with Mr. Tynsdale?"

The young woman in question wore a gown of white tiffany tucked up over a pale blue petticoat, altogether in Elsie's style, and she wore also a straw hat with a gauzy veil, scarcely adequate to disguise her features. But more than that, even at a distance, Sera knew her cousin's posture, her movements, her—well, some traits are simply indefinable, and Sera knew all of Elsie's. Yet hadn't she left Elsie, pale and exhausted, sitting in the garden at Mothgreen Academy, with the solicitous Jed at her side . . . not more than an hour since?

As the girl in white and the itinerant preacher turned down a side street, Sera hurried to overtake them and gain a better look, and Skelbrooke, perforce, came along with her. "It *is* Elsie," said Sera, as they turned a corner. "But how comes she to be with Mr. Tynsdale, whom she knows to be dangerous and deceitful?"

She called her cousin's name but received no answer, Elsie and the clergyman continuing on, quite oblivious to her cries. Sera and Skelbrooke had closed the distance to less than fifty yards when Moses Tynsdale and Elsie climbed into an old-fashioned cabriolet drawn by two horses, and set off at a great pace. But as she stepped into the carriage, the girl had turned her face in Sera's direction, and Sera had recognized not only her but also the odd blankness of her expression.

"She looks just as she used to do, when Lord Skogsrå was magnetizing her," said Sera, with a sinking sensation.

"It is evident," said Skelbrooke, detaching his arm from Sera's "that Euripides Hooke has her somehow in his power . . . equally evident that we have just witnessed an abduction. I will pursue them in Mr. Herring's gig."

Sera ran after him down the street, glancing back over her shoulder as she did so, searching the street for a glimpse of a passing constable. Naturally, there was no lawman on hand in this moment of need.

"*I* shall come with you," said Sera, climbing up into the gig beside his lordship.

"I beg your pardon, Miss Thorn, but you must do nothing of the kind," he said. "I fear that I shall be driving headlong into great danger."

"Do you think I care anything for that, when Elsie may have need of me?" Sera asked.

Lord Skelbrooke sighed deeply and flicked the reins. There was plainly no time for them to argue the matter.

But as they bowled down the road in the direction of Moonstone, with the cabriolet still a long way ahead of them, he said: "Once I have managed to regain your cousin, you may do all you like to offer her comfort. But until then, I beg you—nay, I must command you—not to interfere in my attempt to rescue Miss Elsie. Though you may mean to aid me, you will only hamper my efforts."

"I am well aware of that, and I promise not to interfere," Sera said breathlessly. "Being 'only' a female, I have no experience of—of dueling and brawling."

"Dueling and brawling?" Lord Skelbrooke raised a shapely eyebrow, his hands tightened on the reins. "Is that how you imagine we men keep ourselves occupied? What poor creatures you must think us! Or is it only me you consider so—so lamentably violent in character?"

"Well," Sera temporized. "I don't suppose that boys like Jed have much opportunity to behave so . . . they are far too busy getting their living. It is probably only the gentlemen who have the leisure to occupy themselves in that manner."

The cabriolet had disappeared around a bend in the road, which skirted a hillock covered with low brush. As they, too, rounded the bend, they were astonished to see the cabriolet stopped in the middle of the road, apparently waiting for them. Lord Skelbrooke reined in and managed to bring the gig up at a safe distance.

"The blinds are drawn. This looks very much like a trap," he said, pulling out a pistol and cocking it. "Are you quite certain that it *was* your cousin? I see that you are—and surely it would take more than an altered face, a mimicked walk, to deceive you.

"Trap or no, we can hardly leave Elsie to the mercy of her abductors," he added grimly. "And I believe I am equipped to handle Mr. Hooke and whatever confederates may have been riding concealed in the cabriolet." Jumping lightly down into the road, he pulled out a second, larger pistol. "You, however, are not to follow me under any circumstances, and had far better occupy yourself with turning the gig around."

"I will not increase your danger by disobeying you," said Sera, as steadily as she could. "But my lord . . . do take care!"

As Skelbrooke advanced toward the ominously silent cabriolet, Sera climbed down, took the horse by the bridle, and coaxed him to turn back in the direction they had come. She was heading back toward the gig when the doors of the cabriolet suddenly burst open and Tynsdale jumped out, followed by two rough-looking men clad in buckskins and armed with stout wooden clubs.

Sera watched over the broad back of the horse as Skelbrooke came up short, then gestured with one of his pistols. "Two of you are dead men," he announced coldly, "unless all three of you throw down your weapons immediately."

A shot came whizzing out of nowhere, striking him in the shoulder, spinning him around with the impact, and knocking him to his knees. The larger pistol fell from suddenly slackened fingers, exploding harmlessly in the road. While Skelbrooke slumped forward, for the moment dazed, one of the bearded ruffians stepped up, whipped around his cudgel, and brought it crashing against the side of his lordship's head. Sera watched impotently as Skelbrooke pitched face-forward and lay very still on the ground.

Glancing frantically about to see where the shot had come from, Sera looked up the hill just in time to see a third figure in buckskins, standing in the bushes, discharge the second barrel of his flintlock rifle. Again, his aim was accurate. The gig horse collapsed in the traces, felled by a ball between the eyes.

Sera did not scream—though she was strongly tempted. Instead she climbed hastily into the gig and snatched up Jed's fowling piece from under the seat. But then, realizing the futility of any attempt to hold off four men with a single weapon—particularly one loaded with bird shot—she threw down the gun, gathered up her skirts, and jumped from the carriage. Landing in the gravelly road, she stumbled, recovered, and took off across the fields in the direction of Mothgreen Academy.

She had run perhaps a quarter of a mile over wretchedly uneven ground, stumbling and tripping, hampered more than a little by her long skirt and petticoats, when she heard shouts and pounding footsteps closing rapidly behind her. She ran on without slackening her pace, still determined to outdistance her pursuers. Even when she heard the more solid fall of approaching hoofbeats, and guessed that someone had unhitched the lead carriage horse and come galloping after her, she continued on doggedly, though her breath was ragged and she knew that she was nearly spent.

A strong arm came down and swept her up, struggling wildly, onto a broad grey back. Sera scratched, bit, and gouged at her captor's eyes.

"I have only to release my grip on you, you deplorable vixen, and you will undoubtedly break your back, if not your neck, falling from the horse," hissed Mr. Tynsdale.

Realizing that he spoke the truth, Sera ceased to struggle, and instead clung tightly to Tynsdale's coat while he brought the horse around with some little skill (they were riding bareback) and headed back toward his confederates. But when the pace slowed and the horse came to a halt, when Tynsdale prepared to dismount, Sera squirmed out of his grasp—unfortunately landing in the arms of one of the bearded roughnecks, who not only stank of bear grease but handled her none too gently in his efforts to subdue her. He finally succeeded by the simple expedient of pulling her arms sharply behind her and maintaining a hard grip.

Moses Tynsdale dismounted at his leisure and looked her over with an appreciative eye. "What a glorious creature you are!"

Sera, with her hair tumbling down, the right side of her face smarting from an open-handed blow, and her dress ripped and falling off her shoulders, did not *feel* glorious. "If you dare to lay so much as a defiling hand on me . . . !"

Tynsdale only grinned at her, in a thoroughly insolent manner. His hat had blown off and his dark hair was ruffled by the wind of their wild ride; his white teeth flashed in his sunbrowned face; he did not look at all like the clergyman she knew, but like an unknown and altogether more elemental, more *dangerous* individual entirely.

"I believe that a rape—of sorts—is intended. But I, alas, am not the man destined to enjoy you. Do hasten to bring me the spirits of mandragora, Hancock, before the young lady does herself any serious damage."

"If you are not abducting Elsie and myself on your own behalf," said Sera, trembling with indignation, "then who *is* responsible for this outrage?"

Again there was that flashing smile. "Miss Elsie, in fact, has not yet been abducted," said Tynsdale, as one of his henchmen produced a reeking piece of cloth. "As for you: I am taking you to Stillwater Hall at the behest of a gentleman who admires you most ardently. A gentleman by the name of Jarl Skogsrå."

Someone shoved the rag over her face, and the world began to grow grey around the edges. Tynsdale's voice continued on mockingly, as the darkness enveloped her. "Only fancy, Miss Thorn . . . or should I say Miss *Vorder*? You are soon to be a bride!"

31.

Which finds Sera and Lord Skelbrooke in Desperate Straits indeed.

Sight and sound returned slowly, and with them came a whirling vertigo. Sera lay quite still until the room settled around her; then she sat up slowly and carefully and studied her surroundings.

She had been lying diagonally across a big four-poster bed, as though someone had brought her there and simply tossed her down. The bed was in a dim, high chamber, very warm and humid, and the velvet bedcover smelled strongly of mildew. The only light came filtering in through a tall lattice window, mostly obscured by thorny black-berry vines.

"And so you finally awake. How do you do, Miss Vorder?" The voice, so cold and precise, was familiar, though Sera could not immediately place it. In a deeper patch of shadow across the room, a lean figure rose from a chair and glided in her direction.

"Thomas Kelly . . . it *is* Kelly, is it not?"

For answer, the sorcerer bowed his head. "Indeed . . . I apprehend that it was Caleb Braun who told you that, after the regrettable incident with the poker. How does Mr. Braun, I wonder?"

"I have not the least idea," said Sera, removing a strand of dark hair that had fallen across her face. "I've not set eyes on him since that day you mentioned. Though I am naturally relieved," she added tartly, "to discover that you know no more of his whereabouts than I do." She stifled an urge to ask about Skelbrooke, to plead for reassurance that he was still alive. She knew that any such show of weakness would do neither of them any good. "But really, Mr. Kelly, this is most unexpected—I can scarcely call it a pleasure. I understood that I was to meet Jarl Skogsrå."

Kelly continued to regard her with those odd eyes of his. "Mr. Hooke told you that, did he? I had no idea he had such a loose tongue. But yes, you shall meet Jarl Skogsrå presently. Skogsrå, the Duchess of Zar-Wildungen, and I have recently joined forces . . . a natural enough consequence of our shared objectives.

"I hardly need to tell you that the Jarl is very eager to see you," Kelly went on. He put a hand on the nearest bedpost. "But I wanted to speak with you privately first. Poor Skogsrå is likely to become rather emotional—one might almost say irrational—at the thought of your approaching nuptials. And we had hoped to welcome you here much earlier . . . so inconsiderate of you not to go into Hobb's Church for the Midyear's festivities, or again on Sunday for the holy services. You put poor Skogsrå into a fever of impatience."

Mr. Kelly smiled mirthlessly. "But then, I need not tell you. You were present, as I was not, when he sought to marry your cousin Elsie. I have been told that his actions on that occasion were exceedingly rash. But what, after all, can one expect from a troll in the grip of his overmastering obsession?"

"I hope," said Sera, putting her feet on the floor and managing to stand, though her knees still felt deplorably weak. "I hope that you are here to tell me exactly what I may expect of this one."

Kelly inclined his head. "I must suppose you mean to inquire about the wedding ceremony itself. You could hardly wish to discuss the intimacies awaiting you in the bridal chamber afterwards. Well then, I shall—"

"—I *mean* to inquire: by what means does Haakon Skogsrå imagine that he can possibly induce me to consent to marry him?" said Sera, reaching for the support of a bedpost. This action brought her much closer to Kelly than she would have liked, close enough to catch the odor of balsam and natron, and the cloying breath of corruption beneath. As soon as she was steady again, she stepped stepped away.

"I have—I have studied the subject of troll weddings and I am well aware that the species of matrimony which Skogsrå intends requires a consenting bride. And I believe that I have already proven myself immune to Jarl Skogsrå's powers of suggestion.

"I hope you do not mean to threaten me," she added, dark eyes flashing, "for the truth is, I would far, far, rather—"

"—die. That is the usual response, I believe," the sorcerer finished for her. "Pray do not play the heroine with me, Miss Vorder. Perhaps you *would* rather die than suffer the troll's loathsome embraces, but I remind you that Miss Elsie Vorder is also in our power, to say nothing of your paramour, Lord Skelbrooke. I feel certain you would not wish to see harm come to either of them."

Sera shook her head—which was a mistake, as it made her feel dizzy all over again, and caused her to reach for the bedpost once more. "I am not altogether certain that you *have* Elsie, and as for Lord Skelbrooke . . . your ruffians may have killed him, for all that I know."

"Miss Elsie is here and Lord Skelbrooke has so far been spared. The greatest care was taken to capture him without killing him," said Kelly. "I think you might at least be grateful for that."

"Nevertheless, I will not discuss the matter further," Sera insisted, "until I have first seen both of them alive."

"Very well . . . if you would have it so," said Kelly. He crossed the room, opened a door, stuck his head outside, and issued some low-voiced orders. Meanwhile, Sera glanced desperately around the shadowy bedchamber, looking for anything she might use to defend herself.

Kelly turned away from the door. "You search for some heavy object with which to strike me over the head. That trick will not work a second time, for you will find nothing of the sort here. I am become more cautious, you see. And you possess an indomitable spirit, Miss Vorder, but just at the moment, I think not nearly the strength necessary to make an escape.

"You will feel much better if you will just take a seat on the bed and await further events."

Recognizing the sense in this, Sera did as he suggested. A minute later, the door opened wide, to admit Jarl Skogsrå and Elsie—and a moment later, a very pale and shaken Lord Skelbrooke, who came in with his hands shackled together in front of him, at the end of a pistol in the steady grip of the rugged Mr. Hancock. Skelbrooke was in his shirt sleeves, with one arm in a sling, and Sera could see that his brocade vest and linen shirt had been stained by a copious flow of blood.

Because Tynsdale had alerted her to some possible deception, Sera took a closer and more careful look at the young woman in white. She realized, with a shock, that it was not Elsie, after all. "You attempt to deceive me, but I know my cousin better than that. This woman does resemble her . . . indeed, the resemblance is quite remarkable: she even stands and walks like Elsie. And yet—"

"—and yet, on closer examination, your intuition tells you that this is not she," Skelbrooke finished for her, leaning wearily against the wall.

Jarl Skogsrå made a sound of disgust. "I told you how it would be. They are more different, the two of them, Elsie Vorder and my Cecile, than you and the Duchess like to imagine."

Mr. Kelly fixed him with a hard gaze. "Lacking your intimacy with the monster—and only claiming the briefest acquaintance with Miss Elsie—I am not disposed to contradict you."

Skelbrooke drew in a sharp breath. "This is not some woman you have disguised by your arts: it is Elsie's double, a figure of clay that you have animated in her image with a few drops of Elsie's blood. No wonder you were fooled, Sera, if only for a time."

Kelly bowed stiffly from the waist. "You are very knowledgeable, very perceptive . . . Indeed, I wonder that a man so clever and experienced as yourself chanced to fall into our simple little trap. I must suppose that it was overconfidence that brought your downfall."

Lord Skelbrooke, meeting Sera's anxious gaze, shook his head. "My arrogance rather," he said, sick with the knowledge of his own failure. "I cannot ask your pardon, Sera, for I do not deserve it. But I do offer my most abject apologies for bungling the matter so thoroughly."

"Pray do not regard it, my lord," said Sera, attempting a brave smile. "I do not hold you in any way to blame."

"Very touching," sneered the Jarl, throwing himself down into the chair that Kelly had vacated earlier. "Oh, but exceedingly moving. Well, as you have guessed, we do not have Elsie in our power. But as for your lover . . . you see that we have him entirely at our mercy. He shall die if you do not consent to marry me."

"He lies," said Skelbrooke. "They cannot mean to kill me themselves. There can be no doubt that I am reserved for the Duchess's personal revenge."

"We do not act on the Duchess's orders," said Skogsrå, ignoring Kelly's signal for silence. "The Duchess was called away . . . her servants have been dismissed during her absence . . . our own men brought in—"

"In that case, I am as good as dead already," Skelbrooke said bitterly. "You will hardly leave me alive to tell the Duchess what you have been doing while she was away. She has her own plans for Sera, Elsie, and me . . . and I fancy that you are spoiling them all." He looked across at Sera, and his eyes grew tender. "Dear heart, you must decide for yourself whether you wish to prolong your life—and perhaps gain some narrow chance of escape later on—by marrying Lord Skogsrå. But do not do anything of the sort on my behalf, I beg you. I am fully resigned to die."

"You are a fool," Kelly told the troll. "Pray hold your tongue after this, and allow me to arrange the matter, as I have promised. You are quite right, Lord Skelbrooke, you are doomed in any event. But the manner of your passing is still open to question. Your death can be quick and merciful—if Miss Vorder chooses wisely—or else lingering and painful—if she refuses to cooperate. I hold no personal malice against you, but do not imagine on that account that I would hesitate to put you to the cruelest torture to gain my ends. As for Jarl Skogsrå . . . I think you comprehend the warmth of his regard!"

"Sera," said Skelbrooke, speaking through his teeth. He grew paler with every passing minute, and beads of perspiration formed on his brow. "Whatever they do to me, you must not regard it. Believe me, I have suffered far worse, in the past, than anything they could possibly contrive for me."

"Do you think so?" said Kelly. Reaching into a pocket in his waistcoat, he brought out the little box that was not a snuff-box. "But we do not intend to exert our persuasions immediately. Yes . . . I know what this box contains, as I know something, also, of the action of the drug. I can see that you miss it already.

"We can afford to wait another four and twenty hours—not only to give you and Miss Vorder ample opportunity to contemplate your fate—but also because, by the end of that time, your mind and body will betray you, your senses will become so extremely heightened that even the mildest discomfort will trouble you exceedingly, while as for the exquisite tortures we mean to inflict on you . . . well, I leave you both to imagine."

On Kelly's orders, the buckskin-clad Hancock produced a second pair of fetters and fastened them on Sera. Then she and Skelbrooke were escorted down two flights of stairs to the cellar and into a storeroom.

The room was dirty and smelled of damp, lit only by a barred window high in the wall, at ground level. There was a straw tick on the floor, stained with blood . . . some blankets . . . and Skelbrooke's hat and coat . . . also very bloody. Sera realized that while she had rested unconscious up above, his lordship had been less comfortably confined down here.

"I wish you joy of each other's company in the time remaining to you," said Kelly, standing in the doorway. "Comfort each other in whatever manner seems best to you . . . the strength of your attachment can only aid our purpose. But do not deceive yourself, Lord Skelbrooke, that you can rob Jarl Skogsrå by depriving Miss Vorder of her virtue, for I must tell you (and you will pardon me for speaking so plainly) that though he certainly intends to make her his wife in every sense of the word, he does not care a pig's a-- about her maidenhead."

Lord Skelbrooke and Sera sat silently, side by side, on the mattress on the floor, while the light coming in through the barred window grew fainter, and evening shadows gathered in the locked room. After about an hour, Moses Tynsdale came in with a laden tray and a lighted candle.

He grinned at Sera. "Your bridegroom is naturally solicitous."

"Mr. Tynsdale . . . it may amuse you to contemplate the fate which no doubt awaits me. But perhaps you do not know that they intend to *murder* Lord Skelbrooke. Abduction and deceit are obviously not beyond you, but I should never have taken you for a hired killer."

Tynsdale stood in the doorway for several minutes, his dark gaze fastened doubtfully on Skelbrooke's face. "You are correct. I am a spy, not a hired killer. In order to maintain the rôle I have assumed—how convenient a cover for my true activities his lordship can tell you—I have worked much mischief . . . yet I daresay no one has taken any serious harm. If Skelbrooke must die, I shall make every effort to see that I am not selected to do the job. I may even feel some slight regret—in light of our former association—after his passing, that it was I who brought him here. But it will not trouble me for long . . . believe me, I have far worse things on my conscience. Were that not so, I should still be in solemn fact the clergyman I pretend to be. And as for helping the two of you escape, as you seem to be suggesting, my goodness does not extend nearly so far."

He placed the tray on the floor, near the foot of the mattress, and left the storeroom, locking the door behind him.

Sera examined the contents of the tray. There was a wooden tankard filled with water, and a covered plate containing quite a good supper: beef and eggs and bread and fruit. It appeared that Lord Skogsrå was indeed solicitous. It would not suit his purpose to have his bride fainting from weakness in the middle of the ceremony.

"Lord Skelbrooke," said Sera, as they shared the meal between them, "you would not have your pocket watch or—or anything similarly useful about you?" She felt reluctant to speak too plainly, for fear someone was listening at the door.

"No," said Skelbrooke bleakly. "I regret to say that Euripides Hooke relieved me of all such . . . useful items."

They ate in silence for a time. Then Skelbrooke lay back on the mattress with a deep sigh.

"My lord, you look so pale and you tremble so violently," said Sera. "I am convinced that your wound troubles you exceedingly."

"The ball was removed and the wound cleaned and bandaged while you were upstairs. It does not trouble me very much. The symptoms you notice are the effect of the Sleep Dust . . . or rather, the result of enforced abstinence," said Skelbrooke. "I have now been some twelve hours without the drug. The habit has been growing on me, over the last two years especially, and I am accustomed to take a pinch in the morning and in the afternoon, and a larger dose before I retire. I neglected to take the afternoon dose because—well, it scarcely matters."

"You did not take a pinch this afternoon because you were with me, and you did not like to take out the box, for fear I should see and disapprove," said Sera, with bitter self-reproach.

"As you had every reason to do. It is a most pernicious habit, for all that I told you ôtherwise." He winced as he shifted his position on the mattress. "It is only right to warn you that my condition is like to grow very much worse before the end. But Mr. Kelly was entirely correct: another day must pass before the hallucinations and the other . . . unfortunate effects begin. When that time comes—when that time comes, I beg you will discount anything I may say to you, as the ravings of a madman. I shall not care for anything or anyone but myself, my . . . awareness of self . . . being so acute. But whatever they may do to me, whatever I may ask of you, you must not do anything against your inclination."

Sera turned her face away, so that he could not see how profoundly his words had affected her. "Lord Skelbrooke," she said very steadily. "I shall not deceive you. I had far rather die than marry Lord Skogsrå and submit to his—how peculiarly and dreadfully appropriate the phrase!—his carnal appetites. But I shall not stand by and watch them abuse you, when my compliance may spare you pain. I love you, my lord, far too well for that."

32.

In which Jarl Skogsrå becomes Singularly persuasive.

They passed a long, miserable, restless night on the straw tick, lying on their backs side by side. Once, Sera woke to find the bed next to her empty; she heard movement in the darkness at the foot of the mattress. When she spoke his name, Skelbrooke whispered back reassuringly.

He lay down beside her again and spoke directly in her ear. "I did not wish to say anything earlier, for fear we were somehow watched or overheard . . . perhaps I should not speak now, lest I raise false hopes when I have not formulated any plan. Though my pistols and pocket watch and other weapons are gone, there remain several small items sewn into the seams of my coat. One of them, a magic talisman dedicated to Triunc, the Patron Fate of Prisoners, I have removed and hold in my hand.

"How I may use it to our advantage," he whispered, "I do not yet know. But I am skilled in the use of talismans and the spells associated with them. I may be able to accomplish something. But if I do not"—Sera felt something small and cold pushed into her hand—"here is a vial of poison. Sera, you are not to do anything rash! You cannot poison Skogsrå by swallowing *this* before he feeds on your blood—but if you should find an opportunity to slip the contents of the vial into the wedding cup before Skogsrå drinks . . ."

"Yes," Sera whispered back. "I understand." And she slipped the little glass vial inside her corset, next to her heart.

In the morning, as the light began to creep back into the room, my lord lay very still and silent on the mattress, staring up at the ceiling, his mouth set in a hard straight line, and his lips very white.

Sera bent over him. "Lord Skelbrooke . . . Francis . . . is there anything I can do to ease the pain in your shoulder?"

"Yes," he said softly, and surprised her by taking a hold of her hair and drawing her face down to his for a long, hungry kiss. Glad to offer what comfort she could, Sera responded in kind.

"Sera . . ." he whispered, between kisses, " . . . I am not yet so ill as it might appear. The pain is only a minor distraction. But it is necessary for me to concentrate . . . while I still can . . . to gather my mental forces, to activate the talisman."

"In that case . . ." whispered Sera, drawing a little away, " . . . I will not distract—"

But his fingers remained tangled in her hair. "In that case," he said against her mouth, "you may kiss me once or twice more . . . and then cease to so pleasantly distract me."

There was a faint click, the sound of a key turning in the lock, and the door creaked open. Skelbrooke released her. Blushing hotly, Sera sat up, just as Skogsrå entered the storeroom prison.

"I see you are taking Mr. Kelly's advice," said the troll. Though he spoke lightly, a frown appeared between his eyes, as though his proprietary interest in Sera might be stronger than his confederate supposed.

He closed the door behind him, leaned up against it, with his arms folded across his chest. "Well, well, I shall not allow it to trouble me. Indeed, I come to make a bargain with you, one you may like better than Mr. Kelly's proposition. You wish to save Lord Skelbrooke's life . . . I wish to marry you as soon as possible. Kelly does not dare to offer you the life of your paramour, but I may—yes, I may!"

"I do not understand you," said Sera, straightening the rags of her gown as best she might.

"Then I shall explain it. Kelly does fear the anger of the Duchess, should she return and discover how we have interfered with her plans—this is precisely as Lord Skelbrooke says." Without unfolding his arms, the troll made a slight bow. "But I . . . *I* do not intend to be here when she arrives, so it does not matter to me what she thinks. I have not—I have not been quite myself of late, and your blood, my Sera, will serve as a kind of medicine by which I may regain my strength. Then

I and the golem Cecile will go away from this place. For that reason, I am able to bargain with you: consent to marry me this afternoon, and I shall set Lord Skelbrooke free, directly afterwards."

Sera glared suspiciously up at him. She did not rise, but remained seated with her hands in her lap, the chains hidden in the folds of her skirt, for the iron cuffs shamed her, they made her so utterly helpless. "In despite of Mr. Kelly? I do not believe that you would do that. He is such a dangerous man."

"Ah," said Skogsrå, bending forward, lowering his voice to a confidential half-whisper. "He is indeed . . . not only dangerous, but treacherous as well, and I do not trust him, no, not I. Why, I ask myself, does he delay and delay? Yes, he wishes to make a kind of experiment of Lord Skelbrooke, to watch him deteriorate as the craving for the drug grows. But the Duchess may return sooner than we think, and I must be well on my way before then . . . I must be far beyond her reach."

The troll let out his breath in a long hissing sigh. "This," said Skogsrå, "should concern Mr. Kelly as much as it concerns me—for if the Duchess overtakes me, shall I not tell her of Kelly's complicity? Of course I must do so; I will not take all the blame for myself. Yet Mr. Kelly is not concerned; Mr. Kelly makes no push to bring this thing off. It would seem that this sorcerer, this walking dead man, neither wishes me to escape nor to be captured alive. When the Duchess returns, we will all be dead: myself, Mr. Tynsdale, the pair of you, as well. Then the Duchess depends on no one but Mr. Kelly, who claims the credit for striking me down in the midst of my disobedience. An act of good faith, as it seems, which will only be prelude to further betrayal when he finds the Duchess no longer of use."

Sera's heart was racing at this chance—this very slight chance. But she made a great effort to conceal her excitement, lest the troll realize how desperately eager she was to believe him.

"I do not understand you," she repeated. "Why should Mr. Kelly wish to betray the Duchess?"

"I do not perfectly understand this myself," said Skogsrå, unfolding his arms and shifting his position. "There are things which happen here that no one confides in me, but I know there is something afoot. The Duchess says she is on the verge of a great discovery—Mr. Kelly pretends ignorance, but I have seen his face in an unguarded moment. *I* know the look of a man ruled by an obsession, and I think the Duchess has stumbled on something that touches on his ruling purpose . . . the thing for which he died and came alive again. Something went wrong, Miss Vorder, when your grandfather revived him—that much I know. And he has not so very long to seek this something he wants, because he is slowly rotting from the inside out. Now it appears that the Duchess pursues the same goal. So he allows her to seek this thing, to use her wealth and influence to buy men and ships—then he will step in, at the end, this selfish Mr. Kelly, and claim all the spoils."

By this time, Lord Skelbrooke was sitting up, and listening as intently as Sera.

"You might wish to ask, if he means me to die, why lie to me and beguile me by pretending to aid me?" the troll continued. "He might strike me dead with a single touch. But it amuses him to manipulate us all, to observe our behavior, after he initiates the action. We are all matter for philosophical experimentation as far as Mr. Kelly is concerned. And he thinks me too stupid to guess what he intends, too dull of comprehension to appreciate the subtle workings of his mind. But I am more clever than he and the Duchess are willing to allow, and I am perfectly capable of seeing through his plot. For which reason"—the troll paused impressively—"if you are willing to bargain, by the time we are married . . . there will be no more Mr. Kelly."

Sera took a deep breath, released it slowly. "But that is impossible. That is, if you mean to kill him, I do not see how you hope to accomplish it. We know that he is impervious to fire and to poison, that physical violence will stun but not kill him. How, then, can there be 'no more Mr. Kelly'?"

The troll took a limping step or two in her direction. "Lord Skelbrooke has provided me with the means to destroy him . . . Yes, the exploding pocket watch, the mechanism of which Mr. Hooke so kindly explained to me. Is it likely, do you think, that Mr. Kelly can survive exploding?"

Sera and Skelbrooke exchanged a glance. "No," said his lordship, "I rather fancy that he cannot."

"Nevertheless," said Sera, "even if you should first eliminate Thomas Kelly, how can we possibly trust you to keep your end of the bargain? You betray the Duchess . . . you betray Mr. Kelly . . . how can we expect you to keep faith with us?"

"It does not matter if you trust me or not," said Skogsrå. "You must bargain with me simply because . . . because you are unlikely to find any surer means of escape. Once I have killed Mr. Kelly, you will at least know that I am so far sincere in my intentions. Marry me this afternoon, Miss Vorder, and as soon as I have toasted our union in a goblet of your blood, I shall not only set Lord Skelbrooke free . . . but you as well."

Sera drew in a startled breath. "I shall go free as well? You do not wish to—to keep me as your wife?"

"It would be amusing to do so, but I think . . . over all . . . more trouble than it would be worth," said the troll, with a bow. "Indeed, dear Sera, I have long admired you. It was you I should have wished to marry in the first place, had the Duchess not chosen poor Elsie for me instead. You do appeal to me strongly on a carnal level (I mean that in every sense of the word), but my affections are already otherwise engaged."

"But I should not *really* be free," said Sera. "I would still remain bound to you in some way, as poor Elsie remains in your power. Can you deny that it was you who came to Elsie in her dreams at night?"

"That was not due to any tie between us, believe me. That came as a function of my . . . congress with the golem. They are in some sense the same person, you know. But I was not fully aware of the implications until the evening you summoned my spiritual form to Mothgreen Hall. But you, you shall be entirely free. Yes, I swear it. Moreover, when I take Cecile away with me, Elsie will receive some measure of freedom as well."

"Why then—" began Sera. But Skelbrooke interrupted her, speaking urgently. "You must not believe him, Sera. He will not keep his word."

"Perhaps he will not," said Sera, refusing to meet his eyes. "But we must rely on him to do so. As he points out, it is your . . . our . . . only chance of leaving here alive. Of course it means that you and I cannot marry . . . and I shall quite understand if—if you do not feel the same about me afterwards, Lord Skelbrooke. Indeed, considering—considering the vile nature of the union I am about to enter into, I should not blame you at all." Here she faltered, and required a moment to regain her composure, before going on.

"Very well, Lord Skogsrå, I will marry you. Make . . . make whatever arrangements are necessary."

Thomas Kelly sat in the dining hall at the head of the table reading by candlelight a musty old volume that one of the servants had unearthed for him somewhere in the house. Every now and then, he took a sip of wine or nibbled a piece of bread.

He looked up, without much interest, when Skogsrå entered the room. "You are rather late this morning. Did you eat in your room?" But then he caught sight of the object in the troll's hand. "That is Skelbrooke's watch, is it not?"

The troll smirked at him. "You need not fear . . . Mr. Hooke has disarmed it by removing the explosive. Do you think me such a fool as to play with a live grenado?" He began fiddling with a tiny gold key. "I am attempting to discover how the mechanism works . . . It is very complex, I think."

A gleam of suspicion appeared in Kelly's dark eyes. "Ah . . . of course, Lord Skogsrå . . . no doubt you would wish me to demonstrate for you?"

The Jarl bridled, as though much offended. "Thank you, no. You think this is beyond my powers of comprehension, do you? Let me tell you, I grow tired of being treated as though I had no brains at all!" And he moved toward the other end of the table, still tinkering with the watch and the key.

"My apologies," murmured Kelly, going back to his book. "I should have known that even such a simple stratagem was beyond you."

But he looked up a minute later when he heard a small click, followed by a sharp thud, as the watch landed on the table in front of him . . . looked up just in time to see Skogsrå dodge behind a high-backed chair at the other end of the room, and catch the brilliant, burning flash as the watch exploded.

The troll emerged from his hiding place and surveyed his handiwork with considerable satisfaction. Mr. Kelly's chair had been reduced to a heap of smoking splinters, as was much of the table. As for Kelly himself . . . small bits of bone and flesh were scattered all about the room, but there was surprisingly little blood.

Skogsrå gagged, drew out a handkerchief, and held it over his nose. The air was thick with smoke, and reeking with vile odors: the sharp, acid scent of explosive powder, and the stench of mortifying flesh. Looking down, the troll discovered a nasty-looking stain on the skirt of his coat.

Jarl Skogsrå shrugged. He had intended to change his costume before the wedding anyway.

Down in the cellar, Sera and Skelbrooke felt the building rock with the explosion. Shortly thereafter, a smell of smoke and picric acid wafted in through the barred window. "It would be too much to hope for," said Skelbrooke, with a savage little laugh, "that Skogsrå underestimated the range of the blast and destroyed himself, too."

An hour later, the troll and Moses Tynsdale entered the store-room prison. Skogsrå carried two pistols, and Tynsdale the key to Skelbrooke's chains.

Tynsdale unlocked one iron cuff and roughly jerked the injured arm out of its sling. "Put your arms behind you." My lord obeyed, and his wrists were chained together once more. Sera thought she caught a glint of metal between his fingers, but in the dim light nobody else seemed to notice.

"We heard the blast," said Skelbrooke. "Yet . . . you will forgive me . . . that is really no proof that Thomas Kelly is dead."

"He was dead to begin with," said Skogsrå. The troll had dressed for his coming nuptials in the beautiful green and scarlet uniform, with white lace at his throat, gold tassels on his boots, and a scarlet ribbon tying each golden lovelock. He looked very gay and debonair. "But of course you may view the remains if you wish . . . there is not much left of him, I fear, but some of it you may recognize. I think we can spare my betrothed, however. She will trust you to make the necessary identification."

Sera shook her hair out of her eyes. She did not at all wish to make "the necessary identification," but Skelbrooke looked so ill and unsteady already. "I am not afraid—" she began, only to be interrupted by Skelbrooke.

"I am well accustomed to such sights, Miss Vorder," he said softly. "I will view the remains."

"Miss Vorder must occupy herself dressing for the wedding," said Skogsrå, as they left the storeroom and climbed the stairs. At the ground floor, the party divided. Taking one of the pistols from Skogsrå, Tynsdale led Skelbrooke away, while the Jarl and Sera continued on upstairs.

The troll threw open the door of the same bedchamber that Sera had occupied before. "You see that your wedding gown awaits you. Also, water to wash in . . . a hair brush . . . silk patches . . . and other such feminine trifles. Please make use of them; I wish you to look your best," he said, as he replaced the pistol in his coat pocket and unlocked Sera's fetters. "I regret there is no woman to assist you in dressing: the Duchess, of course, travels with her maid, and poor dear Cecile is rather hopeless . . . But if you have need—"

"Thank you," Sera said coldly. "I am accustomed to dressing myself. I daresay I shall manage."

"Then I will leave you alone—cautioning you against any foolish conduct, the penalty for which must inevitably fall on Lord Skelbrooke." And so saying, the troll bowed and withdrew, closing the door behind him.

Sera felt for the little vial of poison at her breast. *I will keep faith with Skogsrå, if he will keep faith with me. I have promised. But if he should betray me . . . if any ill should befall Lord Skelbrooke, I shall* find *an occasion to use this poison.*

Wishing to be further armed against treachery on the part of the troll, Sera searched rapidly through the toilet items on the worm-eaten oak dressing table, for something—anything—she might use against her captors. But she found nothing. Then she turned her attention to the costume laid out for her on the bed. Not a pin, not a brooch . . . And her hairpins were no good at all, they were so blunt and the wire so soft and thin. She might do more with her fingernails, if it came to that.

She could hear Skogsrå's limping footsteps as he paced the landing outside her door. He would return soon, and she must be dressed . . . She did not like to think what might happen if he opened the door to find her half clad.

Reluctantly, she washed, brushed her hair, and dressed for her wedding.

The gown was cream brocade with a low, square neckline, so heavy and outdated in style it must have been fifty years old. Perhaps it might once have been white. The bodice was long-waisted, embroidered with pearls and clouded rhinestones, and the whole gown trimmed with yards and yards of pale spider lace, growing ragged in places. Where it had come from, Sera could not guess, but it had evidently been made for a larger woman—this gown had never graced the tiny form of the Duchess of Zar-Wildungen, that much was certain.

Her bridegroom had also provided a veil and a wreath of dusty silk flowers—the colors were garish, it had not been made for a bridal wreath at all—and a diamond necklace and a matching pair of bracelets. These jewels Sera did recognize. She slipped them on with a shudder, remembering that Lady Ursula had borrowed and worn them at that mockery of a wedding feast back in Thornburg.

As her bridegroom evidently meant her to arrive bedizened, Sera made use of the haresfoot, the rouge, and the patch box, fastening a bit of black silk under one eye, another, dagger-shaped, at the corner of her mouth. This marriage was such a mockery and a farce, it suited her fancy to paint herself like an actress or an opera dancer. At last, she pinned on the veil and the wreath.

The dusty veil blurred her vision, giving her surroundings a quality like the landscape of a dream—or a nightmare. Moving as one in a trance, she walked to the door and threw it open.

33.

Which finds Sera's friends in a state of Deep Distress.

At Mothgreen Hall, the ladies and Mr. Jonas sat in the parlor (impatiently or tearfully, according to their various temperaments) waiting for Mr. Herring and Jed to arrive with word, any word, of the missing pair. At the sound of a carriage rattling up the drive, Elsie leaped up from the sofa and flew to open the door. Jedidiah and Mr. Herring walked in looking sad and discouraged. Else made a tiny sound in her throat.

"You did not find them?"

Jed shook his head ruefully. "No one was able to tell us anything but what we knew already: how they went to Mistress Morgan's and then to the bookshop; how they climbed into the gig and apparently started home—though they never arrived or were seen afterwards. We did find the carriage about five miles east of Moonstone . . . without a trace of Sera, Lord Skelbrooke, or even the horse."

"The Duchess has them—there is no doubt of that," moaned Elsie, throwing herself back down on the sofa. "There is no telling what dreadful thing she has done to them. If only there were something I . . . that *any* of us could do!"

"If the Duchess has them, they're in no immediate danger, not until the Duchess catches you as well." Jed sat down on the sofa beside her, took one cold little hand tenderly in his. "Lord Skelbrooke knows her mind, and he was convinced, you know, that the Duchess wanted you all together in the same place, meaning to work her revenge in one fell blow. So the only thing you *can* do is stay here safe, where our friends can look after you, and buy us the time we need to find Sera and his lordship."

"Yes, I know," said Elsie, wringing her hands. "But it seems such a weak-spirited thing to do. It seems as if all I ever do is mope about, letting the rest of you coddle me. I wish I could be as brave and strong and . . . and as forceful as Sera."

Mr. Jonas slid down from his own seat and stumped across the room. "Your present disability," said Mr. Jonas, "if I may venture an opinion, does not result from any natural malady, but comes from malign forces at work against you.

"And when I first met you, Miss Winter, you did not mope about, as you put it, but worked for your living and supported yourself quite independently. Nor should you reproach yourself because you have a gentle disposition," he added kindly. "Or because you are too wise to relieve your own anxiety by careering around the countryside in search of our absent friends, putting them and yourself in even greater jeopardy."

Elsie managed a tremulous smile of gratitude. "Indeed," said Miss Barebones, clutching a damp handkerchief in one hand, "I think we may yet entertain some hope of dear Sera's safe return, so long as it appears that she and Dr. Carstares are together. He seems such a capable man."

Jed also smiled, with an obvious effort. "You might just as well say that we may dare to hope for Lord Skelbrooke's safe return, so long as *he* has *Sera* to look after him!"

The sense that she was moving through some horrible dream remained with Sera as she walked down the long creaking staircase with Jarl Skogsrå and into a large, mournful chamber on the ground floor.

Lord Skelbrooke forced an encouraging smile as she entered, but he looked so strained and hollow-eyed, her heart sank at the sight of him. Mr. Tynsdale stood behind an improvised altar: a small table draped with a scarlet cloth, on which someone had placed a pair of dripping tapers in tarnished gilt candlesticks, a heavy wine goblet of chased silver, a prayerbook, and—rather a sinister touch—a pistol carefully set within Mr. Tynsdale's reach, and a long-handled knife.

At the sight of the knife, Sera shuddered, guessing how Skogsrå meant to employ it. Moses Tynsdale looked very neat and correct in his black coat, immaculate white linen, and clerical gaiters, but Sera remembered what Skelbrooke had said, "*No sooner ordained than defrocked.*" She opened her mouth to protest, then thought better of it. What did it matter, after all? It might be that even a defrocked minister would serve for a troll wedding.

Skelbrooke's haggard look continued to disturb her, as did the violent trembling of his limbs. "Lord Skogsrå," she said, with only a tiny tremor in her voice, "I wish you would remove Lord Skelbrooke's irons and allow him to assume a more comfortable position. I feel sure the wound in his shoulder must cause him considerable pain, so long as he is forced to keep his hands behind him."

"His discomfort will soon be over. For now, I prefer to see him as helpless as possible," said the troll. He spoke steadily, but his hands shook and he was nearly as white as Skelbrooke, in the grip of that strange excitement that always preceded a ritual blood-letting.

He took Sera roughly by the arm and pulled her toward the altar. In a daze of fear and disgust, Sera listened as Tynsdale read the wedding service. She gave her own responses in a low voice, heard Skogsrå reply, his voice rising high with excitement. At her bridegroom's command, she dutifully extended her arm, watched numbly as he took up the knife and skillfully opened a vein.

Then he lifted her wrist to his mouth, kissed it, and murmured a few words. "It is a spell to make the blood flow more swiftly. I am not much versed in magic . . . but this spell I know." Carelessly, he allowed the knife to fall to the floor.

Still unable to speak or move of her own volition, Sera watched her blood drip into the silver-chased goblet. Mr. Tynsdale moved uneasily in his place behind the altar. Perhaps he had not really known, until now, at what kind of service he had agreed to officiate.

When the goblet was nearly half full, and the crimson flow of blood from Sera's vein had grown sluggish, the troll dropped her hand. Trembling in his eagerness, he lifted the cup to his lips and swallowed the contents in one deep draught. Sera felt hot tears sting her eyes, her limbs grow weak, so deep was her sense of violation. *I shall never be clean again . . . not while Skogsrå lives*.

Unresisting, she allowed the troll to take her into his arms and press his blood-stained mouth against hers. "And now, my Sera," said Skogsrå, producing the pistol from his coat pocket, "I shall make you forever . . . exclusively my own."

He was turning away from the altar, intending to blow out Skelbrooke's brains, when his intended victim (suddenly and mysteriously free of his shackles) snatched up the knife from the floor, dodged around behind him, and stabbed the troll full between the shoulders. With a wrenching cry of anguish, Skogsrå dropped to his knees.

Moses Tynsdale, after a startled moment of hesitation, reached for the gun on the altar. But Sera recovered from her shock and surprise more swiftly, and snatching up the heavy silver goblet, she struck him a hard blow above the ear, momentarily dazing him. By the time that he could think or move again, she already had the pistol pointed at his head.

Sera allowed herself a momentary sideways glance at Skelbrooke, who had just jerked the knife out of Skogsrå's back, and with ruthless efficiency was now cutting the troll's throat. Jarl Skogsrå sank to the floor in a welter of dark, stinking blood.

Skelbrooke stepped forward and took the pistol out of Sera's hand. "How . . . how did you manage to free yourself at just the right moment?" she whispered. There seemed to be no air in her lungs at all.

"The talisman of Triune allowed me to open the cuffs, though it took many hours to summon up enough power to do so. As to acting just in time . . . I had a strong desire to spare you the ritual blood-letting," he added, in a low voice. He leaned against the table for support. "But I dared make no move while Skogsrå had the knife, or his hands on you."

He spoke to the erstwhile clergyman. "You are very fortunate, Euripides, that I do not kill you, too. Yet I have an impression you were not thoroughly acquainted with the motives of your confederates . . . that you were, in short, swimming in deep waters, well over your head. That is a habit of yours, is it not?"

"A habit of yours, also," sneered Tynsdale, with the pistol still in his face. "Though I must confess that I lack your good fortune in contriving to avoid the full consequences."

Skelbrooke was putting most of his strength into keeping the pistol steady. "I shall leave you here to explain matters to the Duchess. We shall see then if your luck has improved. If you will be so kind as to sit down in that chair over there . . . the one with the rungs on the back . . . and your arms behind you.

Yes, just so. Sera, you will find that the cuffs I wore were not harmed by my spell . . . they remain in perfect working order. Please pick them up and fasten Mr. Hooke to his seat."

This Sera did as swiftly as she could, looping the chain around two rungs of the chair before snapping on the second cuff. His lordship took a handkerchief out of Tynsdale's own pocket and stuffed it into the prisoner's mouth.

"One moment," said Sera, and Skelbrooke waited while she snatched off her veil, ripped a piece off her petticoat, and bound up her wrist. Then, hand in hand, they hurried out of the room.

But out in the corridor, his strength failed him and Skelbrooke stumbled, only managing to save himself from a fall by leaning up against the wall of the passage. "Your wound is bleeding . . . you need to rest," said Sera.

"There is no time for that," he replied, summoning up a ghastly smile. "We do not know if Hooke's henchmen are still on the premises. One of them may arrive on the scene at any moment. I shall, however, require the support of your arm."

Once out of doors, they headed for the stable. They found the cabriolet inside, as well as both of the horses. "The one with the blaze on his forehead allowed Mr. Tynsdale to ride him yesterday . . . I believe it is not always so with carriage horses? But I don't see how we can manage without a saddle . . . you half fainting and I in a skirt," said Sera, lifting a saddle down from its stand as he spoke.

"You will have to tell me, sir, how this ought to be done, for I have never gone riding in my life before . . . that is, not until Mr. Tynsdale snatched me up before him," she added breathlessly, as she heaved the saddle onto the grey's back. "Elsie was always too sickly to learn, so of course Cousin Clothilde would not hear of it that *I* should have a horse or learn to ride."

With Lord Skelbrooke's instruction, she managed to saddle the horse, to lead him from the stable and out to the yard. With rather more difficulty, she mounted, then reached down a hand to help Skelbrooke up behind her. My lord put his arms around her, took the reins into his hands.

"You must watch how I manage him, Sera. I am very much afraid . . . that long before we reach Mothgreen Academy . . . I shall be in no state to guide him."

• • •

By the time they reached the road leading away from
the marshes, Skelbrooke leaned heavily against Sera's back,
shivering and sweating, muttering incoherently in his pain
and delirium, and Sera was forced to take the reins. But the
grey—perhaps sensing her inexperience—refused to go where
she guided him, ambling off in the direction of Moonstone.

"Very well, you wretched creature," said Sera, after several
futile attempts to turn him around, "take us to Dr. Bell instead.
That will serve as well . . . or better than the other. Though I
don't imagine that has occurred to you, or that you mean to be
any help at all."

The ride to Moonstone was endless. The road remained
discouragingly empty, they passed no other riders or carriages
along the way. It was sunset when they finally came into the
town, and Skelbrooke had passed from muttering to raving
aloud. But on the streets of Moonstone, Sera enlisted the aid
of a stout gentleman in a flowered waistcoat who took charge
of the horse, leading him right up to the doctor's door.

The gentleman rapped a brisk tattoo with his walking stick.
A minute or two passed, then the door opened, and Dr. Bell
appeared. Between them, the two men hauled Skelbrooke into
the house.

Sera slid down from the saddle unassisted, felt her legs suddenly go weak beneath her. She, who had never swooned from
weakness in her life, collapsed in a faint on the doctor's doorstep.

34.

Wherein Skelbrooke unburdens his Heart, and Elsie speaks her Mind.

Francis Skelbrooke suffered horribly in the days that followed, as he lay sweating and hallucinating in a bed at Dr. Bell's. The wound in his shoulder was healing nicely, but his mind and his nerves were aflame, and every discomfort was magnified a hundred times over.

"He begged me, during a brief lucid moment, not to allow him the Sleep Dust," Dr. Bell told Sera. "He wishes to overcome his addiction to the drug. It is a vicious habit, I must allow . . . but what principally seems to trouble him is a guilty idea that he might somehow have spared you the worst of your ordeal, had his need for the Dust not weakened him."

The doctor studied Sera with shrewd yet sympathetic eyes. "You are welcome to stay here, if you wish, and help me to nurse him through the worst. My old housekeeper will lend the arrangement sufficient respectability. But I must tell you, Miss Thorn, that the suffering—nay, the *ravings* of your friend—Mr. Carstares or Skelbrooke, or whatever his name is, will distress you very much. Nor will he recognize you most of the time, or take comfort from your presence."

"Nevertheless, I shall stay on," Sera replied, grimly determined. "If he knows me one hour out of four and twenty, then I mean to be there."

Naturally, she had promptly sent word to her friends at Mothgreen Academy, assuring them that she was safe and that Skelbrooke was in good hands. Her first night at Dr. Bell's, Jedidiah and Elsie drove over, to embrace Sera and weep tears of relief, to listen as she recited the whole story of capture and escape, and to shake their heads and declare their sympathy for Lord Skelbrooke. Though they tried to convince Sera to go back home with them, she steadfastly refused.

For two days, Skelbrooke remained in a delirium, tortured not only by his withdrawal from the drug, which caused him to cry out again and again that his internal organs were all on fire, or that worms were feeding on his flesh, but by visions of his tormented past. Sitting by his bedside, listening to him rave and weep, Sera gained a fair idea of what that past had been . . . and of the events which had led him to adopt such a violent way of life. Though shocked and horrified by much that she heard, she thought it a pity that the innocent mistakes of the boy (for he could not have been any older than she was now) should inflict such an agony of guilt on the man.

On the third day, his mind cleared briefly, and he gazed up at Sera with a welcome look of recognition. "Sweet Sera . . ." he said softly. "Can you ever forgive me?"

"Indeed, Lord Skelbrooke," she said unsteadily, "there is nothing for me to forgive."

"I think there must be," he said, "or it should be 'Francis,' not 'Lord Skelbrooke' . . . having already once admitted that you loved me."

Tears suddenly filled her eyes. "Francis, then, if you would have it so."

He took her hand and kissed it, on the palm, and on the wrist where the scar was. "You were entirely wrong, you know . . . What Skogsrå forced you to do in no way diminishes my regard or respect. Indeed, how could I judge you? And if you were ever truly his bride . . . you are his widow now . . . and I want very much to make you my wife. But what you may think of me—"

"I am glad to hear you say so, Lord Skelbrooke," said Sera, "for I have quite made up my mind to marry you."

While all these stirring events took place, it had clearly been impossible for Jed and Mr. Jonas to launch their expedition as planned. Once the crisis was over, the most propitious time to sail had passed. So the *Otter* must needs remain in port, and Captain Hornbeam and his crew—impatient at yet another delay, unwilling to remain so long unemployed—had to be paid a full four weeks wages by the Guild, for doing nothing at all. During all this time, the Duchess apparently held her hand, and Mr. Tynsdale had disappeared, taking his backcountry confederates with him.

Elsie—as might be expected, following Jarl Skogsrå's death—slept peacefully each night. Rather more surprisingly, she completely recovered her health and her spirits in the course of something less than a week.

"It would seem that the Duchess has removed the golem from her unhealthy proximity," said Mr. Jonas, upon being consulted. "Or else—but that would be rather too much to hope for—or else the monster, which the Duchess had apparently assigned to Jarl Skogsrå's care, has 'died' of neglect."

At last the moon began to grow again, and Jed, Mr. Herring, and Mr. Jonas wheeled their fantastic machine down to the dock one morning, and with the help of a crane and a great deal of rope, lifted the mighty engine on board.

The ship was provisioned and ready to depart. Jed, Mr. Jonas, Miss Barebones (acting, she said, on behalf of Uncle Izrael), and Elsie boarded the same afternoon; Sera and Lord Skelbrooke arrived in a carriage that evening. Skelbrooke was on his feet now, weak in body but recovering in mind and spirit. He leaned heavily on his walking stick as he climbed the gangplank.

They found Jedidiah and the gnome with Captain Hornbeam in his cabin, deep in consultation, around a table scattered with maps and charts and navigational instruments. They must chart their course very precisely, explained Mr. Jonas, with the ruby spectacles on his nose. Or at least . . . as precisely as they possibly could, considering the somewhat doubtful precision of their ancient map of the islands.

With the morning tide, the *Otter* set sail. In the late afternoon, Sera and Skelbrooke took a stroll on the deck, up in the wind with the booming white sails. Already, he looked stronger, as though a good dose of salt air was all that he needed to complete the cure.

"You may think me impatient if you like, my Sera," said his lordship, leaning up against the rail. "But I would like to marry you before we return to Hobb's Church. If we succeed in raising the island, we might marry in the temple. Since modern charts record no such place, that location is officially designated as the High Seas, and the Captain could perform the ceremony quite legally and properly."

"Lord Skelbrooke," said Sera, with the wind blowing her dark curls into her eyes. "I have no wish to be married in a pagan temple, I thank you very much! If you wish to marry me immediately—and I confess that I have no objections— you might just as well do so here on the ship. Elsie and Jed are all the family that I have left in this world, and they are on board to witness the ceremony. You have only to choose the day."

"Tomorrow, then, on the bridge . . . we shall make our vows between sea and sky. Yes, it is a pretty fancy, and it appeals to me greatly," said Skelbrooke.

The next morning Sera dressed for her wedding in a gown of figured muslin and a straw hat adorned with red roses and cherry-colored ribbons. This hastily arranged shipboard ceremony spared her those painful associations that a white gown and veil, a wedding performed by a clergyman, must inevitably conjure up. Skelbrooke, of course, would realize this, and that explained his haste to be wed. She was grateful for his consideration—and strangely, rather close to tears. She had fancied herself in love for a long time now, but this shattering emotion was something new.

They assembled on the bridge at noon. Elsie was the bridesmaid, Mr. Jonas the groomsman, and Jed gave Sera away. Of course there were no fresh flowers to be had, but Miss Barebones had stripped two of her own bonnets and one of Elsie's to make two very charming bouquets out of silk blossoms. The groom arrived in a coat of pale blue watered satin and a froth of white lace, but he had dispensed with his powder and patches, in deference to the simplicity of the ceremony.

"You'll take the very best care of her, my lord," Jed whispered fiercely. "Or you'll have to answer to me."

Skelbrooke smiled up at him. "My dear Jedidiah, I shall cherish this lady with all my heart and my soul . . . but as to anything else: I rather fancy that Sera will take care of herself!"

The Captain performed the service, if not gracefully, at least with a rough and hearty good-will. Between sea and sky, with a brisk salt breeze fluttering her cherry-colored ribbons and whipping a more brilliant color than usual into her cheeks, Sera married Frances Skelbrooke. Captain Hornbeam placed her hand in that of her new husband, and Lord Skelbrooke raised her fingers to his lips.

"If you continue to weep, sweet Sera," murmured his lordship, "I shall shortly be obliged to do so as well."

Then hugs and kisses were exchanged all around (this last taking some time, as all the sailors who had been allowed to witness the ceremony insisted on paying due homage to the bride—and Sera, too blissfully happy to stand on her dignity, was for this one occasion willing to oblige), after which, Captain Hornbeam invited the wedding party down to his cabin for cakes and wine.

But Elsie and Jedidiah lingered on the deck after all the others had departed. Jed was thinking deeply, and Elsie, too, appeared to have something on her mind. At last, she could remain silent no longer.

"Jedidiah Braun, if you do not immediately ask me to be your bride, then I shall be obliged to propose to *you*."

"No need of that," said Jed, with a blush. "I've been contemplating something along those lines, and I fancy I can handle the matter myself. Do you want me to go down on one knee and propose to you in form?"

Elsie bit her lip to keep from laughing. "You may ask me standing or kneeling or sitting on the deck . . . just so long as you do it."

"Well then . . . if you think me gentleman enough to be your husband, I expect I had better do the thing properly, as a gentleman would," said Jedidiah, assuming the customary posture, and looking up at her with a roguish twinkle in his eye. "Miss Vorder . . . nay, Elsie. I hope I may call you by your given name? You can scarcely be unaware that those feelings of friendship which formerly animated my bosom have deepened into something warmer . . . stronger . . . more profound and lasting. Yes, Miss Vorder, it is love that makes me bold! Dare I hope, dearest Elsie, that you will consent to be my wife?"

"My gracious, how impertinent you are become . . . to mock me this way when I am so very much in earnest," said Elsie, tipping his hat playfully over his eyes. "Of course I will marry you, you wretched boy, if only to keep you in line!"

Several hours later, alone in the cabin they were now to share, as he attempted to unravel the intricacies of Sera's corset, Skelbrooke said, "I wonder, my love, if you have any idea what a wicked rascal you have married?"

Standing barefoot in her petticoats, with her dark curls tumbling down around her shoulders, Sera smiled into his eyes. "Indeed, my lord, I have every hope . . . that I am about to find out."

Skelbrooke burst out laughing. "My dear Sera, what an extraordinary girl you are. Won't you even *pretend* to be apprehensive, for the sake of propriety?"

Sera put her hands on his bare shoulders. Stripped down to his linen breeches, he looked broader and more substantial than in his satins and velvets, yet she was also aware, as she had never been before, of his terrible vulnerability. "Do you doubt my virtue, my lord?" she said, her smile growing quizzical.

"Not for a moment," he murmured, drawing her into his arms. "But while I confess that it was your *goodness* that won me . . . I admit that I married you in the hopeful expectation that you would prove to be very 'bad' in my bed."

The *Otter* arrived in due course and good time at the desired longitude and latitude, and there she dropped anchor. "In another six and thirty hours, the moon will be so full, she will aid us in our efforts," said Mr. Jonas. "The day after tomorrow, just at sunrise, we shall begin to raise the island!"

But the very next morning, Captain Hornbeam assembled the gentlemen in his cabin, "for a private word . . . and not to disturb the ladies' peace of mind."

Jed, Mr. Jonas, and Lord Skelbrooke (vastly elegant, this morning, in black and silver) took seats around a table under a hanging oil lamp. Captain Hornbeam sat down in an armchair which had been bolted to the cabin floor. He took out a short-stemmed pipe and a pouch of tobacco.

"Any of you gentlemen care for a smoke? No . . . Well, you'll not take offense if I indulge. Tobacco clears the mind, they say." The Captain loaded his pipe as he spoke. "Well now . . . where best to begin? I guess you know there was questions asked, the whole time we was outfitting this vessel. Then things got quiet for a long time. But from the hour we left port, all the time we was moving, there were a ship following right along behind us—always just in sight of our lookouts . . . as we must a been always in sight of theirs. It didn't concern me none, so long as we had the wind in our sails— any ship on the coast might choose this same course, perfectly innocent and all. But then we come here and we dropped the anchor, and blamed if that other ship ain't moved around to the north a bit, and dropped her anchor, too."

Mr. Jonas—who was standing, not sitting, on his chair—leaned forward over the table. "Pirates, do you think? We carry nothing of value . . . not anything to attract freebooters."

"No, sir," said the Captain. "For there ain't often pirates in these waters. Besides that, some of the men think they recognized the ship. So I got to thinking about them competitors you mentioned . . ."

By now, it had been necessary to acquaint the Captain and crew with some part of their intentions—the men might have protested the scheme had they not regarded the whole enterprise as something of a joke, so hare-brained and impossible that nothing either good or bad was likely to come of it. Yet Captain Hornbeam still considered that there had to be some further motive behind all the secrecy.

" . . . yes, them competitors of yours—would they be likely, now, to commission a ship and come sailing after you?"

Skelbrooke frowned, suddenly remembering something that Skogsrå had said about the Duchess: something to the effect that she was hiring ships and men.

"They might at that," said Mr. Jonas. "And this ship . . . if your men have indeed recognized it . . . it is one that our competitors might easily hire?"

"The *Black Bear*, under Captain Kassien. Yes, they might," said Hornbeam, setting fire to his tobacco. "Captain Kassien, he's generally for hire, he is."

Skelbrooke stiffened in his chair. "The *Black Bear*, you said? I know that ship. I wonder," he added meditatively, "if it would make any difference (should it come to a fight) if Mr. Kassien and his crew knew that I was on board the *Otter*?"

"If it comes to a fight, we'll be mightily inconvenienced, but I ain't too worried," said Hornbeam. "Captain Kassien, he knows how to appear quite the fine gentleman on shore, oh yes. Very spruce and sober he is, when calling on the merchants, and they're eager enough, them as don't know him, to hire Mr. Kassien to ship their goods all along the coast. But the men, they all know him for a drunkard and a Sleep Dust addict, and a man who takes unnecessary chances. He generally sets sail undermanned, with a crew of drunkards and other such trash, what can't get a berth on a decent vessel."

Lord Skelbrooke shook out his ruffles, appeared to be considering the effect of black lace against the unusual pallor of his hand. "I am—to some extent—sorry to hear that. I knew Mr. Kassien when he was First Mate to Troilus Diamond. He was then, as now, addicted to the Dust, but he was always sober."

"Yes, sir," said Captain Hornbeam. "Troilus Diamond were a hard man . . . cruel hard, and none too honest . . . but he run a tight ship. He kept Mr. Kassien off the bottle, I reckon. It weren't no kindly act of the Fates as give Captain Kassien his own ship."

"No," said Skelbrooke, with that same thoughtful look. "I have always supposed that the Fates, in doing so, had my own welfare in mind."

35.

In which Earth and Sea divulge their Secrets.

At sunrise, two sailors removed the yards of canvas which had swathed the island-raising engine since it first came on board. Then crew and passengers alike gathered around—curious and skeptical, but withal rather impressed and intrigued by the grandeur of the mechanism—to await the arrival of Jedidiah and Mr. Jonas.

They did not remain long in suspense. Mr. Jonas soon arrived on deck, red side-whiskers bristling, looking every inch the magician in a robe of crimson satin which had been fantastically embroidered with all manner of curious symbols worked in gold thread. On his breast glittered many orders: Supreme Knight of the Burning Water, Grand Commander of the Order of the Shadow of the Sun, Initiated Master of the Arcanum of the Humid Path, and many more. In one hand he carried an ornate ebonwood staff, much taller than himself. Behind him walked Jed, a mere Entered Apprentice, looking a bit embarrassed in his finery, similarly but less gaudily attired in a trailing garment of silver and sky blue, and an immense powdered wig.

Sera, who stood watching on the deck hand in hand with her new husband, could not repress a smile. "I wonder, my lord, that you are not tempted to put on your own robes of power and join them at their conjuring tricks."

"I carelessly left my robes of power—as you so gracefully term them—back at the lodge in Thornburg," said Skelbrooke. "Even without them, I should be tempted to do my part. Alas, I fear my powers of concentration are no longer to be relied upon."

Sera gave his hand an encouraging squeeze, wishing she had remained silent. Dr. Bell had warned her that it would be many weeks—perhaps many seasons—before Skelbrooke would be quite himself again, and further, that his craving for the Sleep Dust would remain strong for many years. In some sense, his addiction would never be cured. Nevertheless, she had resolved to stand by him, whatever the future might bring. The more so, because she remembered something that Hermes Budge once said to her: that Lord Skelbrooke might yet be healed and redeemed by the love of a good woman.

While Jed used a pump to start the flow of animating embryonated sulphur through the tubes, Mr. Jonas bathed the magnets in an attractive water, in order to increase their power. Then they both made a series of very careful adjustments to the smaller mirrors and lenses, directing their invisible beams of force toward the place (about half a league distant) where the sunken island was supposed to lie.

There followed many ritual words and mystic passes, a long, solemn, complex ceremony which kept Sera and the sailors diverted for perhaps an hour, before interest waned and most everyone became bored and drifted away. But Elsie, Skelbrooke, and Miss Barebones, all taking an intense interest in the procedure, stayed on to observe.

In fact, there was little to be seen after that, for the process must be a slow one for safety's sake, and the island raised by careful degrees. The rest of the morning passed without any indication whether the machine was actually working.

A little after noon, however, the action of the waves increased, became quite rough, for all that the wind was utterly calm. The anchor chain began to hum, as though some tremor or movement down on the ocean floor agitated the water and vibrated the anchor, causing the chain to sing. At last the violent slapping of waves against the hull brought Sera back on deck to see what was happening.

"If you are actually accomplishing . . . what you mean to accomplish," said Sera, "I do hope you are not about to bring disaster down on all of us."

"If the waves rise so high they endanger the ship, we can regulate the attraction by removing some of the magnets from the machine," said Mr. Jonas. He had abandoned his magician's robes, and was now more conventionally dressed, gnome fashion, in a sober black suit and a tall stove-pipe hat with a silver buckle. He had spent most of the morning running about, from the place where his engine reposed on the main deck, to a vantage point up on the bridge, and his stiff satin vestments would only have hampered his movements. "Until then, we shall proceed as planned."

At nightfall, Mr. Jonas and Jed uncovered the big bronze mirrors, aligned the bars to which the coils of silver glass were attached. Up until that time the moon had aided them in their efforts by causing the tide to drop; but now that Iune was rising and the tide as well, it became necessary to enlist her magnetic forces to counteract her effect on the waters. As a final adjustment, Mr. Jonas twisted two copper wires together and sprinkled the mated disks of silver and zinc with saltwater. All the metallic parts of the engine began to shoot eerie blue sparks of electrical energy.

Everyone, passengers and crew alike, gathered by the rail or climbed up in the rigging to see what would happen now. An immense yellow moon rose in the east. The waves also rose higher and higher, but the Captain advised that the ship was not in any *immediate* danger.

"Look there," cried a sailor, one of the sharp-eyed lookouts. He pointed to the exact place where a shimmering image of the goblin moon danced on the purple waters. "I think I seen sommat . . . sommat like the hump of a whale."

Everyone watched breathlessly. Soon, they could all make it out: a great, dark, irregular mass rising slowly, slowly out of the water.

"You done it," said the Captain, in reverent tones. "Burn me if you ain't gone and done it, the thing we all swore was impossible!"

"Indeed," said Mr. Jonas, standing on tiptoe to peer over the ship's rail. "It would seem that we have. Let us hope that we do not live to regret our success."

The ocean now became so rough and violent that, on the Captain's advice, Mr. Jonas detached the copper wires (he received a shocking jolt of force in doing so, but that he had expected), removed a few of the lesser magnets, and made a number of fine calibrations in order to slow the ascent of the island.

"Jed," whispered Elsie. "I thought you said there was a temple at the top of the hill. If so, why don't we see its outline silhouetted against the sky?"

Jed had long since followed Mr. Jonas's example and doffed his flowing robes. "Not precisely at the top," he said. "It's supposed to be located on the western slope *near* the top of the hill, where it's not so rocky and there used to be a natural spring of fresh water that they pumped into their buildings through copper tubes. Or anyway, that's what the stories say. Our temple, if any part of it still stands, will be coming out of the water now, but the bulk of the hill shadows it. We may see something when the moon rises higher."

At midnight, they were able to see some sort of irregular building gleaming white in the moonlight upon the slope. Jedidiah removed one of the larger magnets and Mr. Jonas covered one of the mirrors trained on the moon, in order to stabilize the island.

"It is time for those of us who mean to go ashore in the morning to retire," said Mr. Jonas. "I know that we shall all find sleep difficult, but we must get what rest we can."

In the morning they lowered the longboats, and a number of the hardier sailors volunteered to row them ashore. Captain Hornbeam and his lookouts promised to keep an eye on the other ship, to signal if the *Black Bear* so much as altered her position, and to intervene if she approached the island. "We'll send up a rocket, if it comes to a fight," said the Captain.

And satisfied with these precautions, the landing party climbed down to the boats and began the long row to the semi-submerged island.

"We may safely explore only today. We *might* do so, at some risk, tomorrow," said Mr. Jonas, as they rode through the waves. "But as we cannot precisely calculate the magnetic force exerted by the moon, or predict the consequences once that force begins to fade, it were best to err on the side of caution. We must not remain on the island a minute after midnight."

As they drew near the island, they were able to see that strange growths of kelp and green seaweed covered most of the hill. The temple, as expected, lay in ruins.

They ran aground on a pebbly shelf and climbed out of the boats, the gentlemen lending a hand to the ladies, while the sailors unloaded the tools and the lanthorns they expected to need. Then they climbed the slope to the ruined temple. Columns, walls, roofs, and statues—of marble, and obsidian, and rose-hued porphyry—all lay tumbled about as though scattered by some giant child who had tired of playing with them. Yet it was evident, even so, that all the buildings and courts had been carefully arranged according to some precise plan. One great statue, remarkably well preserved though it stood on a tilted base, depicted a majestic figure with four pairs of wings beating the air behind him like a storm. He stood, poised upon a globe of the earth, holding in one mighty hand an open book, and in the other a pair of calipers.

"Is it . . . a statue of one of the Seven Fates . . . here in a pagan temple?" asked Elsie, a puzzled frown furrowing her brow.

"It is meant, I fancy, to represent the demiurge Protœcleptius, otherwise known as the Evening Star, to whom this temple was dedicated," said Mr. Jonas.

For a time they were all content to wander among the tumbled stone buildings and simply marvel at what they saw, but eventually everyone got down to work, making a diligent search of the ruins, hoping to discover some vault or tomb like the Spyglass Hill catacombs, where (they fondly hoped) tablets of stone describing the secrets of the Panterran race might still be found.

They continued on in this fashion for several hours, then stopped for a picnic lunch. Everyone ate hastily, for the seaweed and kelp covering nearly everything had begun to dry in the sun, and truth to tell, nobody found the stench particularly appetizing. But as the others dispersed afterwards in their various directions, Sera remained seated on a marble block, deep in thought.

"Your meditations appear to trouble you, Lady Skelbrooke," said his lordship, coming to look for her. "Will you share them with me, my love?"

Sera sighed and shook her head. "I was trying to imagine how all this looked before: the temple and the gardens and the statues and all. And I thought—I thought how I wished my grandfather were here with us," she said wistfully. "He used to spend days, even weeks, deciphering a single page of ancient writing . . . years translating a single manuscript . . . yet here we have only to look around us in order to discover things that even the most vivid description could not possibly communicate."

Skelbrooke perched on the block beside her, raised her hand to his cheek. Off somewhere to the right, somebody began to shout, and then others took up the triumphant cry. His lordship dropped Sera's hand.

"It would seem they have found the vault," he said, jumping to his feet. "Will you come and look?"

They arrived at the spot at the same time as Miss Barebones and a number of sailors. Jed, Elsie, and Mr. Jonas came hurrying along a moment later. Two of the sailors had discovered a pair of iron doors—though so much stone and rubble lay across the doors, it would clearly be impossible to open them without first shifting a good deal of rock. Nevertheless, everyone was so elated by this discovery that they all set eagerly to work with picks and shovels, levers and fulcrums.

When the last rocks had been shifted, the gravel all cleared away, Mr. Jonas fastened a rope through the ring in the center of each panel. Four sailors heaved the doors open, thereby uncovering a round shaft, like a well. A circular staircase built into the walls of the shaft led down into darkness.

"The air—if the seal was good and there *is* air at the bottom instead of water—the air may be filled with poisonous vapors," said Mr. Jonas. He instructed the men to lower a candle in a bucket at the end of a rope, down the shaft until it struck bottom. When they pulled the bucket back up to the surface, the candle still burned brightly.

"Very good," said Mr. Jonas. "Then with our torches and lanthorns, we, too, may descend. But let us exercise reasonable caution. Allow me to go first. When exploring underground, it is always best to allow a gnome or a dwarf to lead the way."

With wildly beating hearts and bated breath, they followed him down the stairs: Jed and Elsie, Miss Barebones, Sera and Skelbrooke, and then the sailors—except for two burly seamen who were left behind to watch for a signal from the *Otter* announcing they had been forced to engage with the other vessel.

The steps wound down and down for what seemed a very long time. Sera reckoned they were now well below the level of the water, down in that part of the island that the ocean still claimed. At last they reached a great underground chamber, not unlike the Hobb's Church catacombs, but on a much larger and grander scale.

"You see there was no damage here," said Mr. Jonas, in reverent tones. "There were mighty spells at work here. In very truth, this must be the Vault of Secrets." He turned to Jed. "You and I, Jedidiah, are made men. Our fame, if not our fortune, is assured. My dear boy, I heartily congratulate you, for you have risen by your own efforts, and now the whole world must acknowledge your merits." Elsie slipped her hand into Jedidiah's. "Indeed, Jed I always believed in you," she whispered. "But even I never dreamed such a spectacular success."

The gnome bent to examine the floor beneath his feet, walked about with his nose almost brushing his toes. These mosaics were finer and more complex than any they had seen before, depicting a grand and glorious clockwork cosmos: flaming suns, pale moons, rainbow-hued planets, and fire-tailed comets, with their courses, rotations, and perturbations all clearly and meticulously diagramed.

He unbent and turned toward Elsie. "It is well, Miss Winter, that you brought your pastels and your sketchpad with you. When we have seen a bit more, I wonder if you will come back here and copy as much of this design as you can, that I may study it later?"

Farther along, they came to another set of double doors— this time constructed of great planks of polished whalebone— which, opening easily, revealed to their delighted eyes a veritable treasure-house of inscribed stone tablets arranged on mighty tables of rock. Everyone . . . pigtailed sailors, the dignified gnome, the two young gentlemen, and the ladies in their wide skirts . . . crowded into the room to take a look.

"I shall examine these very carefully—and you must help me, Jedidiah and Lord Skelbrooke—to determine which are the most likely to yield the knowledge we seek," said Mr. Jonas. "We cannot take all of them back with us in the boats, so we must choose wisely.

"No . . ." he added, in response to Jed's inquiring look, " . . . of course we cannot do so many rapid translations, but you can see that many show diagrams and plans, symbols and magic squares. You may choose according to these. Then we shall begin to move them, one by one, with the greatest care.

It may be, you know, that we are not meant to have them, and we must be alert to any impending catastrophe which might result from their removal."

Yet when the time came, they moved the tablets without incident, and loaded a great number into the boats. With the weight of so much stone aboard, some of the passengers were required to stay behind. It was decided that Mr. Jonas ought to go, to make certain the tablets received proper handling, and Miss Barebones confessed she had grown a trifle weary, with all the activity and excitement. But Sera, Jed, Elsie, and Skelbrooke declared they were eager to stay behind and continue their exploration of the catacombs.

"We shall return by sunset, I hope," said the gnome, as he took leave of them down in the vault. "But if we should be delayed for any reason—if we should not return much before midnight—you must keep a careful eye on the time and wait for us down by the water."

Lord Skelbrooke and Jedidiah took out their pocket watches (Skelbrooke's timepiece, recently purchased, was quite an ordinary chronometer, innocent of explosives), to make certain they were both still working.

"Very good," said Mr. Jonas. "Then I shall leave you two sailors to keep watch up in the temple, a lanthorn and extra candles for each of you, and I will return as soon as I may."

Elsie took her sketchbook and her pastel crayons out of her reticule and sat down in a welter of skirts and petticoats to make sketches of the floor, while Sera and the gentlemen examined the carved pictures and symbols and the ancient letters on the tombs and catafalques. Sera was particularly intrigued by a line of pictures—she supposed they adorned the tomb of some great inventor—that seemed to depict a number of machines: wind-driven carriages and steam-powered chariots, and a curious device that seemed to be made up largely of graduated lenses, the purpose of which she could not make out at all. She called Jed over for an explanation.

Jed mentally translated the inscription, spent several minutes contemplating the picture, while Sera waited impatiently. "I'll tell you what it is—it's a writing machine, for carving on stone tablets!" he said at last. "These lenses . . . the large one at the top is ordinary glass, those in the middle are quartz, and the tiny ones are ground from Balthorian crystals . . . they concentrate the rays of the sun smaller and smaller, until the heat's so intense it burns through solid rock."

He joined Sera examining the tombs along that wall, all the pictures of men and women in tottering hats and headdresses—in the odd yet oddly familiar styles of a bygone age—all the marvelous machines and inventions of a lost civilization. Meanwhile, Lord Skelbrooke, ever the magician, concentrated on some esoteric diagrams in another part of the cavern. A quiet hour or so passed in this manner, until Skelbrooke called out to the others to join him by a stone coffin.

The coffin had been beautifully carved with magical and alchemical symbols, and a band of lettering all around the top. But considering that the Panterrans had been full-sized Men, it enclosed a space so small that it could only contain the remains of a very young child.

"I do not entirely comprehend the writing, but I believe . . . I am all but certain that this box was never meant to house a body," said his lordship. "I believe that it may, in truth, contain something of great value. Pray bring your lanthorns a little closer, ladies . . . and you, Jedidiah: help me to lift the lid."

The lid was heavy, but manageable. It came off to reveal a glitter of gold and gemstones. Lord Skelbrooke and Jed hastily lowered the lid to the floor, then Skelbrooke reached inside the stone box and drew out a small ivory coffer, set with rubies, emeralds, sapphires, and diamonds, all flashing and scintillating in the light of Sera's and Elsie's lanthorns. The other three watched breathlessly as he opened the jewel-encrusted cover.

On a bed of crumbling fabric lay a single large gemstone of unusual color and lustre, a rich shade somewhere between red and purple, with a golden fire burning at its heart.

"Seramarias," said Skelbrooke, in a low, shaken voice. "It is your namesake, Sera." A sigh passed among them. Elsie leaned against the marble coffin for support, and Sera felt dizzy, too, her heart pounding so hard that she thought it must burst. And Sera knew in that instant that she was the alchemist's granddaughter in every sense of the word—she desired the Stone with all of her heart.

> "Radiant Seramarias, whom men have Sought
> Through all the Ages of the circling World
> Nor Kings, nor Emperors, nor Potentates
> For all their Glittering store of Treasure
> Not one Stone so Precious or so Pure
> As blood-bright Seramarias, with her Heart of Flame—"

Skelbrooke's quotation came to an abrupt end, as a sound reached them from the foot of the circular staircase. They had not heard anyone descending the shaft, and it wanted an hour until sunset and the return of their friends.

"Do not be so foolish as to reach for your weapons, gentlemen," said a sweet, childlike voice. "We are both armed, and our pistols are aimed directly at the young ladies' heads."

The Duchess of Zar-Wildungen stepped into their circle of lanthorn-light, and with her came Moses Tynsdale. There was a rustle of movement, and the ape Sebastian came around from behind the Duchess, clinging to a portion of her wide skirt.

But Skelbrooke had moved so quickly that a small pistol of walnut and brass already gleamed in his hand. "As mine is aimed at your head, Marella," said his lordship coldly. "It would appear that we have reached a stand-off. Our friends will soon arrive, however, to shift the odds in our favor."

"They must first get past my men up above," said the Duchess. "I fear that we handled your sailors rather roughly, but I believe that no permanent damage was done. How very surprised they were to see us! Did you expect us to bring the *Bear* in with all her guns roaring? We came in longboats, the same as you did, and your lookouts never spotted us."

Sera and her friends exchanged embarrassed glances. Somehow, it had never occurred to any one of them that the Duchess would arrive without fanfare and blazing cannons.

Skelbrooke's hand tightened on the hilt of his pistol. "We have nothing to fear from her," he told the others. "She will not shoot any one of us. That would go against her pride. To gain her revenge by so simple and crude a method would be unworthy of the Duchess of Zar-Wildungen."

"But I no longer desire revenge," said the Duchess, smiling. "It is 'Radiant Seramarias' I must and will have."

36.

In which the forces of Nature and magic prove Capricious.

The Duchess continued to smile that same peculiarly benign smile. "I have suffered much," she said, "but I am willing to forget my many wrongs, if you will yield me the Stone. Yes . . . Seramarias will pay for all."

Skelbrooke shook his head slowly. "The Stone is beyond all price—but what is that to a Fee in pursuit of revenge?"

"It is something. Not so much, I will admit," said the Duchess. "But *you* value the Stone, it will pain you to lose it—and that is something, too. By depriving you, I gain some part of the moral satisfaction I seek." She took a step closer, so that the lanthorn lit her features more clearly. She still smiled, but her delicate face had assumed a wistful expression. "And circumstances favor you. The Duke is dead . . . Therefore, in some sense, the Gracious Lady, the Duchess of Zar-Wildungen, is dead as well. If I am to rise like the phoenix from the ashes of my old life and begin anew, I can better do so unburdened by old debts, old hates, old loves. Give me the Stone, dear children, and you need never again fear my interference in your lives. I give you my sacred word."

The others shifted uneasily, exchanged sidelong glances. "Indeed, Godmother," said Elsie, "I wish that it were so. I never did you any wrong that I knew of, but still I would be glad to buy peace with you. If only your word could be trusted."

"You will pardon our cynicism," added Sera, curling her lip. "But Jarl Skogsrå also spun a plausible tale, back at your house in the marsh, and he meant only treachery from the beginning."

"Nevertheless, I believe we may trust her," Skelbrooke said, much to the surprise of the others. "It is not in the nature of

Fee or Farisee to lie about matters of justice or revenge. Yet we cannot give you the Stone, Marella. No one here has wronged you, save I myself perhaps. And the price you demand is much too high."

The Duchess frowned, gave an impatient twitch to her skirt. "Too high a price for peace of mind? Unless I gain satisfaction here and now, I shall hound you all the days of your life. You will never know a moment's safety, a night of sweet, unworried repose. I am long-lived, I can torment your children and your children's children . . . it is not a prospect to which I look forward, I own, but it is something I should be impelled to do, unless you choose wisely and free us all."

Sera's first elation at finding the Stone was beginning to fade. She wanted Seramarias, but not so intensely as before. And when she thought of all the Stone had cost her in the past, what it had cost her own people and Jed's as well, the price it might still exact . . . She looked across at Jed, and saw her own trouble and confusion reflected in his eyes. The family curse—that was what Seramarias had been, and must always be, unless she found the wisdom and the courage to renounce it.

Sera touched her husband lightly on the arm. "If you think that she may be trusted, then you may give her the Stone, for all it means to me."

"For my part," said Jed, "I'd sooner give it up." And Elsie said so as well. But Skelbrooke only frowned.

"Sera, the Stone is more than your namesake. In some sense, it is your birthright. It is the thing for which your grand-father sacrificed all . . . his good name and his fortune . . . the inheritance you were entitled to . . . and he would want you to claim the Stone, of that I am certain. Were you not thinking of him, only today? Were you not wishing—"

"If Seramarias is mine to claim, in either my own name or my grandfather's . . . then I gladly relinquish that claim," Sera interrupted him softly.

His lordship looked pained. "This irrational prejudice against all things magical."

"It is not a matter of prejudice," insisted Sera. "Do you want to hear me say that I understand your desire for the Stone? I do, and I did from the beginning. You were not far wrong when you said that I set my mind against all things magical, for fear of animating my own interest. But if you imagine that Seramarias can somehow set things right . . . blot out the years of poverty, the hardships, the disappointments, the many, many blows to my foolish pride . . ." For a moment, her voice faltered, then grew stronger. "It cannot do any of those things, Francis, and even if it could . . . I have everything that I want or need *now*. And I am not such a fool as to sacrifice my present happiness, all for the sake of the dead past."

As she spoke the last words, a tremor rocked the chamber. "The moon is diminishing," said Jed, catching Elsie by the hand. "As it moves away from the earth, it ceases to exert so strong an attraction. We don't really know . . . we've only been guessing . . . how long the machine all of itself will prove strong enough to keep the temple above the water."

"Then you had better make up your mind swiftly, Francis," said the Duchess. "If I leave the catacombs without the Stone, you will never again hear me offer terms of peace."

Another quake, this one much stronger, shivered through the island.

"It seems Mr. Jonas miscalculated, and we've not nearly so long as we thought," said Jed, as the underground chamber continued to rock and sway. "The island may be sinking."

Moses Tynsdale, who had hitherto remained silent, leaned over and spoke in the Duchess's ear. The Duchess shook her head emphatically.

"You are quite certain, Sera?" said Skelbrooke, very pale and distressed. It was plain that Seramarias meant more to him than it ever could to her. "You are willing to give her the Stone?"

"I am," said Sera, stamping her foot impatiently. "Please do not delay any longer, or we shall all drown along with the temple!"

A difficult internal struggle followed. "Very well," said Skelbrooke, at last, holding out the bejeweled ivory casket. "You may take Seramarias. All debts shall be paid, all wrongs mended . . . on both sides."

In the ruins above, no one could find the sailors they had left on guard, or the Duchess's men who had overpowered them. "Let us waste no more time looking for them," said the Duchess, clutching the ivory casket against her bosom. She had entrusted Sebastian to Moses Tynsdale, who carried the indigo ape in his arms. "It is likely that my men took yours with them and went down to our boats . . . I fear they are not to be wholly trusted, however, and may have deserted *us*. Let us hope that your friends are more trustworthy, and that they are coming back for you as promised."

They ran down the slope, between the broken buildings and statues, through the gathering evening shadows, as the island continued to rock. Much to their relief, they found Mr. Jonas and several sailors along with two of the longboats waiting on the shingle.

"All debts paid . . . all wrongs mended?" said the Duchess, suddenly doubtful.

"I have said it," replied Skelbrooke, helping Sera into the boat. "Give me your hand, Marella, and—"

But just then, perhaps reacting to the excitement around him, the blue ape struggled out of Tynsdale's grip, leaped to the ground, and ran back up the slope.

"Sebastian, my dear!" shrieked the Duchess. Declining Skelbrooke's offered hand, she started off after the ape. His lordship made to go after her, but Sera retained her hold on his hand.

"You do not risk your life and our future to save her, my lord. We may forgive her the wrongs that she did us, but we need not forget them."

"We must wait a bit, in any case, and give her the opportunity to return on her own," said Skelbrooke. The sailors had already launched one of the longboats, clambered in, and were rapidly rowing away. Jed, Mr. Jonas, and Moses Tynsdale pushed the other boat into the water, climbed in with the young ladies, and each took up a pair of oars.

Several minutes passed, during which the island experienced repeated shocks. "The sea is rising, we have no hope of arriving safe back at the ship if we do not go immediately," said Mr. Jonas. "Nor do I think that Captain Hornbeam will wait for us much longer, before moving his ship to a safer position."

Still Skelbrooke hesitated. "I will remind you that the Duchess and I arrived in a longboat of our own," said Tynsdale. "Which we left on the other side of the incline. It is possible that the men *did* wait for her, and that she has already regained her pet and headed in that direction. We might wait for her until the waters overwhelm us, and she would never come."

Reluctantly, Skelbrooke climbed on board and took up the fourth pair of oars.

Captain Hornbeam had waited for them, but the sheets and the sails were rigged, the anchor raised, and the *Otter* ready to make way, as soon as all were safely on board. "A most extraordinary adventure," Mr. Jonas was saying as he climbed over the rail. "You must not repine over the loss of the stone. With the knowledge we have gained we can construct mighty engines . . . flying ships . . . underwater vessels. Even without Seramarias, I believe that the *real* adventure is only beginning."

"Preacher Tynsdale . . . now, where in tarnation did you come from?" asked the Captain, as the clergyman's head appeared above the rail.

"From the depths of the earth," said Tynsdale. Arriving on deck, he removed his wide-brimmed hat with a sweeping gesture. "I cannot say that I enjoyed my visit overmuch, but at least I emerged alive." He turned to Skelbrooke, who had followed him up. "Was it your intention that I should also be included in the general amnesty . . . or am I to spend the rest of our voyage in chains down in the hold?"

Skelbrooke considered for a long moment. He knew Hooke for a thorough-going rogue, yet it was impossible to gaze on his former associate without a strong impression: *There but for the inexplicable whim of the Fates go I.* "In return for satisfying my insatiable curiosity on one or two points, you shall be included."

The longboats came up and were lashed to the sides. The ship started to move.

"You may ask your questions and I shall engage to answer them," said Tynsdale, with a bow. "As I explained to you before, I am not generally employed as a kidnapper or thief. The sale of information is my usual trade."

Skelbrooke smiled faintly. "How came it that you were still in the Duchess's employ?"

"I was able to convince her that I believed I was acting under her orders when I abducted you and your lady. That was not so difficult: I can always contrive a great show of sincerity—particularly when I am telling the truth. I did believe that I acted in accordance with the Gracious Lady's desires, I did not know that you were meant to die, and I was unaware of Skogsrå's precise intentions toward the lady. Indeed, I was not even aware that he was a troll, until he drank Miss Vorder's blood."

He made a deprecating gesture. "I do not say this to excuse my actions . . . of which I am not particularly ashamed . . . only that I take some pride in my work, and wish to provide you with a complete account."

Sera whispered something in her husband's ear. His lordship nodded. "But tell me, Euripides: the Duke of Zar-Wildungen— is he really dead?"

Tynsdale leaned comfortably against the rail. "To the best of my knowledge, he is. But of course, you can ascertain the truth of that easily enough, by asking your friends in Wäldermark."

Jed, who stood nearby, holding hands with Elsie, put in a question of his own. "What of the monster . . . Miss Vorder's double? Did the Duchess bring her on board the *Black Bear*?"

"She did not," said Tynsdale. "Cecile is dead . . . or rather, she lost what little claim to life she ever possessed. At the Duchess's orders, Hancock and I took Skogsrå's body out into the marsh and dropped it into a swallowing bog. The monster was so distraught, we allowed her to follow along behind us. Indeed, we could none of us manage her after he was dead. How were we to guess that she would wade into the quagmire after him . . . or that once there, would refuse to respond to our efforts to save her?

"She was up to her waist in mud, when apparently her semi-immersion in sand and water induced her to return to her own elemental form. Yes . . . she turned back into clay before our eyes," added Tynsdale, with a shudder. "It was not an agreeable thing to witness."

With another bow and a flourish, Tynsdale strolled off. Sera frowned at her husband. "Shall he really escape the consequences of his villainy?"

Skelbrooke shook his head. "Do not be deceived by his manner. A man with his memories, his causes for regret, carries torment with him wherever he goes. Escape punishment? It is not in his power. Believe me, for I speak from bitter experience."

Elsie and Jed joined Sera and Skelbrooke by the rail. "Cousin Francis," said Elsie. "You do believe what the Duchess told us—and if she survived—that she will trouble us no more?"

"I shall be utterly convinced of that as soon as I know for certain that the Duke is truly dead. I learned a great deal about Fairy nature during an extended visit to Mistress Sancreedi. As I was confined to my bed at the time, she had ample time to lecture me on a number of subjects." His lordship sighed deeply. "It seems that those of fairy blood have a tendency to respond to catastrophic events in a most curious way: their personalities disintegrate, nay, fragment is perhaps the better word. After a prolonged period of confusion, the personalities once more blend, and a new life begins.

"I was treated to this lecture," his lordship added, with a quaint little shrug, "because Mistress Sancreedi imagines that all this has something to do with *me*—with a certain instability of character which you might perhaps have noticed. She has somehow gained the fantastic notion that my family has been concealing a significant strain of fairy blood, all these years. When I quote genealogies at her, she only replies that bloodlines have always been an obsession with fairies."

"And how long," said Sera, arching a dark eyebrow, "is this period of confusion she mentioned likely to last?"

"Sometimes for a period of years—but rarely more than six or seven," said Skelbrooke, slipping an arm around her waist. "By her reckoning, I must already be recovering from my bout of madness, and in another year—at the very most—I shall make you a most respectable husband, dear Sera."

"I am sure that I shall believe that when I see it," Sera said tartly, though she smiled when she said it.

"Indeed," said Elsie quite seriously. "I do hope that the Duchess may live *her* new life as a better woman."

"As to that," said Skelbrooke, "these hybrid fairies do not live by our standards. Neither human nor fairy, they must create their own morality. I do not believe the Duchess ever violated her own precepts. And we are aware that many people in Thornburg only knew her as a kind benefactress. Had you not been the innocent cause of an insult she had suffered, had she become in truth your godmother, I believe she might have been kindness itself to you.

"In her new life," said his lordship, "I should imagine she will be in many ways the same Marella: by turns generous and good, wicked and cruel . . . a creature of infinite caprice to our way of thinking, but ever true to her own nature."

Captain Hornbeam invited his passengers to dine with him that evening. But after the others went down, Sera and Skelbrooke remained on deck a little longer, wishing to snatch a moment apart from their friends, after the excitement of the day. The sky was still a sunset purple, and they watched through the rigging as a vast yellow moon, only slightly lob-sided, rose out of the water. The *Otter* left a golden wake behind her, like a path leading to the moon.

"Now that you have had ample time to think of it, do you not regret your decision to relinquish the Stone?" Skelbrooke whispered in Sera's ear.

"I do not," she said very earnestly. "I spoke the truth, there on the island. I am perfectly content with all that I have now, and with the prospect of our future together."

He caught her hand in both of his and leaned against a mast. She moved in his direction, and their eyes met, sharing a smile of pure delight.

"Please believe me, my lord, when I tell you," said Sera, "I have never been happier in my life."

MICHAEL MOORCOCK

"A major novelist of enormous ambition."—*Washington Post*

THE CLASSIC ELRIC SERIES!

Elric, cursed and beloved of the Gods, follows his black hellblade Stormbringer across the myriad planes of Earth and Time—and to the countless hells that are his destiny!

__ELRIC OF MELNIBONE, BOOK I	0-441-20398-1/$4.50
__THE SAILOR ON THE SEAS OF FATE, BOOK II	0-441-74863-5/$4.50
__THE WEIRD OF THE WHITE WOLF, BOOK III	0-441-88805-4/$3.95
__THE VANISHING TOWER, BOOK IV	0-441-86039-7/$3.95
__THE BANE OF THE BLACK SWORD, BOOK V	0-441-04885-4/$3.95
__STORMBRINGER, BOOK VI	0-441-78754-1/$3.95

And look for THE FIRST NEW ELRIC NOVEL IN 12 YEARS

THE FORTRESS OF THE PEARL

__ 0-441-24866-7/$4.50

For Visa, MasterCard and American Express orders ($10 minimum) call: 1-800-631-8571

FOR MAIL ORDERS: CHECK BOOK(S). FILL OUT COUPON. SEND TO:

BERKLEY PUBLISHING GROUP
390 Murray Hill Pkwy., Dept. B
East Rutherford, NJ 07073

NAME_____

ADDRESS _____

CITY_____

STATE_____ ZIP_____

PLEASE ALLOW 6 WEEKS FOR DELIVERY.
PRICES ARE SUBJECT TO CHANGE WITHOUT NOTICE.

POSTAGE AND HANDLING:
$1.00 for one book, 25¢ for each additional. Do not exceed $3.50.

BOOK TOTAL	$ ____
POSTAGE & HANDLING	$ ____
APPLICABLE SALES TAX (CA, NJ, NY, PA)	$ ____
TOTAL AMOUNT DUE	$ ____

PAYABLE IN US FUNDS.
(No cash orders accepted.)

277